NO COINCIDENCES

TESSA D'ERRICO

Copyright © 2023 by Tessa D'Errico

First Edition

Cover Design and Art By Ana Grigoriu-Voicu

All rights reserved. No part of this book may be reproduced in any form or by any electronic or mechanical means, including information storage and retrieval systems, without written permission from the author, except for the use of brief quotations in a book review.

This is a work of fiction. Any resemblance to actual persons, living or dead, events, or locales is entirely coincidental.

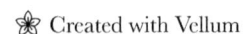

Created with Vellum

for every college girl who's walked home from the bar alone and drunk after a long night

chapters

part one
the first day

1. Bleachers — 3
2. Refills — 18
3. On Writing — 34
4. Sick — 43
5. Fake ID — 54

part two
ten months older

6. Interviews — 61
7. Storm — 72
8. Staying In — 85
9. Yes And — 99
10. Blood In the Sink — 111
11. Just Friends — 123
12. No Charge — 134
13. Things Get Bad — 142
14. Papers — 156
15. Like Back Then — 163
16. Laundry — 173
17. Waiting Room — 182
18. Better Days — 194
19. Black Dress — 202
20. Sleepovers — 213
21. Captain Wentworth — 223
22. Halloween — 235
23. Wallow — 242
24. The Blueprint — 253
25. Door's Unlocked — 257
26. Drunk Girls — 268
27. The Rough Draft — 277

28. Gas Station Tequila	282
29. Bruise	292
30. International Affairs	300
31. In The Elevator	305
32. Aftershocks	321
33. New Years' Resolutions	325

part three
eight months older

| 34. London | 333 |

| Acknowledgments | 339 |
| About the Author | 341 |

part one
the first day

"It's too dangerous to fall so young"
Lucy Dacus, *Historian*

"In the beginning I was so young and such a stranger to myself I hardly existed"
Mary Oliver, *Upstream*

bleachers

. . .

THIS IS ONE OF THOSE THINGS THAT, EVEN IN THE MOMENT, I know I always will remember.

Not in a good way, in a first-major-screw-up-of-my-college-writing-career way. I peek at my watch, I don't even have time to pull my phone out of my back pocket to check the time, as I whip myself down the concrete stairs of my dorm building. Our elevator is something out of a horror movie, so I refuse to use it. A choice I'm now rethinking as I race through the six flights between my room and the exit.

Sam, the editor-in-chief of our school newspaper, is the one who assigned me this article. He said that I should be at the soccer field to interview the freshman on the men's team twenty minutes before practice was over. Ideally, this would give me enough time to introduce myself to the guys and start pulling them for interviews as they warmed down. Sam contacted their coach; everything was supposed to be perfectly set up for me. Until I lost track of time hanging up posters on the confusingly damp and disgustingly sticky white brick walls of my dorm.

I gain some real speed when I start taking two steps at a time. I'm about to hit the third-story landing when I trip and fall. All of my weight falls on my knees as I slide across the concrete, effectively breaking the fall. I barely stop to take in the damage before I keep marking on, I am a girl on a mission and cannot be stopped by a scraped knee.

I have had one dream career my whole life – political communications. It started when my grandmother introduced me to *The West Wing* as a kid. My grandmother and mom immigrated to the US right after my mom was born, and my grandmother became engrossed in American politics. She passed it on to me, buying me American Girl Doll books and letting me pick which documentary to check out at the library on Snow Road. I loved history, but something clicked when I saw Allison Janney as CJ Cregg on my tiny living room TV. She was tall like me and smart like me and, as I watched CJ address a busy White House Press Room, I knew she was exactly what I wanted to be.

And what does every great future journalist or speech writer do to cultivate her skills? She writes for her college newspaper, obviously. She does not lose track of time trying to decide whether double-sided tape or Scotch is best for hanging posters, making her late to her first assignment. I'm not doing great.

By the time I get to the field, I'm officially twenty-six whole minutes late. It's over. I've ruined the whole thing. The field is empty. I look for any signs of life – a spare uniform, a water cooler – and see nothing. I really blew this. Fuck. Only now, in my state of despair, do I notice my bloody knee and untied shoelaces. I can't do anything about my knee right now, but I can at least tie my shoes.

I sit down on the first bleacher I pass, and realize how out of breath I am, heaving deep in and out as I double knot my laces.

"Um, you good over here?"

I jump at the sound, which only makes me more out of breath, and turn around to see the most attractive man I've ever seen.

He's still in his practice uniform, and it makes him look tall. Or maybe he always looks tall, I don't know. A streak of mud covers his left forearm, and an angry red scrape covers his right. Obviously, he's on the soccer team and way too attractive to be talking to me, a political communication major with time management issues.

I've seen him before, I realize. It was in the cafeteria on Friday when my roommate and I tried to grab lunch before the first session of freshman orientation started. I noticed him the second I walked in. Tall, athletic in a way that looks like it's out of necessity rather than vanity, with an air of confidence that's very hard to fake. He seemed like my type. I got scared though, and never tried to talk to him.

I shake my head vehemently. "No, I'm okay. Really."

He cocks his head and gives me a funny look. "You don't look okay," he tells me. What every girl wants to hear.

My tight upper lip and uneasy expression forces him to quickly correct himself, saying, "I don't mean your appearance, seriously. Just...your knee is covered in blood."

I instantly relax. It's a bit pathetic how relieved I feel. "I was in a rush, and I fell. It's nothing life-threatening."

He nods and gives me a tiny smile. "Would you like a band-aid?"

I bite down a laugh. The offer is so genuine and innocent, nothing I would've expected from someone like him. "If you have one, sure."

His shy, tiny smile breaks into a wide grin as he slides onto the bleacher next to me. "I do."

I tell him to use his best judgment in picking which

band-aid I should use and I don't flinch when he asks if he can put disinfectant on my gash. I stretch my leg out until it's nearly in his lap and watch him intently spray it until enough is applied to his liking. His focused face is cute.

"Thank you," I say quickly, trying not to give myself away, pulling my leg back into myself. "You didn't have to do that."

He shrugs and I'm wondering why he hasn't gotten up to leave yet. Doesn't he have somewhere better to be?

"Why were you in such a rush?" he asks, and I'm surprised he was listening closely enough to remember I ever said I was in a rush.

"It's embarrassing," I respond, itching the spot on my neck where my necklace hits my skin. "But I was supposed to interview the new players on the soccer team, and I got here too late and missed it."

He laughs, and I realize I've never thought a sound was attractive before. "You're *that* girl? We were wondering why you didn't show up."

I roll my eyes at him gently and hope he knows I'm teasing. "Great. Way to make me feel better about myself."

"Well, I'm a new player on the soccer team. Can you just interview me now?"

I stare at him, trying to hide my shock at his offer. "That would be great, yeah."

"You're a first year too?" he asks me now.

After recently deciding the word "freshman" was sexist, our university adopted the term "first-year." Because, obviously, the word "freshman" is the most sexist part of higher education.

I only nod. He doesn't say anything. Does that mean it's my turn?

"How was your move-in?" I ask stiffly.

"I've been here since the beginning of the month for

soccer, so it feels like years ago honestly. How was yours though?"

For eighteen years, I made hating change a definitive part of my personality. The last days of summer felt like a countdown to my execution. But once my parents and I brought the last box up to my new room, all the anxiety I had pent up disappeared. It was almost embarrassing. I didn't call my parents for two days after they dropped me off. I thought it symbolized something, a new life without fear of change. It didn't symbolize anything. All it meant was that I was too caught up in the adrenaline of orientation to remember to pick up the phone.

I don't tell the boy standing across from me any of this though, I just tell him moving in "went well."

I ask him the questions *The Clocktower* gave me: What is your name? (Reed Callaway) What position do you play? (Center midfielder) How long have you been playing soccer? (Since he was four) What is your hometown? (Alexandria, Virginia.) I ask my final question, and think I can predict his answer, "What is your major?"

It's got to be sports management, right? That's every college athlete's major. Maybe exercise science.

"English. I think I wanna go to law school," he answers.

I don't hide my shock very well, and he starts laughing. He's *really* laughing. I almost feel like I should apologize.

"I know it doesn't scream *soccer player*, but I've always been…" He pauses to find the correct word and looks at me like it will be spelled out on my forehead. I feel entirely too seen. "…a wordy person," he decides.

I nod. Me too.

I record Reed's answer in my chicken scratch handwriting. I include what he says about being a wordy person.

I'm mid-sentence when he takes the notebook and pen out of my hands.

"Your turn," he says.

"Excuse me?"

"It's only fair. Let me ask you the questions now," he says and gives me a cute grin. I bet this works on a lot of girls because it is working on me.

"Fine," I say, relaxing and leaning back onto my hands.

"Your name?"

"Halle Hevko."

"Halle Hevko." He repeats my name back to me, slowly, like he's trying to memorize it.

I watch him delicately copy my name down but stop him when I see he's spelled my name, *Hallie*.

When I correct him and tell him there's no *i*, he says, "Ah. That makes more sense. No *i* seems more intellectual. It fits you."

He gives me another incredible smile. It's like nothing I've ever seen before. Neither is his light brown hair, a little out of control from his earlier practice, and his light brown eyes that are running over me, his broad shoulders and the soft way they're dropped as he leans over my notebook that's resting on his knees. There's an incredibly attractive boy sitting next to me. And he's holding *my* notebook.

"What position do you play?" he asks.

"I don't play soccer."

He laughs. "What position do you think you'd play?"

"What do I *look* like I would play?" I counter.

He studies me for a few seconds, eyes skimming over every part of me, down to my white tennis shoes, before answering. "Striker."

"What does that mean?"

"You are in the running for worst sports journalist of

the year. Do you know anything about soccer, Halle Hevko?" He says, setting my notebook in between us.

"Not really." I shrug. "I kind of got thrown into working on this column at the meeting today. I thought I would be the only freshman there, but a guy named Danny showed up before me and was able to pick first. He's doing some extended piece on the inflation of our meal plan with the editor-in-chief. And I'm writing a blurb on the freshman soccer players."

I look away from him, embarrassed, realizing I've talked entirely too much — answered his question in far too many words. But Reed surprises me, gently nudging my foot with the side of his cleat to bring my attention back to him.

"For what it's worth," he says sincerely. "I'm glad you're here. You should come to some of our games. You gotta learn the game if you're gonna be a sports journalist."

Is he flirting with me? Should flirting even feel this natural? If he is flirting, I need to revisit the early parts of our conversation and rethink every word he's said to me so far. But I can't do that right now, so I just smile.

"Where are you from?" he asks. His foot is resting quite close to mine, a result of his nudging me, proof he ever did it at all.

"Cleveland."

"What's your major?"

"Political communications."

Reed laughs. "I'm very familiar with your kind. Let me guess: You wanna work for the DNC, you think bipartisanship can solve everything, your idol is Donna Moss, and you'll marry a Kennedy."

I stare at him blankly, trying not to give it away that he perfectly described me. I obviously love *The West Wing* and

I have a Jackie O poster hanging in my bedroom back home. I've never thought I should be ashamed of those two things until this exact moment.

"Maybe I'm more like CJ than Donna," I tell Reed.

"I'm just teasing," he says easily. "You wanna change the world. I think that's cool."

I'm sure at this point he knows I'm attracted to him.

I don't want to look away from him. He's resting his elbows on his knees and his face in his hands. He's studying me again, and I wonder if he's noticing the same things about me that I'm noticing about him. He looks like he was class president in high school, but I think all soccer players look like they could've been class president.

We talk about our families, what type of cars we drive, and how we take our coffee. He tells me both his parents are lawyers. I tell him I'm the first person in my family to go to college. There's a sense of warmth and familiarity between us that I've never felt with a stranger before, which is surprising, knowing the stranger is an attractive boy who I should be nervous around.

"Well, if you want," Reed says after a while. "I can grab the other first years for your interview."

There are other boys on the team that aren't Reed. I forgot about that. As much as I want to keep talking to Reed alone, I can't write the article I'm here to write with only one interview.

"Yeah, that'd be great. Let them know I only have five questions. It shouldn't take long."

Reed nods and leans in, settling right around the empty space above my shoulder before he whispers, "Some of these guys are assholes. Fair warning."

I laugh as he pulls away. "I can handle myself. I am a serious sports journalist after all."

"Then I guess I should let you work," Reed says with a dramatic sigh. "I'll see you around."

"Sure." I smile. "See you around."

I shouldn't believe him. I shouldn't hold out hope that I really will see him again, but I do.

Addy, my roommate, enters our room huffing and puffing from her trip up our six flights of stairs.

We've only unpacked the essentials. Open suitcases and plastic storage bins have made a maze out of the dorm. Addy and I are some of the lucky freshmen, mostly honors students, who get to live in the only freshman dorm with private bathrooms. The only con is the creepy elevator. That and our neighbor, Tori. She tried to hire a locksmith to replace all her locks on move-in day, only for our RA to tell her it would break her housing contract. Tori threw a fit, returning later with a box full of alarms and locks from Home Depot. Addy and I looked it up - the nearest Home Depot is a whopping *seventy-five* minutes from campus.

"I got us a dorm-warming gift." Addy giggles, pulling a comically large bottle of vodka out of her backpack.

"How did you get that?" I ask. We are not 21. I don't know anyone who's 21.

She smirks and plops down onto the futon next to me. "My friend from high school, Luke, goes here and knows some upperclassmen. There's also a party this weekend he said we can go to."

Addy is from the suburbs of Nashville, and you can tell by the way she talks. I saw her unpack a pair of cowboy boots earlier. I'm almost positive her glasses are fake, but I didn't ask. We're pretty close considering we've only known each other for thirty-six hours, but not close enough to ask if her glasses are fake.

She sets the vodka bottle on the top of her dresser and doesn't mention it again. I stare at it. I wasn't a big drinker in high school, but there were a few grad parties this past summer where I indulged in one too many hard seltzers. I've never had vodka before though, and it feels like trying it would be a rite of passage I need to accomplish. Something to cross off my list of things other people my age do. One more thing to solidify my place in the world as a college freshman. Reed flashes across my mind, and I imagine him at a big party on campus, talking to girls and taking shots with them. I bet he likes parties. I've made up my mind.

A few hours later, Addy and I are on opposite sides of the futon with an empty pizza box in between us when I realize I have reading due for the first day of class tomorrow. A lot of reading. Addy, a nursing major, has assignments too. I skim through the online textbook for my composition lecture, trying to gather enough notes to make it look like I read thoroughly without actually doing that. We work until midnight, watching reality TV reruns and taking notes together. Before I check the clock again, we're both twitching to keep ourselves awake. Addy crashes on the couch. I don't feel comfortable enough to wake her up, so I shut the lights off and make my way to bed.

I hear Addy shuffle into her own about twenty minutes later.

―――

I LIKE A LOT ABOUT BEING A COLLEGE STUDENT.

I like that campus is small, but not so small that it feels suffocating. I like the freedom – walking back to my dorm at three in the morning after getting Diet Coke from the vending machine across campus with Addy and knowing there will be no consequences.

I like falling asleep at night to the sound of traffic and distant bells from the clocktower, even though the bells are always two minutes ahead. I like that our campus is a weird mix of buildings that were built one hundred and fifty years ago and buildings that are brand new. I like watching the packs of boys that walk across campus with their floppy hair, five-inch inseam shorts, and quarter zips. I even like the food served in the caf.

The only thing I don't like so far is the mandatory orientation session my advisor is holding tonight. To make it worse, I misread the email and show up at seven instead of eight, so I sit in the hallway of the academic building playing on my phone to kill time.

My mood changes when I see Reed Callaway walk into the lecture hall. I pray he doesn't pretend to not know me, and hope he'll sit next to me. He does. He smiles and waves before he easily slides into the seat next to me.

"I almost forgot about this meeting," he tells me. "I was about to take a nap."

"At least you didn't show up an hour early." I give him a sarcastic smile.

"You did not."

"I did." I nod solemnly as he starts to laugh quietly.

"Wow, Hevko." He smirks and shakes his head. "How will you ever be a sports journalist if you can't read a schedule correctly."

"Trust me, I don't plan on writing for the sports column ever again."

"I'm just teasing, Halle."

Of course, he remembered my first and last name, he'd be stupid not to considering the amount of time we spent talking about it. But that doesn't make him saying my name feel any less amazing.

"Did you finish the article?" he asks.

"Yeah, I actually finished it after the interviews Sunday night."

"Can I read it?"

I turn to face him, skeptical, and ask, "You want to read a biographical article about yourself and your four teammates that you already know?"

"No. I wanna read your writing."

I roll my eyes at him but open my laptop and show him the article anyway. It doesn't take him long to read it, and he slides my laptop back to me when he's done.

"You should be proud of that," he says seriously.

I am. After deciding to include Reed's description of himself as "wordy" in my article, I was able to find little quirks for each player. Things that made them seem like more than just a soccer player. Ben grew up in a south-central Appalachian city and when his parents could no longer afford to pay for his childhood soccer league during the recession, he watched reruns of international games and tried to copy the players' kicks. Harry is a graphic design major because his parents didn't allow him to apply for the visual arts program, and his passion for art is contagious. Elliot thought he would go to college on a track scholarship until the high school soccer coach saw him in a pickup game at a homecoming tailgate his freshman year and told him he was built to play soccer.

I took the crap questions I was given and turned my article into something insightful. I am proud of it.

The meeting starts and our advisor goes over a long list of campus resources and contact information. Then she opens the floor to questions. My peers rattle off the most stupid questions I've ever heard. Whenever someone asks something totally ridiculous, Reed nudges me with his foot to signal he thinks it's dumb. He's able to keep a straight face as he does it, but I stifle a laugh every time.

We aren't dismissed until 9:30. Reed waits for me to pack up my bag and we walk out together. I hear a few sirens close to campus, but I don't think anything of it until Reed asks me, "Where are you living?"

"York."

"Let me walk you."

I feel like the sirens are following us. We walk past the upperclassmen apartment complexes, the Newman Center, and the campus bookstore until we finally reach York. I swipe my student ID to unlock the door to the building and hold it open for Reed to enter behind me, but he shakes his head.

"I'm in Baker Hall, actually."

My eyebrows shoot up involuntarily. Baker Hall is literally next to where our lecture was, at the other end of campus. I assumed he lived in York when he offered to walk me back.

"You didn't have to walk me all the way back here," I say. We're hovering in the doorway.

"If I had told you I was in Baker, you wouldn't have let me walk you back."

I am a self-proclaimed stubborn, obstinate, headstrong girl. So, that is a fair assumption.

However, the more time I spend with Reed, the more I think I would give up any self-sufficiency to spend time with him. At this point, he's the only friend I've made that isn't Addy. But I do want him to believe I'm an independent girl who refuses to be escorted home, so I play along.

"Probably," I say. "Do you wanna come up to my room?"

He looks amused. That came off way more suggestive

than I meant it to. I need to fix this before he thinks I'm about to jump him.

"I'll introduce you to my roommate," I add quickly.

He agrees, and we ride my elevator from hell up to the sixth floor and pass Tori's door (which has a do not disturb sign on the handle, like she's staying at a hotel) and eventually reach 601. I open the door to see Addy sitting on our futon with a girl I have never seen before.

"Reed, this is my roommate Addy." Addy gives a small princess wave while the stranger stares. "And … company."

Addy is looking at me like I've brought an alien home, and I'm looking at her the same way. I try to communicate telepathically and tell Addy to *please for the love of God*, introduce me to this girl on my couch before Reed thinks I'm rude or an idiot, and it works.

"This is Isabel, I met her in my psych lecture." The girl waves as Addy explains. "She lives in our hall, with *Tori*, isn't that too funny?"

Isabel has dark flat hair and a cool smile that forms a tight line. She looks like a fellow tall girl, so I instantly feel some solidarity with her. But she's lanky in a way I've never been that makes her look taller than she is. I would have never been friends with her in high school.

"Don't worry," she says flatly. "I think Tori's weird too."

Reed asks to use our restroom and once he's gone, Addy stands up dramatically and waves a finger at me.

"You are supposed to tell me when you meet a hot guy," she whisper-screams.

Isabel nods. "He is the cutest guy I've seen on campus so far."

My stomach is turning inside out. I was stupid to assume I'm the only one who would ever notice how amazing Reed is, right? I feel like someone just read my diary.

I offer to walk Reed out and I shut the door to 601 behind us. I could lie to myself and say it's so we could talk in private, but really, it's because I cannot watch other girls admire Reed in front of me without vomiting.

"That's a lot nicer than the communal bathrooms in Baker," he jokes.

"I'm surprised they put the athletes in the worst dorm on campus."

"It's just a soccer thing I guess, the upperclassmen say it'll humble us. I think it's hazing. When we hang out, it will for sure be in your dorm."

I want to squeal. I think I might bite my lip at some point to stop myself from making any noise, but I don't remember clearly because I half blacked out from the adrenaline rush of hearing Reed talk about us hanging out again.

We don't touch when he leaves, but he says, "See ya, Hal," in a long drawl, like he's enjoying what he's saying. I want to record it and set it as my alarm clock.

Addy and Isabel, who had their ears pressed to the other side of the door, drag me inside where they demand every detail about Reed. I happily give them like I'm filing a missing person's report on the guy. Isabel says she immediately assumed we were dating because of how he was looking at me and was surprised to hear we had only just met. That makes me happier than anything ever has.

I think Reed is what I like most about being a college student.

refills

. . .

My *literal* first Friday of college was spent unpacking and listening to my orientation leaders, so I've decided today should be considered my first Friday of college. My classes pass by in a lull. Nothing gets interesting until lunch.

Addy sits down at the table that's become "our table" with a boy I've never seen before. He's attractive, but not my type. He looks nothing like Reed. He seems like the confident type— I'd call him arrogant if I was in the mood to be judgy.

"Guys, this is Luke!" Addy practically cheers. Luke gives us all a wave, opening his mouth to say something, before Addy talks over him. "He's my friend from high school! He's gonna bring us to a party tonight."

The party in question that Luke ends up leading us to later is at a house off campus.

"Whose house is it anyway?" Isabel asks as we reach a crosswalk.

"Lacrosse guys," Luke says cooly. "I'm one of their

team managers. It's just gonna be the lacrosse team and the guys they're friends with, maybe the soccer team."

The soccer team? I can't tell if my chest is tightening out of excitement or nerves.

"Halle!" Addy screams. "Reed might be here!"

"Thank you," I mumble sarcastically. "I had not yet thought of that."

I've developed a full-blown crush on Reed. The type of crush where you hope you might run into them everywhere you go. So, even before Luke told us the soccer team might be at the party, I had imagined what it would be like to see Reed there.

We hear the party before we see it, and from the outside, the house looks like all the others surrounding it, except for the two boys in lacrosse hoodies sitting on the front porch. They both stand and greet Luke.

"You know the rules," the one on the right says.

"Rules?" Addy asks.

"Any guy who's a NARP needs to bring two girls to come in," the guy answers.

"What the fuck is a *NARP*?" Isabel asks flatly.

"Non-Athlete Regular Person," the two boys on the porch answer in unison.

"I brought three girls!" Luke says defensively.

"Yeah, we can count," the guy on the left says. "Come on in, let's get the ladies drinks."

Inside, the house looks like every movie I've ever seen about college. People fill the living room wall to wall, the windows have cardboard taped over them, and when the song changes to an old rap song, the room explodes with cheers. I'd be having fun if I wasn't painfully sober.

"Pigsty," Isabel says next to me as she wipes the table at the base of the staircase, filled with beer and seltzers, with one quick finger to inspect its cleanliness.

"What did you expect?" I ask.

She doesn't answer me, instead saying, "You know why all this booze is free right? They're trying to get us drunk enough to sleep with them. So, the booze isn't *really* free because they think we'll pay them with sex."

"I plan on taking their free booze and not having sex with any of them so, stick it to the man I guess," I say.

"You don't think you'll have sex with Reed if you run into him tonight?" she asks casually.

I freeze and remind myself that Isabel does not know that I haven't even had my first kiss. The only person here who knows is Addy — it came up on the first night we were here, when we stayed up talking about the crushes we had in high school.

Even Addy knowing my secret felt like one person too many. College is supposed to be a new start. I can't go around telling people I was the girl no one had a crush on in high school.

"We just met," is all I can manage to croak out.

Isabel shrugs. "It's college."

Addy and I have hung out exclusively with Isabel this week. She doesn't like Tori very much, so she comes over to our room a lot. She's very blunt. I'm not used to it yet.

We drink like it's the end of the world and make friends with anyone who takes the time to talk to us. I wonder if I'm doing a good job hiding how drunk I really am until I scan the rest of the party and realize everyone here is probably thinking the same thing.

We haven't left the living room yet, so I drag Addy and Isabel with me to explore the rest of the house. I'm looking for Reed, but I don't tell them that. The only other room on the first floor we can find is the kitchen, which while still crowded, is significantly quieter than the living room. Despite the crowd, I spot Reed leaning against a counter talking to Ben, who I recognize from my interview. Addy follows my gaze.

"Go," she says, pushing me in his direction. "We'll be in the living room. We won't leave without you…unless you leave with him first, obviously." She winks at me before leaving.

Now that I'm alone in the room, I have no choice but to talk to Reed. I take a deep breath, making my way across the kitchen. Before I'm within ten feet of him, Reed notices me. I see his face light up, and it gives me instant satisfaction, like he's flipped a switch on my mood for tonight.

"Halle!" He waves me over to him and Ben.

"I didn't know you would be here," he says once I reach him. He leans over to give me a friendly, tame side hug. He smells like cologne. Expensive cologne. I've never noticed that before.

Reed's tall, but so am I, so the few inches he's taken off his height by slouching against the counter has nearly put me level with his steady brown eyes.

"Addy's friend from high school needed to bring girls to get in," I explain.

Reed rolls his eyes. "I already hate this guy."

"Hey, if he hadn't used me for my gender, you wouldn't have seen me tonight," I say, making a small attempt at flirting to test the waters.

I'm not sure whether I should blame my newfound confidence on the alcohol or my excitement that Reed is here. I really was lucky enough to end up at the same party as him. He's smiling at me with eyebrows raised, looking interested that I made the first move.

"Good point," he says, before shifting to Ben. "You remember Halle, right?"

"Of course," he says, reaching past Reed to shake my hand politely. "How'd the article turn out?"

"Pretty good! Our editor wants to go over it at our next meeting. It should be in next week's issue."

"She's being humble," Reed says after a swig of beer. "I read it, it's amazing."

Reed's not-so-subtle insinuation that he and I are close enough for him to have read my unpublished article, the odd territorial sense of it, makes me feel better than I'd like to admit. All I can manage is a tight-lipped smile of gratitude until Reed reaches out to me and rubs a careful hand from my shoulder down to my bent elbow. After that, I'm trying to get my jaw from unhinging itself.

"Are you drinking tonight?" he asks.

I nod.

"Let's go get refills."

With his hand delicately placed on the small of my back, Reed leads me to a dining room off the kitchen. The entire room is filled with alcohol. A table with beer, a table with seltzers, and a table with liquor and mixers. In the middle of the room sits a large trash can filled almost to the top with what looks like fruit punch, but I know a batch of jungle juice when I see it. I grab a red cup, but before I can fill it, Reed pulls the cup out of my hands.

When I turn back to tell him I'm a big girl who can handle my jungle juice, he silently points to a sign I hadn't noticed. It's handwritten in marker on cardboard, and there's an arrow pointing to the jungle juice. Under the arrow, it says: FOR GIRLS ONLY!

"They put a shit ton of energy drinks in it," Reed explains, hovering over me. "So you don't feel like you're drunk. And if you don't feel like you're drunk, you'll keep drinking, and if you drink like four cups of this, you'll blackout. And if you blackout…"

Reed trails off, letting me assume the end of his sentence was nothing good, before he hands me another can of seltzer, unopened. I pop the tab and take a sip.

"Thanks," I tell him. I'm not just being polite; I really mean it.

He shrugs. "Yeah, anytime. Someone's gotta show you the ropes."

I roll my eyes, trying to lighten up our conversation. "You've been here, what, two weeks longer than I have?"

He smiles. "Two weeks feels like a whole semester in college, I swear."

Together, we decide to merge back into the living room, where a few of the lacrosse players are pushing the furniture against the wall to create a makeshift dance floor. Bodies crowd it immediately, and Reed snakes a hand around my waist to steady me as people push past us.

"Wanna dance?" His mouth is practically next to my ear, but the room is so loud he's yelling. When I turn to face him, he looks nervous. That's new. It's kind of hot.

I smile and nod and he drags me to the center of the crowd. Dancing with Reed is about as exciting as I imagined it would be, but also way more fun. I like that neither of us are taking this too seriously, that we're both singing along to the songs as we dance and laugh with each other.

But once the music changes to an R&B song, something a little sultrier, I feel the whole room slow down. My hands that were draped lazily around his neck involuntarily tighten and his hands do the same where they hold the backside of my waist. A moment passes between us as we look at each other and wordlessly acknowledge what's about to happen. He kisses me. It starts off sweet but once I feel it quicken, I don't stop it.

In high school, I had always been thankful that my friends who had boyfriends never talked to me about the guys they kissed or what it felt like. But now I'm mad that no one told me how good this felt. If I would've known, I would've done this a lot sooner.

I feel lightheaded. I think I'm shivering. I'm hyper-aware of every spot he's touching on my skin. Our kiss is sloppy, and I feel his hands move up my body, one reaching up to the side of my neck and chin, the other running over the lower seam of my cropped tank top that barely covers the underwire of my bra. He pulls away and rubs his thumb along my jaw.

"Do you wanna get out of here?"

Uh-oh.

I do wanna leave, but how do I tell Reed that I wanna leave with him and go make out until my lips fall off, but *not* have sex, without telling him that he was my first kiss? Are there any rules on how long you should wait after your first kiss before you have sex for the first time? Like waiting to swim until twenty minutes after you've finished eating. I need to stall.

"Yeah, I just..." I stumble for words and try to ignore the concern etched on Reed's face. "Let me tell my friends I'm leaving."

I practically run away from him as I scan the crowd for Addy and Isabel, but it's nearly impossible to see with so many people moving. I pass through the dance floor, not finding them, but spotting the front door of the house.

Perfect, I can go outside and figure out what I'm gonna do in the quiet of the porch, then come back in and face Reed again.

When I reach for the door's handle, I'm taken aback when someone grabs my hand to stop me. Naively, I think it might be Reed catching up with me, but I look up and see that it's actually one of the boys from the lacrosse team that was on the porch earlier. One of the boys who was deciding who could come in.

"Everything okay?" he asks me.

I'm taken aback, and trying to decide if he genuinely cares, so I shrug and stare at him blankly.

"Just looked like you could use a friend." He chuckles softly and sticks his hand out for me to shake. "I'm Aaron."

I comply and shake his hand limply, letting his aggressive grip do all the hard work.

"Well, it was nice to meet you Aaron, but I'm on my way out."

"On your way out this early? What, a stupid boy upset you?" he asks with a megawatt smile. He looks at me like we're old friends in cahoots together. Or like he's my mentor, prepared to pass on his sage advice.

I take a step back. "Something like that."

If I was sober, I would be smart enough to lie – to stop entertaining his small talk and bolt.

Aaron leans against the door and shakes his head. "You gotta stay away from the freshman boys. Nothing but trouble."

"And you're what, a sophomore?" I joke dryly.

"A *junior*. But I'm old for my grade," he replies quickly. "A guy my age would never let a girl as pretty as you walk around this party alone. It's not safe."

"Yeah." I try to smile, but my patience with this guy is wearing thin. "That's why I was leaving."

"Oh, don't leave yet honey." He lazily grabs my hip and pulls me closer to him. "I haven't even gotten your name yet."

I ignore that and shimmy out of his grip, just for him to grab me again.

"I really have to go," I lie. "My friends are waiting for

me back at the dorm and I'm really just not having as much fun as I thought -"

Aaron cuts me off. "Stay. Let me mix you up a drink, you'll be having fun in no time."

Before I left for college, I bought the mace, and I watched self-defense videos. I learned to never set my drink down anywhere and to hold it, so my hand covers the top. But no one ever told me I'd have to deal with anything like this, or how to do it.

"No." I push myself away from him again and stand my ground. "I need to leave. I can't stay."

Just like that, Aaron totally drops the bit where he pretends to be on my side. He crosses his arms and plants his back against the door. His eyes darken as he stares me down.

"I can't let you."

"I'm sorry." I gape. "Did you just say you can't *let me* leave? What's that supposed to mean?"

"Girls aren't allowed to leave our parties until two a.m."

What the hell is wrong with this guy? Is the whole lacrosse team like this? I would blame it on the alcohol, but I can tell Aaron is sober by the way he's carrying himself.

"Halle! There you are!" A distant voice behind me shouts.

I don't have to turn around to know it's Reed. When he reaches me, he looks from me to Aaron and back to me. He doesn't say anything, but he gives me another look-over like he's checking for injuries.

"You okay?" he asks, expression tight, "Did you find the girls? You were gone for a while, I got nervous."

Behind him, Aaron snorts.

Reed turns around slowly to face him. "Problem?"

I answer him before Aaron can. "He won't let me leave. He said girls aren't allowed to leave until two."

I say it hoping it will fire Reed up, and he'll do all the yelling at Aaron, so I don't have to. Reed stares at Aaron like he's weighing his options.

"Why are you being such a dick, man? Come on, Hal, let's just get out of here."

"You're going to regret disrespecting me, freshman!" He yells at Reed.

I roll my eyes. "What are you gonna do? Never let us into another party again?"

"Fine, bitch," Aaron screams, this time to me, specifically. "Fucking leave, never come back to this house."

"Gladly," I say with no smile, escaping onto the front porch with Reed behind me.

I don't realize I've started to cry until I feel the heat on my face. Reed looks worked up, but easily turns off his anger to tend to me, frantically wiping the tears off my cheeks. He looks as freaked out as I feel.

"You good?" he asks.

I nod, but I know I'm not. I think about Aaron's stupid hands grabbing me, how it felt to be called a bitch in earnest for the first time, and how embarrassing it is that I'm eighteen years old and just had my first real kiss tonight. How could all that *not* make me cry?

Reed wordlessly wraps me into a hug, letting me calm down as I press my face into his chest, but it's obvious he has no idea what to say.

I'm surprised Reed and Aaron's encounter ended without any fists flying, that he's out here with me, instead of inside picking a fight with Aaron on my behalf. When I was younger, I thought I wanted a boyfriend who would get in fights for me. Maybe I don't really want the boy throwing punches for me, maybe I want the boy who comes outside to check on me first and cares more that *I'm* safe.

The adrenaline of the moment and the alcohol I've consumed are not mixing well. I feel like I'm about to topple over.

"What was that about?" Reed asks, breaking our bout of silence.

"They wouldn't let me -"

"I meant earlier." He cuts me off, shutting his eyes tightly and pinching the space between them. "When we were ... fuck, I don't know, you just seemed kind of freaked out, I didn't make you uncomfortable, did I? I'm sorry if -"

I interrupt. "It's not your fault. I wanted, *want*, to leave with you."

"What's up then?"

I take a deep breath and prepare myself for the embarrassment, and for him to turn around and tell me he doesn't want me anymore.

"That was my first kiss," I tell him.

He doesn't say anything, instead closing the gap between us and slowly bringing his hand to my face. We're right where we left off.

"I don't believe you," he says sweetly.

"Why would I lie about something that embarrassing?" I scoff.

He smirks. "That was my really lame attempt at saying you are a very good kisser."

I smile and feel the heat in my cheeks but blame it on the alcohol. "All of my guy friends in high school were gay. We used to make out at parties as a joke," I explain frantically.

Reed presses a kiss to my jaw, and says, "I'm gonna need their contact information," while his lips are still pressed to my skin.

"Why?"

"To send them formal thank you notes."

I laugh.

"So, this means you don't have some loser boyfriend back home you're hiding from me," he says.

"Correct. What about you, secret girl back home?"

"No. I wouldn't do that to you."

He's being too sweet for me to process.

"I never had anyone even close to a boyfriend," I say, purposefully changing the topic to pause his affection before it becomes unbearable.

He makes a funny face and tilts his head.

"What?" I ask. "I don't look like a girl who's never had a boyfriend?"

"You don't. I'm surprised."

"You're only surprised because you didn't know me in high school. Boys didn't wanna date me. My mom said I was too intimidating, but I think I just wasn't cool enough."

"I don't believe you." He sing-songs with a grin.

"It's true! I had crushes on guys and would try my best to talk to them, but I'm pretty shy so it never really worked out."

"Bullshit, you are not shy."

"I'm shy around boys I have crushes on," I say without thinking.

"You're not very shy around me, do you not like me or something?" He laughs.

"No, that's not what I meant. It's different with you, obviously, if I didn't like I wouldn't…I wouldn't be -"

"I'm just kidding," he says, adding after a beat. "I know. Can I kiss you again?"

I nod. If our kiss on the dance floor was good, this one

is great. Fantastic. And this time when he asks me if I want to leave, I say yes.

"I should actually tell my friends where I'm going," I say in between kisses.

He nods. "Let's go find them."

But the thought of going back into the house makes me dizzy.

"I don't wanna go back inside," I say.

"I shouldn't leave you alone out here," Reed responds, looking around the empty yard like he's expecting some unseen trouble to creep out.

"I'm better off out here than I am going back in there. Please," I tell him.

He looks me over, performing some weird risk analysis inside his head, before agreeing. "Okay. I'll be back."

I sit on the porch step as I wait and rack through my brain, looking for any evidence that the past hour has changed me. Growing up, I thought that my first kiss would change a chemical compound in me. I don't think it has. I thought my first kiss would make me feel mature, but I've never felt younger. I feel giddy.

Reed returns after an indeterminable amount of time and holds out a steady hand to help me up.

"I found Addy," he says, "who, interestingly enough, was engrossed in a conversation with Ben."

"They were probably talking about us."

"Oh, they were for sure talking about us."

"Were those guys still by the door?" I ask quietly.

"Yeah," he says seriously, "but I told Addy and Ben about it, so if your friends decide to leave before two, Ben said he would make sure they get out okay."

"Thank you."

Reed shrugs. "Least I can do."

He's not standing as close to me as he was, and he keeps kicking the same dirt with his foot. Something's off.

"Are you mad about something?" I ask, trying to think of what could have happened in the few minutes he was gone that would've upset him.

"It's nothing." He pauses as his eyes meet mine. "It really sucks that happened. It's like all this good happens, and then this dark stain washes over the night because of some asshole lacrosse player."

"Make it up to me then," I say quickly as I look at him before my brain can filter the words flying out of my mouth or process the insinuation.

"What?" he asks, looking very alert.

"Make the bad stuff up to me. Let's get out of here and you can replace my dark stain with something better."

He grins mischievously. "I can do that."

Reed and I walk through campus, being nosy and trying to spot which dorms and apartments still have their lights on. Our hands are locked together.

"Once it hits two or three," Reed tells me, "you'll start to see people walking back from house parties and bars. Other than that, it's dead."

Pretty dead is an understatement. Campus is a ghost town right now.

We reach York and I swipe us in, even though Reed stops outside the front door.

"You're not coming up?" I ask, disappointed.

He smiles. "Go change into something warmer and meet me in the yard, under that big willow tree behind the Clocktower."

I've never been so frustrated with how slow this elevator is. I rip off my party clothes and replace them with a university sweatshirt and pajama pants. I don't even stop to check my appearance in the mirror.

I have to stop myself from running to the yard. True to his word, I find Reed sitting on the grass under the semi-privacy of the willow tree, with an oversized blanket in his lap. Is that his comforter?

Like he's reading my thoughts, Reed explains defensively, "It's the only blanket I own!"

"I would've brought a blanket if you asked," I laugh as I slide onto the ground to sit next to him.

He shrugs. "Didn't think about that."

Reed pulls the comforter over the both of us as we lay in the grass. We make out for a while. Reed repositions us so that he's on top of me, and he's doing that thing again where one hand is against the bottom of my face and his thumb is running across my jaw. I'm obsessed with it. When he moves his hand so that it's nearly covering my whole throat, I decide that's the thing I'm obsessed with. He pauses and I take the time to catch my breath.

"Pretty girl," he mumbles, almost more to himself than to me, before tucking a stray piece of hair behind my ear. "I don't know why this feels so different with you."

"It's all the experience I have," I say sarcastically and wink.

"Can only go up from here, really," he says, kissing me quickly, "Practice makes perfect."

We alternate between kissing and talking, listening to the bells from the clocktower ring every fifteen minutes. Some conversations last longer than others. Both of our favorite books are books that we read in AP Literature — *The House of the Spirits* for me and *The Kite Runner* for him. We both hated our high school chemistry teachers. We gush over Stephen King and Reed promises to lend me his copy of *On Writing*.

"You'll have to remind me though, I'm awful at

remembering that kind of stuff," he adds before kissing me again.

I'm so comfortable with the pattern we've fallen into. I can't remember anyone's name except Reed's, and I have no concept of time. My whole body shakes whenever we kiss. I start really shivering in the middle of a kiss, even though I'm not cold, and Reed breaks it to pull the comforter tighter around me. He takes a quick glance at his phone and laughs.

"I have practice in three hours," he says before reaching back over to kiss me.

I stop him before he can. "What?"

"It's four a.m. I have practice in three hours."

"You need to sleep."

"No, as long as I leave this exact spot by six thirty -"

"Reed," I say sharply. "I will not let myself be the reason you pass out on the field in the middle of practice."

"Fine." He grunts as he sits back up. "Can I see you tomorrow? I wanna do this again when we're one hundred percent sober."

Our kiss goodbye outside the door to 601 lasts ten minutes.

When we finally separate, I go inside and catch a glimpse of my reflection in the bathroom mirror. I'm blushing. I fall asleep smiling.

on writing

. . .

I wake up to Addy standing over my bed, hands on her hips.

"You had your first kiss last night, didn't you?" she asks threateningly.

"How'd you know? Do I look like a new woman?"

"No dummy," she says as she sits on the end of my bed. "You kissed in front of the whole party."

That does not sound like my best idea now that I'm sober.

Addy picks up Betty, my well-loved stuffed puppy that I forced my mom to let me bring to school, and fidgets with the stuffed animal's ears. "I approve of Reed," she says absentmindedly.

I shoot her a questioning glance, hoping she'll elaborate and be as excited to talk about my new favorite person as I am.

"He ran around the whole party looking for you after you left him, it was darling. And Ben told me Reed talks about you. A lot."

"Does he now?"

"He asked Ben for advice on asking you out. For real," she tells me, in her flat, faint accent.

I can get behind that. But last night, Reed didn't ask me out. He asked to see me again, but I thought he made it clear he wanted to keep it casual like we did last night. It's easy to convince myself I'm okay with that arrangement.

Addy says, "We're going to the caf. You're coming, I don't care how hungover you are."

I don't feel as hungover as I deserve, but I look like I had a rough night, even though I had the opposite. I went to bed without taking my makeup off, so there's eyeliner smeared under my eyes. I have a hickey on my collarbone, easily covered with a t-shirt. I'm more upset about the mosquito bites covering my arms and legs in big red splotches. I must have been violently itching them in my sleep because it looks like I've been mauled.

Over stale sandwiches, I hear about the drama of the party I missed. My friends left a little before three, and Ben walked back to campus with them. They hadn't even gotten off the block yet when a police car pulled up to bust the party. Addy calls it dumb luck; Isabel calls it good karma.

It's painfully obvious Addy has a small crush on Ben, but we can't convince her to admit it. All we can coerce out of her is that Ben is "just a really sweet guy." Before we leave our table, Reed texts me to ask if I want to meet him tonight.

The first thing he does when I see him later is hand me his copy of *On Writing*.

Reed and I walk to his dorm in a comfortable silence and my hand goes to my neck, fidgeting with the necklace I have on. It's a small sun-shaped charm my best friend from high school, Emmy, got me as a graduation gift.

"Stop doing that," he tells me.

"What?"

"Itching your neck like that. Jesus, you're gonna make yourself bleed," he says, gently reaching over to pull my hand off my neck.

I didn't realize I had been doing it, but Reed's right, my neck is covered in red tracks. Itching the front of my neck has always been a subconscious nervous tick of mine. I'm doing it now because I can't quiet the nagging voice in the back of my head telling me that something changed in the past twelve hours and he's somehow less interested. I'm too young to be this happy being with someone and keep it forever. The voice in the back of my head quickly shuts up when Reed reaches out to hold my hand confidently.

Reed and Ben's dorm room is much smaller than Addy and I's. Ben isn't here, and when I ask Reed if he'll be coming back soon, he tells me not to worry about it.

I thought seeing Reed's room would peel back a layer and help me understand him more. Because that's how my room is. I upheave my personality onto any space I can. My wall is covered with posters and pictures of my friends from back home. My laptop case has so many stickers on it that you can't tell what color it is. I have a growing collection of pins on my backpack.

Reed's room is nothing like that. His walls are blank.

After a few hours of making out and making small talk on his bed, my lips feel numb, and Reed walks me back to York. He's waking up early for an away game tomorrow, which means I won't see him until the team returns Monday morning. It sucks, but I'm weirdly excited. I've never had the chance to miss someone before.

When I come back to the room, Addy and Isabel are halfway through a six-hour reality tv binge. I join them, thinking of nothing except for Snookie, Abby Lee Miller, and Lauren Conrad – until I remember Reed's copy of *On Writing* is still sitting in my tote. I pull it out during a commercial break and find the whole book, every page, is annotated. Passages are underlined in uneven lines, his small handwriting in black ink leaking through the pages. There's a little piece of paper inside the front cover with a note:

FOR THE BEST WORST SPORTS JOURNALIST I KNOW

THE CLOCKTOWER STAFF MEETING STARTS AT NOON, AND I don't wake up until 11:00. I skip my usual stop at the campus coffee shop to be early for the meeting, only to find I'm still the last person to arrive. Everyone is editing or starting new projects. Our editor-in-chief, Sam, waves me over to his desk when he sees me walk in.

"Halle, right?"

I nod uncomfortably. Sam looks totally relaxed and has a cheeky smile plastered on his face.

"Come sit down." He gestures over to his desk, which is really just a normal table with a chair on each side. "Sorry, I'm still learning all the first years' names."

There are only two first years, including myself, on this whole staff so far. I fake a sympathetic laugh.

"So." Sam slides a piece of paper across the desk that I immediately recognize as my article. "I have your article here, great work by the way, but you're gonna have to rewrite it."

Bit of an oxymoron there, Sam.

"Excuse me?" I ask, in my most polite voice possible, although it still comes out a little rude on accident.

"We're just not really looking for any pieces like yours

right now. If you want your article published this week it's gonna have to look more like this." He slides another piece of paper to me. It looks like a template. "Ya know, more like a Q and A. Just write what the question was and what each player answered. No need for the fluffy stuff."

All I can do is nod in response as I feel my throat close.

"Get it to me by five and we can still put it in the issue," Sam says cheerfully.

I take the papers he hands me and get the hell out of there and to the bathroom before I break down crying. Why did Sam have to make "fluffy" sound like a bad thing? Jesus, a robot could have written the article he was looking for.

It only takes me five minutes to pull myself together and head back to the meeting. Projects are assigned for the next week, and I'm given the choice between an article on the upcoming student council elections or a blurb for the back page covering the campus welcome week fair that just ended. I pick the back page option and hope my work won't be too fluffy for Sam.

I leave the meeting in such a bad mood that it takes a conscious effort not to take it out on Addy and Isabel as we eat an early dinner. I wish Reed was with us and that I could rant to him about it. I know we haven't been together long, but I feel like I can already predict what his response would be, something that's sympathetic without sounding too much like pity, something supportive without sounding phony. I think about texting him, but when I open our conversation, I see that the only texts there are the ones we exchanged yesterday discussing what time we wanted to meet.

Two texts. I'm obsessed with this guy, and I only have two texts to show for it.

It only takes me twenty minutes to write the article

Sam was looking for and I email him the attachment with no context or explanation, hoping he gets the message that I'm pissed off. I'm not sure if he does, because he replies:

Thanks, Hallie! Amazing work! Look for your article in the sports section this week! Can't wait to work with you this year!

Sam is, at least, true to his word. Next week, my article is printed on the bottom of a page below a piece of last year's star basketball player's career-ruining injury. I don't even see the article until Addy points out the newly replenished stack of *Clocktower* copies in the student center on a Wednesday. She aggressively grabs the top copy.

"Halle! You made this! That's your name!" she says proudly, waving the paper dramatically.

I don't feel a spark of joy seeing my name in the size six font under the title. That's not my article. It's Sam's. The more I look at it, the more I feel sick to my stomach.

As if that isn't bad enough, when Addy, Isabel, and I meet Ben and Reed for lunch, Reed walks up to the table with the damned newspaper in his hand. He drops it forcefully onto the table in front of me while I'm mid-bite into a slice of pizza.

"What happened to your article? They spelled your name wrong. *Twice*."

Sadly, he's right. The article is credited to Hallie Heykoy. Hallie Heykoy sounds like a nice girl — I hope she's doing well.

All I can do is shrug at Reed as I swallow my bite of pizza. I don't see the point in getting worked up over it. It's irritating, but the article's already been printed so there's not much I can do anymore besides hope it never happens again.

Reed looks at me in total defeat. "You didn't tell me they made you change it."

Well, now he's just making me feel bad. I do feel a little guilty about never telling him, but in my defense, what would he have even done to solve it if he knew? Talked to Sam on my behalf? God no.

We drop the topic once Addy chimes in with a story about the vision board she's planning on pasting over our dorm walls. But I have trouble focusing when all I can think about is if Reed would've reacted any differently if I had told him about it in the first place.

———

Reed and Ben decide to throw their own, tame, dorm party to celebrate Reed's birthday - September 10. He was born in 2001, so the day before 9/11, and he never shuts up about how he was *technically* alive on 9/11 so he can't relate to any of us "youngsters" born after. But he, obviously, has no memory of the day, so it's a weak argument.

When Reed first made the plan for his birthday party, I offered to come over earlier in the day to help him clean up and get the room ready. When I get to his room in Baker, his door is propped open. I let myself in.

Reed's sitting on the end of his bed, holding his phone to his ear. When he sees me come in, he waves and says into the phone, "Yeah, I've got to go, Ben just got back to the room… Okay, bye, Mom…Yeah. Love you too."

My stomach drops as I realize he hasn't told his parents about me. I should never have assumed he had, just because I've told my mother almost everything about Reed since we met.

"Hey." He greets me, shoving his phone back into his pocket. Something's off. He's jumpy.

"Are you okay?" I ask.

He smiles at me, but I can tell it's fake. "Totally. Thanks for coming over early by the way."

Yeah, I'm not gonna let him change the subject that easily. "That was your mom on the phone?"

"She called to wish me a happy birthday," he says, sadly, with the disposition of a kicked puppy.

I sit down next to him on the bed. "Everything okay? You seem kind of upset."

He heaves a big sigh. "It's fine. Sometimes I just don't think my parents are very nice people. That's all."

"Do you want to talk about it?"

"Not really."

I wish he would talk to me. I wish I felt comfortable easing the information out of him, instead of letting it go. I want to tell him his parents must be at least a little bit good if they raised someone like him.

We set the room up, people start arriving, and the party starts. He loves my gift, a copy of *A Farewell to Arms* I found at the used bookstore in town, and kisses me when I give it to him. Our friends give Reed a cake with no candles, we make each other stupid cocktail concoctions, and Reed spends most of the night introducing me to his friends with his arm lazily draped around my waist.

We don't talk about his parents again. I'm too afraid to bring it up. I regret that.

———

The next night, a little past 2 a.m., Reed and I sneak onto the soccer field.

"Are we going to get in trouble for this?" I whisper after he's done helping me over the fence.

Reed hops over, landing next to me with a thud and a smirk.

"No," he says, deadly serious. "I don't know if you knew this about me, Halle, but...I'm a college athlete so-"

I cut him off with a push to his chest and a sharp laugh, before continuing onto the unlit field. "You're such an asshole."

"-I can get away with anything," he finishes, even though he's laughing now too.

He finds a soccer ball somewhere and teaches me how to kick it properly, so I can kick it more than a foot away. Apparently, you kick a soccer ball with the side of your foot. Never knew that.

He tells me he's gonna teach me how to do a step over and then score and doesn't give up on me even when I confuse my left and right.

"Okay." He heaves, standing in front of the goal in a fighting position. "Pretend I'm a defender."

"Will I be tested on all of this or something?"

He straightens up, relaxes from his guarded post, and shrugs. "I thought it'd be fun."

Now that I've got him distracted, I kick the ball like he taught me to, do the step-over thing and score, even though my kick makes me lose my balance and fall flat on my ass.

Reed crouches down next to me immediately, running his hands up and down my legs and ankles like he's checking for any injuries, "Shit, are you okay?"

I laugh, unfazed as Reed looks at me in total confusion.

"I scored," I tell him smugly between wheezes. "You got distracted and I scored."

He looks at the ball still in the net and shakes his head. "Playing dirty. Think that means I've taught you all I know."

I'm still laughing as he helps me up.

sick

. . .

It's the last week of September, and I have the worst flu of my life.

Addy comes back to the dorm after class complaining of a headache. I don't think much of it when she decides to take a nap and skip her afternoon classes. I ask her if she needs anything and she says no before knocking out.

But by the time my last class of the day is over, I think I might pass out. I feel shaky and sick all over and feel like I'm using all my energy to drag myself from the academic mall back to York. I know it's a fever.

I crawl into bed and text Reed, knowing he's at soccer until ten and won't see it until he's on his way over.

Reed and I have been exclusive over the past almost month, but we aren't exactly dating. We had made plans to hang out tonight and usually, our plans for nights when he comes over after soccer practice almost exclusively consist of making out (some days getting to second base) on my bed while Addy goes over to Tori and Isabel's.

He never stays overnight, it's a line we don't cross. At first, I thought he was the type of person that didn't like sleeping in front of people, being vulnerable like that. But the other week we took a nap together. So that rules that out. Even if he's in my room until two a.m. on nights like these, even when I offer, he doesn't sleep over.

I know texting him and letting him know that I'm sick is somewhere in between a gamble and a test. I know what I'm really saying is: I can't make out with him until my lips hurt tonight. I know that if he doesn't come over, it means he doesn't see our relationship as anything but physical. I can't lie, it makes me nervous. I almost decide not to send it, but I do.

Addy and I sleep for hours, though sleep isn't the best word to describe the awful state of waking up repeatedly because I'm shivering. In one of my spurts of consciousness, Addy sits up straight in her bed and looks at me with pure panic in her eyes.

"I'm gonna puke," she says, though it comes out quickly like it's all one word. She runs to the bathroom and slams the door behind her. She pukes, and from my bed, it sounds like a baby dinosaur dying.

Isabel grabs dinner for us, dropping it in take-out boxes outside our door. She refuses to open the door out of fear of contamination. Neither of us eat it.

Then I puke. And I really hope my puking doesn't sound as bad as Addy's did. I can't stop until the toilet bowl is filled with bile. Once I recover, I mix Theraflu my mom forced me to pack into a cold glass of water. I'm very thankful for her right now.

Reed knocks on our door at 9:45, waking me up. I have no idea how he got into the building. It looks like he was in a rush to get over here, he's still in his uniform. His duffle bag is in hand, even though he usually goes back to his dorm and showers before coming over.

"Jesus," he says softly, looking me over carefully. He

takes in my pale face and the hoodie plus two blankets I have over my shoulders and shakes his head.

"Do I look that bad?" I groan.

"No, but when I get a text from you saying you 'aren't feeling great' I was expecting a runny nose or something... not *this*."

He follows me in, trailing as I drag myself to the sink to grab my third glass of Theraflu for the night.

"I guess like half the campus has the same flu. Our captain said his girlfriend had to go to the health center." He stops talking to watch me sip my glass. "You do know that stuff is supposed to be heated up, right?"

"I think we're past that point now." I swallow another oversized lukewarm sip and force a tight-lipped smile.

He nods seriously and I don't know why he's looking at me like I'm a Victorian child with a case of tuberculosis. Do I seriously look that bad?

"I think maybe we should go to the health center," he says slowly.

"Don't be ridiculous." We walk toward my bed, passing Addy who's been sleeping on the bathroom floor for the past hour after another wave of nausea. "I'm awake and walking around, aren't I? How bad can it be?"

He sighs out of, what I interpret to be, disappointment. "Seriously Hal?"

Arguing with him is useless, so I only shrug in response as I squirm onto my bed. He takes a deep breath and settles next to me, pulling me to him and kissing my forehead.

"Just don't want you to be sick," he whispers sweetly.

"I know." I match his hushed tone and press every ounce of my weight I can into him, not because I *need* to lean on him, just because I like how it feels. "And I know

I'm being a pain in the ass, but I really do appreciate you coming over."

"Always. But if your fever gets higher, we're seeing a doctor," he says, his voice suddenly serious again.

"What are you gonna do about it, take my temperature?" I tease and stick my tongue out at him.

"Hell yeah," he growls in a way that's so overtly sexual it's funny, as he playfully slides his finger on the hem of my shirt. "I'm gonna take your temperature, I'm gonna take your temperature so fucking hard-"

"Reed!" I laugh and push him off me before he starts to kiss my neck. "Stop, you can't be touchy, you're gonna catch my germs."

"Don't care. And I was serious about taking your temperature by the way."

"We don't have a thermometer," I argue.

"Ben has one, I'll run back to our room and grab it now. I'll just take your key with me."

"Don't leave me," I whine.

"You know I'll be back," he says. When he stands to leave and I shiver in response to missing his body heat, he slides Betty the stuffed dog under my arm.

"Try to get some sleep," he says while he absentmindedly smooths the blanket out with his hand, never breaking eye contact with me, "Hal, I won't be upset if you're asleep when I get back, you know? I don't want you to feel like you have to stay awake to entertain me or anything. I just want you to feel better."

I feel my heart try to escape through my rib cage. I wonder if he knows how much what he just said means to me. Have I ever said anything that's made him feel even a sliver of this incomparable adoration that I have for his understanding of me and how my brain works?

"Can you take Addy's temperature too? And ask her if

she needs anything? She's probably more sick than me honestly."

He nods seriously, processing his task, before grabbing my hand to kiss the back of it and running out of my room.

I fall asleep while Reed is gone. I only wake up when Reed shoves a thermometer under my tongue. In my state of half sleep and half not, I can't quite place his expression, his furrowed eyebrows, and the tight line his mouth is settled in.

"You look flustered," I tell him.

"Yeah, your fever went up."

"Up from what?"

"I've been taking your temperature every hour," he says, "this is just the first time you've woken up."

"I don't believe you." I rearrange myself so we're both sitting up. "I'm a very light sleeper."

Reed smiles a bit. "Did you not know the Theraflu you were drinking was nighttime Theraflu?"

I did not.

I pale. "Obviously not! I had like three full glasses of that, I could have overdosed!"

Reed laughs and reaches an arm behind me to rub my back. "You weren't gonna overdose. And if you did, I would've pushed my fingers down your throat until you puked all of it up."

"Aw, that's so romantic."

In the dark of my room, I swear I see Reed blush. "Yeah, yeah that's me, romantic and all."

I laugh, maybe a bit louder than I planned on laughing, and look over at Addy's bed to make sure I didn't wake her. I didn't, she's out cold. Reed hands me two pills and a bottle of water from my nightstand that I'm certain were not there when I fell asleep. He pushes my hair back from my face so he can kiss me quickly.

"Stop kissing me," I argue. "You're gonna get the flu."

All he does is shake his head. "Go back to sleep."

I have the worst night of sleep. To make things worse, every time I wake up, Reed's awake too. He always tells me not to worry and to just go back to sleep, but I feel so awful. I'm thankful he's here, obviously, but nothing he says makes me feel less guilty about taking up his time and keeping him from falling asleep.

The sun is rising when I finally wake up and find Reed dead asleep for the first, miraculous time. More good news — I feel like my fever broke, even though it's been replaced with some major congestion issues. I can feel every liquid in my head draining down the back of my throat. Addy's still asleep too.

I'm able to squeeze out of bed without waking up Reed. Success! I check the time, and it's around 7:00 am, a socially acceptable time to shower. I need one, now that my fever's gone, I feel disgusting.

I wash up and change into my never-seen-in-public sweatpants. I already know I'm not going to make it to my classes today. When I'm out of the bathroom, I grab some of the pills and water and wake Addy up to give them to her before she immediately falls back asleep. I turn around and see Reed's sitting on the edge of my bed, rubbing his eyes.

"Hey," he says, his voice still strained with sleep. "How are you feeling?"

"Better." I wring my wet hair out with a towel, noticing how exhausted Reed looks. "You should go back to your room. Get some real sleep."

"Do you want me to leave?" he asks.

"No," I answer honestly and quickly, hanging the towel over the back of my desk chair.

"Then I'm not leaving."

I roll my eyes. Stubborn man. "Are you not going to class? What are you even going to tell your professors?"

Reed shrugs innocently. "That my best friend has the flu," he says sincerely.

It shouldn't be, but somehow these words mean more to me than anything else he's ever said to me. I don't care that he's never referred to me as his girlfriend, because he just called me his best friend, and for some reason that means more to me.

I convince him that I can handle myself for the time it takes him to go back to his room to shower, put fresh clothes on, and pick up his homework so he at least gets *something* done. While I'm waiting for him to come back, Addy wakes up and jumps in the shower, still making some odd puking noises, and I try to sleep through them. I can't. So, I pull out my laptop and work on my latest *Clocktower* article.

When he comes back forty-five minutes later with his backpack, I'm still working on my article. Addy's finally awake, watching a reality dating show on our TV and sipping on a cup of tea. When he sits down Addy looks at him quizzically.

"Were you here earlier?" she asks him quietly.

When he nods, she raises her eyebrows. "Holy shit," she says, "I totally thought I dreamt that."

Reed spends the rest of the day with Addy and me, offering to go pick us up food and medicine before we even ask him to.

He never gets my flu, and he tells me it means we're destined to be together, that God made us immune to each other's germs on purpose.

REED LOVES MY FRECKLES. *LOVE* LOVES THEM. I HAVEN'T gathered the courage to tell him they only exist when I'm tan and coming from summer, and that they will fade by October. He calls me *freckles* sometimes, though the way he says it makes it sound less like a nickname and more like an I love you.

"Alright freckles," he says as we stand at the counter, ordering lunch from the Ross Cafe and Diner, a small family-owned place uptown. "You order first."

I order a chicken sandwich with extra lettuce, no tomato, with chipotle mayo, and iced green tea to go with it. Reed copies my order exactly.

When I laugh at him, he just shrugs and says, "What? It sounded good."

We eat our lunch at a big corner booth. I didn't realize it when I invited Reed here, but this is the first time we've been off campus together. It's a date but it's not a date.

"How'd you find this place anyway?" he asks me.

"This is where my parents and I ate when we first toured campus," I say before swallowing.

I was planning on coming here alone until I ran into Reed while walking across the yard and asked him to come with me on a whim. I was just going to grab a sandwich to go. It sounds kind of stupid, but I thought it would remind me of my parents. I've felt homesick this week. At the start of the semester, college felt like summer camp. But that feeling wore off recently and it was a little jarring, like a bad hangover.

Apparently, I don't hide my overthinking well, because Reed nudges me with his foot.

"You look tense," he says plainly.

"Sorry." Suddenly embarrassed, feeling bad that my

own overthinking is interrupting our time together, gulping a third of my iced green tea down at once.

"Do you wanna talk about it?" he asks slowly.

"I'm just homesick, I guess." I sigh.

When I look at Reed to see his reaction, he's staring at me with his eyebrows raised, waiting for me to go on like he knows there's more, so I explain to him that most of my high school friends went to college close to home, so they all get to hang out together on weekends. I feel left out, I think. And that it kind of sucked when I was sick the other week and my parents weren't there to take care of me like they used to be. I miss watching TV with them at night and stuff. I miss my cat. I miss my queen-sized bed. There're all these restaurants back home that I'm craving, and I get so sad when I realize I can't eat there. I tell him I miss going to the mall. I miss driving my car. I feel sick whenever I walk into a grocery store near campus that looks like my grocery store at home. There's a moment when I walk into the store that my brain tricks itself into thinking I'm home, and that when I walk out of the store I'll be getting in my mom's car and driving home with her, not that I'll have to walk back to campus alone.

I tell him everything until I'm out of breath from talking.

"Sorry," I say quietly. "I probably just unloaded a lot on you. I feel like I've been talking forever."

Reed shakes his head slowly. "I like it when you're chatty."

I try to fight a smile that peeks out anyway before I reach for my sandwich again, as Reed not so subtly sneaks a picture of me.

"Hey." I protest softly, even though I'm not sure why I say it. I'm not upset he's taking my picture.

Reed smirks and turns his phone towards me, showing

me the picture. "What? You look cute, I want to remember it."

I guess I do look cute in the picture, only in the way that anyone who sees the picture would know that I wasn't posing. I grew up in a house where my parents were too busy to be insecure about their appearances, so I've never thought about how I looked for enough time to lack any confidence. But seeing that the way Reed sees me is an odd boost to my self-esteem.

When we get back to campus, I'm still feeling a little bit down. The sandwiches didn't help cure my homesickness like I thought they would. Being with Reed helps a little though.

"Do you wanna watch your show?" he asks me, picking up the TV remote before settling next to me in bed.

"*My* show?" I'm already under my comforter, clinging to Betty like the stuffed animal will cure all my problems.

"Your show," he repeats, using the remote to pull up the list of *West Wing* episodes on the TV.

I've never been in love, but I imagine this is what it feels like — having someone who knows you very well.

Reed stays and does homework from my bed while I go through half of the first season's episodes, eventually falling asleep before nine.

I wake up sometime in the middle of the night to find Reed asleep next to me. When I check my phone for the time, I see that he's posted that picture of me from lunch today and tagged me. It's included in a slew of photos from the past few weeks, along with a picture of him and Ben in their soccer uniforms, a picture of the whole team on the field, pictures from his dorm room birthday party, and a picture of him and I sitting on his bed talking that I didn't even know existed. I blame Ben. It's innocent enough, we're on top of his comforter and barely touching while we look at each other, but the message is loud and clear. We're more than friends.

His caption: ***For everyone who's asked — yes, I am liking school so far***

Even though he's so passed out that he's snoring, I roll over to give Reed a tiny kiss on the cheek anyway and hope he dreams about it.

fake id
. . .

I think it's sweet that Reed doesn't wanna rush me or pressure me into doing anything I'm not comfortable with, but I wanna have sex with him this weekend.

He's been away for a series of soccer games, including a game against our university's rival. His parents were even able to come to a few games, which I know made him happier than he let on. I haven't heard from him since this morning, but I'm not worried. I know the team is playing right about now. Besides, Reed and I are in a good place. He never ignores my texts without a warning. They're supposed to get back to campus around eleven tonight and Reed and I have already made plans to see each other.

Isabel, Addy, and I get an exciting piece of mail and run across campus in the early October chill to pick it up before the mail center closes for the weekend. Our fake IDs are shipped to us inside a pair of fuzzy socks. I am officially twenty-one in the state of Maine. There's a bar called Laundry Room that a sophomore in Isabel's history class said is loose on fakes, so that's where we're heading tonight.

We pass on dinner in the caf because, apparently, Laundry Room also serves pizza. I'm wearing the same outfit I wore to the lacrosse party a few weeks ago, which is probably the most basic outfit I own because I have no idea what college freshman girls wear to bars that also serve pizza and have stupid names. I don't wanna stand out too much.

We walk to the nearest gas station and Isabel is the only one brave enough to use her fake. When she purchases the two bottles of Malibu and three packs of seltzers, the man wearing headphones working behind the counter doesn't even ask to see her ID. We make it halfway to campus before realizing we don't have any bags to hide our copious amount of alcohol in. The plastic bags the gas station provided are not doing us any favors. Addy and Isabel hide in an alley behind the library while I run to York to grab an empty backpack. It doesn't hold all of it, so I end up clutching one of the Malibu bottles under my (Reed's) sweatshirt and running past the RA desk in the lobby. The RA on duty doesn't even look up.

Addy and Isabel start the pregame immediately after we get to the room. Luke, Addy's lacrosse manager friend, and his roommate, Teddy, invite themselves over, but won't be at Laundry Room because they're going to a party at the lacrosse house. We're kind of friends with Luke and Teddy now, but Reed and Luke don't particularly get along, so Addy and Isabel see Luke and Teddy a lot more than I do. Sometimes hanging out with them feels disorienting. It makes me feel like I'm in high school again, which is not a feeling I particularly enjoy.

If I am going to have sex with Reed tonight like I plan to, I need to be a comfortable level of drunk. Tipsy enough to have courage, sober enough to avoid turning the whole night into a serious mistake. So far, the only drink I've had is one cherry-flavored seltzer. My cheeks are a little flushed, but I barely feel buzzed. So far so good.

Isabel, the all knower, tells us we shouldn't leave for the bar until ten, otherwise, we'll show up too early and "totally look like freshmen." I watch my friends get more and more drunk and anxiously watch the clock. I want Reed to be here. I would never whine about missing Reed to Addy and Isabel. I'm afraid that admitting how much I missed Reed would be some ultimate betrayal of feminism or the power of female friendships. So, I sit on the end of my bed and miss him alone.

The room has a renewed energy once it hits ten as we map out a bus route to Laundry Room and Luke and Teddy say their goodbyes. Seemingly immediately after their exit, as I'm sliding on my shoes, there's a knock on the door.

In a moment of sheer panic, Addy, thinking the knock was an RA, picks up every seltzer in sight and dives under her desk.

It's not an RA, it's just Reed. It's Reed. My Reed, who for some unknown reason seems unable to make eye contact with me.

The happiness I feel when I see him is immediately replaced by the sinking feeling that something is wrong. He should be kissing my cheek, telling me about his tournament, and complimenting my outfit. Why won't he look at me?

"What's wrong?"

It's the closest I can get to asking him *what the hell is wrong with you.*

"Dumb soccer stuff," he replies barely loud enough to hear over the pregame playlist of rap music Addy manufactured. The Reed I've known for the past few weeks would be jumping into a story that he's been waiting all day to tell me right about now. Seriously, what the hell is wrong with him?

"Can we talk in the hall really quick?" He hastily adds.

Oh, Jesus Christ.

This is where life as I know it ends, in the hallway of the sixth floor of York Hall. I bite back the lump in my throat as Reed tells me exactly what my worst insecurities told me he would.

"I think we should take a break from seeing each other," he says, emotionless. "This thing we have… it's just moving really fast, and I think we both need time to focus on things that aren't each other… fuck, Halle I -"

"What are you talking about?"

He meets my eyes for the first time since knocking on the door. He looks hurt, which just confuses me more. I think about him being so gentle with me, being so supportive of my work on *Clocktower* even if it meant not seeing him for a few hours, taking care of me when I was so sick I couldn't even function — and none of it makes sense anymore. My first kiss, the first boy who ever made me feel pretty, and my best friend on this campus are all about to be gone. I'm so mad, I can feel my skin set itself on fire.

He doesn't seem to have an answer to my mostly rhetorical question, and I'm too hurt to have anything else to say.

I reach for the door I had left ajar, and he stops with a gentle tug on my wrist. "Halle, I promise I'll explain. I just need to think for a few days. Can we talk then?"

"Talk to me about it now."

He shakes his head. He can't. And if he can't talk, I don't have anything to listen to.

I think I'm in shock. I feel like I've been hit. The longer I stand here and look at him, the more it hurts. I don't think I could do anything, *ever*, to hurt him more than how badly he's just burned me.

"Fuck you."

I shut the door behind me. I've never said that to anyone before and meant it. The words taste bad. I don't turn back to see his reaction.

Inside, I hastily explain the conversation to Addy and Isabel who are too drunk to realize I've started crying. I feel lightheaded, cold-blooded. No one says much, but Addy hands me the bottle of Malibu she was about to put in the closet.

I flick off the cap in one swift motion and chug.

part two
ten months older

"God, who am I?...Girls, girls everywhere, reading books. Intent faces, flesh pink, white, yellow. And I sit here without identity: faceless. There is history to be read... centuries to comprehend before I sleep, millions of lives to assimilate before breakfast tomorrow...I'm lost."
Sylvia Plath, *The Unabridged Journals of Sylvia Plath*

"I'm nineteen and I'm on fire"
Lorde, *Melodrama*

interviews

. . .

For someone who hates surprises, I feel like I get surprised a lot.

My birthday fell on the first day of finals week of the spring semester last year, and while I tried to convince my friends that I didn't want any attention drawn to it, they ambushed me at midnight with a cake and a bottle of Moscato. The cake had two candles on it, a 1 and a 9. 19. I blew out the 1 and wished for all memories of Reed Callaway to disappear from my brain. I blew out the 9 and wished for Reed Callaway to text me happy birthday. Neither wish came true.

While I was home for the summer, I worked at the Rock and Roll Hall of Fame, working the front desk and selling tickets. When my last day for the season arrived, I didn't tell anyone. I didn't want it to be a big deal because I'm coming back next summer, so it wasn't *really* my last day. When I clocked in, my manager surprised me with a cupcake and a card signed by the guest services team, wishing me luck for the upcoming school year.

Things like that are why I'm surprised, but not

surprised when Reed Callaway sits next to me in my first class on the first Monday of sophomore year. It's bad enough that he's in the class at all, but then he has the nerve to plop down into the seat next to me like we're best friends. It just feels like some shit that would only happen to me.

I already hate this class, and I can't blame it all on Reed. Dr. Wells, the professor, tells us if we ever emailed him outside of business hours, asked for an extension, or asked a question he had already answered, he would take a percentage point off of our final grade.

I almost say something to Reed, it feels weird not even saying hi to a man who knows so much about me, but Dr. Wells said if he caught any of us talking, he would (you guessed it) take a percentage off of our final grade. That doesn't mean I can't look at Reed though. It's what he deserves, sitting next to me like this and looking so attractive. He knows what he's doing.

This isn't the first time I've seen Reed since the night he ruined my life outside room 601. Unfortunately for me, Addy and Ben stayed friends, even after losing me and Reed as a mutual connection. Sometimes, they would try to *Parent Trap* me and Reed into hanging out, but it never worked. We would catch glimpses of each other, but we never spoke or stayed in a room together for longer than five minutes. Ben and Addy's tricks stopped by winter break. I grew to miss them.

It became common to run into Reed at bars the following spring semester, so common that I would've thought he was stalking me if he had ever actually tried to talk to me, which he only tried to do once. We were at Laundry Room, and he tried to get my attention as I walked past the bar. All I said was, "I'm not drunk enough to talk to you" and then I kept walking before he could respond.

Even though we aren't talking, seeing Reed always makes me oddly pleased. He's so good-looking. Seeing him, reminding myself he was attracted to me gives me an ego boost.

I like to think he's analyzing the same things about me that I am about him – my outfit and my hair, trying to figure out how I'm doing. I'm not stupid, I can feel him looking me over and watching me regurgitate Dr. Wells' words into my notebook. But I learned a long time ago that trying to predict Reed's actions is rarely productive and always exhausting.

"Everyone needs to take out their computer as we go over the syllabus, I did not bring printed copies," Dr. Wells tells the class.

I pull out my laptop and hold down the power button. My screen stays black. I hold down the button again, with a little more force, just for the screen to stay dark. I try to run through my actions last night - I finished the Moshfegh book Isabel lent me, my roommates and I watched a bad Netflix original and loved it, and I went to sleep before midnight. I can't remember charging my laptop.

Fuck. Inconvenient, but if I can feign looking at my computer, Wells won't notice. I'm sitting in the back of the lecture hall for God's sake.

"Alright, we're going to go around the room and take turns reading the syllabus, just go down the rows and read one sentence each. We can start in the back," he adds.

This man is seriously out to get me. The back row has started going down the line and every sentence is one sentence closer to my death. I keep pressing the power button, hoping my laptop will have a Jesus on the third day moment, but all I see on the dark screen is the unflattering reflection of my defeated face.

The girl two seats to my left is taking her turn and I think I'm about to break out into hives until stupid-fucking-hero-complex *Reed Callaway* slides his computer over so I can see the screen.

He's even highlighted the sentence I'm supposed to read.

I hate him. I read my stupid sentence and he reads his, a stupid smile plastered on his face the whole time. When class is eventually over, I break out into a near sprint and am the first to make it out of the set of double doors. I don't slow down until I'm sure Reed is nowhere to be found.

I go to the gym after class, a habit I formed late last year once I realized that the gym is a Reed-free zone. The athletes have a private gym in the athletic complex, so they never use the rec center. Today, Addy meets me for a Pilates class. She rushes out to meet one of her advisors after, but I'm feeling restless, so I stay to walk on the indoor track for a few minutes.

I make my way back to Prez, the dorm hall that will be my home for sophomore year, alone once I'm done, and when I'm crossing in front of the yard, I almost get hit by a car.

There's a brick path that people, mostly parents touring campus with prospective freshmen, think is a street because it connects to the first major road next to campus, but it is not a street. There's even a sign that says PEDESTRIAN TRAFFIC ONLY.

I turn around to see what the ass who almost hit me looks like, only to see it's *Reed*.

I swear to God, this day can't get any worse. It doesn't help that I look like a complete mess. My face is red, my hair pointing out in all directions possible, the ugly shorts and a tank I only wear out in public if I'm going to the gym.

"Halle!" he yells, rolling down his window with a fat smirk on his face. "I've been trying to track you down all day."

Since when does he have a car on campus? I forget there's nearly a year's worth of things about him I don't know. It's a Jeep, by the way. Reed Callaway drives a Jeep. You learn something new every day.

Reed looks me up and down, and when I just stare at him instead of responding, he fills the silence. "You bolted out of class this morning."

I shrug and feign obliviousness. "So what? I had somewhere to be."

"I'm starting to think you're trying to avoid me," he says, still smirking.

I have to come up with some way to change the topic or blame this all on him before he realizes he's right. "What do you want? Besides run me over with your car and ask me stupid questions."

He sighs. "Let's grab coffee."

I laugh stiffly. "Why would the two of us grab coffee?"

Talking to him is doing things to me that I don't like. I feel myself blushing, speaking to him in a slightly higher voice than normal, like I'm a fan meeting her celebrity crush. Is it possible that his voice has gotten deeper since the last time we spoke? Are his shoulders wider?

Reed puts his car in park. "Because Wells' class is gonna be a pain in the ass and working together would do us both a lot of good. And we can only work together if we're on speaking terms."

That's how I end up in his passenger seat.

He lets me pick the music and drives with the windows

down. And he's a safe driver. Actually, I can't remember a time I've ever felt unsafe with Reed. Maybe that's why I can't shake my feelings for him. I go a whole day without thinking of him, but the moment my head hits the pillow at night, he's all I can see. Sometimes, if I can't sleep, the only way to get myself to drift off is to pretend he's in bed next to me. How pathetic is it to imagine him behind me, rubbing my back and telling me to quiet my thoughts and go back to sleep?

But none of that has ever been enough to erase the resentment I harbor for him. My life went downhill quickly after Reed broke up with me. I have an overwhelming fear that letting myself talk to Reed regularly would stop me from growing. He'd be too supportive, too fussy if he knew the bad side of me. I don't want to need him.

Reed drives us to the Ross Cafe and Diner. We go straight to the take-out counter and Reed offers to order first because I can't decide if it's too late in the day to have a double shot of espresso.

"Chicken sandwich, double lettuce, and no tomato, with chipotle mayo," he says calmly to the girl behind the counter.

"That's my order," I remind him, trying to ignore the new tightness in my chest.

He nods and looks a little embarrassed. "I know, I order it every time I come here."

I feel like I've been hit. "You come here? By yourself?"

I haven't been here since the last time I was here with Reed. I never wanted to be reminded of how good that day was.

"Yeah," he responds so quietly I barely hear it, "a lot, actually."

The satisfaction of knowing he comes to the restaurant I introduced him to and orders my sandwich, presumptuously without being able to separate it from me, makes my body burn up head to toe. Whether he knows it or not, he's just confirmed that I take up the same amount of space in his mind as he takes in mine. It's a great feeling that I have no use for. Knowing what Reed thinks about me hasn't changed anything about our relationship or who we are.

I should order the double shot espresso after that, I've decided.

We take our coffees and matching sandwiches to a park on the water that always smells a little bit like weed. I'm not dressed for air conditioning. We sit on a bench, close but not too close. We talk about our classes and our summers. Reed's excited for the soccer season and I'm not excited about going back to work on *The Clocktower*. It's kind of nice to catch up with him.

In another life, there's a version of me who would consider this the perfect end to my first day of sophomore year. Early dinner from one of my favorite restaurants with my boyfriend in a park on the water. But that's not this life.

"Do you have a boyfriend?" Reed asks, cutting through our content silence.

He has a way of ruining things, doesn't he?

"No," I say slowly, half a bite of my sandwich still in my mouth, "but I have a feeling you already knew that."

He laughs with a hefty shrug. "I keep tabs on you Hevko, so what?"

"I guess I can't judge. I also happen to know that you don't have a girlfriend."

"Oh yeah? Who's your source?" he asks.

"Ben," I say smugly.

He smirks. "Poking around, looking for something to be jealous of?"

"No, it's called curiosity." I take a breath and hesitate before I continue. "*But* since you brought it up, there have been other guys, I guess, since we stopped seeing each other. Nothing serious."

It's not a lie, exactly; more like a total understatement of the truth. What he doesn't know won't hurt him. I don't think Reed *wants* to hear my definition of "other guys." The ones I made out with at Laundry Room every weekend of last year, most of whose faces I can't recall, all of whose names I've forgotten.

It was fun for a while. It became who I was – the girl in my friend group who got too drunk and found a new guy to make out with every night, who liked dancing with boys who weren't afraid to put their hands on me.

But the high from the attention never lasted long, and the anxiety of waking up and not knowing what I'd done the night before killed most of the fun I had.

The worst of it was the morning I woke up in the morning back in the dorm, to Addy asking me how I felt about losing my virginity. I thought she was joking until she showed me videos of the night before of me talking about how badly I wanted to have sex with this senior and eventually walking into his bedroom with him. The worst part was that I had this huge smile on my face.

Watching the video felt like watching someone else, and it's easier to pretend it was someone else. Afterwards, I told Addy I would never drink again. She said, "That's what everyone says. Don't lie to yourself."

She was right. I drank myself through the rest of the semester, but I was able to restrain myself from getting into any more trouble with boys. I don't want this semester to be like that. I won't let myself.

Reed's smiling at me behind his sandwich from the other side of the bench. "Of course, there have been other guys," he says decisively. "I'd be surprised if guys *weren't* all over you. You're amazing, Hal."

"Yeah, well none of them ever treated me as well as you did."

That slips out, unfiltered and unplanned. I should not have said it. His stunned face confirms it – I really shouldn't have said it. But it's better than saying, *If I'm so amazing why aren't you still with me?* Which is what I wanted to say, and what I've always told myself I would say when I imagined what it would be like to talk to Reed again.

Reed isn't smiling anymore.

"I'm sorry," he says.

"Don't be."

I can tell he feels bad. And I don't feel bad for making him feel that way.

He musters up a smile again, though it's not the same as it was before, it doesn't quite reach the rest of his face.

"Is one of those other guys Luke Allen?" he asks slowly, almost sarcastically.

My jaw drops. "Who told you?"

It's, embarrassingly, true. Lacrosse manager Luke dramatically proclaimed his crush on me a few days after Reed and I stopped talking last year. The longer it went on, and the more ridiculous his advances got, the more I started to believe it was all a joke. A mean, hidden way to make fun of me.

Flirting with Luke can be fun when he's not being a jerk. We've never had a conversation about our feelings, but we've had some decently hot make-out sessions. He's tried to push things further, but I always shut it down. I just don't feel like I need sex, and I have no impulse to do it with Luke even if I wanted to. I like him but I don't. Sometimes I think something's wrong with me. He's a fine guy and I know he likes me. But still, I can't.

Reed laughs lightly. "No one told me. I was just guessing. Come on, he's *always* liked you. He hated me last year, and it was because he thought you should've been with him, not me."

"If you knew, then why didn't you say anything when we were together? You could've asked me to stop hanging out with him. I would've if you asked."

"I'm not a very jealous guy," he says down into his coffee, looking like he's trying to stifle a smile. "And this is gonna sound so asshole-ish, but…I guess I always just knew you were mine."

Reed's more observant than I give him credit for, I used to tease him about it back when we were together. He's able to put feelings into words that I've only ever processed as memories. The feeling of being in a dorm, packed wall-to-wall, and making eye contact with him. Knowing that every girl in the room could ask him to dance and knowing that he would politely decline. At the end of the night, it would be us, drunk in my room, arguing over who pays for the pizza we order, and who is more drunk until we fall asleep — his hand trapped in my hair and my makeup staining his shirt. It's a feeling I miss. I always knew he was mine back then.

It looks like rain, so we decide to head back. Which is good because I'm itching to get out. I don't know how much longer I can sit next to him if he's gonna look at me with all the love in the world, while we casually talk about the other people we've been seeing.

When we reach campus, I ask Reed to drop me off by the door of my dorm building so I have time to put on presentable clothes for my job interview. Attached to the student center is our campus' only sit-down restaurant, The Lighthouse. It takes a lot of meal swipes to cover the check, so most students only come on special occasions. Or late at night on weekends when the caf has closed and the intoxicated masses want food. It is always busy. The Lighthouse is hiring, and over the summer I learned how effective work can be in distracting me from my own awful life. Working is like free therapy. Solving other people's stupid problems instead of my own? Sign me up.

"You're gonna do great," he tells me as I open the car door.

I shrug before gathering my bag. "Thanks. And thanks for paying for the food too."

"Yeah, anytime."

I get a good look at him before I shut the door. The sun's hitting him in the exact right spot, flooding his hair and making it look lighter than I've ever seen it. He looks beautiful. It makes my stomach hurt. He's looking at me with his whole heart, how he used to look at me last year. I need to shut this down. I cannot put myself in a position where he can abandon me like he did last year.

I look away from him to center myself, but when I look back at him, his face, his look of adoration, hasn't changed a bit.

"We are not friends," I tell him quickly. "You know this doesn't make us friends now, right?"

All he does is smile at me. "Let me know how the interview goes, Hal. I'll be mad if you don't."

I close the door. He puts the car in drive.

The interview is easy and quick. They're very understaffed. I get the job, and the manager adds me to the schedule for tomorrow so I can start my training in time to work the weekend. Reed's the first person I text.

Just two words: ***got it***

He responds instantly like he was waiting for it: ***Knew you would. Congrats***

storm

. . .

Dorm is a loose word for our room, which is a refurbished four-bedroom pre-war apartment. Our university bought the building, now called Presidential Hall, about ten years ago when enrollment increased so quickly, they didn't have time to build a new dorm block. Prez, as it's more commonly called, is a sophomore-only dorm. It's the tallest building on campus. When I toured campus for the first time, I remember looking up at it and thinking it looked like a skyscraper. It looks much smaller to me now.

Addy, Isabel, and I live with two girls that we became friends with last year, post-Reed break up: Nadia Javadi and Michaela Bak. Nadia is the type of girl that's intimidatingly pretty, she has a warm smile that takes up her whole body, making her shoulders pop up. She also sneezes alarmingly loudly. It woke me up the first night we spent in the dorm. Mic is a history major with a focus (likely obsession) on World War I who recently broke up with her boyfriend from freshman year. She will make sure you know that by starting every conversation with it. Other than that, she's quite sweet.

I love our room. Having a full kitchen is great for nights when we want to ditch the dining hall food. We ask the internet for recipes, make grocery store runs, and cook together while Nadia plays jazz music from her phone and Isabel gives her dramatic recreation of an old-fashioned swing dance. The window in the kitchen faces the back side of campus, so Addy and Isabel can lean their upper bodies out and smoke without fear of being seen by any university faculty. The front door to the apartment makes a definite squeak when it's opened, but it's kind of nice to hear when my roommates are coming and going.

And Tori is our neighbor again, funny enough, and we don't find her intolerable anymore like we did in the first few weeks of freshman year. She's one of those people that, if you don't have to live with her, is *incredibly* entertaining. Once we moved into Prez and found out she was in our hall, we invited her over for dinner. We had a good time.

After my interview at Lighthouse, I come back to the dorm and see Michaela hunched over the stove, cooking a recipe she learned from her dad. My other roommates are gathered at the kitchen table. Isabel's munching on a family-sized bag of pretzels. Mic tells her not to ruin her dinner.

I tell them I got the job, and they all congratulate me.

"You should tell Luke about the new job," Addy says. "He was asking about your interview. He genuinely seemed interested. It was surprising but kind of endearing."

"Huh," I say, only half interested. I think about my day with Reed, and how much it made me realize I can't keep pretending I want to be involved with Luke long-term.

Isabel laughs. "Oh come on, Ice Queen. Don't do to Luke what you do to every other guy. You're always looking for something to find wrong with him."

Despite my proficiency in finding guys to drunkenly make out with, Isabel started calling me 'Ice Queen' after a few guys asked me on dates or showed interest in me, and I gently shut them down. But Isabel said I was "unnecessarily cold" to them when I rejected their advances, hence the nickname. It only happened twice, and I really did shut them down gently. The guys were nice, but it just gave me the worst stomachache to think about going on a date with them. Isabel won't give it up though.

"I'm not an *Ice Queen*," I defend. "I just have high standards. There's nothing wrong with that. And every decent guy on this campus either has a girlfriend, is gay, or is super weird. Or he's Luke."

"Right, because you've met every one of the single decent guys on this campus," Addy says sarcastically.

"I have," I reply. "This campus isn't *that* big."

"You know that's stupid right?" Isabel adds. "You're limiting your prospects when you have that mindset."

I shrug and steal a handful of pretzels from her. "This way I can't get hurt again."

Isabel rolls her eyes.

Once Mic is done cooking, we all eat together, and watch a couple of episodes of the newest show on TLC, before everyone peels off to do their own thing.

My own thing to do right now is to finish unpacking. A few boxes are stacked on top of my desk. One is filled with books, and the book on top is Reed's copy of *On Writing*. I never gave it back to him last year. I packed it with the other books I brought back to campus, thinking I would run into him and return it. But I was lying to myself when I packed it. I never actually thought I would see him; I just like holding the book in my hands. I like reading his notes in the margins. I like remembering how good my life was when he gave it to me.

I flip through the pages, not realizing how long I've been reading until Addy starts getting ready for bed.

In the middle of the night, I wake up to Addy calling my name in the distance.

"Halle, come help me figure out what's making this noise in the kitchen!"

The noise in question is an awful scraping, clanging, and overall upsetting combo that can be heard from every part of the dorm. We put our ears up to every wall and appliance to search for the source until Addy reaches the fridge.

"Jesus Christ," she groans, "it's coming from our fucking ice machine."

When I eventually fall back asleep, I dream of performing an interpretive step routine to the rhythm of our ice machine's thuds.

———

THE WALLS OF MY ACADEMIC ADVISOR'S OFFICE ARE BLANK. I can't tell if it makes the room feel smaller or bigger.

The advisor the university assigned me last year was a man named Mark. I hated him, so I requested a change and was reassigned to Julia. Typically, Julia only advises students in the English department, but since Mark is the only advisor for political communications majors, English was the next best thing. Julia is also the closest thing I have to a therapist right now.

"You had a few hiccups last year," she says, looking over my grades from last year.

Hiccups is one word for it.

She's the only person, besides my parents, who knows that I'm on academic probation and at risk of losing my scholarship. It came as a bit of a shock to me, honestly. I never checked my grades last year. I think that's because deep down, I knew they'd be awful. I didn't know that my GPA was below the scholarship requirement until the school sent a letter to my house over the summer. That's another reason I hate Mark, the guy who was supposed to *advise* me couldn't have given me a warning.

So, that's why Julia is on my ass about keeping my grades up, and I honestly need it. It doesn't feel great to know that I'm the first girl in my family to go to college and I'm on the verge of flunking out.

"So you'll reach out if you're struggling, right?" She adds.

"Of course," I nod. Though, I hope to never need to. If I can get through this year without begging a professor for an extension, this year would be perfect. My long-term goal is to make it onto the university's dean's list, but we'll see. Baby steps.

"How's your work on the *Clocktower* going?" she asks me.

I shrug. "It's fine."

"You don't sound very passionate about it," she says.

"I'm not."

Julia laughs a little, in the same way my mother would if I were having this conversation with her instead. "Then why do you do it, Halle?"

"I want to work in political communications and *Clocktower* is kind of the only communications-related club here."

"I'm worried about you prioritizing your writing for *Clocktower* over your schoolwork. Isn't that part of the reason your grades slipped last year?"

God no, I don't care about *Clocktower* that much.

But I'm not going to tell Julia that the biggest thing keeping me from academic success last year was going out with my friends and getting blackout drunk every single weekend.

But this year that'll change. I have a secret plan that not even Julia knows about – I'm done drinking for good. I refuse to blackout and fuck up my life because I'm bored or looking for an escape.

But I haven't told anyone about my plan. It feels like telling any of my friends would spoil it, like how you're not supposed to tell anyone what you wish for when you blow out the candles on your birthday cake. Plus, there's my overwhelming fear that if my girls find out I don't drink anymore, they'll stop inviting me to go out. Or that they'll think my not drinking means I'm secretly judging them for their blackout or back-out style of drinking.

———

THERE'S A HURRICANE HITTING THE SOUTHEAST TODAY which is turning into a thunderstorm on campus. My phone is filled with notifications for severe weather, high winds, and flooding. All of these seem like very abstract concepts to me until I step out of Julia's office and feel the heavy air on my shoulders. The weight it holds, the warning of a storm. I speed walk from Julia's office to Prez. The first crack of thunder erupts as I shut the door behind me.

I can hear my roommates from down the hall before I unlock the door. I collapse on the couch and don't notice Reed is in the spot next to me until he pushes a plastic cup into my field of vision.

"Wine?" he asks.

"No thanks." I shake my head and try to hide my surprise and suppress the urge to tell him to get out. Reed is *here*, on my couch, drinking my wine. "I didn't think you drank wine."

"That's all you guys have in this apartment," he says, a bit more snark in it than I'm used to hearing from him.

I pick up the throw blanket that lives on our floor and snuggle into it. Spending a half hour talking about my failure with Julia is tiring.

I realize Reed's shoulder is about an inch from my head. I can smell him, his cologne, his shampoo. I could so easily close this gap, one inch, and melt into him. He probably wouldn't even flinch. He'd probably put his arm around me and pull me closer. I can't let myself. I won't.

Ben is here too, sitting in between Addy and Nadia on the second couch. Isabel and Michaela are sitting on the floor, using the coffee table to eat dishes of pasta. Why Reed and Ben were invited, I have no idea. Ben's come over a few times since the start of the semester, to do homework with us or make a weak attempt at flirting with Addy that we all pretend not to notice, but he's never brought Reed with him. He's never even mentioned him.

"There's some pasta left on the stove, Hal," Isabel says with her mouth full.

I practically feel Reed's uncomfortable shift at her use of my nickname. I don't think he's ever heard anyone call me *Hal* before that wasn't him. He coined that nickname, no one in college started using it for me until after he did. Knowing Reed, he probably feels like that means he owns it.

Isabel is the best cook of all of us, so I don't hesitate to fill a plate and scarf it down. By the time I've finished, everyone has spread out. Ben, Addy, and Nadia are watching TV, Mic and Isabel are cleaning the kitchen, and Reed is alone on our balcony. I see him leaning on the railing.

Following Reed to the balcony is not a difficult decision. I open and shut the sliding patio door behind me. He looks over his shoulder to see who's joined him but doesn't particularly acknowledge my entrance. I slide up onto the space next to him against the railing.

"I feel like I don't know you anymore," he says seriously.

I freeze. Where is this coming from? When I saw him the other day, our conversation was light, at least it was light compared to the intensity in his voice right now. I'm worried one of my friends said something about how I acted last year. I try to think of a way to justify myself, my chest is tightening, and I feel like if I try to talk about last year I'll start crying.

Reed starts laughing, breaking me out of my trance. He's laughing like he's just told an inside joke. If he noticed how freaked out I was, he isn't letting me know.

"You guys are friends with Tori now." He cackles. "What the hell? I must know nothing about you anymore."

I try to laugh convincingly, ignoring the feeling of my heart hitting my rib cage and the anxiety that he could still bring up something I don't wanna talk about. "Remember all those extra locks on her door last year? Well one-night last semester, she lost the key to one and we had to help her break into her room. It was a trauma-bonding experience. We're sisters for life now."

"That and your hair's lighter," he says.

It is. I started dying it for the first time after we ended things. It was that or bangs. "It's just a couple of highlights."

"Still. Lighter." He shrugs.

"I'll probably keep it this way for a while."

He nods like we're talking about something much more

serious than my hair color before turning his head out to look over the balcony.

"Look." He points over the edge of the railing before saying, "You can see the storm over the water."

You can. The rain looks almost like fog sitting under the dark clouds from way back here. Lightning hits the water. We watch it in silence, listening to the thunder and blurry but comforting sound of our friends on the other side of the door.

I want to ask him why he came over, why he decided to join Ben tonight. He had plenty of excuses to come over before but never did. But I don't ask him anything.

"It looks like it's getting closer to us," I tell him.

"Yeah, it does," he responds flatly.

"So we should probably go back inside soon."

"Yeah, we probably should."

When I pull back the handle of the sliding glass door, Reed is still watching the water. I don't ask him to follow me.

―――

"The reason you guys broke up is so stupid."

Ben and I are the only ones still awake. I don't know how anyone is asleep, the storm is so loud it sounds like someone is doing construction on the whole building. The walls shake with the thunder and the lighting makes it look like someone flipped on every light in the room. All the girls are asleep in their beds, except Mic, who fell asleep in one of the living room armchairs.

Reed and Ben live in Prez with some of the other guys on the soccer team, and they're on our floor. And apparently, no one thought to tell me this until tonight. So, Reed went back to their apartment to go to bed, which is only six doors down.

Ben and I are absentmindedly watching the reruns Isabel had turned on hours ago while Mic softly snores in the chair next to us. I don't remember the last time I talked to Ben alone, and I forgot how funny he is. He's similar to Reed in so many ways — they both have the same sunny outlook on life, but Ben takes things less seriously than Reed does, and he is way more outgoing than Reed. When I first met Reed, I assumed he was a very friendly person because of the warmth he always treated me with. Turns out, he just acted like that because he liked me. In most settings, Reed is a reserved person. Ben is the one who makes all their plans, and does all the talking.

"I don't know," I respond to him simply.

I've spent the past almost year thinking about why Reed could have ended our relationship. I've thought about every possible reason — not attracted to me, embarrassed to be seen with me, wanted to sleep with another girl, was sleeping with another girl and didn't know how to tell me — it's a pretty long list. I don't feel like rehashing those possible reasons with Ben.

"You don't know? Like you don't know if it's stupid?" Ben asks.

"No," I say. "I don't know why he ended things at all."

Ben's eyes almost fall out of his head. "Reed never told you?"

"No, he didn't."

"Wow, okay," he says, releasing a heavy breath and putting his cup on the coffee table. "This is a lot to process."

"How do you think I feel? This is the first time I'm hearing about any of this. I just thought he got bored of me or something."

"I don't even know where to start."

"Just tell me." I'm trying not to explode, I'm so anxious about what he could say.

"Remember how we were at that tournament?" I nod, so Ben keeps talking, "All he could talk about the whole time we were gone was you. He was so excited to see you when we got back. Then when we were playing our last game, the student section for the other team started getting really rowdy. And they started saying shit about all of us, but then they started talking about *you*. I guess they looked Reed up online before the game and found pictures of the two of you. Reed started playing like total shit after they started shouting stuff. And we ended up losing. He freaked out about it. He said it wasn't just about the student section, that it was his fault for thinking about you too much when he should've been thinking about the tournament. He told me he was gonna talk to you and tell you that you two could only talk to each other if he wasn't in season, but that he still really liked you or something. I told him you would never agree to that, but he didn't care. He didn't want thinking about you to fuck up a game again. He's an idiot, right?"

I could run down the hall and confront Reed about it right now if I wanted to. I could yell at him for being so stupid. I could rip him to shreds, yell at him until my throat is raw, and he'd let me. But if he still hasn't told me about it, there must be a reason. I should respect that, I guess. I'm in shock, trying to grieve the year Reed and I could've had together if he had just been honest with me, and if I could've talked him out of it.

"Any time we would see you out at a bar or I would hang out with you and Addy," Ben continues, "Reed would get so sad after. I never got it. I'd be like 'Just try to talk to her or apologize' and Reed would get all pissy and be like

No, you don't understand it's too late. Eventually, I let the whole thing go because every time we talked about it, I wanted to bang my head into the wall."

Before I can agree that this all makes me, also, want to bang my head into the wall, the TV cuts out. Then the lights. We've lost power.

"Addy and I have some candles in our room," I say, standing, looking for the easiest solution.

In the shadows, I barely see the outline of Ben shaking his head. "Don't worry about it, I should probably go to bed anyway. And don't tell Reed that I told you any of that, at least not right now."

"Yeah, of course."

Before Ben can reach the door, there's a knock and I hear Reed's voice on the other side of the door. "Hello? Are you guys awake?"

Ben opens the door. Reed's not the only one in the hall, illuminated by phone flashlights as people flood the hall, wondering if their room is the only one without power or if anyone knows when the power will be back on. Reed is stretched over the door frame, wearing blue plaid pajama pants and a soccer t-shirt from last year. I know it's from last year because I remember borrowing it. He looks surprised that anyone answered.

"Just wanted to make sure everyone was okay," he says sincerely, quietly.

"The power's out man, it's not like the building's burning down," Ben responds.

Reed shrugs defensively. "You never know. Someone could've been stuck in the elevator, the AC is out, people's key cards stop working…"

He trails off and I see his glance shift to me. He's looking at me like he cares about me, which takes me by surprise. You'd almost think he came over to check in as an excuse to talk to me. And for the first time in almost a year, Reed makes sense to me.

I don't see him as a stupid boy telling his freshman-year girlfriend, they can't be together because he's afraid of commitment or wants to be like his friends and hook up with a different girl every Friday. Instead, I see a boy who's played soccer his whole life and has never thought about putting anything above it before, let alone a *girlfriend*. I see a boy who's naive enough to think he could convince a girl to only talk to him five months of the year because he really likes her, but he has no idea how to like her without giving something up.

I hug him, in a friendly way, so my arms drape around his shoulders instead of slipping tightly around his waist like they itch to. It's not until he hugs me back, gently pressing my face into the top of his chest, that I realize this is the first time I've touched him since October of last year.

"Thanks for checking though," I say into his shirt. I feel him almost brushing his hand over my hair, a small action that used to be habitual, before immediately pulling it away. His touch feels like fire, I'm almost glad that he pulls away.

"Anytime," he tells me.

staying in
. . .

It's a Friday night. I should be out with my friends, but I'm sitting in my bed thinking about Reed. Pathetic, I know. I don't need anyone to remind me how pathetic I am.

This is why I have not told any of my roommates about Reed's visit during the power outage the other night. If I told them how often I thought of Reed, I think they'd make fun of me. Isabel thinks I should hatch a plot to make him jealous. Addy thinks that I should never think of him as a romantic prospect again. We didn't even meet Nadia and Mic until after Reed stopped talking to me, so they don't know him well.

So, when Addy strolls into our room to tell me that Luke's been asking her if I'm mad at him and avoiding him on purpose, I'm not in the mood to pretend.

"Not on purpose, but maybe I am. I don't know," I respond.

"You at least need to give him a chance," Addy says to me from the other side of the room, sitting on the edge of her bed. "You can't compare every guy to Reed. Luke's not Reed."

Like I wouldn't move on if I could. It's not my fault Reed is stuck in my head. "But Reed is the only guy I've ever been serious with. If Luke can't treat me as good as Reed treated me or better, he's not worth my time. And so far, he hasn't! Sure, we've fooled around a little and it can be fun to flirt but anytime I ever need Luke or wanna talk, he disappears. Reed's not like that."

"Reed broke up with you out of nowhere and still hasn't developed the basic communication skills to talk to you about it himself," Addy says sharply.

"Well, everything except for that part."

Addy rolls her eyes and pushes herself up. "Don't count Luke out."

Isabel, walking past our room, overhears her. "What's this about Luke?"

Addy shrugs. "I think Halle and him together would be an adorable couple if she gave him a shot."

"Cute," Isabel says dryly, cementing herself in the doorway with her arms carefully crossed. Isabel is always able to look me directly in the eye when staring me down. She's a dance major, the prima ballerina type. No matter what she does, she always looks ready to move, like a choreographer has told her to stand there.

"Well, I came over here to say that I think *Nadia* is Ben's new girly pop," she says inconspicuously.

"What?" Addy and I both almost scream.

We've been developing a theory that Ben is hooking up with some mystery woman for quite some time now. He's been bailing on some of our group plans without reason – which obviously means he's hooking up with someone. What else would be more important than us, his only friends that are girls and not on the soccer team, other than *sex*? Isabel and I wonder out of pure curiosity. Addy, I'm guessing, is jealous. She still hasn't admitted she has feelings for Ben, but anyone could figure out she likes him after watching them interact for maybe thirty seconds.

Ben has been acting weird. But I would've never guessed Nadia was his girly pop. She talks about a lot of things, but boys are not one of them. She is laser-focused on her nerdy work as a musical composition major.

"What makes you think that?" I ask.

"She's been sneaking off after dinner every night. And Ben is always busy when we ask him to hang out after dinner. The timing is impeccable," Isabel explains flatly.

"I don't know," I say, "She's probably practicing or studying."

It's not surprising that none of us know the intimate details of Nadia's life. Until we all moved in together, I saw the five of us as two separate groups. There's me, Addy, and Isabel, and then there's Mic and Nadia. The two groups started blending when we moved in, but it's not the same. I know every form of birth control Isabel has ever used and how Addy's parents met, but I don't know Nadia's or Michaela's middle names.

Realization washes over Addy's face. "I know where she is! She's with her orchestra friend, they go to the music building and tune their violins together."

Isabel's eyebrows furrow. "Is that a metaphor for something sexual?"

"No, they seriously just work on violin stuff together."

"Interesting." Isabel walks away with an odd look of determination that makes me almost worried for Nadia. Knowing Isabel, she's about to set up camp outside the music building and look for Nadia herself. I truly don't have an opinion on all of it, except that I don't wanna live in a dorm room where Nadia is hooking up with Ben. Addy would be inconsolable.

Luke knocks on our front door twenty minutes later.

"Ladies," he says. He doesn't even address me directly. "Who wants to go to the lacrosse house?"

We all collectively share a groan.

The ice machine deposits a new batch with its signature thud and Luke practically jumps. "What the fuck was that noise?"

"Ice machine," all five of us mumble in unison.

"Give it up, Luke," Addy says, unpacking the contents of her purse and attempting to organize them. "We're not going."

"Oh, come on," he says defensively. "The freshman that I'm hanging out with and her friends bailed on me. If I don't find girls to bring, they won't let me in."

What freshmen is he *hanging out* with? I have Addy and Isabel in my ears telling me I need to reach out to Luke and try harder, but I have Luke in front of me openly talking about the other girls he's seeing. This may be my last straw with Luke. I need to talk to him ASAP and end us for good. At a time when my roommates aren't all in the room with us.

"They still do that not-letting-boys-in-unless-they-bring-a-girl shit?" Addy asks while pouring a can of Diet Coke over ice.

Luke nods slowly like he's waiting for us to catch up.

"No way Luke."

"*Please.*" He melodramatically drops down to his knees in front of her and paws at the hem of her jeans. "Addy, baby, I need this."

Addy, maybe too aggressively, pulls him up off the floor by the collar of his polo shirt. "Get up, loser! Deal with it.

You can go one night without the lacrosse house. Get a fake ID and go to a bar like the rest of us."

Beside me, Isabel perks up. She's an incredible dancer, but not the greatest actress, so her pretending that she just had a brilliant revelation looks like something out of a cartoon. "Nadia, you should totally go with Luke, you'd love it…Unless you have *other* plans?"

Nadia, who had been sitting on the couch scrolling on her phone, turns, looking surprised that Isabel addressed her by name. "Actually, I do. I'm meeting a friend tonight."

Addy and I exchange suspicious glances, while Isabel's gaze stays locked on Nadia.

"A friend?" she asks bluntly.

"Correct, a friend," Nadia responds, not budging.

Isabel does something I don't see her do often: she gives up. Rolling her eyes, she turns from Nadia to Luke. "Alright dingbat, let's go."

I feel betrayed. I feel like I've been shot straight through my chest. Addy and Isabel slip on their shoes.

"Wait, you guys are both going to the lacrosse house now?" I ask.

"Obvi," Addy says, grabbing her purse from the counter. "I can't leave Isabel alone with Luke. She'll never come back in one piece."

"I'll come too!" Mic says cheerfully.

The thought of poor, innocent, still-heartbroken-over-her-ex Michaela going to the lacrosse house makes me sick. They're gonna eat her alive.

"Am I the only one who remembers what happened the last time we went there?" I ask.

Addy shrugs. "It's one night."

I thought we were all in this together, a room of feminists agreeing to never go back to a house so sexist that it will probably end up in a *Law and Order: SVU* episode one day. Am I the only person in this room with a brain?

The thought that Luke is the one who invited us makes me wanna go even less. And if I'm not willing to go to a party to spend time with him, my feelings for Luke are clearly very minimal. Sorry, Luke. You were cute while it lasted, but I don't think our connection is very strong.

"We'll text when we start to walk back! I'm leaving the door unlocked so I don't have to bring my key," Addy says in lieu of a goodbye. Isabel blows me a kiss, and Michaela copies her.

Nadia nearly follows them. "My friend is waiting for me," she says.

"Sure," I say, trying not to sound too bitchy as she shuts the door behind her.

I'm alone. And I feel Caesar-level betrayed.

The first thing I do to cheer myself up is bring *The West Wing* up on the TV and put some frozen mozzarella sticks in the oven. Then I light a candle that's supposed to smell like sea salt, dolphins, and a fresh breeze – but all it smells like is sunscreen – and put it on the coffee table.

I'm not alone in the room often, and I'm starting to enjoy it. I aimlessly walk laps around the kitchen, then the living room, just because no one is around to ask me why I'm doing it. I lie on the carpet of the living room to eat my mozzarella sticks. I've never been in this exact part of our room before, I realize, lying in this particular way. From this angle on the ground, looking out the window, I see less of the buildings surrounding us and more of the sky. I like it. If I roll my head from one side to the other, I can see under our couch. God, has anyone ever cleaned under there? I add "clean under furniture" to my never-ending, never will be written down, internal to-do list. As time passes, the stray thoughts I have about what my friends are doing right now or what freshman girl Luke is flirting with wane.

After I'm done eating, I take the goddamn longest shower. I take my sweet time washing my face. I floss. I even remember to wear my retainer. This is turning into the best night of my life.

The next episode automatically starts itself – Josh, Toby, and Donna miss the motorcade during President Bartlet's reelection campaign. The stakes are very high.

The front door creaks open with its typical ugly scream behind me. I turn, expecting to see my roommates returning earlier than expected, but it's Reed. He scans the room uncertainly until his gaze settles on me. He smiles.

God, he looks drunk. Very attractive, but also drunk.

"*West Wing?*" he asks, walking toward me.

"How'd you guess?" I tease.

"This spot on the couch," he mumbles lazily as he takes a spot next to me. "You always sit here when you're watching your show."

He's right, every time he's come over to work on homework or steal some of our food, I've been in this exact spot on the couch, watching my show. I never thought he would notice something like that.

"Where's Ben?" I ask, hoping to gather some evidence to bolster our theory about him and Nadia.

Reed shrugs. "Haven't seen him. I just got back, but he left the club a while ago."

That could mean anything. Oh well, at least I tried. I really can't picture a world where Ben and Nadia get it on, nor do I want to. I turn my attention back to the TV.

"You guys need to stop leaving that door unlocked. You don't know what type of creeps live in this dorm," Reed says tensely, picking up a blanket that was on the couch and throwing it over himself, then throwing the excess over my legs. Guess that means he's staying. Our legs being covered by the same blanket feels entirely too intimate.

"Talk to Addy about it," I respond, half distracted by the blanket situation, "she's the one who left it unlocked."

Reed's eyes, half droopy from drinking, narrow as he surveys the room critically. "Where is everyone?"

"Lacrosse house," I say bitterly.

"Wow. Fuck that," Reed says passionately.

I should've known he would be the only one to understand. "That was more or less my reaction."

He goes to put his feet on the coffee table but stops when he sees the lit candle. "I didn't think we were allowed to have candles in this building."

"Oh. We aren't."

He laughs, a boyish giggle, and it makes me blush. "Wow. A three-wick candle burning and *The West Wing* on a Friday night. Hevko, you really are like a new person now."

He's joking but I don't laugh. It makes me wish I never lived last year and embarrassed that Reed knew me while I was a train wreck. In a better universe, I wouldn't have met Reed until after I got my partying phase out of my system.

He tries to change the conversation, vaguely gesturing toward the TV. "This the episode where they try to make college cheaper?"

I try and fail to hold back a smile. Reed's the only friend I've ever had who has also watched *The West Wing*. Yet he still refers to it as "my" show. Last year, I thought that meant something. "That's the next one. But it kind of comes up toward the end of this one."

"I remember watching this episode as a kid. When my parents would turn on re-runs, you know? And I used to think college was so far away, like something another version of me would have to go through, not *actually* me.

Now I don't know, I never thought about all this." Reed's face grows redder the longer he goes on. He giggles again. "Ignore that, I don't know what I'm saying. I'm drunk."

I find it endearing, to see him vulnerable like this. "No, go on."

He takes a deep breath, the one someone takes after a workout or before a big presentation – pure adrenaline. "I never thought about how thankful I'd be. What kid would, right? I had friends in high school and they're great people and all, but I never imagined I would have friends as amazing as Ben and Harry." He breathes again, and it fills the whole room. "And you. If I went back in time and told my fourteen-year-old self he would meet you, Halle I-"

"You can't say that type of stuff." I cut him off unabashedly and rip my legs out from under the blanket, suddenly very concerned with the direction this conversation is going in.

I've daydreamed about him saying something like this to me for almost a year, but when it happens, I can't seem to stomach it. Where was this a year ago? If he feels this way about me, why did he let me go so quickly? I remind myself that he's been drinking, and this conversation is probably only something he'll be embarrassed by in the morning.

"What do you mean?" He scoffs. "Hal, I'm serious. I have never known another girl like you. You're intelligent and driven and the funniest person I know and fucking beautiful and you're just…" He trails off, reaching across the couple of inches that separate us to tuck a stray piece of hair behind my ear. "Perfect."

I laugh in his face, watch the bit of hope leave his eyes, and ignore the guilt that settles in my stomach knowing I caused that. "You must not know me very well if you think I'm perfect. I am not perfect."

"You are to me. That's my opinion. You can't tell me my opinion is wrong."

"Reed!" I successfully quiet him for long enough to push myself from the couch. I need to put some distance between us before I explode. Once I'm in the kitchen, I fill a glass of water to the brim. "Stop, you're drunk. You don't mean that."

He follows me into the kitchen, slowly, until he ends up in front of me as I lean against the counter. "I'm not that drunk."

Deep down, I know he's right. But it's easier to pretend he's very drunk. So drunk that he won't remember this tomorrow.

I hand him the glass through the three inches that separate us. He takes it but doesn't drink it.

"I'm not exaggerating," he says softly. "I think your freckles are perfect. Particularly this clump of three right here." He runs a delicate finger across the top of my cheek, under my eye, and presumably over the freckles he's talking about that I've never noticed myself. His touch is so soft, barely existent, but his fingers move down my neck and my side until they rest on my waist. "I think these satin pajama pants you own in five colors are perfect. And, Jesus, your hips are perfect. I'm obsessed with your hips."

I squirm with the urge to tell him that I think his arms are perfect. I'm obsessed with his hair and the way he never cuts it too short. His calves are perfect. I've never thought more about someone's legs ever than I've thought about his. But I can't.

"I don't think we should do this," I whisper.

I'm worried I'll have to clarify, but Reed seems to understand exactly what I'm saying. "Tell me to leave and I'll leave."

I don't have a response. I don't want him to leave. My mouth is dry as I grasp at words that don't exist.

"I'm sorry," he says, "about everything. And for what it's worth, I think about what I did every day. I miss you."

"You miss me?" I'm not sure why I sound defensive. I believe him.

"All I do is miss you."

He gently brings his hands to each side of my face, and I'm certain he's about to kiss me. I've never realized how badly I'd been waiting for him to kiss me one more time, but I can't even enjoy the moment because all I'm thinking about is the fact that the *one* night I wear my retainer, Reed Callaway decides to kiss me. His lips are an inch from mine.

Until the front door flies open.

Reed and I instinctively jump apart as Luke, the last person I want to see right now, strolls into the apartment like it's his own. If he noticed Reed and mine's almost kiss, he isn't acting like it. He drops his wallet onto the kitchen counter, burps, then turns to us.

"Halle, baby, Addy said I could spend the night. Teddy's being a douche and locked me out, so I need somewhere to sleep."

I let the silence stretch for a beat too long to be casual, trying to think of how to talk myself out of this. How am I supposed to explain to Reed that I'm 100% done with Luke while he's standing right next to us – or tell Luke whatever small spark we had is over while Reed is in the room?

"Yeah, sure," I respond, trying to ignore Reed rolling his eyes. "I can pull out the bedroll for you, hold on a sec."

I cross the kitchen to get to our hall closet, where we keep said bedroll, when Luke stops me by grabbing my waist.

"I see how it is." He nods toward Reed, who is watching us darkly. "Sharing your bed with someone else tonight?"

"What the hell is that supposed to mean?" Reed yells, which me and Luke both ignore.

I push him off me and am taken aback when he almost falls over. He must be more drunk than I thought. I don't know where all this is coming from, Luke and I have never *once* shared a bed. I don't even sit next to him if I have a choice.

"Get out Luke. You can't stay here," I tell him.

He laughs. "You're not the only one who lives here, baby. So not until Addy tells me to."

"Jesus, Luke." Reed scoffs. "Have some decency and leave."

"Why? So you two can sit here and make out? No, I need a bed! How about you fuck off back to your own room, Callaway."

"Guess that's my cue to leave," Reed says bitterly. "Since this is *your* room, Luke."

"You don't have to," I say, reaching for his arm as he walks toward the door. I want him to stay. I don't wanna deal with my drunk friends, or with housing Luke on my living room floor. I want Reed to stay and distract me from all that. "Please don't leave."

He opens the door and gestures for me to follow him out into the hallway. Once the door shuts behind us. He sighs in relief.

"I can't stay Halle," he tells me plainly. "But if he keeps talking to you like that, or he touches you again, call me. Okay?"

"Reed, he wouldn't..."

He shakes his head. "I'm not just saying this. Call me.

If it's late and I'm not answering, come pound on the door until someone answers."

"Okay. Goodnight, I guess."

Reed smiles at me and opens the front door, holding it open with one arm and pulling me closer to him with the other. He holds me tight against him and kisses the top of my head. It feels like it happens in slow motion before he eventually pulls away.

"Night, Hal. We'll talk later," he promises, before he ushers me back inside and shuts the door behind him. All I can do is watch him leave and feel my muscles twitch as I fight my urge to chase him down the hall.

Tonight started as my quiet night in. What the hell happened?

I'm only alone in the room with Luke for another thirty seconds or so before Isabel, Addy, and Michaela stroll in. Mic has thick streams of mascara running down her cheeks.

"What happened?" I ask, rushing to give Mic a hug that she melts into.

"Nothing," Isabel responds. "The police got called on the party and she got a little spooked."

"Is everything okay?"

Addy shrugs. "Some freshman girl called them because she thought her friend had been drugged."

"But she hadn't, it was just all the caffeine in the jungle juice," I assume.

"Exactly. So, I don't think anyone will get in trouble."

"Load of horseshit if you ask me." Luke, who has grabbed a bag of chips from our pantry, chimes in. "Just some frosh looking for attention."

Isabel and I scoff, while Addy's eye roll is a bit milder. "Go to bed Luke," she says. "Take my bed and quit this conversation while you're ahead."

"That comment put him ahead?" Isabel laughs dryly.

Luke shrugs innocently, and scuttles into my and Addy's bedroom without another word. Isabel brews a pot of tea and offers a cup to Michaela, but she tells us all she wants to do right now is sleep.

Once she's gone, I say slowly, "I'm about to tell you two things that you're gonna assume are related, but I promise you they're not." They both look at me warily but don't object, so I continue. "I've decided I just don't like Luke enough to have a crush on him… and Reed came over tonight while you guys were gone."

"Did you invite him over?" Addy asks, shocked.

"I have my fucking retainer in right now, do you think I invited him over?"

Isabel has a distinct look on her face when she is judging someone and making fun of them inside her head. It is hilarious to watch her give it to other people but absolutely humiliating to be on the receiving end of it, which I am right now. That's just how Isabel is; she talks with her whole face, and every thought she has is always visible.

"Well, how did it go?" Addy asks.

"He kissed the top of my head on his way out."

Isabel and Addy both gasp and lean forward.

"That's a boyfriend thing," Isabel whispers.

"He's totally still in love with you," Addy adds.

"Sure," I respond, not so convinced. I don't know what could convince me he won't leave me again.

yes and

. . .

I have been working on my paper for Dr. Wells' class for almost six hours. I'm locked in. I've been in the same uncomfortable chair in the student center since my classes ended at one o'clock. I like it better than the silence in the library. Plus, I'm invested in the daytime soap opera playing on the television mounted in the corner. I'm not very confident about everything I just wrote, but it's getting late and I'm ready to throw in the towel.

On my way back to my room, I run into Reed. Just my luck. Of course, Wells' class comes up in our small talk, and I end up telling him about my day spent in the student center, which leads to him saying we should proofread each other's papers tonight before we turn them in, which leads to me inviting him over to my room. It's always a slippery slope like that when it comes to me and Reed.

If I had half a brain, I would've never invited him over. I'm too tired for this. I've been having weird pseudo-nightmares this week so I haven't gotten more than five hours of sleep a night. I don't feel up for entertaining company right now, even though it's Reed.

When we get to my room, I try to weave us through my roommates without any questions from the peanut gallery. And fail.

"Hey, lovebirds." Isabel laughs.

Reed plays it off well, laughing with her and rolling his eyes. But I'm more offended – what's so hilarious about me and Reed hanging out?

When I roll my eyes and keep trudging to the bedroom, Addy shouts after me, "Luke said you've ghosted him! What the hell?"

Once we're in the safety of Addy and I's bedroom, we exchange laptops so we can look at each other's work. We both sit on my bed. I only make a few changes to his paper, mostly grammar. When I'm done, I look up at him and see he's still intently reading my paper. He looks focused but relaxed, and I see him nod a little whenever he reads something he likes or agrees with. I like looking at him when he doesn't know he's being watched.

He finishes reading, tells me it looks good and there are only a few changes he would make to help my arguments sound more succinct. I tend to ramble when I write, and over-explain things. Reed has the same problem, he's just better at stopping himself.

"I'm sorry about Luke, the other night," I tell him. "That was really awkward, wasn't it?"

He shrugs. "I'm the one who should apologize. I shouldn't have let him talk to you like that."

"Well, *I* shouldn't have let him talk to me like that," I respond. He's staring at me. "Anyway," I say. "I wanted to let you know that I ended things with him. We don't have to talk about it, but I wanted to keep you in the loop."

I notice Reed tamp down a smile. "Is that what Addy was talking about when we walked in?"

"Yeah. I don't know what he told her, but I didn't ghost him."

I really didn't. I asked to talk to him alone the other day and we had a very long conversation about how whatever was going on between us needed to die. Well, it was less of a conversation, and more like me talking at Luke for fifteen minutes as he looked at his feet and nodded repeatedly.

"That's good though," Reed says, fidgeting with a stray thread on my comforter. "I think you did the right thing."

He leaves my room after, and even though I want to ask him to stay, I know I have no valid excuse. On his way out, as he's saying goodbye, his gaze lingers on my bookshelf, studying something quickly, but long enough for me to notice. He shakes it off and continues his way out.

After he's gone, I stare at the bookshelf for a good ten minutes. Trying to see it through Reed's eyes, figure out what he could've been seeing that would make him stop dead in his tracks. It takes me a while to catch it, his copy of *On Writing*, tucked in between an Intro to International Relations textbook and a Meg Cabot novel. I wonder why he didn't ask for it back.

———

DR. WELLS, AS HE SAID IN HIS SYLLABUS, HAS OUR PAPERS graded seven business days after the deadline. He posts our grades online, and I only know when they're posted because Reed texts me to let me know.

Almost excited to see what I got, I grab my laptop and plop myself down onto the couch. Moment of truth.

The 58 on my computer screen is not bigger than any of the other numbers, but in my mind, it fills up the entire page. I failed the paper. *Failed*. This year was supposed to be the year to get my grades up, to not be stressed about losing my scholarship, and I failed the first paper of the year. I feel my chest tighten, the tears well in my eyes, but hold myself together as I hear the door open behind me.

It's Isabel and Nadia, laughing as they drop their backpacks by the kitchen counter. I quickly shut my laptop and take a deep breath to pull myself together.

Isabel says, "We're going out tonight, and you're coming."

"It's a Wednesday," I say dryly. Even in my near-alcoholic phase last year, I never went out on a school night, not even a Thursday.

"It's Wine Wednesday at Laundry Room. Drinks are dirt cheap."

"I don't know," I say as Nadia walks into her bedroom.

"Come on," Isabel says, now that we're alone. "Come with. All of us going out without you would be weird. With you coming, it would be a party."

I almost say no again, but then I think about that stupid 58. Maybe a night out will help. Even if I'm not drinking, just hanging out with my friends is better than sitting in the dorm wallowing.

"Okay," I tell her. "I'll go."

Isabel squeals and throws her arms around me, "Wear something sexy. I don't wanna pay for a single drink all night."

We take a bus to Laundry Room, which is in a gentrified part of downtown and surrounded by similar joints. The bar makes a feeble attempt at being true to its name, with a few washers and dryers acting as tables and signature shots named after laundry related items ('fabric softener' is the one I used to order.)

When Addy offers to grab the table shots, I shake my head.

"I don't need one tonight."

I'm trying to softly drop my newfound sobriety, and see how my friends would react to one night of not drinking before I tell them my real plans.

Addy carefully taps my arm. "You sure? Everything okay?"

"Yeah." I smile. "Just not really in the mood."

Nadia scoffs. "God, Halle. You used to be *fun*."

An icky feeling crawls across my skin and I don't think before I say, "Okay then, get me a shot."

The girls cheer, except for Addy who gives me a funny look. But she doesn't say anything as she leaves and comes back to the table with five shots of tequila. When we all take them, I throw mine over my shoulder and shockingly get away with it. No one seems to notice as I make a fake face of disgust and chew on my lime.

Isabel squeals with excitement and throws her arms around me. "This is gonna be the best Wine Wednesday ever! Are you feeling it yet Hal?"

"Totally," I lie.

Isabel pulls away to put her hands over my cheeks. "Your face is already *so* red. Get ready to be wasted tonight."

There's only one way I make it out of this night without starting any fights. I took one improv class in high school and I'm about to see how much it taught me because the only way I see out of this is to pretend to get blackout drunk. Easy.

So far so good. The next step for my plan to work is to get everyone else so drunk that they won't be thinking about how drunk or not drunk I am.

"Let's get another round!" Nadia says.

Biggest thing I remember from improv class? Always respond with *yes and*.

"Yes! And let's do shots!" I say, way too enthusiastically. My friends cheer in response.

I offer to grab them for us and ask the bartender to pour me a shot of water. She doesn't ask questions.

This is turning out to be easier than I thought it would be. Just being around this many drunk people makes me feel a little drunk myself, though every few minutes something breaks my act and reminds me how sober I am, like feeling the sweat from someone's arm as they're passing me stick to my own or hearing someone slur their words. None of my friends have seemed to notice my sobriety, I think I may be pulling this off.

And I'm also shocked to say that I'm having fun tonight. We're trying to find an open spot on the patio when a wise, albeit drunk, foreign exchange student grabs Isabel's cheeks and screams "There is no better place to live than an American college!" I laugh so hard that I almost throw up. Laundry Room is filled with students; people we know from classes and people we know because we met them here. I decide to dance with my friends instead of complaining about the music or thinking about how I'll probably have a headache later tonight.

I'm having so much fun that I don't see Reed walk in, only noticing him and Ben when I follow Addy across the patio on our way back from the bathroom.

"My favorite boys!" Addy exclaims, running to greet them. I stray behind, noticing that they're sitting at a table with a few girls I don't know. I don't like that. I especially don't like the girl that's cuddled up to his side – a smiley, clear-skinned, virgin brown hair beauty. A total foil to my resting bitch face, the acne flare-up on my cheekbone, and brassy fake blonde highlights. She touches his upper arm sweetly as they both laugh at something Ben says. I quickly catastrophize and imagine her to be a secret girlfriend

Reed's been forgetting to tell me about. They probably go on cute, quirky dates, like going to a farmer's market or something, where he pays for the stupid homemade body butter she picks out. And after the farmer's market, they head back to his room and have mind-blowing, incredible sex where they're so loud all his roommates complain behind his back about it and all of her friends ask her how she got lucky enough to find a boyfriend like him.

I snap out of my horrible vision when I notice Reed noticing me. Jesus. I am a miserable, jealous person. No wonder I'm not the one sitting next to him. At least he looks happy to see me, signaling me to join the table with a sharp nod of his head and a smile.

"I didn't know you guys would be here!" Addy says excitedly, sounding as drunk as ever. It's gonna be hard to match her energy.

"Hey," I say, peppy, trying to sound as drunk as I can without being ridiculous.

There's a flicker of something in Reed's eyes, maybe suspicion, but it leaves as quickly as it had arrived. "This was a last-minute plan," he explains, "the club we usually go to is closed and we wanted to go somewhere for Harry's birthday."

Were Ben and Reed planning on going to the club with these girls? Probably. I feel sick. I shouldn't be surprised. Girls love Reed. I would know.

I only feel worse when the girl sitting closest to Reed nudges him flirtingly and says, "Reed, honey, don't be rude! Introduce me, dummy!"

Hearing her say something so humiliating for him almost makes up for how shitty I feel watching him talk to another girl. Almost.

I've only seen Reed look this embarrassed a handful of times in the time I've known him, and he takes a deep breath in preparation before saying, "Um, sure. This is Liv." He gestures to the girl next to him, who flashes a cool smile, before turning to Addy and me. "Liv, this is Addy and Hal." It takes a solid three seconds to notice his use of my nickname before he hastily corrects himself. "Halle. Halle Hevko."

Liv purses her lips as she looks me up and down, as if she's heard of me before, and is just now placing a face to the name. Or maybe she hasn't heard of me before and it was Reed's use of a nickname or the way he said my name that cued her into the fact that we have a history. Either way, now she knows exactly who I am, I'm sure.

Her icy glare intimidates me, along with the fact that she is genuinely more attractive than me until my epiphany comes - I hold all the power here, not her. She probably really likes Reed. She probably really wants to date him. And as far as she knows, I might be the reason he isn't dating her. I'm the ex he can't get over, the girl he compares her to, and we never even had sex! God, I must be terrifying.

I know I have two ways to proceed: I can either play her game and say something bitchy, or I can take the high road.

I smile and offer my hand. "It's nice to meet you Liv."

She looks like I just smacked her across the face or something as she weakly shakes my hand, and I realize I made the more satisfying choice. Reed snickers.

Something about this exchange must have eased his tension because now he's acting like a normal person.

"Did get your grade back on that paper yet?" he asks.

Why did he have to bring that up? I was starting actually to enjoy this night.

I roll my eyes, in an overly dramatic way so he'll know I'm not seriously annoyed with him. "I think you need a hobby or something. You talk about Wells' class way too much."

He laughs warmly. "Just checking."

"Ladies of room eight o' six," Isabel screams from the other side of the patio. "Get your asses over here, they're playing our song!"

Addy expels a drunken squeal, and I have no choice but to imitate her, so I don't look like the odd one out. I see that same undefinable look of recognition flicker across Reed's face, but this time it stays. I follow Addy back to the rest of our group before I can decide what he's thinking about.

I try to dance with my friends, but it isn't fun anymore. The reality that I have a failed grade waiting for me in my room is catching up to me and seeing Reed here with another girl didn't help. Isabel is the closest to me, so she's the one I let know that I'm stepping out to the patio.

"Why?" She yells. "Trying to find a cig? I have some with me."

She shoves a cigarette and a pink lighter into my hand, and I play along. Going out to the patio for a drunk cigarette is a better reason than for no reason at all. When I step out the back door to the patio, I don't see a single familiar face.

I take a drag and cough a fit. Jesus, I don't think I've smoked a cigarette since February of freshman year. I'm still coughing, so hard it's embarrassing. Of course, it's at this moment that Reed enters my field of vision, looking over my body with dark eyes. Did he follow me out here? I'm both happy and insecure that he's seeing the 'something sexy' Isabel convinced me to wear, which is a low-cut shirt I borrowed from her closet. Reed and I lock eyes and his dart to the cigarette in my hand. I go for a second hit anyway, keeping the smoke inside my mouth and blowing it out instead of inhaling it so I don't cough.

"You smoke now?" he asks, void of any emotion or indication of how he would feel about my answer.

"No," I say densely, keeping eye contact as I take a long, albeit fake, drag.

Reed shakes me off with an eye roll. "So," he says over the music. "Tell me why you're at a bar on a Wednesday night pretending to be drunk."

Busted.

"Is my acting that bad?" I ask, fidgeting with the cigarette clasped in between my thumb and forefinger.

He shakes his head quickly. "It's that not bad it's just…" he pauses for a while, like he's not sure if he wants to finish his sentence, and softly chuckles before continuing, "*I think you need a hobby or something.*" I laugh at his impression of me, and he stops to listen to my laugh before continuing. "I was suspicious before, but after that, I thought: *That's Halle for sure. There's no way she's drunk.*"

I don't get it. How can he know me so well and not be too proud to hide it? And at the same time, sit with other girls and make plans with them. He didn't mention anything about going out for Harry's birthday the last time I saw him, which is when he helped me with my paper. That stupid paper is ruining everything.

"You got me," I confess.

"Why pretend? Trying to get some fool at this bar's attention?" he smirks.

"Yeah totally," I say sarcastically. "You know me, acting drunk to get male attention is totally my forte."

"I'm serious, Hal," he whispers. My face flushes and I can't even blame it on any alcohol. "What's going on with you?"

"Nothing." I avoid looking at Reed's face because I

would probably break and tell him the truth. "I just felt like going out with my friends."

"I feel like you're lying to me."

I roll my eyes. "Reed, I can't do this tonight. Go back to Liv and enjoy the rest of your night. Stop fussing over me."

I'm sure there was a time when this bar had ashtrays, but that's not true anymore so I have to stomp out my cig on the cement like the miserable person I feel like. Reed doesn't say anything as my heel grinds the cement and I walk away.

Inside, I see my friends have migrated to a table.

"I'm gonna grab another drink," Nadia says, standing up so quickly that the chair flies out from under her, "Someone come with."

I offer to join her and when we fight the crowd to get there, Nadia orders and settles on a set of stools, slouching over the bar while we wait.

"Sometimes I don't like Isabel very much," she says, unprompted, which makes me suddenly very uncomfortable but also interested. Damn, this girl has loose lips when she's drunk. Noted. I'm surprised she would even admit this to me. Does she not realize how close Isabel and I are?

"What do you mean *sometimes*?" I ask.

Nadia sighs loudly. "It's just like…she acts like she's so much better than us. Like she's not *special* for listening to Fiona Apple, that kind of shit – you know?"

Her words slur together, and when the bartender brings her a vodka Diet Coke, she downs all of it to punctuate the end of her monologue.

She leaves the edge of the bar without waiting for me, and I start to follow before realizing I left my purse draped on the back of the stool. I run back to grab it and speed up to catch up with Nadia.

Before I reach her, my foot catches on a stray table, and I fall. Too shocked to put out my hands and break the fall, my face hits the dirty floor with a definite thud. My lips feel wet and stupidly, I think at first that it might be someone's drink on the floor that transferred to my lip. I touch my hand to my lip and pull it back to see bright red. Nadia rushes to my side and helps me up and is asking more questions than I can process. I shake my head over and over.

"I'm gonna clean up in the bathroom," I tell her. "I'm fine. I'll meet you back at the table."

She nods, not questioning me too much in her drunken state, and leaves to go back to the patio. Once she's out of sight, I start crying. I'm not sure why, I'm not in that much pain and I'm not drunk. Maybe it's the adrenaline. Maybe it's because of that stupid paper I failed. I don't have time to overthink it, I run to the bathroom before anyone can stare at me for too long.

blood in the sink

. . .

I USUALLY LOVE THE THIRTY SECONDS I HAVE TO MYSELF when I pee in a bar bathroom. The best ones are the ones with the toilet and sink behind the same door, so I don't have to make conversation with the other drunk girls at the line of sinks. That's how the bathroom at Laundry Room is — the toilet and the sink are both behind one door.

I lock the door behind me and look at myself in the mirror. My hair is matted, mascara smudged from crying and wiping my eyes, and my lip busted. I look like the worst version of myself.

I've been in here for five or so minutes and I cannot get my stupid lip to stop bleeding. I didn't know there was this much blood in my face. The sink is filled with blood and won't drain fast enough. There's a knock at the door, not the first one since I've been in here.

"Occupied," I shout lazily, all attention focused on the wet paper towel pressed to my lip.

I feel like I have to catch my breath when I hear Reed's resonating voice. "Hal, it's me. Open up."

I open the door to see Reed hanging himself across the

frame, blocking my view of anything that isn't him – taking up as much space as possible.

He looks upset. I don't get it.

"I heard you were hurt," he says. He's looking at me too closely. I squirm.

His gaze shifts to my lip as he steps closer and closes the door behind him. My gaze shifts to the floor in front of the sink because all I know is that right now, I cannot look at him. He tilts his head in either disbelief or amusement at my obvious discomfort with his coming to check on me, I can't tell.

I'm trying so hard to resist the urge to fall back into old habits, to let him clean my lip for me and tell me everything will be okay. I can't. I know deep down, that if I let him take care of me tonight, I won't be able to stay away from him anymore. He is only one kind deed away from me throwing away all the work I did to try to keep him out of my life, to keep myself from depending on him.

Throwing the bloody paper towel in the trash can next to me, I turn away from him.

"Look at me," he takes my face in both his hands. With anyone else, this would feel like a violation of personal space, but nothing with Reed feels like that anymore. He tilts my chin up so he has a better view of my lip, which, in a moment of absolute stupidity, I think means he's about to kiss me. He does not.

"It doesn't look too bad," he tells me, assessing the injury.

"It stings. And it won't stop bleeding."

He grabs a clean paper towel, pressing it against my lip until the bleeding slowly stops. It's probably only a minute, but it feels like we're standing there staring at each other in silence for hours, his fingers pressed to my lip.

He's officially fixed my problem. And he's done it

better than I could've. I'm done for. My final wall has been torn down, and that, along with the reoccurring thought of my failed paper, makes me break into an abrupt sob.

It makes poor Reed drop his calm, caring demeanor, as he rubs his palms up and down my arms like he's checking for another injury. Feeling his warm hands on my shoulders makes me shiver. "What's wrong?"

I heave air in, trying to suppress another sob, but failing.

"I can't tell you everything. It's too embarrassing," I barely gargle up.

There's a violent knock on the bathroom door that makes me jump and effectively shuts our conversation down. Reed knocks back on it until the knocking stops.

"I'll cut you a deal," he tells me as I rub at my now puffy eyes. "I'll give you a ride back to campus, but we're talking about this."

"Can you imagine what my friends would say if I told them I was leaving with you?"

"I think I have a pretty good idea." He flashes me a cocky smile, something I don't see often. I can't lie, it's really hot.

"You guys drove?"

He nods.

"And you haven't been drinking?"

"Correct."

I almost cave. Not taking the bus home or paying for a cab sounds really nice. But, since I like to ruin things, I have to ask, "What about Liv and the other girls you were with? Are they gonna be in the car too?"

Reed laughs hard. "We didn't come with them. I know Liv from my stats class, and she invited us to sit with her and her friends when she saw us walk in."

"Liv has a crush on you, just so you know."

"I know. She's told me before. But do you really wanna talk about Liv right now?"

"No, you're right." I sigh. "Okay. Let me tell my friends we're leaving. But they're gonna interrogate me and it's gonna be all your fault."

"I'll take the blame if it means you don't have to keep using your pitchy, fake drunk voice for the rest of the night."

"You said it wasn't that bad!" I scoff, trying not to laugh as we exit the bathroom together.

He smiles warmly. "It's not bad, just weirdly pitchy."

My friends react exactly how I thought they would when I tell them that I'm leaving with Reed. Isabel takes a condom out of her purse and shoves it in my back pocket. I try to tell them it's not like that, but no one believes me.

When I find Reed to let him know I'm ready to leave, Reed is standing next to Liv and her friends' table. When he sees me approach, he smiles and puts his arm around my waist to pull me into him. Liv looks like she could kill me. Ha. I win.

"We're gonna head out," Reed says, "but I will see you in stats."

"Right," Liv says stiffly.

As we walk away, but before we're far enough to be out of Liv's line of vision, Reed holds me tight to his side and uses his other arm to gather my hair away from my face.

I can't see Liv's face, but I wish I could. She's probably about to burst.

Is that why Reed's doing all of this? Is he only treating me this way so some girl from his stats class will see us acting like a couple and leave him alone?

"That was a nice little show," I whisper, trying not to sound too bitter, as we reach the parking lot.

Reed stops, still holding me so that I stop with him. He

brushes his hand under my shirt before tickling my hip until I giggle. "Who said anything about a show, Hevko?"

I smile. I hate him.

Reed puts the windows down and takes the long way back, driving around the perimeter of campus to reach the student parking garage instead of through it. He finds a spot and we shuffle out of the garage, which is so far from the main part of campus that we have to cut through the block of off-campus student housing to get there.

When we make it back to my room in Prez, I flip the kitchen lights on and drop my keys in our bowl on the counter. Reed tosses his car keys in it too. He stares at me over the counter.

"Spill. Start at the beginning, why were you pretending to be drunk?"

I sigh and migrate to the couch, trying to put some distance between us, but he follows me. I sit on the edge — in a rigid way that I've never sat in front of Reed before. He crouches down and rests his hands lightly on my kneecaps, so close to my face that he's all I can see. I start to tear up again, feeling absolutely ridiculous, waiting for him to say something to break the silence. But he doesn't, just stares at me and waits for me to start talking.

"I'm not drinking because I just don't like who I am when I'm drunk, and I'm so over the 'we only drink to get drunk' vibe. I wasn't planning on keeping it from my friends forever, I was just trying to find the right time to tell them. Until Nadia made a stupid comment about me not being fun anymore. And I know I shouldn't let it affect me like this, I know, but I decided to just *pretend* to be drunk so everyone would still think I was the same fun Halle they became friends with last year."

Reed nods. It feels good to talk to him about my trial

run at sobriety. I originally wanted to keep it all my little secret, but he doesn't count. He's like an extension of me.

"So, Nadia made a stupid comment, that's why you were on edge all night?"

I shake my head. "It gets worse. I failed that paper we turned in for Wells' class. Which especially sucks because I'm on academic probation and I *really* can't afford an F. And now my lip is busted because I tripped over a chair. I'm not even drunk! What type of clumsy loser trips and falls when she's not even drunk?"

"But I read your paper. It was great," he says.

"That's what I thought too."

"You need to talk to Wells, go to his office hours, and ask him why you got such a low grade. Ask to redo it and if he can't give you a straight answer then you know he's grading you unfairly and you can go to your advisor-"

I scoff. "I don't think I could go to a meeting with Wells without crying."

The front of my hair is sticking to the caked tears on my face. Reed notices and reaches up to pull them off and gather my hair behind my neck. He looks at me with that dumb look guys get when they're about to kiss you, but he doesn't kiss me. When he doesn't kiss me, I feel sinking disappointment. Then I'm mad at myself for feeling it. What's wrong with me? I'm at risk of losing my scholarship, my *education*, the only thing I've always wanted, but all I can think about is whether a boy is about to kiss me or not.

Reed's hand lets go of my hair. I forgot it was even there.

"And you're on academic probation?" he asks.

Damn. He went so long without mentioning that part of my monologue that I thought he didn't catch it.

"I was booted from the honors program and I'm on

academic probation for my scholarship, so I need to keep my grades up. None of my friends know that either. The only people that do are my parents and my advisor...And now you, I guess," I say quickly.

The room is silent as Reed's mouth drops in surprise. He finally shakes off his eye contact with me before pacing around in front of the TV with his hands clasped behind his neck.

This isn't the reaction I expected. I guessed he'd either talk some sense into me or comfort me. I'm not sure where his complete surprise falls on that spectrum.

"You have to have below a two-point two GPA to be on scholarship probation," he says. I realize he probably meant it to be a question.

I nod in confirmation, yes, my GPA was that low, which seems to distress him even more, as he dramatically drags his hands down his face.

"Why are you acting so weird?" I ask. His reaction is only making me feel worse.

"You're smarter than me," he says. Like it's an absolute.

I shrug, and my hand runs up my throat and neck as I start to feel itchy. "Not according to my transcript."

He's quiet for an uncomfortably long time, moving to the other end of the counter, before asking the one, single thing I hoped he wouldn't. "Is this because of me? What I did last year?"

"No," I tell him quickly, and I'm not lying. I've always been smart, but I've always had focus issues. I didn't stop doing my homework because Reed stopped talking to me. It was my problem, and I fixed it.

Well, I thought I had before I failed this paper.

He nods, unconvinced, fixating his eyes on the floor.

"It's not your fault. I have issues when it comes to school, always have, way before I even knew you."

He looks at me with uncertainty, but I don't care whether he believes me or not. I'm more concerned with the fact that I just ruined the image he had of me in his head. He probably doesn't want to be friends with someone dumb enough to be on academic probation.

"We can look at your paper together tomorrow," he says, with a sense of finality, walking toward me. He grabs my hand and stops it where my nails are sharply scratching my neck, squeezing it, and placing it back at my side. The gentle act, and the natural way he did it, reminds me of last year. Anything that reminds me of last year usually makes me sad. But this doesn't. "But tonight, we're not gonna think about it."

Reed channel surfs for a while and settles on a Hitchcock movie playing on Turner Classic Movies. Our thighs rest only half an inch from each other, even though the whole rest of the couch is empty. *I wish we were sitting even closer;* I realize. I shouldn't be thinking that. I don't care about what he said when he came over and professed his feelings for me in his cute tipsy rambling voice. He hasn't brought it up since so he must not want me like that anymore, and who can blame him after seeing what a train wreck I am. He's just trying to be nice. Still, I want him. The realization makes me shiver.

"Cold?" Reed asks.

It takes me longer than it should to realize he's responding to my shivering. Sometimes I forget that other people can see things like that, and they're not inside my head.

"No," I respond.

He ignores me, grabbing the blanket draped over the

back of the couch and clumsily throwing it around my shoulders.

"There," he says plainly, looking me over like he's proud of his choice.

I smile at him, but it gets interrupted by a yawn. I try to hide it behind my hands, but he notices and slides a throw pillow between us.

"You should try to sleep," he says, almost demanding. Maybe it's because I was thinking about how close our thighs are a minute ago, but I find his strong tone very attractive right now.

So, when he stretches out his legs, sinks into the couch, places the pillow on the bottom half of his chest, and taps it like I'm meant to lay my head down there – I do. Neither of us speak. I try to focus on the movie, the Old Hollywood hero who I recognize but cannot name is mistaken for a spy. Anything is better than thinking about Reed right now. Feeling his chest through the pillow is all I could've wanted out of tonight and somehow too much. If I try hard enough, I can almost hear his heartbeat. My hands rest on his arms. Either I'm cold or he's warm because his skin feels scorching under my palms.

We shouldn't be cuddling like this. I know that for certain. But I'm so tired and he's so warm. I fall asleep before those worries can stop me.

I have a nightmare where I'm stuck in a horror movie. I'm the final girl, living in a haunted house where some type of zombie virus is infecting everyone I love. So I trap them in the basement and run out the front door.

I wake up in a daze, having no clue how long I've been asleep. Each of my limbs feels tangled with Reed's. I'm afraid to move and wake him. Plus, I'm still thinking about my nightmare. I don't like to move after I wake up from them. I've had nightmares every night this week, but never the same one. This one tonight feels noticeably spookier, even though I don't know why. Usually, they're variations of getting so drunk I accidentally ruin my relationship with my friends or being trapped under someone and not being able to see his face. The zombie horror movie nightmare is new. I don't know why I let it scare me, sounds like it would make a shit horror movie anyway.

I turn my face towards Reed. He's wide awake, staring at me. I think he woke me up. He probably wants me to get off him so he can sleep in his own bed. I scramble and try to pull myself up when I feel his hands gently tighten around my waist like a cryptic hint telling me not to move.

"What time is it?" I ask.

"Twelve forty-five," he says. "No one else is back yet."

"You can head back to your room. I'll be okay."

He shrugs. "I'm comfy here."

I don't believe him for a second, but before I can argue, he says something else.

"I woke you up because you were talking in your sleep. It kind of sounded like a nightmare."

I hate lying to Reed. But if I'm honest with him, he'll ask me why I'm having nightmares. And I can't tell him that my theory is it has something to do with my drunken escapades and having sex I don't remember, which would require me telling him I had sex with someone who wasn't him. He would know what type of party girl slut I became, the type of drunk girl who can't remember losing her virginity. Not telling him that tonight. Preferably, not ever.

"What do you mean it sounded like a nightmare?"

"I've never heard you talk in your sleep before."

"I don't remember anything," I say. "You can leave if you want. Really."

He shakes his head, running a hand through my hair delicately. "Go back to sleep, Hal."

The shrill beep of my scheduled weekday alarm wakes me up. My bones ache, feeling a little like shit from sleeping on a couch with another person.

Reed's gone, which is a little disappointing, but good because I don't want to talk about last night. Reed now knows my biggest secrets, and it doesn't feel weird. It feels so right, it's confusing.

I don't have class until noon, and it's nine, but I decide to stay awake instead of trying to get an extra hour or so of sleep in my bed.

Addy comes out of the bedroom as I scour the pantry for a bagel. She's wide awake and ready for the day, already dressed in her scrubs for her nursing lab.

"Why was Reed sleeping on the couch with you? He said he was worried about you, did something happen last night after you left Laundry Room?" she asks.

"I failed a paper. It's fine. He's making a bigger deal out of it than it is."

Before Addy can counter me, there's an incessant pounding on the door. I open the door to see Reed with two cups of coffee in his hands and a goofy smile plastered on his face.

"Good morning," I say skeptically.

"What time do you have class?" he asks.

"Noon."

"Perfect, go get dressed and meet me back out here."

Once I'm ready, Reed hands me the second coffee and tells me to follow him. We walk across campus and toward the academic mall until we reach a small building in the front.

"This is where Wells' office is. He has drop-in office

hours until ten and if you would like to go in, I will wait out here until you're done. Deal?"

No one's ever done anything like this for me before. No act of love has ever been this practical. How did I ever convince myself it was easier to live life without him?

"Deal." I nod.

"Does that mean you're gonna go in?" he asks, seeming almost excited for me.

"I guess."

"You got this babe." He pauses and his face turns a bright, firetruck, red like I've never seen it before.

"Thanks," I say. "For last night too."

"I'll always look out for you Hal," he responds, gaining his composure back, "I don't think I'm wired to do anything else."

Now I'm the embarrassed one, his words throwing me off guard.

"Hopefully I won't take too long," I say.

He shrugs. "Take all the time you need."

I give him one last smile before I turn toward the door. I wonder how I'm supposed to get through this meeting when all I think about is how good it felt to hear Reed call me "babe."

just friends
. . .

Reed insists on helping me with my paper in the days after meeting with Wells. My roommates are already starting their Friday night pregame, so we decide to work in his room, which I've never seen before. The bedroom he has to himself is different from the room he shared with Ben last year. Instead of blank walls like his room last year, he's put up a few movie posters, a Kendrick Lamar album cover, and a poster advertising a Fleetwood Mac concert in Pittsburgh, in 1975. I like them. I like seeing that he's confident enough now to advertise his interests in things that aren't soccer. Sometimes, last year, I felt like he was afraid to admit to his teammates that he found anything other than soccer even remotely interesting.

He has a Scottish flag hanging on the wall behind his bed, which I find more interesting than I should. Reed's mother's side of the family is almost one hundred percent Scottish, he told me last year, and on one of those ancestor tracing sites they discovered they were very far and very ambiguously descended from some famous Jacobite leader. And his family ate that shit up.

It's always been weird to me how Reed thinks of his heritage as something akin to a fun fact. My family is Ukrainian, but I've never seen it as anything interesting, it's simply part of who I am, inseparable from the rest of my characteristics. When I'm listening to my grandmother talk about "the old country," the rare occasion when my parents and I attend a mass at Saint Josaphat, or when someone asks where my last name came from, I don't think to myself, 'Ah yes, I am Ukrainian, thank you for reminding me because I had forgotten that,' I just do it because it's what I do. I don't need a Ukrainian flag on my wall.

Reed has a lot of pictures hanging up, too. There're pictures of him with his parents and his two younger sisters, pictures of him and Ben with other guys on the team, and a few pictures of him in high school with his friends from back home. I never knew that version of Reed, I realize. That's weird. I feel like I've known Reed my whole life.

Selfishly, I scan the pictures looking for my face and am very surprised when I see it. It's nothing special or personal, just a picture Reed took of everyone who came to his birthday party last year to send to his family, to "prove he had friends," so he said. It should mean nothing to me, he probably didn't even think twice about me being in the picture, but it makes me feel a little lighter just looking at it.

Reed sits with my laptop in front of him, staring at it with furrowed brows as we split the space on his bed.

"I think it's good," he says.

"But does it *effectively portray an understanding* of the material?" I mock.

When I visited Dr. Wells during his office hours, he had given me a long list of broad criticisms of my failed paper, none of which I understand. He said I could turn in a corrected paper for partial credit, and I've been procrastinating doing it because I don't understand his criticisms. I was hoping Reed would, but he doesn't totally get it either. But two brains are better than one, and we're slowly making our way through my paper. I could never explain to him how thankful I am that he's helping me with this, so I never try. I hope he knows.

"Well, I'm not endorsing giving up," he tells me, handing me back the laptop, "but I don't know what else you could add. It all looks good to me."

I feel ready to give up. We've been working longer than I thought we would, and I don't know what else I can do to gut this paper. I've nearly rewritten the whole thing. I've also had a killer headache all day and feel a total burnout coming on. Like no matter how many naps I take, I can barely keep my eyes open.

"I'll turn it in on Monday." I sigh dramatically. "But for now, I'm going to eat a nice, large caf dinner."

"I'll come," he says cheerily, hopping off the bed when I do.

I shoot him a glance, not knowing whether he's joking or not, and he responds with a teasing smirk.

"What?" he asks suggestively. "Am I not invited? Got a date or something?"

I roll my eyes. "No, I don't have a date, obviously. You can come."

The caf is serving a pasta dinner and we eat at one of the small tables in the front. We talk about his soccer season so far and my job. We sit at the table talking long after our plates are emptied.

Reed's teammate, Elliot, abruptly joins us at the table with two full plates of food.

"Sup," he says nonchalantly. "Glad to see you two are shacking up again."

I choke on my Diet Coke. Reed laughs casually.

"We're just friends," he replies quickly.

I feel seasick and dumb. *Just friends*. Right, how could I ever let myself be naïve enough to think we're anything else? He goes out of his way for me and spends time with me and looks like he's about to kiss me any time we're alone together. Where could I have possibly gotten the idea that we were more than friends from? I want to bang my head on the table, but I restrain myself.

So, I smile instead. "Right. Who says you can't be friends with your ex who never even officially asked you to be his girlfriend?"

Ha. Two can play this game. From across the table, Elliot gives me a fist bump.

Reed is quick to change the subject. "Did you guys figure out what you're doing tonight?" he asks Elliot.

"We can't go to the lax house anymore, so no."

Now I'm interested. "Why?"

Elliot looks at me with pity, like he feels bad that I'm not cool enough to have heard this piece of gossip yet.

"I don't know *why* they're doing it," he says, "But the girls' volleyball team is boycotting their parties. And if they're not going, the girls' soccer team won't go either. What does that leave me with? The swim girls and the golf girls. I'm not wasting my time if those are the only girls going, fuck no."

If true, the girls' volleyball team boycotting the lacrosse house's parties is huge news. I should be thanking Elliot for showing me I have better things to focus on than thinking about Reed, especially if we're only *friends*.

"About the girls' volleyball team," I say to Elliot. "Do

you think they would mind talking to me about this boycott?"

It's not often that I'm excited for a *Clocktower* meeting. This moment should be celebrated. I walk into our usual Sunday morning meeting with an extra pep in my step.

Elliot was able to put me in contact with two seniors on the volleyball team and they agreed to meet me for coffee. They had a long list of stories from the past four years of parties but told me their final straw was a few weeks ago, the party my friends went to where the police were called. A freshman on their team passed out and Aaron took her up to his room to lie down then refused to let any of her friends check on her or help her get back to her dorm. He tried to tell them it was "his job" to take care of her since it was his house.

I tell Sam the whole vision I have for this article, it's an opinion piece — "What the boys who throw parties need to change if they want girls to keep showing up." I figured out that I can talk about my experiences at lacrosse house, and what the girls on the volleyball team told me, without naming the lacrosse team specifically, and everyone will still know exactly who I'm talking about. I think I can make this work.

Sam thinks otherwise.

"I don't know," he says sheepishly from behind his stupid makeshift desk. "Do you really wanna be the girl that messes with the lacrosse team?"

"You'd rather ignore it?"

Sam shrugs. "Maybe one of the guys from the sports

page could write it. They might be better at subtly calling out the lacrosse team without… offending them."

"They're gonna be offended no matter who writes it," I counter. "This is my article. I know I can make this work."

I can tell Sam is resisting the urge to roll his eyes as he awkwardly crosses his hands on top of the table. "Fine," he says unconvincingly, "Get me a draft by the end of the week and we'll talk then."

I spend all day and half the night working on my draft. It's better than anything I've ever written before. I stay up until four a.m. working and forget to set an alarm for Wells' class on Monday. I don't feel guilty, the article is more important. I figure since I already missed Wells' class, I may as well miss my other ones too, and I spend six hours holed up in my room until I've perfected the draft. This is the best thing I've ever written.

I'm not the only one who thinks it though, which fuels my ego. When I take it to Sam, he reads it carefully and stares at me with wide eyes once he's done.

"I have a few small notes but overall, you did a great job," he says in disbelief. "This is incredible."

I'd be offended, thinking he was insulting everything else I've written for him if I didn't know myself how much better this is than the filler articles I've been signing up for. He lets me know that my deadline for the finalized piece is next Monday, and he's sending the issue to the printers Tuesday morning. We both leave the room smiling, which is a first.

On Wednesday, I wake up with a blinding headache and a stomachache. It's almost enough to make me skip Wells' class, but since I missed Monday, I know I need to go.

I sit next to Reed like I always do. He had a tournament out of state and didn't get back to campus until

Monday night, so he wasn't in class either and has no idea I ditched. Thankfully, he doesn't ask me what Wells talked about. I'm not in the mood to be reprimanded by Reed, an unforeseen consequence of telling him about my scholarship probation.

After class, Wells calls my name and gestures for me to come to his desk. I exchange a wordless glance with Reed, knowing it means he will wait for me outside the lecture hall.

"Miss Hevko," Wells says in his usual noncommittal and monochrome tone. "I graded your revised paper and wanted to tell you before I update your grade, your final grade on the paper ended up being sixty-five percent. Feel free to come and see me during office hours before you turn in your next paper if you're worried about this happening again."

Sixty-five? What the fuck? That's a high D, and while I appreciate Wells letting me rewrite it in the first place, I don't feel like it was worth all the pain I put into that paper.

Reed's outside, of course, already poised with a question. "What was that about?"

I make a split-second decision not to tell Reed about my grade. I don't want him to be disappointed in me or feel like he wasted his time. Plus, I haven't talked to Reed much this week. He's had soccer, I've had work, and my *Clocktower* article. It just doesn't feel like a conversation the two of us should have right now. It's not a big deal, and I've been trying to rely on him less since his total denial of our relationship in front of Elliot.

"Nothing, he had a question about my paper."

Reed doesn't ask any further questions, but I can tell he's suspicious of me, which makes me feel guilty about lying.

"Are you gonna make it to my birthday party?" he asks, smiling.

"Wouldn't miss it, called off work and everything."

Reed wants a small gathering, not a party, for his birthday, so he planned his birthday dinner at Taco Loco. The Lighthouse has been understaffed since a mass exodus of freshmen that quit last month, which has nearly doubled my hours and made calling off almost impossible. But I fought tooth and nail to get the night of Reed's birthday off and won.

Reed and I go our separate ways to go to our next classes, but I can't pay attention to anything. Three ideas have been bouncing in my head all day: my incurable body aches, my abysmal Wells paper, and the deadline for my article. I feel like I can't function. When my classes are over, I nap until dinner. Addy asks me if I want to go to Pilates with her and I decline.

When the weekend eventually comes, I work until ten on Friday and Saturday, both nights coming back to my room after my shift and trying to work on the final draft of my article. I end up staring at the screen until three a.m., too burned out from work to think about writing. Good thing I have Sunday off. A whole day off seems so foreign, I'm not sure what I should do with it. I sleep most of the day until Addy wakes me up accidentally when she comes into the bedroom and mills through her closet. When she sees me in bed, she pauses.

"Are you not coming?" she asks.

"What are you talking about?" I respond with a yawn.

"Reed's birthday dinner," Addy says slowly, and then laughs at me when my eyes nearly pop out of my head.

"Don't tell me you forgot about it. We need to leave in like ten minutes."

I did forget about it. I totally forgot today is Reed's birthday. I've been so busy, I just forgot what day it was. I feel awful, it's five o'clock on Reed's birthday, and I haven't even talked to him. I had a whole plan to see him this morning so I could be one of the first people to wish him a happy birthday, write him a heartfelt card, and dress up for his dinner, but it's too late for any of that now. I'm a horrible person. No wonder he doesn't want to date me. I get ready quickly, throwing my bedhead into a braid and copying Addy's outfit because I don't have the mental energy to come up with one of my own.

I don't know how, but I end up with a seat next to Reed at the largest table Taco Loco has. Addy, Isabel, and I are the only girls here. The rest of the table is filled with Reed's teammates - Ben, the other sophomores, and a few upperclassmen that Reed is close with. It's both a reward and punishment to sit next to him. I get to spend time with one of my favorite people, but what are we supposed to talk about? That I've barely been able to pull myself together and go to class, that I have to turn in the best article of my Clocktower career tomorrow and have seemingly forgotten how to write, or that I work so much that I go to bed dreaming about seating people and wiping tables down?

The table orders a pitcher of strawberry margarita, and I gag a little. Tequila and I do not get along. Anytime I have ever thrown up from drinking, it has been from drinking tequila.

Reed is busy trying to entertain the whole table and the two of us don't have time to talk, besides small talk and tagging onto the ends of funny stories the other tells. It's not until later, after we eat our entrees and after our friends have ordered a third pitcher of strawberry margarita and after they have convinced the Taco Loco employees to let them use the karaoke machine, that Reed and I *really* talk.

"I feel like we haven't seen each other in a while," he says.

"Yeah, I've been at work a lot, we're pretty under-staffed."

"Do you wanna work on the Wells paper this week?"

Seems like forgetting things is becoming a recurring theme in my life. I forgot about our next Wells paper — I was too focused on the first one. I try to hide my surprise, I don't wanna disappoint Reed or make him feel like it's his fault for not reminding me of the paper earlier.

"I'm off on Tuesday and Wednesday, we can do it then," I say quietly, trying not to give myself away as someone who totally forgot we even had a paper due.

Reed sees right through it. "You forgot about it."

I don't respond, suddenly becoming very interested in the chips and salsa I'm eating, as Reed studies me patiently, like he has all the time in the world to wait for my response. I look up from my chips mid-bite and accidentally meet his eyes, and the look in his eyes makes me break. He doesn't look like he wants to jump at the opportunity to judge me or tell me what to do, he looks like he's just interested in what's going on inside my head.

"Maybe. I've been hyper-focused on this assignment for *Clocktower*. I haven't had the brain power to think about much else."

"Oh, is that why you've been ignoring me?"

My face flushes as I turn to him again, expecting to see him angry. But really, he's just smirking at me like he won. I feel like I've been caught stealing a cookie from the cookie jar or something – pure shame.

"I haven't been ignoring you on purpose."

I have.

Reed shrugs. "I'm free Tuesday. Let's work on the paper then."

I only have enough energy to respond with a nod. Isabel and Addy start the chorus of an old country song, and we pause our conversation to watch them but never start it up again.

no charge

· · ·

It feels like the world is about to end on Monday night when it's 11:35 and I'm supposed to email my article to Sam by midnight. I'm tired, and not in the mood to write. I know if I just had another day, twelve hours even, I could crank this out and nail it. Just not right now.

I call Sam and he answers on the first ring.

"Where's my article?" he asks.

"I know, that's what I'm calling about." I'm exhausted. Even I can hear it in my voice. "I need a few more hours. What time do you have to send the issue to the printer tomorrow? I can get it to you before then for sure."

He sighs. "If you can get it to me before seven o'clock, I can add it in before I send the final issue. And you know I'm only doing this because it's a goddamn great article, right? Never expect an extension like this again."

I take a breath for what feels like the first time all night.

"Thank you. It'll be worth it, I promise."

I immediately fall asleep on the couch after our call and wake up to the 5 a.m. alarm I set. I pick up my laptop and work on the article down to the wire, emailing it to Sam by 6:54.

Phew. Now that the article's done, I don't have a good reason to skip classes. So I go and immediately regret it. I feel like a zombie. All I can think about is my article. Will Sam like it as much as the first draft? Will people understand that I'm talking about the lacrosse team?

When I get back to Prez, all I want to do is take a nap on the couch with *Friends* running as background noise. Which I can't do because Luke and his roommate, Teddy, are sitting smack in the middle of it.

"Can I help you two with something?" I don't know what they're doing in my room. No one else is here.

Luke twists around to face me. "We're waiting for"

"Addy," Teddy cuts him off and bro-claps his shoulder.

Luke rolls his eyes at him but keeps his focus on me. "Right. Waiting for *Addy*."

I could escape to my bedroom, but I don't feel great about leaving these two out here alone to mill about the room.

"Anyway, how have you been?" Luke asks as I sit on the loveseat across the room.

"Fine. A little overwhelmed with school but fine."

Teddy smirks mischievously. "Overwhelmed? Luke said you're a *comm* major."

I don't know Teddy well, and only as Luke's roommate, not as an individual. From what Addy's told me, they're always fighting. That's why Luke's so buddied up with Aaron and the other guys on the lacrosse team. I've always thought Teddy is a little sleazy, but I've never told anyone that.

"I'm actually political communications. Lots to get done tonight."

Luke and Teddy share a sneaky grin that makes me

sweat as Teddy reaches into his backpack and pulls out a gallon-sized Ziploc full of pill bottles. Oh hell. He digs around for a beat, unscrews a childproof cap, and hands me a blue capsule.

"Forty milligrams Adderall. Guaranteed to get all your shit done in one sitting," he tells me.

I stifle a laugh. Is this how other people see me, someone who would buy Adderall? "What does Adderall even go for nowadays?"

Teddy shrugs. "First timer's sale, no charge."

"Yeah right," I scoff.

"Seriously. Take it. Let me know if you want more."

Maybe I am someone who would buy Adderall. The more I stare at the pill, the more tempting it gets. Teddy makes it sound so easy, like some type of magic.

The front door opens, and I clench my hand around the pill to hide it. It's Addy, who notices Luke and Teddy in the living room and waves.

"Well, we better go," Luke says hastily. The two boys stand, practically pulling each other up from the couch and rushing out of our room.

Addy watches them leave and stares at me. "What did they want?"

"They said they were waiting for you."

"Weird."

I trail Addy into the kitchen as she opens the fridge.

"You're a nurse," I say.

"Nursing student," she corrects me.

"Same difference. Do you think I'll die if I take this Adderall Teddy gave me?"

I open my sticky palm to show her the pill. She sighs, sounding a little like my mother.

"I don't think you'll die. But do you really need to take it?"

I shrink behind the door of the fridge, trying to avoid eye contact with her. I don't appreciate the judgment. "I'm working on a big paper tonight."

She slams the door shut.

"I can't tell you what to do," she says, "but even if it works, it might make you sick."

I take the pill with a swig of Diet Coke and Addy leaves for Pilates. She invites me but I pass. This paper is more important.

An hour later, I feel nothing. All I've accomplished is creating a document with the title 'PAPER TWO' and staring at the blank screen.

I finally write a rough thesis but stop typing when a wave of nausea washes over me. Like, debilitating and horrible nausea. Addy was right, I feel sick. I have the chills and the shakes like I have a fever and have to shut my laptop and close my eyes to try to center myself. That's unsuccessful. If anything, closing my eyes makes me feel worse. Food. Food should help, right?

I stumble to the kitchen. A protein bar is the first thing I can get my hands on, so I nearly swallow it whole. That doesn't help either. I'm thinking about my next steps when there's a knock on the door. Maybe Addy forgot her keycard. I check the peephole and jump when I see Reed.

I forgot we made plans to work on this paper together.

I open the door and fake a smile. "Now might not be the best time to work on the paper. Can you come back tomorrow?"

He looks me up and down, gripping the straps of his backpack, and pushes past me into the threshold of my room. Point of no return.

"I can't tomorrow," he says, dropping his backpack onto the kitchen counter. "I have practice. And you said you had work tomorrow."

"But you could come over after my shift's over."

He pulls out his laptop and settles into a stool, barely looking at me. "Don't you get off at like eleven? I can't start working on a paper that late. With practice and all this homework, I'm like a grandpa nowadays, in bed by ten-thirty."

I can tell he's trying to joke around with me, but I don't care. The only thing I can think about is how awful I feel. I sit on the farthest stool from him, my knee bouncing.

"What's wrong with you?" he asks, any sense of joking around now gone.

"Huh?"

"You're wired."

"You're being dramatic," I say, standing up to grab a glass of water. Water will help. "I am not *wired*. I'm just ready to get this paper over with. So let's get it over with."

I gulp from the cup quickly as Reed glares at me from across the counter. We fall silent, the only sound in the room is the sound of me gulping. I feel out of my own body. Everything's blurry but not blurry in the literal sense of the word, just muddled.

After a painfully long time, he asks, "Are you on something?"

"No." I scoff. I don't think it's too convincing, but at least I tried.

"You're acting like you are. All jumpy and shit."

I'm about to defend myself when another bout of nausea hits me. This one's bad — feels like I'm being kicked in the chest *bad*. I'm going to throw up and doing it in front of Reed would be mortifying so I need to excuse myself and run to my bathroom.

Except when I open my mouth to speak, I can't. Without thinking, I turn around, grab the trashcan we keep under the kitchen sink, and puke. I haven't eaten yet today, so it's just water and the remains of the protein bar.

I can't look at Reed right now, so I refill my water cup and chug until I shake the vomit aftertaste. He's not saying anything, but I can feel his eyes burning into my shoulder blades. When I finally turn around, he doesn't look shocked, instead like he knew all along this would happen. I don't know if he did, but he's doing a damn great job of looking like it.

"What'd you do?" he asks, toneless.

"Adderall. Teddy offered it, I thought it would help."

He slams his elbows onto the counter and buries his face in his palms.

"Jesus, Hal," he mumbles, barely audible. "You're so dumb."

I suddenly feel sick again. He could've said anything, *anything*, to me other than that, and I would have accepted it. But being called dumb? I can't handle that today. I step away until my back hits the sink. I'm as far from him as I can be without running out of the room.

"I only took it so I could work on this paper and get a good grade. Doing everything I can to do better in school makes me dumb now?"

He looks at me like he knows he screwed up – raised eyebrows and frantic hand gestures. "I didn't mean it like that," he tells me.

"Please leave," I croak.

"I can't leave! You just puked your guts out."

"I want you to leave."

He stares at me in shock, then around the rest of the room like he's looking for another reason to support his argument for staying. But it doesn't take long for him to give up, grab his backpack from the counter and run toward the door like the room's just caught on fire. He pries it open but looks back at me one last time before leaving.

"Fine. I'll leave. But *this* is not you – you know it and I know it. Get your shit together."

The door slams behind him. And I don't get to tell him how wrong he is. This is me, the best I'll ever be. If he doesn't see that, it's another sign a relationship between us could never work. It feels like I've been getting a lot of those recently.

All I feel like doing is crawling into bed and crying, but now that I'm thinking about my paper, it's like my body can't do anything until that's done. I sit on the stool Reed abandoned and don't get up until the first draft of my paper is complete. How's *that* for dumb, huh? Even when Addy calls me and asks me if I want to get dinner with her and Isabel, I tell her I can't. I'm not hungry anyway.

When they get back, Addy practically throws a to-go box onto the counter in front of me. "They were serving chicken alfredo, so we grabbed you some. You need to eat."

I shake my head, barely looking up from my screen. I'm already making headway on my revisions. My laptop's about to die though, and I'm worried getting up to grab my charger would break my flow.

"I'll eat it when I finish this paper. Promise."

"Be careful, it's running right through me." Isabel groans. "I'm going to the bathroom. Be back in like fifteen minutes."

When she starts walking in the opposite direction of her bathroom, Addy stops her. "Wrong way, babe."

She shakes her head. "No, this is the right way. I'm

taking a shit in Nadia's bathroom. She pissed me off yesterday."

Isabel's gone for less than thirty seconds before coming back.

"Follow me, you guys have to come smell her bedroom. It smells like she shoved weed in the vents."

Addy and I follow her into Nadia's empty and unlocked bedroom. She starts totally ransacking the place, leading with her nose like a bloodhound.

"Isa!" I shout. "She could come back any second!"

Isabel shakes her head. "She never comes back before nine."

"Have you been stalking her?" Addy asks.

"No, I've just been paying more attention to her than I normally do," Isabel says sheepishly. "Something's going on with her, I'm just trying to figure out what it is."

Isabel reaches Nadia's bottom desk drawer and all of us shut up. It's full of weed. Like, a lot of weed even for a college student. There's also a pack of Fireball shooters, a condom wrapper, a shoebox full of pill bottles, and a few unopened chip bags. We all gag, before Isabel slams the drawer shut and runs out of the room. We talk for an hour about what Nadia's stash could mean. We come up with nothing.

When Nadia returns, exactly when Isabel said she would, we're watching a movie in the living room. No one says hello to her, and she doesn't greet us. It seems unusually cold. I wonder if she can sense that we were digging around in her room. The room feels tense like a wall's just been put up between Nadia and the rest of us.

But I finished my paper. And that's all I care about.

things get bad

. . .

None of us have talked to Nadia in four days. Or seen her. I haven't seen Reed since Tuesday either, which is only because I ditched Wells' class on Wednesday. I didn't feel like running into him.

But that backfires because when I finally go to class on Friday, the anxiety of seeing Reed after I kicked him out of my room has only gotten worse. I feel sick, which isn't saying much because I feel sick every day now, and I haven't slept more than four hours a night.

When I get to the lecture hall, I immediately notice Reed's absence. Something that should make me relieved but strangely doesn't. He isn't the type to skip class without reason. Is he sick? Or worse, avoiding me like I'm avoiding him? I'd rather see him in class and have it be awkward than not see him and think about all the horrible reasons he might not be here.

I'm itching to pull my phone out of my pocket and text him when the door in the front of the lecture hall flies open. It's Reed, and holy hell, he looks terrible. Disheveled. He runs and slides into the empty seat next to me as Dr.

Things Get Bad · 143

Wells starts speaking and uploading his presentation to the projector.

I know Reed well enough to notice he clearly didn't brush his hair, he doesn't smell like his usual expensive cologne so he must have not put it on, and his shirt is wrinkled to the point of embarrassment. I'm not usually a stickler about wrinkled clothing, so it must be bad for *me* to notice. But, even in this state, he still looks like Reed. He still looks handsome and kind and like the smartest person in the class.

Wells is droning on about the papers we're turning in tonight, "housekeeping" as he calls it. Reed hasn't opened his bag, and doesn't have his laptop out or a notebook or a pen. And he's staring at me.

"I'm really sorry about what I said," he whisper-screams, "but this is ridiculous, I can't let you skip class just to avoid me."

"Let me? Get a grip. You can't tell me what to do."

"Jesus, Hal," he says, and out of frustration, says a bit too loud.

Dr. Wells stops talking, steps out from behind his podium, and clears his throat.

"Mr. Callaway, do you need a refresher on my policy for students who talk during lectures?"

Instead of doing what he should do, which would be apologize and shut up, Reed responds with what I would rank as the number one worst possible response:

"Dr. Wells, you haven't started the lecture yet. We're just going over the schedule."

The entire class stares at him in shock, and by proxy, stares at me. This is humiliating.

"My no talking policy applies to all aspects of the course, Mr. Callaway."

Then, Reed commits one of the only moral sins a

student can do to a professor — he rolls his eyes. "It was important."

Wells is slowly encroaching on us, walking up the steps of the lecture hall like he's stalking prey. "Is my class not important?"

Reed's face flushes red, but he stands his ground. Like the calm, cool, collected guy he tries to present himself as. "That's not what I said."

"Get out of my classroom, Mr. Callaway."

Someone behind us gasps.

Reed laughs dryly. "You can't ask a student to leave, if I want to be here and learn you don't have to right to-"

Wells throws his clipboard onto the steps and the whole room jumps.

"I can do whatever I so please in my classroom!" He screams. "Leave, or I will be calling your coach."

Reed scrambles to grab his bag and steps over the rest of the students in our row. I don't think long about following him out, and we're both in the empty hallway before I realize what I've done. When he notices I followed him, he sighs in defeat.

"You've missed enough class, go back in. I'm fine," he tells me, his voice disturbingly even and quiet.

I gape at him. "What is wrong with you?"

"What's wrong with *me*?" he asks, suddenly loud again. "What's wrong with *you*?"

I shrug. "Nothing."

"So," he says, counting off on his fingers as he lists. "Having a break down at Laundry Room over your grades, skipping classes, not eating, not talking to your friends, having weird nightmares that when I ask you about you start getting defensive-"

"Stop." I cut him off. "That's how I am. I'm messy and

I suck at this whole college thing. I know all that so don't remind me."

"This is not you. I know you and something is wrong."

It's admirable that Reed sees the best in me, even when it's unrealistic. He wasn't around last year; he doesn't know that this level of barely functioning is my baseline. I'm comfortable here. Stress motivates me. Trying to get help, or even talk to someone about my problems, would just eat up time I don't have. The last time I tried to help, in high school, the doctor told me I would grow out of my procrastination. I doubt anyone now would tell me anything different.

"We barely dated for six weeks over a year ago." I bite. "You don't know me as well as you think you do."

I almost miss it, but he rolls his eyes, which pisses me off even more. "Now you're just saying things that aren't true," he says. "You're trying to make me angry so I'll drop this. It's not working."

Well, he's not wrong. I huff in defeat and settle next to him on the bench. The hallway is so empty it echoes. I've never seen it like this.

"We can't keep being friends like this," I admit. "I'm dragging you down. The more time we spend together the worse your life gets."

He shakes his head curtly. "Not a choice you can make for the both of us, Hal."

"It can be if I start ignoring you all the time." I flash him a cheeky smile and am more relieved than I want to admit when it makes him laugh a little.

"You wouldn't."

"I might."

I won't.

———

I would try to ignore Reed if I could, but the guy is everywhere. Like today, when I leave Addy and I's bedroom after a power nap to leave for a meeting with Sam about my article. Ben and Reed are sitting at the kitchen table suspiciously.

"What's up?" I ask, hoping this has nothing to do with me.

"Isa said she'd cook for us if we helped her deep clean your place," Ben responds.

"Fair trade." I would clean for Isabel's food too. Luckily, I live with her, so she cooks for me anyway.

"Are you going somewhere?" Reed asks. "She made it sound like deep cleaning was a roomie thing."

I shake my head as I reach into our designated first aid drawer. "I have to meet with Sam about one of my articles. But I'll be back later."

I avoid eye contact with Reed as I dig out our communal bottle of painkillers and dry swallow three pills. Neither of us has brought up the conversation we had after he got kicked out of class. But I haven't forgotten anything he's said. We're playing jump rope with the line at the moment, and once it's crossed, I'm sure he'll realize I'm seriously screwed up and he'll see I'm too broken to fix. He'll probably never talk to me again.

"You always take three painkillers before a meeting with Sam?" Reed pries.

I narrow my eyes and stare, silently warning him this is not the time or place to get into this. "My head's been bothering me."

He nods, resigned, and I feel like I've won.

Sam asks if we can meet in the caf, disrupting to our normal routine. My sixth sense is ticking, this feels like one of those movies where the couple breaks up in a restaurant because one person is afraid of the other person's reaction, so they want to break up in public. We're meeting at prime lunch time, so it's very loud, but I hear him very clearly when he says, "I need to pull your article."

The phantom sound of glass shattering echoes in my mind. "Excuse me?"

Sam's face is flushed bright red, but he trudges on. "I have a friend who is on the lacrosse team, and he said that nothing good could come from printing this. You don't understand the power these guys and their families have over the school they could get us shut down."

"They could not." I'm already gathering my bag and my coat, mourning the wasted meal swipe that will have counted for nothing once I storm out of here.

"I can't risk it. I was hoping you would understand."

"Do you want to be a journalist after college, Sam?"

"What type of question is that I'm already applying for J-schools and-"

I swiftly cut him off with a hand wave. "A journalist wants to tell the truth. You should think about that. I quit...And you're pathetic."

Charged with adrenaline, I march out of the caf. I feel weird. Quitting feels freeing in a way, but I'm mourning the loss of that article. Sam is censoring an important story, but selfishly, I'm regretting the hours of stress and missed classes, and poor sleep that went into a piece that will never see the light of day.

I mull over my grievances as I walk back to the dorm, and accidentally into the middle of the most heated conversation I've ever seen in 806. I've only been gone for a half hour, and my roommates, minus Addy plus Reed and Ben, are in the middle of the planned deep clean. Our large, funky patterned rug is rolled up in the corner of the living room and the furniture has all been pushed to windows.

"Clean it. Now." Isabel is in a standoff with Nadia, holding a bottle of all-purpose surface cleaner and a kitchen towel in front of Nadia's nose, who is standing with her hands on her hips. Reed and Ben awkwardly stand by the kitchen table, which all of our chairs are stacked on top of. Michaela sits on the kitchen counter, biting her nails, watching the whole encounter like it's dinner and a show.

"It's not dirty," Nadia says sharply, "we didn't *do it* on the counter."

What the fuck did I just walk into?

"But you didn't *do it* on the bed." Isabel bites mockingly. "So where *did* you *do it*?"

"I'm totally lost," I interrupt. "What are we talking about?"

Isabel drops her cleaning supplies on the counter dramatically before turning to me. "Nadia just accidentally let it slip that the man she's been having sex with is afraid of beds. And now she won't admit that they've had sex on every surface in our *shared* space."

"He's not afraid of beds," Nadia protests, "he just doesn't like having sex in them!"

"He has a fear of beds?" I ask and everyone nods in response. "So he definitely has a girlfriend that's not Nadia."

Because duh, that's the bigger problem here. Boys are weird, but they're never *afraid-of-beds-weird* unless they're hiding something. I drop my bag onto the couch and sit down, before quickly picking myself back up after remembering Nadia may or may not have fornicated on it.

"He doesn't have a girlfriend," Nadia says dully, "I would know if he did."

"Would you though? I didn't know my ex was texting other girls when we were together," Mic adds, barely looking up from her homework, seemingly unbothered by the whole ordeal, contrasting Isabel's total breakdown.

"Guys don't just have fears of beds, that's really fucking weird. He either has a girlfriend and thinks having sex with you in a bed would be too romantic for sex with his side chick, or he has intimacy issues that are beyond repair," I say.

Nadia rolls her eyes at me. Reed and Ben slip out of their corner in tandem, clearly looking for an escape route.

"We should go," Ben says, attempting to sound cheerful.

Isabel freezes him in place with one terrifying glare. "No! We are not done cleaning!"

Ben raises his hands in surrender.

Before Isabel can shove the kitchen towel back in Nadia's face, the door opens and Addy walks in, still in her scrubs from her nursing lab. We all stare. She looks around the group suspiciously.

"I'm sorry, am I interrupting something?" she asks.

Isabel raises her eyebrows. "We're deep cleaning. And Nadia is seeing a guy who won't fuck her in a bed."

Addy laughs. "Oh, so he has a girlfriend then?"

I laugh with her, thanking God someone agrees with me, but am cut off by Nadia waving her arms around frantically in an attempt to shut us up.

"Enough!" She screams. "I would know if he had a girlfriend, trust me."

"Are you sure you don't want me to do some digging on this bastard?" Isabel asks, and it seems like a genuine offer. "I'm kind of a pro when it comes to stalking."

"It's true," Addy says. "One time she found a guy I thought was cute's secret Reddit account from when he was seventeen. There was some weird shit on there. Like, weird enough to make me stop thinking he was cute."

"Can you find something on my ex's new girlfriend, Isa?" Michaela asks. "All I know about her is that her name is Alice, and he says he met her at camp when he was eleven but I don't believe him."

Isabel nods solemnly. "I can definitely work with that."

"He doesn't have a girlfriend." Nadia sighs, walking down the hall and toward her bedroom. "And this isn't me admitting to anything at all… but fine, I'll clean all of the surfaces in here."

Isabel looks truly torn between ripping into her again and thanking her for agreeing to take on wiping everything down. She delegates tasks to us, and I am assigned to the bathrooms. Reed casually offers to help me, and Isabel sends us on our way with a bucket of supplies.

He shuts the bathroom door behind us, immediately muffling the sound of the vacuum in the living room. We stare at each other, and I mentally prepare for him to ask me about my meeting with Sam or my headache.

Instead, he asks, "Is Nadia always like that?"

Relieved, I relax and grab the toilet bowl cleaner from the bucket. "Recently? Yeah. She used to be more normal. Before all this boyfriend stuff."

It's hard to slowly lose a friend. I'm not as close with Nadia as I am with Addy and Isabel, but the five of us used to sit around and watch rom-coms and play card games and talk about nothing. Now, it's like living with a nasty ghost. It makes me wonder if I was that bad of a friend when I was seeing Reed last year and is one reason, among many, I'm hesitant to ramp up a relationship with him again. I don't want to lose my girls. I tell myself it would be different because they already know Reed and we've all been friends for so long, but I'm not sure it would be.

I tell Reed the story of Nadia's boyfriend's weird stash we found in her room a couple of weeks ago as I scrub the toilet and he wipes down the sink. I tell the long, dramatic version, and don't spare him any of the gory details. Even when I finish, he's still laughing. It feels good to know I did that.

"You're funny," he says simply.

"Thanks. I guess," I say.

All I did was tell him about how ridiculous my roommates can be. They're the funny ones, not me. I'm just the narrator. Narrators aren't funny. Sometimes, I'm not entirely sure I even have a personality. I'm only made up of what happens to me – the funny stories I collect and the trouble that my friends and I get into.

"You're a good storyteller," he explains, "it's why you're a great writer."

Reed, unknowingly, hit a sore spot. A flashback of my conversation with Sam hits me, and I'm no longer enjoying this moment. I throw my damp sponge back in the bucket, and hear it plop in the water as it lands. I sit on the edge of the bathtub with to pick up the sponge and get back to my scrubbing, but end up sighing and slouching as I stare at Reed kneeling on the cool tile next to me, his forearms pressed against the edge next to me.

God, he looks so much comfier than this bathtub. If this were happening last year, I would have crawled into his lap instead. I need to stop daydreaming like that while he's next to me. Because this isn't last year, and this Reed, the right now version of him helping me clean my bathroom, is the only one I've got.

"You do know you're a great writer, right?" He repeats.

"Sam pulled my article from our next issue," I blurt. "And it's all I've been working on, I've been eating, sleeping, and breathing this article. I worked on it instead of my homework I started skipping classes to finish it. And no one's gonna see it now."

"Wait, why did he pull the article?"

Common Reed occurrence: gather information before providing comfort.

"Someone from the lacrosse team told him he would find a way to shut down the newspaper if we published it. He wouldn't budge and I ended up quitting."

"Bullshit someone from the lacrosse team has any power over the school newspaper."

"That was about my reaction too, but he was acting all serious about it."

"You should find a way to publish it anyway," he says, eyes bright. "A blog or you could post a link to a document or something."

"If Sam's right, I don't want this getting traced back to me."

"But you know he's not-"

"I said *if*!" I half yell. He doesn't get it and I know he never will. Sure, he was there at that party freshman year when Aaron tried to tell me I wasn't allowed to leave. And sure, he's a good guy for saying he'll never go to a party at that house again. But he will never actually understand what it felt like to be cornered by Aaron, alone by the door, knowing no one was around to look out for me. "I don't want this getting back to me."

"But you want people to read it."

"I want people to read it and I want them to stop going to lacrosse parties after they finish it."

Reed brushes his fingers over my knee, feather-like, before pulling them away. He opens his mouth to speak but stops himself, pausing before saying, "I can post it. I mean, I won't take credit for it obviously, I'll just post it."

It's not the worst idea, but I am done dragging him down into my shit. Today is the day that ends. "I can't let you do that. But thank you."

He nods but I can tell he doesn't agree with me. I catch myself thinking about last year again. Last year, he would've fought me on this. Last year, he couldn't understand why I wasn't upset that Sam made me rewrite my first profile on the soccer team and spelled my name wrong.

For the first time, I realize I prefer the right now version of Reed.

He smiles, breaking some of the tension. "Well, even if you don't post it, I'm gonna fall asleep picturing Sam stomping around once he sees you found a way to share it. Instead of counting sheep, I'm gonna imagine that."

"You haven't even met Sam. You don't know what he looks like in the first place."

"I picture him in a scarf. Is he a scarf guy?"

I laugh so hard I snort. "No."

His lips split into a grin as our eyes lock. The corners of his eyes crinkle. "I made you laugh. Perfect. That was the only thing on my to-do list today."

It's the type of thing you shouldn't say to someone you claim to be just friends with, and we both know it. We reach that conclusion at the same time, smiles dropping but never breaking eye contact.

"I'm gonna clean the mirror next," he says, pushing up from the edge of the tub to stand up. He turns his back to me. "That seems like something Isabel would be pissed if we forgot."

THE NEXT AFTERNOON, I GO TO MY SHIFT AT LIGHTHOUSE and what was supposed to be a three-hour shift turns into my manager asking me if I can stay until close, which is at eleven. I stupidly say yes. Saying yes to that one shift turns into one of the worst missteps of my life. I work from three to ten, or later, six days in a row.

My whole life, I've only ever ebbed and flowed through two phases: good and bad. Since I can remember, things are either going good for me or going bad. So, I'm really good at recognizing when things are about to get bad again.

I've been on a downward crawl toward hell ever since I got an F on my essay, but I haven't had the true, achy feeling of things going bad until now. It starts with one or two missing assignments. Small pieces of homework due on Wednesday turn into something I swear I'll get done Friday night. Then, it's the bigger stuff – essays and projects I ask for extensions on. Slowly, over the week, I build up a pile of missing work that I keep telling myself I'll do on my next day off. On my next day off I will do homework all day, and then I'll finally be caught up. Except, every "next day off" I have turns into my manager calling me about an hour and a half before the dinner shift asking me if I can come in. My pile of missing work starts making me feel sick to my stomach and burning a hole in my to-do list as I write the same tasks over and over again, day after day, but never cross out.

Things getting bad means getting used to not talking in class. Making myself small, knowing that when I do try to contribute, one of the boys in my class will raise his hand and repeat my opinion almost verbatim.

And, as someone who can't form a habit to save her life, I know things are getting bad again when I suddenly start keeping a rigorous schedule. I shower in the morning, go to class, take another shower, eat a grilled cheese with tomato soup from the caf, sleep until work starts, go to work, watch movies or read until three a.m., try to fall asleep, fail to fall asleep, repeat.

Indeed, I can feel it in my bones, things are getting bad.

But on my way into Prez after a Sunday evening shift, I see a flyer pinned to the community board in the lobby: ANNUAL OKTOBERFEST COOKOUT SPONSORED BY THE LACROSSE TEAM. FIRST OF THE MONTH AT NOON. 18 AND UP ONLY. MUST BE 21 TO DRINK. TO PURCHASE A WRISTBAND, TALK TO AARON LANDRY.

A pay-to-play lacrosse party. Huh. That's new.

I rip the flyer from the board, a bit torn off the top still stuck to the pin that had been holding it up. I think about my article. If things are getting bad again, it means I don't have much to lose.

papers
. . .

Monday is my first day off, and it's only because I had requested off weeks ago to go to tonight's soccer game. I'm surprised they approved the request. This is the first game of the season I'm going to, and my roommates are coming with me. Except Nadia who, of course, couldn't take one night off from seeing her man who's afraid of beds.

From the time my shift would normally start to the game's kickoff, I consider doing my homework. Just the thought of that makes me ill, so I decide to figure out how to share my article. I need a way to share it that wouldn't leave a trail back to me. *Paper, duh.* The idea hits me fast and I'm immediately angry at myself for not thinking of it sooner. Thirty dollars of my allotted printing money later, I have a decent-sized stack of copies. Once I squeezed the font size down to eight, I was able to fit the whole article on one page front and back.

I'm about to start looking for places I can "accidentally" leave a few copies behind when my phone dings with a text from Reed. I shove my phone down into the back pocket of my jeans. He never texts me these days. Why would he text me? I haven't seen him since the night of the deep clean, besides in class, and I'm usually too tired to chat. I think about last week, us talking in the bathroom, and how bittersweet it felt. We're so good together right now, almost closer than we were when we were regularly napping in a twin XL bed together and halving cookies in the caf to share. What if that's only because we're not dating? He could be texting me to say that after he accidentally let slip that making me laugh was his top priority, he realized we should only ever be just friends. Or he could be professing his love. Or he could be telling me he never wants to see me again. Or that he's actually been dating Liv this whole time and she's saying he can't have any friends that are girls.

I avoid touching my phone for as long as possible. Schrödinger's text message.

I walk the loop around campus from the library to Prez, dropping copies of my article outside classrooms, slipping them under the doors of RAs, and taping them to the windows in the back of the student center. I finally work up the courage to unlock my phone.

I squeeze my eyes shut before opening his text. This could change everything.

But it doesn't. All it says is: *I don't know why I didn't think of this earlier, but you should just print the article out.*

I suppress a giggle, not wanting to be the lovestruck idiot who laughs at her phone in public because of something a boy texted her. I snap a picture of the papers I have left in my hand, and send it, along with: *Great minds, you know what they say.*

He replies: *Exactly. Bring some copies to the*

game. I can slide them into the locker rooms before I leave.

Addy, Isabel, Mic, and I get to the field before the game starts, sitting at the front of the bleachers as the teams come onto the field to settle in and warm up. I brought a tote bag to carry the copies of my article, but it looked weird, so I stuffed a bunch of junk in it to make it look like something I carry every day. I'm not a bag girl. I'm convinced everyone attending the game will be able to tell by the way I walk that I have never carried a tote bag in my entire life. I sit on the end of the group and immediately regret it when Luke, of all people, slides into the open spot next to me.

"Ladies," he says in greeting, looking down the row.

"Your henchman off duty tonight?" Isabel asks dryly.

"Teddy's busy. He's got a date or something," Luke answers, before looking me over in his usual weird way that makes me squirm. "What about you Halle, here for a date? You and Callaway hooking up again?"

I don't have to defend myself because Addy beats me to it. "Jealous?" She smirks.

Luke shakes his head, "Just don't wanna hear about you crying over him whenever he decides to stop talking to you… again."

That hurt, I can't lie. I feel Luke's words deep in my gut, and from his little smug smile, I can tell he knows what effect his comment had on me. Even though I know Reed can't hear our conversation, he turns and looks at the bleachers from where he is on the field like sensed we were talking about him. Sometimes I think he can read my mind a little, or maybe he has a psychic gift. It's frustrating because I feel like I can never figure out what he's thinking, yet he's always one step ahead of my own thoughts. I give him a little wave, which he returns while squinting at us. Then he goes back to warming up with the team like the exchange does not affect him at all.

I can't say it doesn't affect me. The only reason Luke's words are so upsetting is that I know they're not far from being true. Nothing is stopping Reed from deciding to never talk to me again. Logically, I know we are both better people than we were last year. Illogically, I think I should prepare myself for the worst, or maybe I should get one step ahead of him and drop him before he gets the chance to drop me.

I sulk until the game starts, barely listening to whatever Luke and the girls are talking about. Watching Reed play soccer is one of my favorite things. I like watching almost anything Reed does. I like watching him talk to strangers because he always treats them kindly like he would greet an old friend. I like the way his face lights up when he talks about soccer and the admiration he has for his teammates. I like the reactions he has while I tell him stories that prove he's truly listening.

The whole game, all I can do is watch Reed. I almost feel guilty about it. I had forgotten how good he is, but Reed's just that type of person. Everything he does, he does well. If he thinks he can't do something well, he doesn't do it. Maybe that's why we aren't dating.

We win, which is good because I like seeing Reed happy. Once the players finish talking to the coaches and shaking the other team's hands, he runs jogs up to the fence and motions for me to meet him.

Our faces are only a half inch apart as he leans against the metal. So close, the only thing I can focus on is his beautiful dark eyes and how lucky I am that he's looking at me right now. The color from the end of September's cool sunset fades as the field lights kick on.

Reed cordially asks me to wait for him and Ben, so we can all go back to their room and have some celebratory beer. I scrunch my nose.

"I'm not sure if I wanna come," I tease sarcastically. "You know I'm not a huge beer drinker."

Reed rolls his eyes and presses his face even closer to mine, so close I'm preparing for him to kiss me through the fence, until he shifts so his lips are almost against my ear.

"I bought Diet Coke for you specifically. Come on," he says lowly. "I wanna see you."

He backs up from the fence, just as his teammates are calling him back toward the locker room, winking at me on his way out.

I feel glued to the fence, gripping it tightly as I try to figure out what the fuck that means. He wants to *see me*? I need to get my shit straight with Reed, and fast, because clearly, I'm in over my head. I have no idea what he wants from me anymore. I feel like we're speaking different languages.

I walk back to my friends, and Luke who's standing with them, in a Reed-induced haze, and repeat the boys' after party plans to the group. We wait by the locker room doors, and to my surprise, Luke waits with us. I don't know why he's still here. He has to know he isn't invited over to Reed and Ben's. Right? But he never leaves.

Five minutes turn into ten, and Luke is still standing with us. Addy doesn't seem to have a problem as she chats with him, but me and Isabel exchange confused glances every time Addy isn't looking at us. The biggest thing Isabel and I have in common is that we think Addy should cut Luke out. We get it, she was friends with him in high school and he's a connection to home, but sometimes that's not enough. He's a rodent. Seriously, who does he think he is, standing here chatting it up with us while we are clearly waiting for Reed and Ben, who he hates? It's all for attention, I swear. Mic remains oblivious to all of this. She isn't the best at picking up social cues, and she also isn't close enough with Isabel and I to understand what the micro-movements of our eyes truly mean.

Reed and Ben join us a lifetime later, freshly showered and smiling, both clocking Luke's presence before greeting us. Reed gives Luke a not-so-subtle stink eye, while Ben looks like he's trying to stifle a laugh. The whole thing is unbearably awkward.

Reed gives me one of his cool boy nods, which he would never do if Luke wasn't here, and I try not to laugh.

"Did you bring the stuff?" he asks, his voice approximately half a step deeper than it is when I talk to him alone.

I nod and grab the papers from my tote, pressing my lips tight in an attempt to hold myself together. He takes them from me, our hands almost brush but don't, and trots back into the locker room.

He's only gone for about three minutes, where Addy tries to fill the silence by asking Luke about the lacrosse Oktoberfest party. He complains about all of the regulations they need to add to keep the cops away. Ben starts laughing, but no one confronts him about it.

When Reed returns, Luke happily switches gears. "What was that all about? Some sex thing?"

Addy's quickest to respond. "Gross, Luke."

Luke shrugs, like Addy's hint to pipe down, and all of our narrowed eyes pointed at him mean nothing. "No? Some type of secret club then?"

Reed, being the borderline control freak he is, tries to get a grip on the situation gracefully. "Good to see you,

Luke. Ladies," he says, with a little too much emphasis to be considered subtle. "Still coming over?"

The insinuation is not lost on Luke, who physically pulls back from the rest of the group like the words hit him. He puts up a fight, though, retorting under his breath, "Right, can't do anything without the groupies."

He smirks, proud of the lit match he just threw onto the pile of gasoline that has been this conversation.

"What did you say?" Reed says.

Luke scoffs. "I think you heard me -"

And before the pissing match can truly ramp up, it is cut short by Ben, who stands in between the two competitors and shoots a solid, effective glare at Reed. Reed turns around, locks eyes with mine, and quickly looks away, almost embarrassed.

Reed leads the group as we walk back to Prez together, Luke splitting off in the opposite direction toward the off-campus houses. None of us need to guess where he's heading. Addy and Mic catch up with Reed while, Isabel, Ben and I linger behind.

"Why does she waste her time with Luke anyway?" Ben asks the two of us, gesturing vaguely toward Addy's short blonde ponytail bobbing as she walks in front of us.

"We've been asking ourselves that for a while," I say.

At the same time, Isabel responds, "Why do you care so much?"

Ben looks like he's about to break out in hives. "Addy's one of my closest friends. That's why I care."

"Nice of you to look out for a friend like that," Isabel says with a false air of sincerity. Ben doesn't buy it.

"Maybe I'll ask her about it sometime."

"Sure. You do that sometime."

The sun's completely set by the time we reach the front doors of Prez.

like back then
· · ·

Reed unlocks the front door to their room and immediately starts serving beers to anyone who asks. He's a great host. I imagine him in a big house of his own one day, having his friends over for a summer dinner party with all the windows open. I picture myself there too, briefly, before stopping myself.

He brings me a can of Diet Coke after everyone else is sufficiently served and our group naturally falls into the same patterns as always. Elliot and Harry, two other sophomores on the team who live with Reed and Ben, float around the room but mostly keep to themselves. They're both nice guys, but none of us girls have ever been close to either of them. Ben is explaining something about fishing to the eager audience of Addy and Michaela, while Isabel half listens and scrolls through her phone. Reed and I sit at the kitchen table together.

I think it's funny that their room is almost identical to my beloved room 806: the same four-bedroom layout, the same cheap university-issued furniture. Our room is much better decorated though. The only décor in the kitchen and living room combined is a comically large Bob Dylan poster.

I glance at my friends on the other side of the room – Addy with her chin perched on her clasped hands, watching Ben tell some exaggerated tale of him as a kid with intent and admiration. I turn to Reed, who I think, has scooted his chair closer to mine.

"You ever think there's something between Ben and Addy?"

He grins and moves his face closer to mine. "I have never *not* thought something was going on between Ben and Addy."

Call me immature, but I love gossiping, especially with Reed, so I dive into this conversation headfirst. "They always pair off, you know? And earlier, when we were walking here, he was asking me and Isabel about what's up with her and Luke." Reed pulls away. Jilted, I ask, almost too loudly, "What? What did I say?"

"Nothing." He sighs. His voice is calm, but his shoulders and jaw are tight. "I would just like one opportunity to talk to you for real without Luke somehow butting in, even when he's not here."

He's being a bit dramatic. We talk all the time and Luke rarely comes up. Besides, he only came up because we were talking about Ben and Addy. I roll my half-empty can between my palms to distract myself.

"I was surprised you didn't hit him. Earlier. You looked like you wanted to."

"Luke?" Reed asks. I nod. He sips from his bottle and says, "Nah, I wasn't gonna hit him. I was gonna let Ben do it. I don't hit people."

I squint at him, trying to gauge if he's making a joke or is being genuine, which makes him laugh.

"Hal," he says. "When have you ever seen me hit anyone?"

I rack my brain, looking for an example to throw in his face and come up with nothing. Now that he says that I can't think of a time he's hit anyone. I can't even recall a story someone told me where Reed hit someone.

"Is it a moral thing or something?" I ask him.

"Nah," he says slowly. "I just don't like it."

I nod, pretending I understand him, even though I truly don't. I feel like I know Reed a little less every time he tells me something I can't figure out. What type of dude bro college soccer player decides he's against a few punches and slaps?

Ben walks by the table on his way to the kitchen for another drink, pausing when he hears what we're talking about.

"You're telling her the daycare story?" he asks Reed.

Reed shoots Ben a threatening glance, his face flush with embarrassment. "No. I was not telling that story."

"Well, now I need to hear the daycare story."

Reed shakes his head sternly as Ben happily pulls a chair out from the table and settles across from us.

"When Reed was four, he got kicked out of his super preppy daycare because he started hitting other kids. So his parents put him in soccer instead," Ben says.

Reed looks extremely frustrated with Ben, and I'm sure this will be brought up between them later tonight, long after the rest of us leave. I have so many questions.

"So that's why you don't like hitting people? Or that's how you started playing soccer?" I ask.

"Both," Ben answers before Reed can formulate his response.

"Well I like to think there's a little more nuance to it than that," he spits out. "If my parents hadn't put me in soccer, I'd probably be a punk who never learned not to hit people. So I don't really, you know, get in fights as a way to thank the fates or whatever. Let the universe know I recognize what it did for me."

Ben looks at me and raises his eyebrows as if to ask me if I can even believe how ridiculous Reed sounds. It is a weirdly specific rule to give to yourself, especially for someone like Reed who isn't very superstitious. Ben leaves to go to the fridge, leaving me and Reed alone again.

"I guess I don't like Luke because he goes around, talking big talk that he has a crush on you, then talks to you like he did tonight. That's all." He shrugs.

The admission makes my heart pick up. "Nice of you to be bothered on my account."

I know I'm baiting him. I know I'm prodding. I'm just curious to see what he says. I want him to prove Luke wrong, and finally tell me how he feels about me so all the uncertainty can be over and done with.

He doesn't take the bait. "I mean, I can't believe you still talk to him after that night he showed up drunk to your room."

I glance at our friends on the other side of the room and catch Addy and Isabel staring. "If we're really gonna air this out right now. Can we not do it where all our friends can hear?" I whisper.

I assume he'll move on and change the topic of conversation, but instead, he stands up from the table abruptly and nods toward the hallway behind us that leads to his bedroom. "Fine."

We walk to his room, and he shuts the door behind us. It's that simple, but it feels like a lot more. I lean on his door, awkwardly wringing my hands as he turns to face me.

"It's not my fault that Luke comes over sometimes. And

I can't control who my friends are friends with," I say, breaking the tension.

Reed throws his hands up in disbelief. "He's always around! And always finding some weird passive-aggressive way to remind me that *he* was the guy you liked after we stopped seeing each other. That he got months to be with you when we weren't even talking."

"I was not *with* Luke, we talked about this. And you said you weren't jealous."

"I wasn't back then."

Already exhausted, I stare at him in shock. "So?"

"I thought once we started, I don't know, talking or being friends again he would just go away. But he's always around. Like a fly I can't swat."

"I never really notice him."

"But you have all this weird history with him."

I laugh. "History? Seriously? Every time I ever hung out with Luke, or the maybe four times we ever kissed – I came back to my room and had to put my phone in my closet to stop myself from calling you, crying, and begging you to explain to me why everything was so natural with us, but I couldn't make it work with anyone else."

He meets me at the door, and I think he's trying to test me, see if I'll leave, but I stay put until his face can't get any closer to mine.

"They're gonna notice we're missing eventually," I whisper.

He shakes his head at me. "Don't care," he says, tucking a stray piece of hair off my forehead and behind my ear.

Our lips meet, and we kiss softly like we're not sure if the other is really there. We find a comfortable rhythm and it picks up as his hands can cradle my face, and mine brush against the hem at the bottom of his shirt tentatively. He takes a hand off my face and places it over my own, guiding it under the fabric of his shirt so I'm touching his skin. I let him, and I can feel our kiss break and feel him smile against my lips.

"I've missed you," he says.

I know what he means. We see each other nearly every day, but we both know there's always been some piece missing and now it's not anymore. At least not at this moment. I can't bring myself to even think about what this means for our relationship, all I know is that this, right now, feels good and right. Some people just feel like home. Reed's that person for me.

We make our way over to his bed, sitting until he helps me lie down and hovers over me on his forearms. Our kisses are more feverish now, and I swear a kiss has never made me feel like this before, not even the ones I've gotten from him.

I run my hands through his hair. Last year, I did it so much that I could tell how many days it had been since he'd washed it. I wanna be that close to him again.

His hands run from my throat down my chest, over my hips, and to the top of my jeans. A subconscious shiver runs through me, head to toe.

Reed laughs delicately. "Oh, I remember this," he says.

"What?" My head feels light and my cognitive ability to speak full sentences is numbed by the feeling of his hands on me.

"You get really shaky when you're turned on," he teases, as his kisses trail across my jaw, down my neck where he kisses over my pulse reverently.

His hands run over my jeans, his fingers hook around the button, and my nerves light up with excitement. He undoes the button and zipper, his fingers brushing under my underwear before he looks back down at me.

"Is this okay?" he asks, barely above a whisper.

I nod quickly, biting my bottom lip to keep myself from breaking out into an embarrassingly large grin.

He nods too, kissing me fiercely before looking at me again. "You are so goddamn beautiful."

My stomach flutters. I don't remember the last time anyone said anything like that to me.

His hand starts moving, and I close my eyes. But once I close them, I feel like I'm not with Reed anymore. January, last year. My chest tightens. I have no idea what I'm doing. I can't do this.

I don't realize I've pushed Reed off of me until I open my eyes and see him sitting on the other end of the bed.

"Are you okay?" he asks, out of breath.

"Yeah," I respond. My hands are shaking so I shove them under my legs. "I don't know what happened. I thought…nothing. Never mind."

"What? Tell me."

I look at him as he looks at me, and seeing the care in his eyes almost makes me tell him. But I don't want to ruin this. So, I lie.

"This just happened really fast. I'm okay, really, but – maybe we should just kiss tonight."

"You're sure? We don't have to. I know I kind of sprung this on you, you're right-"

I put my hand over his. "I'm sure."

He nods and smiles a little. "Easy then. I could kiss you all night."

"Good."

We both lean forward, connecting again, and I finally feel safe. But before we get too far, there's an incessant, pounding knock on the door.

Reed and I both break apart and stare wide-eyed at

each other, mirrored expressions of pure panic on our faces.

Reed's panic resolves quicker than mine. "Fuck them," he murmurs, moving to kiss me again before I push it away. He complies, swearing under his breath before turning toward the door.

"What do you want?" he yells at whoever's on the other side. He's being a little too harsh, and I lightly slap his bicep to hint at that.

"Uh." I hear Addy's voice through the door. "Is Halle in there?"

Reed looks back down at me and whispers, "Should I tell them? I can cover for you if you don't want me to."

I shake my head. "No, it's okay."

We separate from each other; he helps me button and zip my pants when my hands because my hands are to do it myself.

"Yeah," he yells. "She's in here."

Addy sighs. "Great, can I like, talk to her then?"

I look over myself and Reed, deeming us both ready to be seen. Except for his hair, which is sticking up at every angle possible from where I ran my hands through it earlier. There's not much I can do to remedy that now. I try to push it down as best I can, but fail. My eyebrows press together in frustration, and Reed smiles at me and rubs my worry lines until I ease them.

"I'm here Addy," I say, opening the bedroom door.

It's not just Addy on the other side, everyone is there. Seriously, everyone. Addy, Isabel, Mic, Ben, Elliot, and Harry are standing outside Reed's door, staring at us like we're circus performers. Michaela's face is blank, Addy looks so shocked you would think she just watched someone rise from the dead, and Isabel looks smug like she won some huge bet and is about to cash in big time.

"Nadia called me," Addy says, "and said it's an emergency. I told her we were all on our way back."

"Okay," I say, hoping everyone will leave, giving me the time to say goodbye to Reed in private, Maybe I can ask him what this means for us or ask him if he wants me to come back over later tonight. No one leaves, though. They all stand and stare at us.

I turn around so only Reed can see me and mouth a quick 'I'm sorry' but he one-ups me. He smiles and kisses my forehead, rubbing his hands softly up and down my arms.

Reed smiles at the crowd warmly, not an ounce of guilt or embarrassment on his face.

"Night guys," he says calmly, before retreating to his bedroom and shutting the door behind him.

———

BACK IN OUR ROOM, WE FIND OUT THAT NADIA'S "emergency" is, as expected, about the guy she's hooking up with, whose name she still won't give up. She sits us all down in the living room like she's holding an intervention, on the verge of tears.

She tells us all about this secret drawer she has in her room, where she keeps everything that her man asks her to keep in her room because he's too afraid to be caught with it, mostly weed, she says.

Addy, Isa, and I avoid looking at each other, trying not to give away that we already know exactly what she's talking about because we saw it ourselves because we're awful people who dig through our roommate's drawers.

"But now," she says, her voice breaking, "he's asking me to keep a bunch of Adderall in my room for him to sell and he wouldn't listen to me when I told him I wasn't comfortable doing that."

Isabel is the one who talks some sense into Nadia, reminding her that if this guy really cared about her, he wouldn't put her in a situation that would make her so uncomfortable. She's the last person I expect to calm Nadia down, and the last person I thought Nadia would listen to, but it works. She finally looks like she's not on the verge of mental collapse once Isabel's done talking to her.

I debate texting Reed after our little roommate meeting ends, and ask him if he wants me to come back to his room. But I'm too afraid he would tell me no. That maybe with space he would think it had been a mistake, and I'd be making a fool out of myself for trying. Then I remember how good it felt to touch him again, and I think maybe I should text him. But I restrain myself.

When I finally fall asleep, I have a dream that Reed and I are dating. He takes me out somewhere nice for dinner in his car, and when we get back to his room, we end up on his bed. I can feel his hands running over my thigh, the feeling of his skin under my hands, his lips on mine. But I wake up before anything happens.

laundry

. . .

Addy and Isabel waste no time starting their interrogation of me after my stint behind Reed's closed bedroom door.

I tell them everything the next day as we do homework together at the kitchen table and listen to the myriad of opinions they have on the matter.

"He's using you," Addy tells me at one point in the conversation. "He knows you'll give him attention no matter what, and he likes the attention. You should just stop talking to him."

Isabel nods. "And you don't know if he's talking to other girls."

I shrug, trying to keep my eyes on my reading in front of me, *Macbeth* Act Five, and avoiding looking at either of them. "I mean, I'm pretty sure he's not talking to other girls."

"*Pretty sure*? Has he said those words?" Addy asks. "Has he *literally* told you that you are the only girl he talks to?"

I sift through my memories, trying to think of a time he has, but all I remember are times that he's implied I'm the only girl he talks to, or that he's done things that make me *assume* I'm the only girl in his life, but I can't remember him ever telling me verbatim. I still don't agree with them, though.

"Speaking of men who have girls on the side," Isabel says slyly. "Where's Nadia? I wanna ask her if she ever talked to her boy toy about taking his drug stash out of her room."

Addy rolls her eyes. "She's over at his place. *Again.* And Mic's in the library. It's like she's afraid to be in the room when Nadia isn't here. I don't think she likes it when we talk shit about Nadia in front of her."

"Ugh." Isabel slams her head into her notebook out of frustration. "I can't believe Nadia won't even tell us his name. How have we never seen them walking around together? This campus isn't that big."

"It means she must *really* not want us to know who it is," I say. "Takes a lot to be that sneaky on a campus of six thousand people."

"Do you still think it's Ben?" Addy asks nervously.

"No." Isabel pulls her head up. "I think we would've caught them already. Or Ben would've broken down and told us. Or Reed would've said something to Halle."

I nod in agreement. Reed would've told me by now if it was Ben. We tell each other (almost) everything, Addy and Isabel don't need to know that though.

"That's your problem with Reed," Isabel says, turning to me. "You guys are too close. He talks to you like you're his girlfriend, but you had absolutely no physical relationship until last night. You're basically weirdly close friends who made out once."

"You two have no boundaries, no labels. It's not right. Talk to him about it." Addy encourages.

"What am I supposed to say to him?" I ask. I can't

think of any way to start this conversation with him without totally humiliating myself. I would rather never know how he feels about me than confront him on the off chance that he tells me he doesn't want to be with me. What I have going on with Reed right now is better than not talking to him at all or losing him completely

"You only need to ask him one question," Isabel says very seriously. "*Are we allowed to have sex with other people?*"

"Isa!" I scream. "I'm not even having sex with *him*!"

"You should be." Isabel shrugs. "Fine. Don't ask him. But then you'll never know what he thinks of you then."

"I'd rather not know," I say.

Isabel sinks back in her seat, shaking her head at me shamefully like I've insulted her personally. Addy starts digging through her bookbag, looking for something, and curses when she can't find it.

"I left my textbook at Luke's, I'm gonna go grab it," she tells us.

She leaves, trapping me alone with Isabel, who looks like she's about ready to strangle me.

"Talk to him," she pries.

"No." I busy myself by highlighting a line in the text to avoid looking at her. "It's better this way, trust me."

"Halle, I am going to kill you with my bare hands, I swear. You realize how stupid you sound, right?" She grumbles through a clenched jaw.

I'm about to give up. Maybe I should just lie to her and promise her I'll ask Reed the next time I see him. No, she would see right through me. I decide to just keep quiet, go back to my reading, and pretend I'm too engrossed in it to continue talking about Reed. I feel Isabel's angry stare for a while, but eventually, she too turns back to her homework as we study in silence.

Addy sprints back into the room, panting as she slams the door behind her.

"I..," she wheezes. "Went upstairs and…Nadia came out of Teddy's bedroom…Luke's roommate Teddy is the one Nadia has been fucking…Teddy is afraid of beds."

She takes a massively deep breath, dragging herself back to the table like she's in pain. Isabel and I stare at her in total shock. Teddy and Nadia? I would never have figured that out.

Nadia is gorgeous, but she's a music composition major. She was in her high school's marching band. Not that *I* think there's anything wrong with that, but I assumed Teddy would be the type of guy to think Nadia is too nerdy, too uncool for him, because of her major. A lot of guys on this campus are like that. Even Isabel lies about being a dance major whenever she meets new guys at bars, to avoid both the weird second glances she gets for being in the arts program and the inappropriate jokes about her flexibility. It's so annoying and so high school, but it's how a lot of boys on this campus are. So yeah, Teddy and Nadia being paired up surprises me.

Addy tells us that when she went to Luke's room, she grabbed her book from their living room and stopped to talk to Luke for a few minutes. She heard a girl's voice coming from Teddy's bedroom, which is when she noticed Nadia's backpack in the hallway. She put two and two together and sprinted back up to our room to tell us.

The three of us debrief this breaking news together – trying to guess how they ended up together, why she would keep it from us, and how they got away with hiding it for so long. We speculate but can't come up with any logical explanation.

"Should we tell her we know?" Addy asks.

"If we don't tell her now, it's just gonna get more complicated. The sooner the better."

"Oh." Isabel shoots me a dirty look sideways, "Now who thinks sooner is better when it comes to being honest with people, Miss *'I'd rather not know'*?"

"This is different than me and Reed! We live with Nadia. Her being sneaky around us for no reason makes her an objectively bad roomie." I say.

"And a bad friend," Addy tags on.

"Let me do the talking," Isabel says seriously as if she's debriefing us for combat. "We attack once she walks in. We don't give her the chance to run to her bedroom."

When Nadia eventually comes back to the room, Isabel rips into her.

"Why didn't you tell us about you and Teddy?"

Nadia shrugs like the question is unsurprising. "He asked me not to tell anyone."

"Do Luke and all his other roommates know?" Addy asks.

"Yeah."

"Well, then it sounds like he asked you not to tell *us*."

She shrugs again, making her way to her bedroom. "You know now. I don't see why it's a big deal."

Addy, Isabel, and I go to the caf for dinner so we can continue our shit-talking session without the fear of Nadia overhearing us. The food's bad today and the lemonade from the fountain is so sour it burns.

Speaking of sour, right after we finish our dessert, Luke sits down at our table.

He skips the pleasantries, picking up the crumbled half of a cookie Addy didn't finish and saying, "Aaron's real mad about the article you wrote."

My blood freezes. Next to me, Isabel asks, "What article?"

"How does he know I wrote it?" I zero in on Luke.

"I told him," he replies quickly.

"How do *you* know I wrote it?"

Luke has the nerve to smirk. "Saw you handing them to Reed yesterday at the game."

I've never found him more despicable. "He can't prove I wrote anything. Neither can you."

Out of the corner of my eye, I see Reed and Ben on the other side of the caf walking toward the exit. He sees me and waves, then notices Luke and lowers his hand. He looks sad, that's the only way to describe it. Shit. But he has to know Luke sitting at our table means nothing. It's not like I'm alone with him.

I try to break the ice once we get back to our room and text him: ***Can I see you soon? I feel like we need to talk.***

Reed takes a whole hour to respond, very out of character: ***Not sure. Busy week for soccer, away tournament this weekend.***

Shit.

REED COMES INTO CLASS ON WEDNESDAY ABOUT A MINUTE before it starts, which I assume is because he doesn't want to talk to me.

All he gives me is a polite hello before Wells starts another terribly boring lecture. For the whole dreaded class, I stare at the three inches between our feet and wonder why the two of us keep getting this wrong, why it doesn't ever work with us.

I catch him by the elbow as the lecture ends so he can't run away from me.

"Are you ignoring me because you saw Luke sitting with me in the cafeteria? Are we in eighth grade?"

He deflates and I almost feel guilty that I brought it up. "It's not all about Luke. I got in this fight with my parents about law school yesterday morning and…I can't stop thinking about the way you froze up in my room and-"

I let go of his arm. "We don't have to talk about that."

"Are you kidding? Halle, I don't know what I did wrong, and I don't think this, us, can go anywhere until I do."

"You didn't do anything," I reassure him.

"Who did then?" he asks quickly.

I almost gasp but clutch the straps of my backpack instead. What made him say that?

I shake the question off. "You're right, maybe we should wait until you get back from your tournament to talk."

I push past him down the row and leave before I can see his reaction.

No one else is home when I get back to the room and collapse in my bed. I sob, terribly and in a way that hurts my throat, thinking about the mess I'm drowning in. I don't have Reed and I feel like I never will. I can't get hot and heavy with him without thinking about the secret I'm keeping from him. I have more missing work in my classes than completed work. Luke told Aaron about my article.

All I want is to go back in time and re-do the last year and a half of my life. That would be the only way to fix any of this. What's done cannot be undone.

I DON'T REMEMBER FALLING ASLEEP, BUT WHEN ADDY shakes me awake, it's dark outside.

"Are you okay?" she asks slowly like she's talking to a wounded animal she found in a gutter.

"Fine. Why?"

She stares at me like she can't comprehend the level of denial I'm currently in but keeps her tone nonjudgmental. "Well, you've been asleep since three o'clock. And it's nine."

"I think I'm coming down with a cold or something."

"And you haven't done laundry in over a month. I can't see the floor over here."

I sit up and peer around my side of the room. Sure, it's pretty messy, but it's looked worse. "No, the piles by my desk are clean clothes that I haven't had time to put away."

Addy looks disappointed. "Well, the only other time your laundry has gotten this bad was when Reed broke up with you last year."

"So?"

"So, what's going on with you?"

I shove my head back into my pillow. "Oh, nothing. My life is just falling apart."

I start to cry again, and she rubs my back until I calm down. As I sit up and rub my eyes, she tries to give me a convincing everything-will-be-okay smile.

"I think you need to slow down."

"I don't know how to do that," I admit.

"I think you should talk to a doctor. But not the ones in the student health center, they suck. Because I don't think all of this is you being lazy, I think something more is going on. And you should call off work for the next couple of days. Then when you do go back, stop volunteering to work such long shifts. After you do that, you can email your professors and let them know what's going on and talk to them about when you can turn in your late work."

"After that?"

She shrugs. "We try to make sure we get ahead of it if it starts to get bad again."

We.

I squeeze her tight. "I love you so much."

She giggles. "I love you too."

waiting room
. . .

The next day, I call in sick at The Lighthouse and don't give my manager details. When I talk to her, she even tries to guilt trip me into coming in later tonight, when I "feel better." I almost tell her to fuck off but resist the urge.

I call my mom and cry to her for two hours while I explain the hole that has become my life. She agrees with Addy and makes an appointment for me with the kindest looking physician who had the earliest available appointment, which is tomorrow.

Only problem? It's out in the suburbs. Too far from campus to take a bus.

"Doesn't your *friend* Reed have a car?" My mom asks.

I don't miss the insinuation she adds to the word 'friend' and am not surprised. I tell my mom a lot about my life, but I truly tell her everything, each single detail, about Reed. She is the only person I give the ups and downs to. Most of the time it's because Addy and Isabel stop listening to my stories, a lot of the time it's because I'm looking for advice. My mom's advice is always the same: tell him how you feel before it's too late. I've never taken it, clearly.

"I can't ask him to drive me, that's weird," I respond.

I hear my mom heave a sigh on the other end of the line, "It's not weird. Why would it be weird? You need a ride."

"We're rocky right now."

It would be *so* weird to sit in a car with him. I pull Betty to my chest and absentmindedly pull her floppy ears up and down, repeatedly. It would be weird, right? A ride to the doctors is a lot to ask of a person, right? I don't want him to think I'm just doing this to get attention or as an excuse to talk to him.

"Can you ask him if you can *borrow* his car?"

"That's not a bad idea." It's perfect, actually. I can get what I need and minimize time spent with Reed.

When I get off the phone with my mom, I fight my nerves and go knock on the boys' door.

Ben answers and tells me Reed's in his bedroom and not doing anything he'd be upset I interrupted. I thank him and watch him shuffle to Elliot's bedroom. They probably think I'm about to confront him about our relationship status or something. I wish. Another fight would be less nerve-wracking than asking Reed for help.

"I need to borrow your car," I say as soon as I walk in, before he can turn his head to see me. Once he does, he smiles and checks me out slowly, like we aren't rocky right now. The only light on in the room comes from his desk lamp, hitting him from the front so he looks like a carefully framed picture. His right hand is half suspended in the air, holding a pen like he was about to write something down before I barged in.

He looks at me with amusement, before he fully

processes what I've asked, vehemently shaking his head. "Absolutely not."

"Why not?" I whine.

"Because I like my car and I don't want it to be totaled," he says calmly leaning back in his chair, unmoving as I pace in front of him.

"You've never even seen me drive! Assuming I'm a bad driver is really sexist, Reed."

"Are you forgetting the story you told me about crashing your car... twice in two months?" he says, with a little more sass than I would've liked to hear.

"I was sixteen!"

Reed raises his hands in defense. "It's nothing against you, I swear. But do you really think you would be comfortable driving a car you have never driven before in a city you have never driven through before?"

I'm in the mood to be stubborn today, so I respond quickly. "I can handle it."

I know the look on Reed's face well. It's the same one I see when we're working on assignments together, it's the look he gets when he cannot figure out how to solve a problem. He hates when he can't do that.

"You know I could just give you a ride, right?" he asks.

"Not an option," I assure him.

"Is something wrong?"

"No," I say defensively. "Why would anything be wrong? Am I acting like somethings wrong?"

He vaguely gestures to his own neck slowly then to mine. "Your neck is red. You itch your neck when you're nervous."

Fucking hell. I can't tell one lie around him, can I?

"I was stressed about my homework earlier." Not a total lie.

Reed sighs, giving up. "Fine. Okay."

I squeal. "I can take the car? You're sure?"

Reed laughs. "No no no, you can only take the car *if* you pass my driver's ed test first. Come on Hevko, my keys are out there."

This is a nightmare.

———

"Okay," Reed says as he tosses me the keys. "We're just gonna go around the block and if you can survive three left turns without giving me heart palpitations, you can take the car."

His car is parked in an overflow student parking lot on the outskirts of campus. It's a long, mostly silent, walk there. I take my time settling into the driver's seat, fidgeting with the mirrors and the seat. I'm so ready. I can so do this.

At least, that's what I'm thinking before I press my foot to gas while the car is in reverse instead of drive, and the back of Reed's car slams into a telephone poll. I shove the gear shift into park as Reed and I both stare out the front windshield.

I quickly look at Reed, then look away after I see the look on his face. His eyes haven't left the windshield yet. His jaw is clenched, his shoulders are drawn tight as he leans back against the passenger seat. Fuck — he's mad at me.

I drape myself over the steering wheel, burying my head into it and hoping I will magically be transported out of this car. And I start crying. Not tearing up, no. Full blown, ugly crying. I can't do anything right.

I don't move until I feel Reed start to rub small circles on my back. But when I pick my head, I see Reed still glaring out the windshield, his angry expression unmoving, the total opposite of the sweet small motion of his hand on my back.

I say the only thing I can think of. "I'm sorry," I say it softly, trying not to start crying again. "I'll pay for-"

"Shut up," Reed says steadily and lowly, somehow making the harsh words sound almost like something kind. "I don't give a fuck about the car, Halle."

I only nod, processing his words slower than I should be as I lean my head back against the seat. I'm exhausted from crying, from not eating enough, from not taking my nap today. I can feel it in my eyelids.

Reed clears his throat to break the silence and speaks very slowly. "I feel like this... episode of yours isn't just about the car."

Maybe it's because I'm tired, but something about Reed saying this just sets me off.

I'm mad he is calling my very real feelings about crashing his very real car into a pole an "episode." What the fuck is that supposed to mean?

I'm mad he decided to be all cryptic, to force *me* to make the decision to talk, instead of just asking me if I was okay like a normal person would. All the things I've always liked about him, the fact that he has always let me take charge in our relationship, have suddenly flipped. Is he afraid to just ask me what's wrong? Why I'm *obviously* upset?

I can't believe this is the same man who dragged me to Wells' office hours a few weeks ago. Reed was able to help me in a way that was so ridiculously practical, I could've told him I loved him that day. But since then, all we've done is fight. He notices I'm struggling, tries to lecture me, and then pushes me away.

"I'm done. Forget I ever asked you." The words come out of my mouth as a bite, quicker than I can even remember thinking of them, as I jump out of the car and slam the door behind me.

I check the damage on his bumper and am relieved to see it's less severe than the catastrophe I had imagined it to be. It's drivable. The bumper is a little beat up, but it doesn't look like anything I won't be able to pay for with my savings from working at The Lighthouse. That doesn't make me feel any less guilty though. I walk toward the exit of the parking lot, planning to walk back to Prez alone and sulk in my bedroom.

Of course, *now* Reed doesn't feel like leaving me alone. He sprints ahead to block my path, spinning around to face me.

"Halle," he says, sounding a bit frantic. "I'm so sorry, I didn't mean it like that, I just meant you've been acting weird about getting a ride and I just want you to know you that I don't care about the car, I'm more worried about you. I'll tell my parents I hit the pole and they'll pay for it without even asking for details. I'll drive you anywhere. I don't care how far it is."

He stares at me, awaiting my response. I can't make eye contact with him, I won't let myself, but his eyes dart around, following mine until I accidentally lock in on him.

"Fine." I sigh. "I have a doctor's appointment and I would very much appreciate it if you gave me a ride there. It's too far to take the bus."

Reed looks at me blankly, not looking any more relaxed, even now that I've explained it all to him. "Doctor?" he asks, stupidly.

"Yes, Reed, a doctor's appointment," I repeat.

"Are you pregnant?"

"God! No!" I rub my hands across my neck as it starts to itch. "I've just been really struggling, mental health wise, recently and I wanna talk to a doctor about it. Because I don't know what else to do."

I didn't plan on telling Reed, it just slips out as a defense. But now that I've said it, I feel better. I am a little confused to see Reed looks relieved. I thought telling him would just make him get fussier over me.

"Thank God," he says, letting out an uneven breath. "I thought you were actually sick."

Wow, he really has a way with words today.

"Reed," I say threateningly, glaring at him until he very quickly realizes his mistake.

"I'm sorry! I just really thought you were about to tell me you had cancer or something."

All I can do is lightly roll my eyes at him. I'm very thankful he cares about me but too annoyed and too tired to tell him that. Something about my expression must give away my inner monologue, because Reed softens. He turns back to the car, gesturing for me to follow.

"Come on," he says over his shoulder. "Let's grab dinner somewhere. I don't wanna finish this conversation in a gravel lot."

"What about your bumper?" I protest.

Reed shrugs. "It's not falling off."

I follow him to the car semi-reluctantly, settling into the familiar passenger seat and feeling like I can breathe for the first time all day.

Our drive to Ross Cafe and Diner is silent except for the radio and we soon find ourselves in a familiar corner booth, sitting across from each other with our knees almost touching and matching sandwiches in front of us. I'm not done eating before Reed starts asking the hard questions.

"Why didn't you tell me?" he asks plainly.

I understand why he's pressing; I would be mad if Reed kept something like this from me. And I would be upset if I knew he had been going through something difficult and I hadn't noticed.

"It's embarrassing!" I say defensively.

"It's not embarrassing," Reed says casually, taking another bite from his sandwich.

I don't know how to explain to Reed that he still hasn't seen the worst of me and that if he did, he would find me unlovable. I don't wanna be difficult, but I think I am. I don't wanna be too hard to love. No one does.

"I want you to keep me updated on this type of stuff from now on. Tell me when you're feeling shitty," he says.

"I'm not feeling *as* shitty right now." I smile. I really mean it.

I catch Reed up on everything that led me to this point, telling him everything. It takes a while for me to convince him that there's no one to blame. He wants to blame himself for not noticing. He wants to blame my professors for not filing a student concern report once they noticed my grades dropping. We sit in the booth and talk for a few hours, longer than I thought we would. And while it's not the same as talking to my mom, or Addy, talking to Reed feels good. Familiar in a way I've felt with no one else. I always appreciate his perspective on things. It's different from mine, but also so similar sometimes.

I'm in the middle of a sentence when I get distracted by the song that's just started playing over the speaker.

"This is Fleetwood Mac, right?" I ask Reed, trying to explain why I've gotten off track.

Reed vehemently nods his head, looking offended that I even had to ask. He takes his love for Fleetwood Mac *very* seriously. Last year, I liked to get a rise out of him by asking him if every song we heard out in public was a Fleetwood Mac song, even if it was a top forty pop song or I already knew it was Fleetwood Mac. I always tried to pry into the roots of his obsession, but the only reason he ever gave was that its his parents' favorite band. It's something he shares with his parents. Which is odd, because he doesn't usually talk about his parents like that. I've always been under the impression that they don't share anything.

"How did you *not* know this song is Fleetwood Mac?" he asks, half paying attention to me and half zoned out, methodically tapping his fingers on the edge of the table.

I shrug and suppress a laugh. "I could've guessed it was, but I didn't wanna disappoint the *biggest* fan in the world."

Reed rolls his eyes. "I am not the *biggest* fan in the world."

"You know, I only ever hear their songs when I'm with you."

His fingers pause their tapping as he stares at me. "What's that mean?"

"Nothing, I don't know. Does it have to *mean* anything?"

Reed smiles and says, much more quietly, "You forget I know you, Hal. That type of shit always means something to you. You get it from Isabel."

Maybe I do think that if I listen to Fleetwood Mac without Reed's presence, I would be enacting some type of curse. Maybe I do think the fact that I only ever hear their music when I'm with him is some type of sign. Maybe I never listened to Fleetwood Mac on my own because I knew it would remind me of him. I would never bother trying to convince Reed to believe in the same romantic fate I do. He only believes in that stuff when it serves him.

Sure enough, another Fleetwood Mac song plays in the small room of my doctors office as I sit alone on the crinkled exam table and wait for the nurse to return and take my blood pressure. I wonder if this counts since Reed is here with me but not in the room.

I guess it counts if it's playing in the waiting room as well. I should have guessed that I wouldn't be able to convince him to wait in the car while I was at my doctor's appointment. He insists on sitting in the waiting room. I fought him when he first offered, but now, sitting in the exam room alone on the crinkly paper, I am happy to know I have someone thinking of me in the waiting room, who will be there when I walk out. I picture him how I left him, intently skimming a copy of *Highlights* magazine like its required reading and tapping his foot.

My doctor is nice. She's young, understanding, and asks me a long, long series of questions. I tell her everything. How I can't focus on anything but sleeping and showering, how the stress of work and my now seemingly infamous *Clocktower* article have just been too much.

When I'm finally done talking, she looks at me carefully. "If it's okay with you, I think I'm going to put you on an antidepressant."

I feel gob smacked. "I'm not depressed," I tell her bluntly. "I would know if I was depressed. I'm anxious and I can't focus, that's all."

The doctor looks at me, with what I think might be pity. "Not being able to focus, feeling antsy and unmotivated are signs of depression. I'd like to at least try it. And if it doesn't work, we'll try something else."

It's hard not to listen to her. She is my doctor after all. So I listen and let her write me a prescription for Wellbutrin and assume that means this appointment is over.

"I'd still like to draw some blood and run some tests,"

the doctor says from behind her little computer on the swiveling half-desk attached to the wall. "Sometimes problems like this can come from a deficit of certain vitamins, so I always like to check."

She leaves and the nurse who brought me into the room returns with a needle.

I'm a little afraid of needles and blood work. Well, *little* might be an understatement. I only got my flu shot last year because Addy jokingly called me an anti-vaxxer. To prove her wrong, I went with her to the free flu shot clinic run by the nursing majors. I cried the whole time.

I can do this though. I don't really have a choice. I do my deep breathing, and barely even notice when the nurse pushes the needle into my vein. I can do this.

One more deep breath, and I start to feel lightheaded. Fainting while getting your blood drawn is one of those very specific feelings. The only thing fainting on a doctor's office crinkle paper feels like is fainting on a doctor's office crinkle paper. The slow internal realization of what's about to happen, looking your own demise in the face. I manage to mumble some mostly incoherent words to the nurse, something including the words "pass out" before I fully lose myself.

When I come to, I'm lying down on the now reclined exam table, the nurse standing over me, a sullen look on her face.

"You could've told me you would react like that before I actually drew blood. I would've done it with you already lying down," she says. Maybe it's because I'm still woozy, but she sounds really mean.

"If I had known that was going to happen ahead of time," I tell her, my mouth feeling too dry. "I would have told you."

Then, I swear to God, this nurse rolls her eyes at me.

Addy would never. Next time I need a needle stuck in my arm, I'm making Addy do it.

"Oh, I got your boyfriend from the waiting room. If someone passes out like you did, we can't let them leave alone."

My brain suddenly feels very alert, and I try to sit up to find Reed, but my body can't keep up and I have to lie back down because I feel like I'm about to pass out again. Reed comes to me, standing at my side and handing me a juice box with a soft, uncertain smile.

I don't think he's ever looked at me like this before. I wanna know what he's thinking. It feels distinct from the relationship we've had before this. Like something about him seeing me drink apple juice out of a carton with animated movie characters on it, while a huge piece of gauze is wrapped around the inside of my elbow, and I look completely pale in the doctor's office lighting has fundamentally changed how he sees me. I don't know. Maybe seeing him stand at the edge the exam table, looking at me with such care, has fundamentally changed how I see him.

He intertwines his hand with my own clammy one as I sip the juice box. There is something heavy, unspeakable, probably unnoticeable in the glance the two of us share.

better days
• • •

I won't say Wellbutrin is a miracle drug, but it, along with a lot of reminders from Addy and Reed and my mom to take care of myself, improves my quality of life astronomically over the next couple of weeks.

My professors are kind and more accommodating than I ever imagined they would be. We work together to create a plan for missing work that gives me time, but enough structure to keep me from falling off again. I walk around the strip of stores on the edge of town with Reed while we wait for the auto shop to repair his bumper. Addy spends her Saturday morning helping me carry loads of dirty clothes to the laundry room in our building's basement and helps me fold them, even though she has a lethal hangover. Isabel leaves frozen leftovers in the freezer with my name on them just in case I feel too overwhelmed to cook. Mic invites me to go to yoga with her, and I do. Nadia even smiles at me a little bit more now.

Things are getting good again. And for the first time, it feels real, permanent.

But now that I'm not mega-depressed, I feel the sting of quitting *Clocktower* for the first time. I'm bored.

"I need a hobby," I tell Addy and Isabel as we leave the student center after a productive two hours of studying.

"Start collecting something," Isabel suggests.

"You should scrapbook," Addy says. "I do. It's relaxing."

I shrug. "No, something that'll let me write. I have a *Clocktower*-sized hole in my heart right now."

"Journal," Isabel replies.

"I don't know, I want it to be something I can share. And collaborate with other people."

Addy's eyes light up. "You should start a magazine. Like *Tiger Beat* but for girls on campus."

It's not a bad idea, though I like to think I could create something a little more artsy than *Tiger Beat*. Before I can respond, our path on the sidewalk intersects with Reed, Ben, Harry, and Elliot. Both of our groups stop to greet each other, but Reed awkwardly pushes himself to the edge of his pack so he's standing across from me. It's weird for him to put so much distance between us. He looks nervous. It makes my stomach hurt, worrying he's about to tell me something I don't want to hear.

"Hey," he says, feigning casualness that does not read on his face at all. "We have this banquet for soccer and we each have a plus one. I was wondering if you wanted to come with me."

I blink at him. "Me?"

"Yeah." He smiles. "Everyone else is bringing their girlfriends so-"

He stops himself when he realizes what he's said but recovers well by just smiling at me and pretending that was all he meant to say.

Everyone else is bringing their girlfriends - I will be thinking about that sentence all week. All of his teammates were sitting around talking about bringing their girlfriends to the banquet and Reed thought: *Ah yes, let me bring Halle.* Does that push me into girlfriend territory?

Unseen by him, Addy and Isabel gawk at me from across the sidewalk. They are in total shock, I think Isabel is trying not to laugh, and I'm sure my face would be similar if I didn't have to look into Reed's eyes while he says all this. I deserve an award for not breaking.

"Sounds fun," I tell him, trying not to sound too strained. "I'll go."

"Cool." he relaxes a little. "Two Fridays from now. And it's semi-formal. I'll pick you up."

"Do the rest of you have dates too?" Isabel asks.

Harry says he's bringing Anna, who Reed has told me is his long-time fling. Elliot tells us he's bringing a freshman none of us know.

"I'm not going," Ben says.

The color drains from Addy's face. "Why not? Are you worried about getting a date or something?"

He shakes his head. "Just not my scene."

We talk to the boys for a few minutes before they continue their walk to the caf and we continue ours to Prez.

"Everyone else is bringing their girlfriends?" Isabel teases once we're out of earshot.

"Something you're forgetting to tell us?" Addy asks.

"No," I answer. "I think we just witnessed a Freudian slip in real-time."

Isabel leaves for rehearsal after we get back to the room, while Addy and I sit together and work on the rest of our homework in near silence. Until Nadia starts milling about the living room. We share a subtle glance of wariness once she walks in. Nadia has been a menace to the room recently. Now that we all know about her and Teddy, their relationship is the only goddamn thing she talks about. That and she's just plain mean.

Nadia puts a basket full of laundry on the kitchen table, right in between me and Addy, going back to her room to grab her detergent and then returning.

"Are these Teddy's?" Addy asks, pointing to a pair of white briefs sitting on top of the basket with the end of her pencil.

Nadia nods, "Yeah, he asked me to put a load in while he was doing his homework."

Addy and I stare at each other, unseen by Nadia, both thinking the same thing: There's no way this girl is serious. There is no way she means what we think she means.

I have to ask her, it's too tempting. "Nadia, do you mean this whole basket is full of Teddy's laundry? You're doing his laundry for him?"

Nadia nods pleasantly. When she sees the horrified look on our faces, her face drops. "What? He said we couldn't hang out tonight because he had too much homework and laundry, and I said I would do his laundry, so we had time to hang out."

Addy and I both manage to nod, hopefully with enough understanding to avoid a verbal lashing from her. Nadia takes the basket and her detergent out the door. It takes approximately six minutes to get to the laundry room and put a load in, so Addy and I know exactly how much time we have to digest this and talk about Nadia before she returns.

"Would you ever do Reed's laundry?" she asks me quietly.

I think about it for a while before answering. "I would, I guess if he asked me. But Reed would never ask me to."

EVEN IF REED KIND OF CALLING ME HIS GIRLFRIEND WAS AN unintentional slip of his subconscious thoughts, it gives me enough courage to stop being so skittish about our relationship.

The days between his asking me and the dance, we hang out every night. I come to his room after he's done with practice, and we tell each other all about our days.

"Nadia's doing Teddy's laundry," I tell him. I'm on his bed, sitting on top of the comforter, while he empties the contents of his duffle bag into his hamper.

Reed smirks. "When are you gonna start doing mine?"

I throw one of his pillows at him, going for a headshot, but he dodges it. "Shut up."

He laughs and throws it back at me, being kind enough to aim it toward my feet instead of my head. "It's more likely that I do your laundry honestly."

I'm laughing now too. "I would never trust you with my laundry. You'd shrink my good leggings."

He settles on the bed next to me, and being this close to him feels like taking a breath after being underwater. That's how it feels every time I come over. I want to touch him, and I want him to touch me. But I don't know how to do that without freaking out again, and I don't know if I'm ready to be honest with him.

Friday night, a week before the banquet, I sit in Reed's room while my friends are at Laundry Room. He's at his desk typing, while I sit on his bed with my notebook and copy of *Macbeth*. Drafting essays on paper is the only way I can get anything done. I look up at

Reed, and all I can think about is how I wish he was sitting closer to me.

"Can I ask you something?" I dogear fold the page I was reading and put my book down.

"Oh no," he responds seriously, but when he turns to face me, I see he's smiling.

"It's not bad," I say quickly.

"You can ask me anything. Even if it's bad."

I sigh. "And I'm gonna say things that are intentionally vague, but you can't ask me what I mean or get mad at me for not being more specific."

"Okay, deal. What's up?"

I can already feel myself blushing, all the way up to my forehead like I'm sitting too close to a campfire. "Do you think, when I come over here like this, we can...do more like, touching?"

He looks smug as he shuts his laptop. "Halle Hevko, are you asking me to fool around with you?"

"Don't say it like that," I half-yell, exasperated, and bury my face into his comforter. "Forget I mentioned it."

"Then what did you mean by touching?" When I don't respond or pick my head up, I hear Reed's chair scooch and feel his weight sink into the bed next to me. He gently tugs my chin so I'm only half-pressed into the bed and can see him. "Talk to me."

"I want to kiss you all the time and it's driving me insane, and I want to hang out in your room with you, but I can't get any of my work done because all I'm thinking about is why I'm not kissing you."

He's quiet for too long. "I don't know, Hal."

I sit up to assert some power. "Am I reading this wrong? Because if you just wanna be friends now you have to tell me."

"You're not reading this wrong. I just...it's not fun to

watch your girl look like she's about to have a panic attack when you touch her. I didn't wanna rush you. I was trying to let you make the first move."

"This is me making the first move then."

"You're sure?"

"I know I was weird with you the other day. But it's not your fault and I trust you and I think I'm ready. So let's make out."

———

It turns into a very beneficial week for both of us.

Our hang-outs start innocently enough. I talk to him about Addy's idea for a college version of a teen magazine and what I could potentially do with it. Reed talks about his frustrations with soccer and his parents trying to sign him up for LSAT prep courses even though he won't be taking it for another year and a half. However – our hang-outs always end with him telling me he likes the taste of my lips and me digging my nails into his shoulders. Slow kisses where we break smiling and he tilts my chin to guide me back in. Getting through moments with him without thinking of last year.

Towards the end of the week, there's a night we get carried away and I'm still in his bed after midnight, which doesn't normally happen.

"Stay," he says, lazily drawing circles on my back as I lay on him.

"I should get back soon," I respond, even though my eyelids are heavy, and I've never been more comfortable. "If I'm gone all night my roommates will know something's up."

He hums to himself, unsatisfied with my reasoning. "You still with me?" he asks.

I yawn. "What does that mean?"

"Like, all this." He vaguely motions between us. "You'd tell me if it was too much? Too fast?"

"I would and it hasn't been."

"Good. Stay the night then."

"You know how judgy my roommates are." I groan.

"Hevko, one day soon I'm gonna make us so official that even your roommates won't be able to judge."

The idea of that makes me happier than he probably thought it would.

black dress

· · ·

The day of the soccer banquet comes, and Isabel and Addy tell me I have to start getting ready at 4:00 to look my absolute best, even though Reed isn't coming by our room to pick me up until 7:00. I accidentally burn my forehead while trying to curl one of my shaggy half bangs, so now I have a huge red line to try to cover up. At least I'm wearing my favorite black dress, which is coincidentally the only black dress I own. It's sexy without being controversial, tight but not in an unflattering way where it looks like I bought the wrong size, and long enough to pass for formal attire without being over the top. My Goldilocks black dress.

By the time Reed picks me up, I'm flustered. I'm still excited though. I think I look good, despite all the hurdles. Plus, I have a good feeling about tonight. A fancy dinner where Reed and I are all dressed up feels like it could lead to sex. I feel like I'm not totally crazy to assume that we might have sex tonight. It makes me nervous. Not nervous about having sex with Reed, more nervous I'll do something wrong.

He stands outside my door grinning, his tie hanging undone around his neck as I close the door behind me.

"Want help with that?" I gesture vaguely towards his tie.

"Please."

I get to work, feeling the heat radiating off his neck and trying to ignore how much I'm enjoying being this close to him.

"I know you're an only child and I know you went to public school, so I'm wondering how you learned how to tie a tie." He teases.

I smile. "Model UN, debate team, student government, journalism summer camp – I was surrounded by lots of nerds in ties. Why'd you wait to tie it? Mr. Perfect not good at tying ties?"

He smirks. "No. I am."

I drink him in – paying extra attention to the way our eyes lock and his hands cover mine as I straighten his tie. Screw the banquet, I want to stay here with him like this.

I talk myself out of my trance, dropping my hands from his chest. "All done."

My nerves are humming by the time Reed and I get to the banquet hall.

I feel like a fish out of water. All of the other girls here are serious girlfriends of guys on the team, junior and senior girls who have been dating their soccer boyfriends for years. The girlfriends are all really sweet when Reed introduces me, but I can't help but be intimidated. I'm very temporary compared to these girls. They're all friends with each other, they all sit together at games and get brunch together and talk about their boyfriends. I cannot relate.

He leads me to a big circular table, already filled with his fellow sophomore teammates and their dates. There are two empty chairs across from us, that I assume were meant for Ben and his plus one. I wonder why he didn't want to come; this seems like an important event. It's the first time I've seen any of these guys in ties, the places are set with three forks each, and there's smooth jazz music playing distantly somewhere in the background. A man, I'm assuming one of the coaches based on the way the boys at the table erupt into cheers once they see him, steps up to the microphone to announce that dinner will be served shortly.

Elliot, who sits on the other side of Reed, pokes him with a sneaky finger before pulling a flask shaped like a phone out of his pocket.

"Anyone?" He offers.

Reed shakes his head. "I drove."

"Loser." Elliot scoffs at him before he reaches the flask over towards me. "Halle?"

"No thanks." I smile tightly.

"Come on. Live a little." He laughs, nearly grabbing my glass of Diet Coke before Reed quickly stops him.

"Back off," he says forcefully, putting the glass back in its spot next to my plate. "She doesn't drink like that."

My annoyance that Reed just spilled my dirty little secret about drinking to the whole table is overshadowed by the shrill noise of Elliot laughing harshly.

"Jesus, man," Elliot says. "Like I'm supposed to believe the same Halle we all watched tear up Laundry Room every single weekend last year *doesn't drink* anymore. What the hell would make you stop?"

I stutter and feel my face heat up as I fumble for a decent answer that isn't the truth. I don't realize my knee is bouncing until Reed steadies it under the table.

He answers Elliot for me. "If you knew the whole story you wouldn't be saying shit like that," he says casually. "So fuck off."

We share a weird look, and for a fleeting moment, I think he might know about me having sex last year. I look over at him questioningly, trying and failing to read his mind.

Am I crazy to think he knows? I don't know who would've told him. Maybe I called him or texted him to tell him about it the night it happened and forgot about it. That's totally plausible. I don't know how he found out, but based on the look he just gave me, I think he knows. But if he knows, I don't know why he's never brought it up before.

Our salads are served. I'm interested enough in the stories the boys are swapping about other teams they've played, and the gossip about what seniors are going to play professionally versus which ones that think they're good enough to play professionally but aren't that my suspicions of Reed knowing all about my sex life gradually float to the back of my mind.

The main course arrives – a very dry chicken parmesan but it's good enough for a free dinner. I've almost cleared my plate when Ben walks into the banquet hall and takes a seat at the table. And he has a girl with him. She's a little bit shorter than me but not much with curly blonde hair and a blue bodycon dress that looks very expensive. She looks a little like Addy. None of the boys look as shocked as me to see him, let alone see him with a date, which makes me wonder if he's introduced her to them before. The question on the tip of my tongue is: *What changed your mind about coming tonight?*

But the question Elliot asks is, "What took you two so long?"

Ben shrugs as the mystery blonde girl sits down next to him and straightens out her dress. He doesn't look particularly happy to be here, or be here with her I can't tell, which makes me wonder why he didn't just bring Addy, even just as a friend. It would have been perfect, the two of us could have entertained each other when the soccer talk gets too convoluted for us normies. The four of us could have carpooled. This is so weird.

I excuse myself to use the restroom, making sure to grab my phone from my purse hanging on the back of my chair. Because I'm not going to the bathroom, I'm calling Addy.

There are a group of girls chatting by the plush chairs and mirrors outside of the restrooms, so I sneak out a propped door that leads to a rickey back porch with trashcans and spare catering equipment. It's raining, not a gentle kind either. Even though this porch has an awning, the wind throws splashes of it at me, sticking to my hair and eyelashes. It finally feels like October. The first week or so of this month was uncomfortably warm.

I call Addy. My phone rings, but before Addy can pick up, I hear the heavy door to the patio open behind me. Reed stands there, half outside and half in, with his hands shoved deep in his pockets.

"What's up?" I ask.

He shrugs as he steps onto the patio, the door shutting behind him with a thud.

"Hey, Hal Pal." Addy finally answers my call. "Everything okay? Are you having fun?"

Reed stares at me expectantly, like he's daring me to tell Addy what I really came out here to tell her.

"Sorry, butt dial. Yeah, I'm having fun. I'll tell you all about it when I get home."

She laughs. "If you make it back home, who knows, you and Reed might-"

I hang up on her before she can finish that sentence, on the off-chance Reed can hear her through my phone.

"Didn't know the bathroom was outside." He sulks. "Did you seriously come out here to gossip with Addy?"

"Well, um, not exactly. Can we just talk about this later? I don't wanna ruin your night."

Reed stares at me as I look down at my shoes. "I'm leaving for that tournament tomorrow and I'd rather clear the air before I leave. We're not gonna see each other for a few days." He huffs.

"I've gone longer without you before."

"That's low."

I roll my eyes. "Let's just go back inside."

He shakes his head and leans against the door. "You can't tell Addy about Ben and Meg."

I scoff. "That's her name? So you've known about this?"

He takes a step closer to me and throws his hands up in defense. "He's talked about her a little, but I never knew he was bringing her to this I swear. But...I don't think you should tell Addy about this tonight."

"She's my best friend! What are you talking about?"

"This was supposed to be a good night for *us*. Do something normal and not let our friends' drama get in the way for one night."

"You're being dramatic. It's not drama. I tell Addy everything. Let's just go back and talk about this later."

I push past Reed toward the door, but his words stop me dead in my tracks.

"Of course, how could I forget? You tell Addy *everything*."

My gut aches. "What's that supposed to mean?"

"Nothing." He tries to play it cool, but he doesn't do it well. This, along with the comment he made at the table about me not drinking – I think he knows my big secret. I almost hate him for it, but a tiny part of me feels the worst type of relief. I think my hands start shaking.

"You know about last year?" I seethe. "That's what that was about earlier with Elliot – You know about last year, don't you?"

"I know," he says slowly.

I haven't seen him look this mad in a long time, maybe ever. He looks jealous too. If only he knew how I really felt about it. How has he not read my mind? He must know if it was something I was super happy about or proud of, I wouldn't have tried so hard to keep it from him.

"You don't know the whole story," I tell him quietly.

He shakes his head, still tense. "No, I know. Addy told me last year, right after it happened. She was worried about you. She said you refused to talk about it, and she wanted me to talk to you."

"But you never talked to me about it." I bite.

"That night last year when I tried to get your attention, and you told me you weren't 'drunk enough' to talk to me? Yeah. I was gonna ask you that night if you wanted to talk. But I realized it would've been unfair to force you to talk about something like that with me. I didn't wanna make you uncomfortable."

"Addy told you *everything*. And you still have the nerve to act jealous? You realize I didn't exactly want that for myself either, right?"

"It was supposed to be me and you!" He screams.

"But it wasn't! *You* decided that not me." I match him.

"Well, you let me leave."

"What was I supposed to do? Chase you down the hallway after you left my room and told me you didn't wanna see my face anymore? Beg you to stay with me?" I scoff.

"Yes," he says seriously, "Because I would've if you asked. You know what you do to me, if you had talked some sense into me we could've stayed together."

"Why would I? You decided I wasn't good enough to lose one fucking soccer game over."

He stills. "Ben told you about that?"

"He did. A while ago. And I never brought it up because I didn't want to let last year affect this year, but I figured if we're digging up shit from then I may as well throw that in."

"I'm not the same guy I was last year."

"And I'm not the same girl! You expect me to believe that about you, but you can't see it in me?"

"I thought you would wait for me! And then I hear about you going off and having sex with some guy. You never thought we would eventually get back together?"

"I didn't."

"You're lying."

I start crying, immediately, and escalating quickly, so much so that I think it scares Reed. "You don't get it."

"Get what?" He's barely looking at me but doesn't look as tense as he did before.

I'm starting to get snotty, but I try to hold on to the last parts of my dignity by not sniffing.

"I didn't have sex with that guy because I wanted to. I was drunk. And he was there. And I don't remember any of it. I didn't do it to spite you or to replace you because, honestly, I don't remember why I did it. I can't believe you knew this whole time, and you never said anything. Do you know how much it has killed me to keep this from you? How worried I was that this would make you hate me? You are the *one person* I wanted to talk to about this and the only one I knew I could never tell without having a total breakdown. I think you never asked me about it because it made you uncomfortable. Addy was so fucking worried about me that she reached out to you of all people, did you ever even think about what that meant? I wouldn't talk to any of my friends about that night. I still don't talk about it. And now I have to listen to you throw it back in my face like I'm some kind of whore." I swallow the lump in my throat. "You're just being mean."

When I open the door, Reed stops me by tugging on my arm. It's not aggressive, just a little tug, but it's enough to keep me in place. He still won't look at me.

"What?" I snap.

Now he does look at me, heaving a deep breath and shoving his hands deep into his pockets, "Hold on, I'm trying to figure out what I want to say."

"Oh. You don't know what to say?"

"I didn't exactly script this conversation out in my head," he says. "This isn't really how I planned on this night going. So yes, I need a minute to figure out what to say."

Reed, who usually always knows the perfect thing to say to me, is speechless. I can't believe it. I shrug him off and lean against the door, closing my eyes and trying to transport myself out of my body. I hate this. I hate the feeling that I'm about to lose him. Again. This isn't how I planned on this night going either. The more I think about it, the more tears fall, until I'm holding my breath to keep myself from breaking out into sobs. The lump in my throat hurts.

"I didn't mean to sound like I was just jealous or mad earlier," Reed says lightly after a while, running his hands down his face, "I'm sorry. It's just hard for me to think about. After Addy told me, I went back to my room and threw up. You're right, it makes me uncomfortable. But not because I blame you, because I…care. About you."

"Care?" I smirk.

"Well, there's another word I could use, if you'd like, but I was worried I'd scare you off."

He smiles a little, not enough to make me feel better, but enough to make me realize I haven't ruined us. He knows the ugliest thing about me and isn't running away. He's always known, and he stayed. The thought comforts me but also makes me cry harder.

My cries finally break into full sobs. Reed slides next to me against the door, and I let him hug me and hold my head into his chest, slowly calming down as he rubs my back. I'm enjoying the moment, which feels wrong given the context. But I'm in my favorite person's arms, the rain is pouring a steady and comforting rhythm on the awning above us, and I'm wearing my favorite dress. Maybe we're gonna be okay.

I let go of him once I'm fully composed.

"Sorry, I ruined your night," I say, wiping the lingering tears and raindrops from my cheeks. "All of your plans to woo me and take me to bed have been compromised."

"Take you to bed?" He laughs.

"Am I wrong?" I ask, hoping he doesn't say that I am.

"You're not wrong," he says quietly.

I initiate the kiss. It doesn't take long for it to pick up as his hands into the back of my hair, but after a few seconds, we both pull apart as we remember where we are. We're both smiling, and I laugh when I notice Reed has a little smudge of my pink lip gloss across his lips. My heart picks up looking at it. We stare at each other for a while, listening to the rain pitter-patter.

"Should we head back?" he asks.

"I don't want you to miss the rest of the festivities." I already feel guilty enough about all this.

He shrugs it off. "All they're doing is giving out awards to kiss the seniors' asses. I don't mind missing that."

"That'll be you in two years."

Reed doesn't look so sure. "I guess. But I also can't sit at a table with Ben for the rest of the night and not tell him what an ass he's being to Addy."

I laugh. "If you would've said that when you first came out here, our lives would have been a lot easier."

"Yeah, yeah." He kicks a little puddle in between his feet. "This way ended with us kissing and I don't know if the easy version would have."

"Alright. So then let's leave."

"We can hang out in my room for a bit. Together?" Reed asks carefully.

I bite my lip to stifle another laugh at his poor attempt to glaze over what we both know will happen if we go back to his room together. "Sounds perfect."

sleepovers

. . .

We leave without saying goodbye to anyone and sprint through the rainy parking lot to get to his car.

The short car ride is silent, and so is our walk from the student parking lot to Prez. It worries me until Reed reaches for my hand as we walk, rubbing it with his thumb before dropping it as we pass a large group of freshmen on the sidewalk.

When we get to the eighth floor, we pass Tori in the hall. She looks me and Reed up and down giggles to herself, and keeps walking. Once we make it to his room, he closes and locks his bedroom door behind us.

Reed sits on the edge of his bed while I stand, fidgeting with my dress. He empties the contents of his pockets onto the nightstand — his phone and his wallet and his keys. He takes off his watch too. He loosens his tie and takes that off too. I can't look at anything but his arms. I feel out of breath just watching him.

I sit down next to him, and we both try to kiss each other at the same time, knocking our foreheads instead, which breaks some of the tension and makes us both laugh. We make out for a long while on the bed. Our hands are all over each other, I don't think I've ever felt this good before.

"Can I take off your dress?" he asks, his voice low.

I feel hypnotized, but I manage to nod. "There's a zipper."

I reach for it, but Reed gets to it first, pushing my hair to the side before slowly undoing it, lightly kissing the nape of my neck once it's undone. He strips it off slowly as I unbutton his shirt. We're kissing and he's on top of me. When he reaches for the clasp of my bra, he stops himself.

"Are you sure you wanna do this?" Reed asks me seriously, almost out of breath.

"Do what?" I respond, unable to think of anything but the lingering tingle of where his lips were just on mine.

He laughs. "Have sex."

"Oh," I say. "Yeah. I do."

"You're sure?" he asks again, climbing off me and reaching under the bed, coming back up with a condom in his hand.

"Yeah. I trust you."

He smiles to himself, almost blushing as he looks down at his feet before he sits back down on the bed.

"You gotta talk to me, yeah?"

I nod. I didn't know people were allowed to talk during sex. They never do it in the movies.

It's all more fun than I ever thought sex was supposed to be. He holds my hand the whole time.

After, he lays on his forearms above me as we both stare at each other smiling at each other's flushed faces. I stifle a laugh.

"What?" he asks me.

"That was good. Thanks." The words leave my mouth and I immediately cringe at myself.

Thanks? I am such a fucking idiot. I deserved to be muzzled for that one.

"You're welcome, I guess." Reed laughs easily, only making me feel slightly less embarrassed. "What else are you thinking about?" he asks.

"Nothing," I say.

It's not true. I'm thinking about how stupid I am for *thanking* him for sex, about how much easier that was than I thought it would be, about how much I really really really like him. I'm thinking about how I like him more than another person should ever like any one person.

"Well, don't be shy now."

I grin. "Can we do that again?"

After round two, Reed asks me to spend the night. I borrow one of his t-shirts and use his toothpaste to brush my teeth with my finger.

We hear his roommates coming back from the banquet right before we get in bed, and Reed tells me not to worry about it. He says that they won't bother us, and even if they try, his door is locked.

"I'm gonna grab a glass of water," I tell him. "Do you want one too?"

"I can grab it," Reed says quickly, already moving for the doorknob.

"It's fine. It's not like I don't know where it is."

He shakes his head. "Let me get it for you."

"Do you not want your roommates to know I'm here or something?" I say it like a joke, but I'm not joking. I think it would ruin my night if I found out Reed was keeping me a secret.

"No," Reed says, frustrated. "They're gonna see you in

my shirt and they're gonna know we had sex. They're creeps. I don't exactly want them to be prompted to think about what you look like during sex, okay?"

I roll my eyes. "That sounds like a problem between you and them."

I leave and feel Reed tailing behind me.

Out in the living room, no one seems to care that I'm wearing the uniform of people who just had sex because Ben, Elliot, and Harry are having a quiet argument. They're standing around, holding their coats in their hands with undone ties. Whispering, like they were trying not to wake me and Reed up.

Once Elliot sees us, he lights up, but in a nasty way. He's half leaning over the couch, barely standing, very drunk compared to the last time I saw him tonight. "Oh, there they are. See what I mean!" He yells. "This place is turning into a fucking brothel."

"Hey." Reed warns sternly. I feel like I'm missing out on part of some inside joke.

"Meg's coming over in a little bit," Ben explains.

"And Anna's waiting in my room," Harry adds.

Reed rolls his eyes. "Get over it, Elliot."

Harry smirks. "If you're that lonely, call a hooker, then this place can *really* be a brothel."

Elliot tries to tackle Harry, but in his drunken state, moves far too slowly. Harry anticipates it and punches him first. Elliot falls onto the couch, cradling his cheek. Harry walks back into his room calmly, like it never happened. Ben sighs and turns to me.

"This happens about once a week. Always on Friday nights after they've both been drinking. Such weird timing, right?"

I laugh at his sarcasm before I remember I'm mad at Ben for lying to Addy, but it's too late to take my laugh back now. I do enjoy Ben's friendship. What a shame he's breaking Addy's heart and I'm never going to talk to him again.

Next to me, Reed looks like he's going to be sick. I say goodnight to Harry and Ben, even though Reed doesn't, and follow him into his room.

We lie in bed, my head on his chest, both trying to fall asleep and failing to. We aren't trying very hard though. His hand delicately combs through the knots in my half-curled hair, and we listen to the white noise of his AC unit.

"You feel okay about all this?" he asks. He sounds nervous.

"Yeah," I reassure him. "Why wouldn't I be?"

His hand pauses its work on my hair while he sighs before it starts again. "I don't know. I feel bad about what I said earlier about you having sex last year."

"Don't feel bad." I yawn. "I know why you said it."

"I have a hard time thinking about it. What it would feel like to," he pauses and takes a breath before continuing in a quieter voice, "be assaulted like that and not remember it."

"I wasn't assaulted," I assure him quickly. "I wanted to have sex with him. Everyone that was there said I told them I wanted to do it."

Reed starts to speak, then stops himself, like he physically has to bite his tongue. He's quiet for a while before he says, "Still, something like that has to warp your feelings about sex, right?"

"These are deep reflections for two a.m.," I close my heavy eyes and I hope this is the end of our conversation.

"Humor me."

"I guess I didn't think about it," I say slowly. "It felt like having sex had checked off a box or something. I didn't see myself ever wanting to do it again in the future. I thought

I'd always have a bad relationship with sex. But then I started getting closer to you again and that helped me realize I don't feel that way anymore. What about you? Any two a.m. reflections on your relationship with sex you feel like sharing with me?"

"I don't know." Reed laughs deeply, I feel it vibrate in his chest. "It's different for guys. I guess from the way all my friends talk about it, I always thought of sex as a thing for *me*. Not a thing for two people together. But now I see it as a thing for us, not just me. God, I sound like an asshole."

"No, you don't," I say. "Tonight wasn't your first time, right?"

"I had sex with my high school girlfriend, but it was barely sex. It wasn't like tonight. We tried it like three times just to say we did."

"I never knew you had a girlfriend in high school," I say, trying not to sound hurt that he would keep that from me.

"I was a junior, she was a senior. It was only for like six months. She broke up with me, but it felt like a relief, honestly. I did the shitty thing where I was a bad boyfriend on purpose because I was too scared to break up with her myself. She used to wear these super clunky, loud combat boots." He laughs at the memory like he's remembering it for the first time. "And she wrote poetry in the backs of her notebooks during class."

I relax, knowing now that he never told me about his high school girlfriend because he doesn't think about her. Not because he can't get over her.

"You have a type," I tease. "You only have sex with writer chicks."

"Apparently." He laughs.

"We should sleep," I say once his laughter dies down. I can barely keep my eyes open anymore.

"We should," he says.

The methodical pattern of his hand in my hair doesn't stop, his breath doesn't feel like it's evening out. It's like he's wide awake.

"You're not trying to sleep," I whisper.

"No, I'm not," he says in a matched hush. I can hear his smile in his voice.

"Why?"

He kisses my hair. "Go to sleep, Hal. I'm enjoying the moment. Let me enjoy the moment."

IN THE MORNING, REED'S ALARM DOESN'T WAKE HIM UP, but it wakes me. When he presses snooze in a state of semi-consciousness and rolls back over, I don't shake him awake. He's the type of person who sets his alarms too early. I study the acne scars on his chin, the slope of his nose, and his eyelashes as he sleeps. He's so beautiful.

When he does wake up, he has to start packing for their tournament. But he's in a good mood. I'm happy that he still seems happy about us, and about all the choices we made last night. But knowing we still haven't talked about our labels or boundaries for each other makes me nervous. Isabel and Addy were right, I need to talk to him. Not right now though, not when he's about to leave.

When I make it back to my room, Addy is sitting in the kitchen eating a plate of eggs. She tells me Nadia and Mic are still asleep, and that Isabel woke up early to practice for a callback for her fall ballet showcase. So Addy is the only person who gets to hear my play-by-play account of my night with Reed.

"Thank you?" Addy yells once I'm done with my story, "You had sex, and then you told him *thank you*?"

"It was just 'thanks' actually," I murmur.

"Good lord." She shakes her head. "That's just as bad. You're lucky he didn't kick you out of his bed."

"I didn't think it was *that* bad."

Addy gapes at me. "It sounds that bad."

I shrug. "It was awkward for like a second, maybe. But it's me and Reed, it's hard to feel awkward around him."

"This is a real thing again, you and Reed?"

"I think? I mean it seemed like a real thing since we had sex and all, but we didn't have time to talk about labels or anything."

Addy tsks in quiet disapproval and says, "Halle. Do not put yourself through this again. Just ask him what he's thinking. Or casually refer to him as your boyfriend in front of him, and if he freaks the fuck out about it then you know how he feels."

"Not doing that."

She sighs and shoves a forkful of eggs into her mouth. "I give up on you."

"Addy-"

"I don't mean that I'm not happy for you," she adds quickly. "I love you. And Reed is a nice guy, I guess. But it all feels like deja vu."

My mother's reaction to the news about me and Reed is no better than Addy's. When I call her, she's in the car with my grandmother and puts me on speaker. I don't tell them more than I have to – just that being Reed's soccer banquet date had gone well, I spent the night in his room, and we're in a really good spot with each other. When I finish catching them up, the other side of the line is dead quiet. So quiet, I check to make sure my mom hasn't hung up on me.

"Mom?" I ask, "You there?"

She sighs, deeper than Addy did when I told her the news, "This again?"

"It's different this time!" I say, trying to keep my cool, "We're both a year older now. It's like being in a relationship with a whole new person."

She sighs again and I hear my grandmother yell, "This sportsman with the weird name? Him again?"

"That would be Reed, yes," I say, hoping they can both hear my eye roll through the phone.

"Do not let him fuck you over this time," my grandmother says. "We have to hang up, koshka. We're driving to Columbiana for Christmas in the Woods. We are almost there."

"Okay. Have fun."

"We will," my mother says. "Talk to Reed. I expect an update."

"Mom," I warn.

"I'll talk to you later. Love you."

"Love you too."

Hearing that everyone important to me thinks Reed and I's relationship is going to tank is not comforting. I try to forget about it – it would be good for me to learn not to take other people's opinions so seriously. But then again, I cannot think of one good, healthy relationship that starts with your best friend and mom hating the idea.

I cannot forget about it. I feel doomed.

REED AND I HANG OUT WHEN WE HAVE TIME, HAVE SEX when we can, and do not talk about 'what we are.' I do not ask. Asking that feels like it would put a time of death on everything good we have going.

I hide in Reed's room whenever Nadia goes on a

tangent about Teddy, or whenever she brings him over. We do homework together. We sit in silence together. I work on my magazine proposal in his room. We have celebratory sex when my proposal gets approved by the student activities board. Total honeymoon phase.

Reed has three books on his nightstand - *Carrie*, *In Cold Blood*, and *The Glass Castle*. I read them in chunks whenever Reed falls asleep, and I've finished my homework. Once I finish those, I start bringing over my own books to read when he falls asleep. I have two Meg Cabot books stacked on his nightstand. One day, I take out my oversized hair clip so I can lay down without it stabbing my scalp, and rest it on top of the books. The next time I come over, I set my emergency chapstick next to the books and forget to put it back in my pocket. It all just stays on his nightstand.

I look at it and decide I don't need to beg Reed to tell me what I mean to him. Seeing my favorite books stacked next to his, and an accumulating pile of my junk on his nightstand is enough.

captain wentworth

. . .

I MAKE EVERY SOCIAL MEDIA ACCOUNT POSSIBLE FOR THE magazine and post about looking for submissions every day. Students can submit by emailing the magazine's school-sponsored email (we have a school-sponsored email, isn't that fancy?) or they can drop a paper submission off at our cubicle in the student affairs office (we have our own cubicle!)

The craziest part is, I've been getting a *lot* of submissions. People like my idea and want to be a part of it. That's been the best part so far.

This magazine is slowly becoming my entire personality. Reed takes me to a bonfire held at one of the senior soccer player's houses, and when any one of the players or their girlfriends ask me what I've been up to, gushing about the work I've been doing on my magazine seems to be the only thing I can talk about.

It's a Thursday night, and everyone is worked up because Halloween is next weekend. Two of Reed's teammates are taking turns running and jumping over the bonfire. It's not the type of thing that's spoken about, but we all know the weekend before Halloween will be the last weekend of outdoor parties before it gets too cold. There won't be another bonfire like this until March.

"I'd love to get involved with your magazine. I was an editor of my high school's lit magazine," one of the team captain's girlfriends tells me by the beer cooler. "Reed told me all about it, he said you're aiming for publishing in February?"

She says Reed's been bragging about my magazine and telling everyone all the details, which makes me glow — proof he's been listening to all my blabber.

Her question turns into a twenty-minute conversation, where she tells me she might submit something of her own that she wrote for a creative nonfiction class last semester. We exchange phone numbers.

"I hear you've been advertising for me," I tell Reed once I find him in a lawn chair, sliding into the chair so I'm half on his lap.

"Duh." He grins, sipping from the cup of beer in his hand.

"I think I might get some new staff members out of your recruiting."

"Have you been keeping up with your submissions?" he asks.

I shrug, not sure why he cares. "More or less. I'm caught up on all of the online submissions, but I haven't stopped by the office to pick up the paper ones."

"Nice," he says quietly.

"Why do you ask?"

"No reason. Just curious."

I nod, even though I don't believe him for a second.

Reed and I leave the bonfire after midnight, smelling

like smoke, and part at the elevator to go to our own separate rooms. The front door to 806 is unlocked, not unusual, but I walk into complete chaos. More than usual.

Nadia and Teddy seem to be throwing the rager of the year in the living room. The furniture has been pushed to the walls, music blaring, and the living room is filled with people I have never seen before. I sneak through the crowd, unnoticed, into Addy and I's bedroom.

Addy, Isabel, and Michaela are all huddled on top of Addy's bed. They look like the kids in *The Sound of Music* who are scared of the thunderstorm.

"What are you doing?" I ask.

"Hiding from the demon rave," Addy whispers.

We all hide in the bedroom together until Michaela and Isabel go to bed. Even as Addy and I try to fall asleep, we still hear the thud of the music through the walls.

"I thought they'd be tired by now," Addy says. "They've been going at it since eight."

"Should we ask Nadia to turn it off?"

"You think that would stop her?" Addy laughs. "No, best to not poke the bear."

When I eventually fall asleep, the music is still going strong, buzzing through our thin walls.

In the morning, Addy's 7 a.m. alarm goes off, and she starts getting ready for her lab, putting on her scrubs and braiding her hair. I'm half-awake when she leaves our bedroom, but she wakes me up when she dramatically runs back into our bedroom and shakes me until I'm alert.

"Get out here right now," she whisper-screams, "Look at this."

She drags me into the living room with a terrifying grip on my forearm. It somehow looks worse than it did last night. All of Teddy and Nadia's strange friends decided to spend the night in our living room. There are at least eight people sprawled out on the floor. I know eight doesn't sound like a lot, but eight strangers in our modestly sized living room is *a lot*. Nadia and Teddy aren't in the crowd, they must be in her room. Beer bottles, red cups, and clothes are littered everywhere.

I couldn't have asked for a better start to my Friday morning, personally.

"I have to go like *now*," Addy says, looking down at her watch.

"No." I groan. "Do not leave me with this. What are we supposed to do with these people?"

Addy looks at me sternly. "Don't do anything at all. Isabel has class at nine, wait for her to wake up and see it. Let her freak out about, because she so will, and let her kick them all out and scream at Nadia. Then come out here like you just woke up and pretend you haven't seen any of this."

"What about you? She knows you leave at seven thirty for your lab."

She shakes her head mysteriously and turns off the lights that were left on last night. "Out of sight, out of mind."

Then she leaves for her lab. And I go back to bed.

Around 8:30, I wake up to the shrill sound of Isabel shouting and the scuffling of eight people leaving our room.

I give Reed a dramatic retelling of the story as we lie in his bed doing homework later that day.

"Isn't that so out of character for Nadia, though?" I ask, watching him chew on the end of his pen. "I guess you don't know her as well as you know my other roommates. But still, isn't that so weird?"

"She's in my psych gen-ed. Hasn't been to a lecture in like three weeks, at least."

"Actually?" I sit up a little straighter. "How have we not talked about this before?"

Reed shrugs, still looking at his homework. "Maybe because she hasn't tried to throw the party of the century in your dorm before? I don't know, I've never given it a second thought. I don't really care who goes to class and who doesn't."

"Unless it's me," I tease.

"Exactly," he says seriously. "Unless it's *you*, I do not care who goes to class and who doesn't."

"Should I say something to her?"

"She doesn't seem like she'd be receptive to any advice. Besides, you have better things to focus on. Like looking through your magazine submissions."

I eye him suspiciously. "What is up with you and these damn submissions lately?"

"Just trying to motivate you," he says, feigning innocence.

"Well, you can stop after tonight. It's the first Friday night I have off work in forever, and I'm spending it sorting through submissions with Addy and Isabel, and then watching them get wine drunk."

When I finally leave Reed's room for my own later, Addy and Isabel have already opened the last bottle of Moscato on our bar cart.

"I picked up the paper submissions on my way back from class," Isabel tells me, using her wine glass to gesture toward Addy, who is sorting through a stack of paper on the floor.

"Thanks," I say, collapsing onto the couch. "Reed has been bugging out all week about me going through these, I don't know why."

Addy's jaw drops as she looks from the paper in her hands up to me. "I think I may know why."

She runs to the couch and thrusts the paper into my hands, watching me anxiously as my eyes scan it and I process what I'm reading: It's a submission from Reed. Except it's not a submission, it's addressed to me.

A letter. Reed wrote me a letter.

"A letter?" Isabel asks dryly. "Who is he, Captain Wentworth?"

Addy shushes her.

I read it slowly, trying to ignore Isabel and Addy's stares.

> **HALLE,**
>
> **YOU ALWAYS COMPLIMENT MY WRITING (EVEN THOUGH YOU SHOULD KNOW IT'S NOT AS GOOD AS YOURS), SO I FIGURED WRITING WOULD BE THE BEST WAY TO SAY ALL THIS. I'M NERVOUS I'LL FORGET SOMETHING IF I TRY TO SAY ALL OF THIS IN PERSON. AND THIS WAY, YOU CAN READ THIS ON YOUR OWN TIME AND NOT WORRY ABOUT ME SEEING YOUR REACTION. BUT THIS IS THE ONLY THING I'M EVER GONNA WRITE TO YOU, I SWEAR. I AM NOT THE GREAT AMERICAN NOVELIST YOU THINK I AM, AND THIS LETTER WILL PROVE IT TO YOU.**
>
> **AND BEFORE YOU STOP READING BECAUSE YOU THINK THAT I'M ABOUT TO SAY SOMETHING YOU DON'T WANT TO HEAR, I PROMISE YOU ALL OF THIS IS GOOD. I KNOW YOU. I DON'T NEED YOU TO FREAK**

out and put this down before you get to the good stuff. So don't do that.

Anyway, here it goes – I kind of knew who you were before we officially met, and I hope this doesn't make you think I'm some stalker.

It was last year, move-in day. I was on my way to practice, and I was already running late because I stayed up too late the night before and missed my alarm, then I couldn't get through campus quickly because I had to walk past all the freshman dorms where everyone was unloading their cars. I was in a really bad mood. Then I saw you. You were carrying a box of clothes or something and laughing at something your mom had just said. And I thought you were the prettiest girl I had seen, and you looked so easy to talk to.

I was convinced I needed to stop and introduce myself to you. I made this whole plan in the fifteen seconds I was staring at you to walk toward the door and "accidentally" pass you and offer to help you carry something, but I got too scared. I thought it would make me look super weird, which is probably true. So I kept walking, made it to practice, and thought about how stupid I was for not introducing myself the entire time. I even told Ben about you. He also thought I was an idiot for not saying anything. I thought that was the end of it. That I lost my one chance and would maybe see you

AROUND CAMPUS, BUT NEVER ACTUALLY TALK TO YOU.

WHEN YOU SHOWED UP AT OUR PRACTICE TWO DAYS LATER, I THOUGHT IT WAS FATE. GOD WAS SMILING UPON ME. THEN I KEPT RUNNING INTO YOU AND I THOUGHT IT ALL COULDN'T HAVE FALLEN INTO PLACE MORE PERFECTLY. I STILL FEEL THAT WAY. NOTHING ABOUT LAST YEAR CHANGED THAT FOR ME. WHEN WE STOPPED TALKING, I ALWAYS FIGURED WE WOULD RECONNECT LATER IN LIFE. DIDN'T THINK IT WOULD BE SO SOON THOUGH, I ALWAYS PICTURED MYSELF REACHING OUT TO YOU THE DAY AFTER GRADUATION OR SOMETHING. BUT I'M VERY GLAD IT HAPPENED SOONER.

I KNEW I WAS TOTALLY FUCKED THAT DAY I DROVE YOU TO YOUR DOCTOR'S APPOINTMENT, AND THAT AWFUL NURSE CAME INTO THE WAITING TO GRAB ME BECAUSE YOU PASSED OUT. I SWEAR TO GOD, I'VE NEVER BEEN MORE WORRIED ABOUT SOMEONE IN MY LIFE. I KNEW IT WASN'T EVEN THAT BIG OF A DEAL AND THAT YOU WERE TOTALLY FINE, BUT IT WAS HARD TO HIDE HOW NERVOUS I WAS. I THINK YOU NOTICED BUT I NEVER ASKED. THAT WAS THE DAY I DECIDED I WAS DONE PRETENDING I WAS OKAY WITH JUST BEING FRIENDS WITH YOU.

ALL THIS TO SAY, I'VE BEEN IN THIS SINCE DAY ONE - BEFORE DAY ONE REALLY. YOU'RE IT FOR ME. I HOPE THIS LETTER SPELLS IT OUT FOR YOU. AND IN CASE IT DOESN'T, HERE IT IS IN WRITING: HALLE, I LIKE YOU MORE THAN A LOT, AND WANT TO BE YOUR BOYFRIEND.

YOURS, REED

When I'm done reading, I mumble a quick apology to Isabel and Addy before running out the door and down the hall to Reed's room.

I knock with the letter still in one hand, and Reed opens the door almost immediately like he was standing by it waiting for me. Thank God he was the one who answered, I didn't even think of what I would say if one of his roommates answered the door instead.

Reed looks me up and down, at the paper in my hands and back to my eyes.

"You read it," he says. It's not a question.

I nod quickly, trying to hold myself together.

He grins and hugs me frantically.

I don't go back to my room until the next morning.

On Saturday night, I'm working at the Lighthouse, but all I'm thinking about is my magazine. I'm zoned out when a group of guys approaches the hostess stand.

The tallest one says plainly, "You're Halle Hevko."

I break out of my trance, looking up to make direct eye contact with Aaron. You know, lacrosse player Aaron. The same Aaron that, according to Sam, hates me. Aaron, that I had forgotten about until now.

I pretend I didn't hear him. "How many?"

Aaron smirks at me and my stomach flips into itself. "You're the bitch who wrote that article that got me kicked off the lacrosse team."

I didn't hear about that.

I'm not sure that's my doing. As far as I know, no one read my article. I never heard anyone talking about it. My heart was racing before, but now I think it's stopped entirely. I feel every nerve in my stomach light up and I think I'm about to throw up.

I take a deep breath, trying to get this confrontation over with. "How many people are in your party?"

He leans over the stand, about to say something that I assume to be a threat based on the violent look in his eyes, but he gets distracted by the door opening next to me.

I don't look to see who's walked in.

"Welcome to Lighthouse," I say cheerfully, wary to take my eyes off Aaron. "Take out or dine in tonight?"

I finally turn to smile at the group that just walked in as they approach the stand, only to see Reed and Ben, coming in after a night at some club downtown with the team. I thought they'd be out later than this.

"Hey," Reed says. He looks so happy to see me. He's probably a little drunk.

"Hey," I return. My mind relaxes a little, but my body can't. I'm still in attack mode.

"Your customer service voice is cute," he says.

Still hovering in front of me, Aaron clears his throat. "Are you gonna do your *job* and seat us or not?"

Reed and Ben's happy drunk demeanors immediately snap as they stare at Aaron in disgust, shocked that anyone would ever say anything that rude to me. I shoot them glares, begging them to stay down as I grab menus for Aaron and his friends and quickly show them to a table.

When I make it back to the hostess stand, Reed and Ben are gaping at me.

"Who the hell was that?" Ben asks.

"You look shaken up," Reed says.

"That was Aaron and the lacrosse team," I tell them, arms crossed. "I got Aaron kicked off the team apparently."

The boys shake their heads, as Ben says, "No way that's

true. He was probably just trying to start shit. I bet he's still on the roster."

I shrug. "I don't care if he's on the team or not. I just want him to leave me alone."

"I'll take care of him," Reed says darkly.

Ben laughs, embarrassingly loud, *"Take care of him?* Sure, okay Al Capone, what the fuck?"

I swear Reed blushes, but he recovers quickly. "You good, Hal?"

I try to shake off the nerves in my voice, but I feel like it's stuck in my throat. "I'm good."

I smile at him, but it feels strained. It must look strained too, Reed furrows his eyebrows.

"You still get off a little after midnight, right?" he asks.

I nod stiffly.

Reed takes a sharp inhale. "Cool. Table for two. We're gonna stick around until then. Is that okay?"

Hearing him say that is immediate relief. "Yeah." I smile and grab menus for them. "Thank you."

I mean it. It's barely eleven, Reed offering to stay until we close isn't a small favor. That's a lot of time to sit in a loud restaurant while you're a little drunk.

Reed shrugs. "You can thank us when Aaron leaves."

I seat them close to the front so I can see them from the hostess stand, but we still have to walk past Aaron's table to get there. They stare at us the whole time.

Even after I'm back at my stand, Aaron's staring at me. He stares at me all night. Each time I sneak a glance at their table, he's already looking at me. Whenever it feels too uneasy, all I have to do is look at Reed and Ben and remind myself they're here too. Aaron and his friends don't leave until 12:25, even after one of my coworkers comes to their table twice to remind them that we close at midnight.

Reed and Ben wait for me outside the student center as I help my manager mop and lock up at close. The three of us walk back to Prez together, laughing and talking about their night at the club. I feel like someone's following us. I think I'm just paranoid.

halloween

. . .

Last year, on Halloween, Addy, Isabel, I and dressed as slutty fairies and I got blackout drunk and made out with a man dressed as a Hooter's waitress on the dance floor of Laundry Room.

This year, I have to work on Friday night, and I'm dreading going out on Saturday. Addy and Isabel had to do some heavy convincing for me to agree to Saturday night's karaoke bar plans.

Friday afternoon, in between my classes and the start of my shift, 806 is being torn apart. Addy is digging through my closet, looking for pants to wear with her cartoon character costume. Isabel is trying to brush out the wig for her mermaid costume, leaving blue strands of plastic hair all over the kitchen counter. Michaela is running around trying to throw together a decent costume. She decided to join in on our plans an hour ago after Nadia told her she was no longer staying in with her because Teddy invited her to go out with him and his friends. Reed and Ben sit in our living room, each with a midday beer in hand, watching us all run around with looks of total indifference.

Reed follows me into my and Addy's bedroom to watch me try on the dress I'm borrowing from Isabel for our lame attempt at a couple's costume. We're going as a couple from one of our favorite sitcoms when we go out with the group Saturday night. I'm guessing that about four people will know who we're dressed as.

The dress is black and long-sleeved, and even though Isabel is as tall as me, she's a lot smaller, so the dress looks shorter, tighter, and a little more provocative on me than it looks on her.

I turn to Reed, modeling the dress for him. "It's not too slutty, right?"

Reed looks up from his phone to scan me, before he says, "I mean, you could dress sluttier."

I relax and roll my eyes. "I thought guys didn't want other guys staring at their girlfriends. Territorial, alpha male thing."

His chest puffs up, and I try not to laugh. "If any guy stares at you too long, that's a problem between me and him."

I would find his protectiveness attractive if I didn't know it was total bullshit. I sit next to him on the bed. "What are you gonna do?" I tease. "Hit them?"

He raises his eyebrows. "Just because I haven't hit anyone since I was in preschool doesn't mean I won't."

I laugh. "Sure."

Our conversation is light, airy. I know we're both joking, but it makes my stomach hurt. I would never ask Reed to give up something so integral to his self-image. If he started hitting people who stared at me for too long, he wouldn't be the same person I'm attracted to now. I don't know how to tell him that.

I survive working the Saturday brunch shift at Lighthouse, come back to my room and take a nap, and wake up to find my roommates already getting ready for tonight's plans. We're heading to a karaoke bar we went to for Isabel's birthday last winter. Well, all my roommates minus Nadia. She was supposed to come but texted us this morning to let us know Teddy had made new plans for the two of them.

Reed and Ben bring Elliot and Harry over for the pregame, and Isabel invites them to come out with us. I'm surprised when they agree. We hang out in the kitchen like we do for every pregame. The girls pass around a blunt and the boys bitch and moan about how they can't take a hit because of their drug tests for soccer. We take pictures in front of the big window we always use as a backdrop. We're about ready to start migrating to the karaoke bar when Nadia and Teddy walk in.

Nadia poses at the front door holding a six-pack. "Surprise! Are you surprised to see me?" she slurs.

"Yeah, considering you told us you weren't coming," Isabel says dryly.

She dramatically kisses Addy, who is closest to the door, on the cheek as Teddy follows her around the room.

Addy sneaks up next to me and whispers, "She reeks. Like she's been turkey basted with the dollar beer they sell at Laundry Room."

"Are they dressed as a deer and a *hunter*?" Isabel asks on my other side.

"Somehow both tacky and weirdly violent. Very Nadia," I say.

Isabel checks her phone and whistles to get the attention of the room. "Alright people, cars are here! Move it!"

The karaoke bar is on the other side of town than the bars we normally go to, but the crowd is about the same – a bunch of grossly drunk underage college students. When we walk in, someone is giving an awful rendition of "Thriller," but not everyone singing does Halloween-themed songs. Thank God. There are only so many of those.

Two hours, after many pitchers of Halloween-themed cocktails that I did not drink from, Addy and Isabel are on their third karaoke song of the night, this time they've dragged Mic up there with them. Reed and I are sitting comfortably together at a booth with Ben, Elliot, and Harry. Nadia and Teddy are at a safe distance, grinding on each other on the dance floor even though there aren't many other people dancing. And the song the girls are singing is an absolutely butchered version of "I Have Nothing" which is not exactly a song to dirty dance to, in my opinion. But their usual nasty selves are making it one over there.

This song is longer than I remember it being, but it's almost over when Ben stops in the middle of his story about his tyrannical boss at his high school job to stare at the dance floor.

"Hold on," he says. "I think Teddy just tried to hit her."

He doesn't need to clarify who he's talking about, and he jumps out of the booth to go to them. I follow him. It isn't until we reach Nadia and Teddy that I see what he was talking about – it's almost like Teddy is trying to do some serious damage to Nadia but is too drunk to successfully make any contact. Nadia's sobbing. When Teddy tries to grab her by the neck, Ben steps between them and pulls Teddy's wrists down.

"Dude!" Ben screams over the singing. "What the fuck is wrong with you?"

Teddy mumbles something incoherent and I guide Nadia further away from him.

I don't notice Harry and Elliot are behind me until Ben nods at them. "Help me get him out. Halle, take her home?"

I nod as Nadia leans into my shoulder, still sobbing.

"You got her?" Harry asks me as he passes. I nod. "Good. Bring Reed with you. We'll stay with the other girls after we get him kicked out."

I shuffle back to the booth with Nadia and explain the situation to Reed, who's staring at me like I'm a ghost and looks like he just stepped off the most puke-inducing roller coaster ever built.

"Can you call a car, or do you want me to?" I ask.

My question half shakes him out of his trance as he pulls his phone out of his pocket. "Yeah, I got it."

Not even five minutes later, we're dragging Nadia out to the car and making our way back to campus. Nadia's still crying, but Reed and I are dead silent for the entire ride.

Now that I think about it, it's weird that all of the other boys jumped up to help Nadia while Reed just sat there. That's lame of him. I think about that first party at the lacrosse house, when I thought it was nice that he checked on me outside instead of starting some altercation with Aaron. Now, I just find it odd. That time, he was avoiding a fight for my sake. Tonight, he watched me run towards a fight to help my friend and didn't even follow.

We get Nadia into bed, put a bottle of water on her

nightstand, and lock the door to my 806 behind us as we head to his.

I'm slipping on the spare sleep shirt I keep in his room when he asks, "Are you mad at me or something?"

"Not mad. But it bothers me that you didn't come with us to help get Teddy off Nadia."

He starts folding back the blankets on his bed and awkwardly rearranging pillows. "You know I don't like fighting. Besides, you guys had it covered."

"What if it had been me, not Nadia?" I ask, which is the real question I've had on my mind since. "If I was in some type of trouble, would you really sit by and watch as all your friends helped mediate?"

He rolls his eyes. "I'm not playing the *what-if* game. It wasn't you. If it was, I don't fucking know what I'd do. I've never had to do anything like that for a girl before, I literally wouldn't fucking know what to do."

I didn't mean to start an argument, but it feels like we're in for one now. I'm too tired for this. My shoes gave me blisters, my ears are still ringing from how loud they were playing the music, and a loop of Teddy trying to hit Nadia underscored by "I Have Nothing" is stuck in my head.

"Maybe I should go back to my room," I say, already grabbing my dress from off the floor.

Reed gently cups my cheek, cementing me in place, before kissing me passionately, his other hand snaking around my waist.

"Please stay," he says quietly once we finally break apart. "If you leave, I'm gonna be awake the whole night imagining situations where you're in trouble and I can't do anything about it. But if you stay, I can just roll over and remind myself we're fine."

I nod, taken aback by his honesty.

"I always feel safe with you. I know what I said earlier but, that doesn't mean I don't feel safe around you," I say after we crawl under his sheets.

"You don't have to say that just to make me feel better."

"It's true. Like when we're driving or walking somewhere or out in public. But also when I'm telling you a secret or being vulnerable. I never really feel butterflies around you, and it took me a while to realize that's a good thing."

I feel him looking at me even in the dark. "I never thought about it."

wallow

. . .

REED AND I DON'T KEEP THINGS FROM EACH OTHER VERY often anymore. Maybe it's because we know each other well enough to predict any surprises or because we've had enough drama involving secrets, but we've never been that kind of couple – the kind to plan big elaborate surprises and keep the other on their toes. We're always just on the same page.

He has a game today that I thought I couldn't attend because of a magazine meeting – our first publication date is getting closer and closer, and I just couldn't reschedule. But the meeting ended up taking way less time than I had budgeted for, thanks to my amazing staff, so I got out early enough to rush over to the soccer field.

I've only missed the first few minutes of the game, but the bleachers are full, so I have to sit on the grassy hill next to them, the side closest to our defense. Closest to Reed. I don't bother texting him. I told him I might not make it tonight, so hopefully it'll be a happy surprise for him to see me after the game. The team should win tonight, playing one of the teams ranked lowest in the conference, which means Reed should be in a good mood later.

I'm kind of glad I didn't bring any of my friends with me. Being alone, I can really focus on the game and shamelessly cheer without being told I'm being too loud. It makes me feel more connected to Reed, watching him play. He moves across the field easily, celebrating when his teammate scores a goal but never getting so carried away that he loses focus. The game slows down when the referee gives a yellow card to a player on the other team. I swear I see Reed notice me, but I can't be sure because he doesn't show it. That doesn't bother me, he's got his head in the game. I like that about him. I like it when he's focused.

The score is 1-0 with three minutes left in the first half. Reed has the ball until he doesn't, and he turns to run and regain possession of it. And then he falls. I don't know if it's instinct, how his teammates freeze when they see him, or just common sense, but I immediately know he's hurt. Bad. The referee stops the game while his coach and a few other people run to him. They talk to him for what feels like forever, and I feel my hands shaking.

I'm laser-focused on the field. What am I supposed to do? I see Reed scan the crowd, and I don't know who else he would be looking for besides me, so I give him a wave that he doesn't acknowledge. He talks to his coach for a little longer before two people help him off the field. I feel sick. This is so bad. They lead him back toward the locker rooms and he disappears. What am I supposed to do? Stay here? Call him?

The first half of the game ends and I sit in the grass, too stunned to move. Until a man I don't recognize, wearing a soccer team polo, approaches me.

"You're Halle, right?"

I nod.

He gestures for me to stand. "Follow me."

I follow the man out of the stands and toward the locker room. Even though I know he's most likely taking me to Reed, the whole thing feels so secretive. Like I'm part of some government mission.

The man opens the door to the locker room for me and leaves without saying a word, leaving me alone with Reed. He's sitting on a bench, his leg propped on some boxes in front of him with a large ice bag taped around his knee. All he does is look at me, and I already know that he is out for the rest of the season. I can tell he's devastated. What does a good girlfriend say to that?

"Hey," I say lightly.

He smiles sadly at me, gesturing for me to come closer. I do, still too afraid to be within a foot of him in case I hurt him.

"Did Calvin find you okay?" he asks in an obvious attempt to avoid the elephant in the room. When I nod, he copies. "Cal's a good guy."

"We didn't talk much." I shrug.

"He's one of our sports medicine trainers."

I nod again while Reed looks at the floor. I swear nothing has ever felt more awkward. Am I allowed to touch him? Is he breakable? After what might have been ten minutes or ten seconds of total silence, Reed finally looks at me.

"I don't think about you when I play…ever," he tells me.

"Okay?" I respond quietly, uncertain if I'm going to like where this conversation is going.

"I don't think about anyone. I just think about the game. It's one of the things I'm good at. But when I fell, you were literally all I could think about. I was really hoping you weren't here and didn't have to see that. I knew you weren't sure if you were gonna make it, but I swore I saw you and...I don't know why I'm telling you this."

Reed has just done the hard work of picking at the ice between us, so I feel free to slide onto the tiny sliver of the bench that's open next to him and wrap my arms around his waist. He pulls out his arm to put it around my shoulder and brings me in closer until I can squash my face in his side.

"Does it hurt?" I ask.

"Yeah," he replies. It hurts to hear, but I'm happy he's not lying to me.

"What even happened?"

"It's my ACL," he says. "I'll have to see a doctor to confirm but Cal thinks it's a minor tear. I'll have to get surgery."

I don't respond. Surgery is a big, scary word.

"What's the next hour of your life look like?" I ask.

"Go back to my room. Wallow."

He deserves every right to wallow, but I'm worried about him being alone when his teammates come back to the dorm room to celebrate a win. He's gonna feel like shit.

"How about you let me wallow with you? We can order pizza. Or Chinese."

"Or we can order both," Reed says conspicuously, and when I look up at him, I see he's smiling. Seeing him smile feels like a weight being taken off my chest, and suddenly all of this feels a little more bearable.

A COUPLE OF DAYS LATER, BEN DRIVES REED TO AN appointment with his surgeon, but I have class so I can't join. He comes to my room after looking downtrodden, sighing dramatically as he sits on my desk chair, leaning his crutches against my closet.

"What's wrong?" I ask. "What did they say?"

Huge sigh. "The surgeon thinks I need to take next year's season off since this is my third ACL tear in three years. She thinks I'm gonna get early arthritis if I keep pushing myself."

I don't like the way he worded that like he thinks he isn't going to follow the medical professional's advice.

"Do you not agree with her?"

He shrugs, faking nonchalance. "I mean, I don't really *disagree* with her, but I'm not exactly sure the only solution is to take a whole season off."

"Did you talk to your coach?"

"Yeah." He rolls his eyes. "He thinks I should take next season off too."

"Reed!"

"What?"

"It sounds like you're taking a season off!"

He awkwardly shuffles on his good leg to my bed, lies down, and buries his face in one of my throw pillows.

"I don't want to," he mumbles into the fabric.

I rub his back – thankful he can't see my blank face. I know this all sucks for him, and that it's upsetting, but I can't relate at all. The last sport I played was fourth-grade volleyball, and I hated it, but my mom wouldn't let me quit. So no, I cannot relate to the emotional trauma of having a sport taken away from you.

"Did you talk to your parents yet?" I ask.

Reed had told me earlier that he was going to ask his parents if either of them would be able to come into town when he has his surgery so they could help with some of his post-op care. He wasn't going to ask, but I convinced him he should. Even though his relationship isn't always warm and cuddly with his parents, he said he would feel better knowing they're in town.

"Yeah, I called them before I came here." He flips over so he's looking up at me. "My mom said she, and my dad, can't call off work, and my sisters have an ice-skating competition that weekend after, so neither of them can come."

"Actually?"

"Yep," he says sadly.

"I'm sorry. I can be there if you want. I don't know if that's helpful or not, I know it wouldn't be the same as having your parents there."

He smiles at me. "It does. I want you to be there, but I didn't know if that was too much to ask or not."

Ben drops us off at the hospital but refuses to wait with me for the surgery to be over. When I ask why, all he says is, "Hate hospitals."

Reed and I sit in the waiting room. His good leg bounces up and down, but I know pointing it out would make him feel insecure, so I don't.

"I feel bad making you wait for me. I should've let you take my car, then you wouldn't have to wait."

I shake my head. "I don't mind waiting."

"I mean, I know you're missing class and probably have other things to be doing so I'm happy you're here, but I feel bad."

"I want to be here. I'm your girlfriend. I would've thought you were mad at me if you hadn't asked me to come."

"I was just trying to look out for you. I love you, so I

don't want you to have to stress yourself out over anything or go out of your way."

Did he just say he loves me? Does he even know what he's just said? He doesn't look like he knows, his expression locked with no awareness of his words or any embarrassment for letting them slip.

I guess I've known I loved Reed for a while, but in a way I can only compare to the fondness of swing sets I had as a child. It's something sticky and obsessive and nauseating. It's a fixation. It's love that's clumsy and childish. It's nothing like this love I feel now – watching him fill out paperwork, sitting in a hospital waiting room love.

I place my hand over his, taking a deep breath to hide my nerves, deciding to be brave and say, "I love you."

It comes out close to a whisper, my voice a little shaky, like I'm an actress unsure of her line.

Reed smiles at me like I just told him some amazing news. He tucks a stray piece of hair from my messy ponytail behind my ear and says, "I love you too."

We don't say anything else until the nurse calls Reed back.

THE DOCTORS WON'T LET ME INTO THE ROOM THEY'RE prepping Reed in, so we share a slightly awkward hug in the hallway outside the room in front of three nurses and his surgeon. I feel silly. They probably don't see many girlfriends in these types of situations.

During my first hour in the waiting room, I try to read the literacy fiction, book club bestseller I brought with me, but trying to read about a housewife accused of killing her husband while my boyfriend is in surgery makes me feel like I'm about to throw up.

Thankfully, by my second hour, I'm able to meet Addy in the hospital cafeteria. The children's hospital she's shadowing this semester is attached to the hospital Reed's surgery is at. When I told her I was nervous about waiting for him, she offered to meet me while she was on her lunch break.

"Look at you, spending your day in a hospital," Addy says while taking a slice of the pizza we're splitting. "You're such a good girlfriend."

I brush her off. "He doesn't have anyone else. I mean he has other friends and stuff, but his parents wouldn't even call off work to come stay with him. Or visit him over the weekend."

"I guess they see him as an adult."

"Maybe," I say. "It's been bothering me though. If I had surgery, my parents would at least come for a day or two."

"His relationship with his parents is different from the one you have with yours then."

"It's weird though. Do you not think it's weird?"

Addy makes a funny face before sipping her Diet Coke. "Well, at least he has you then."

"Right."

"And Ben has Meg," she says casually with a light sigh. "Everyone's coupling up."

I am totally taken aback.

"You know about Meg?" I ask her.

"*You* know about Meg?" she counters.

"On accident," I assure her. "She showed up with Ben as we were leaving the soccer banquet. But I didn't want to upset you."

"Why would Ben being with Meg upset me?" she asks innocently.

I stare, trying to gauge if she's messing with me or not.

She's not. I decide to let it go. I don't wanna start a fight with her after she was nice enough to spend her lunch break distracting me. One day, Addy will admit she has a crush on Ben. Today is not that day.

Before I can press Addy, my phone rings. It's an unknown number, but I answer anyway, worried it has something to do with Reed's surgery.

"Hello," a woman's voice says immediately after I answer. "Am I speaking to Halle Hevko?"

"That's me, yeah," I say warily.

Addy looks at me in confusion and I stare back at her with wide eyes. I'm just as confused as her.

"This is Melissa Callaway, Reed's mom, I just wanted to check in on him. He hasn't answered any of my calls or texts all day."

Is she serious? I don't know how she even got my phone number.

"Yeah," I say slowly, trying to sound light and casual without sounding like a total airhead. "He's in surgery right now."

"Oh," his mom says, sounding a little embarrassed, but she recovers well. "He told me it was at one o'clock."

"No, it was at eleven."

Addy's looking at me curiously across the table, trying to figure out what I'm talking about just from my end of the conversation. I look at her in panic, trying to telepathically communicate that I'll tell her everything once it's over.

"Well, the appointment must have been moved since I last talked to him," his mom says.

It wasn't moved. It has always been scheduled for 11:00.

"I think it was." I lie to spare her feelings.

"Right," she says, "Well you just have him call me when he's back. I'm sure he's gonna let you know when he's back on campus."

"I'm here at the hospital with him."

"Oh," she says pointedly. I wait for her to say more, but she does not.

"I'll make sure he calls you when we're back."

"Perfect," she says sweetly. "Thank you so much, Halle."

Once we've said goodbye and the call is cut, I shove my phone back into my purse and stare at Addy in total shock. I tell her everything his mom said.

"I'm on your side now," Addy says once I've finished. "That sounds fucking weird."

After Addy's lunch break is over, I feel a lot less anxious. I kill the last hour by talking to my mom on the phone, and right as I finish talking to her, a nurse approaches me. She tells me Reed's in recovery, that it went well, and starts rattling off a huge list of things I need to know to help take care of him. How often he should ice it, when he needs to see the doctor again, how often he should take medicine, what over-the-counter medicine to look for if what he's taking isn't working, and even how often he should be showering.

"I'm sorry." I stop her. "Is there any chance you can write this down for me?"

She smiles warmly and leads me to the nurses' station. "Of course. First ACL tear, huh?"

"Yeah." I laugh. "I was a speech and debate kid in high school. Not many injuries in that. I'm totally in the dark."

"He should know all of this, but it can be a lot for one person to handle. He's lucky he has someone around to help," she says as she scribbles on a pad of paper.

It's not often that I feel like Reed is the one lucky to have me, not the other way around. I twiddle the paper in my hands as I wait for him and let the feeling sink in.

the blueprint
. . .

I'M IN AND OUT OF REED'S ROOM FOR THE NEXT TWO weeks.

Isabel cooks a few meals that I put in his freezer. Addy explains anything I don't understand what's on the paper the nurse gave me. I never go full Nadia and do Reed's laundry, but I tidy up his room whenever I come over, so he doesn't have to move around so much.

One night, while we're sitting on his bed, he admits that he has absolutely no plan for how to make up the in-class work, notes, and assignments he's missed. It takes a lot of restraint to not lecture him.

"How'd you get caught up?" he asks. "You know, earlier in the semester."

"I begged."

"Seriously, though."

"I am being serious. But you probably won't have to beg because you have a doctor's note, and it hasn't been that long."

It takes three hours, but together, the two of us create a realistic timeline for when he can complete assignments when he'll have time to make up exams and quizzes, and potential times for him to go to each professor's office hours. We start referring to it as "The Blueprint."

It's almost two a.m. when we wrap up and Reed drafts emails to his professors regarding The Blueprint.

"I can't email them, it's the middle of the night," he groans.

"Schedule send it," I mumble, my eyes half open as I curl up on his bean bag chair.

"You're a genius."

"No. I just have a lot of experience sending middle-of-the-night panic emails."

I yawn, which makes him yawn too.

"Stay over tonight," he says.

I haven't been staying because I'm worried if I try to fit into his bed, I'll end up hurting his knee. "Only if I can sleep in this bean bag."

"No, get up here. Your back will hurt if stay on that thing all night."

"You know you need to sleep flat, and you can't do that if I'm shoved in there with you."

"The couch then."

"I may as well go back to my own bed."

He dangles his hand off the bed, letting it hand until it reaches mine on the floor, grabbing onto it. "It makes me feel better knowing you're here. Gives me something to look forward to in the morning."

How can I say no to that? Reed sends me off into the living room with spare blankets and the single extra pillow he has. But I hesitate when I realize I'm not the only person out here – Ben is walking Meg out the front door. Interesting she doesn't get to spend the night or doesn't want to.

Once he shuts the door, Ben awkwardly waves at me.

"Meg seems nice," I say, laying the blankets over the couch. "Why don't you ever bring her out with us?"

"You know why."

"Addy already knows about her, so if you're trying to spare her feelings don't bother."

He freezes. "How?"

"Wasn't me. I think you're underestimating how resourceful she is. Do you wanna know what I think?"

"I have a feeling you'd tell me anyway, but sure."

"You don't want Meg around Addy because you don't want her to know you're unavailable? Or you feel bad?"

He doesn't respond and goes to bed after that.

Reed wakes me up in the morning, and I'm surprised to see him without his crutches.

He beams when I comment on it. "Been two weeks. Need to put weight on it eventually."

I sit up, groggy, and watch him methodically pace in front of me, occasionally stretching his leg. "Good."

"Do you want me to make something for breakfast?"

"If you feel up for it."

"It'll be a good way for me to walk a little. I feel fidgety."

"I can tell. You look like a little kid who has to go to the bathroom."

He moseys over to the coffee table that I used as my nightstand, my phone and my laptop, and the list the nurse wrote out for me sitting in a nice, neat pile. Reed picks the paper up and looks it over front and back.

"What's this?"

"I asked the nurse to write everything that you needed down because I knew I'd forget something."

He looks at the paper, then back at me adoringly. "I love you."

Always a nice thing to hear in the morning. "Love you too."

I leave my advising meeting to plan my spring semester with a pamphlet for the London study abroad trip being offered next fall. Julia recommended me for it and told me all of the credits they're offering match up with what I need to take that semester to stay on track — like it lined up perfectly, like it's meant to be.

The idea of going clangs around in my head for the next few days. I would be away from all of my friends, the best and closest friends I've ever made, but I've never left the country before. Studying abroad is something I always told myself I would do in college.

The only people I discuss the choice with are my parents, who encourage me to just do it. My scholarships transfer, so it's not technically any more expensive than a semester here. I can't say what made me decide to be brave and go, just that it felt like a pull in my stomach that wouldn't ease up until I started filling out the paperwork.

I usually agonize over my choices, and still end up making the wrong ones. Why make myself miserable over this? I want to go. I want to see a sliver of life outside of this small campus that cares about lacrosse parties and articles in the school paper.

I'm going to London next year. I'll figure out how to tell everyone later.

door's unlocked

. . .

I HAVE A HALF HOUR LEFT UNTIL MY SHIFT IS OVER. IT'S A Saturday, and back in 806, my roommates are waiting for me to rush back so we can all go out together.

I'm honestly dreading it. I'm just not in the mood. But I feel guilty knowing my girls pushed back their fun so I could join after work. If I decided not to go, the late start time would be for nothing.

When I get back to the room, Reed and Ben are already here, drinking beers and listening to Addy and Isabel's latest story. I drop my bag on the counter with a thud and heavy sigh that turns the whole room's attention toward me.

The four of them stare at me, expecting a story, or some other explanation for my dramatics.

"Work sucks," is all I say.

Reed wordlessly crosses to me, rubbing my back as I lean against the counter.

Isabel gags. "You two are getting grossly domestic."

I don't have the energy to retort.

"Where are Nadia and Mic?" I ask.

"In the boy's room, no surprise there," Addy responds.

She's right, it isn't a surprise. All Nadia does anymore is hang out with Teddy. Recently, she's been bringing Mic with her to Luke and Teddy's room. I don't know what Mic does while Teddy and Nadia are fucking, or doing whatever they do, but I've never asked. I don't complain about them being gone, it's better than Teddy and Nadia hanging out here.

"Hey," Ben says sternly between sips of the bottle in his hand. "I thought Reed and I were your boys…I thought we were *'the boys,'* not those idiots."

"Yeah, what the hell!" Reed tries to agree sincerely but can't get through it without laughing.

Isabel rolls her eyes. "I'm not entertaining this," she says before she turns to me. "Hal Pal, please go get ready so we can leave."

"Are Nadia and Mic not coming?" I ask.

"They are," Isabel says. "But they're already slow enough. If we have to wait for them *and* wait for you to get ready…we won't leave this room until midnight."

"Fine." I groan. I push off the counter and lug myself to my bedroom, pulling Reed behind me, which elicits whistles and catcalls from our friends.

Reed shuts the door behind us, leaving us alone for the first time all day. It feels like it's been years. I kiss him quickly, just to get it out of my system, and he pulls me back into him by the back of my head into a deeper kiss.

"You know," he says lowly. "We've never had sex in your bed."

"Because I share a bedroom with Addy, dumbass." I offer him one last peck before detaching myself from his arms and going to my closet, pulling out the same blue skirt and shirt I wear every other weekend. I strip and pull the set on, and when I look back at Reed, he has a very specific look in his eyes. Those are sex eyes, for sure.

But I have things to do – makeup to put on and hair to curl. I don't have time for a quickie. I brush him off when he tries to kiss my neck and sit at my desk. I pull my makeup bag out of the drawer, and put my laptop on the ground, fully converting my desk to a vanity. I brush on my foundation, but even after two coats, I still look beat. I somehow look more tired than I feel.

Reed settles on my bed, watching me intently while I do my makeup. When my routine is completed, I still look tired. It's just one of those nights. I don't feel cute. I don't feel like going out. I'm wiped.

I wish going out with my friends didn't make me so anxious. It happens to me often. Usually, I'm able to power through it, and I end up having fun. Not tonight. I have a pit at the bottom of my stomach like something terrible will happen if I leave this dorm room. But it's impossible to distinguish intuition from just being anxious.

"How do I look?" I ask Reed, forcing a thick, fake smile.

"You look beautiful," he replies quickly, but not so quickly that I think he's lying. More like he's very sure.

Frustrated, only with myself, I start aggressively throwing my makeup back into its bag.

"Thanks. I don't feel it."

Immediately sensing my bad mood, Reed jumps up from the bed and stands next to my desk chair. "What's up with you? You never talk about yourself like this."

I shrug. "Bad day at work. I just want to eat and sleep."

Reed brushes my hair off my shoulders and leaves his hands lingering at the base of my neck. "We could stay in," he says, knowingly tempting my introverted side. "We don't have to go out."

"I already told them we would."

"So? Who gives a fuck?"

I shrug his hands off my shoulders and smirk. "You just wanna have sex in my bed tonight."

"I have many motives. I'm a very complicated man."

I laugh, feeling a little bit better about my life than I did a minute ago, and thinking that maybe I can handle a night out. Reed will be there, after all.

"I'm just being dramatic. We should go."

Reed shakes his head at me like he can't believe what he's hearing. "You were at work all night. I think everyone would understand." He pauses for a while, before saying, "I'm not trying to be the type of bad boyfriend who tells you not to hang out with your friends, but I realize that's how this is coming across."

I finish clearing my desk and stand, putting my hand on his shoulder to hold my balance as I slide my first shoe on, then my second. In my chunky heels, I almost match his height.

"We need to go," I say. "I owe it to them."

He rolls his eyes but gives up the argument. We both already know how the other feels, why drag it out? Reed knows I don't like to let down my friends, and I know that Reed doesn't understand why I do things for my friends.

We re-enter the kitchen as Isabel puts her pregame playlist on, and we all stand around the counters chatting and telling stories. I actually feel relaxed. Maybe tonight will be okay.

Until Nadia comes in, with Michaela trailing behind her. Nadia's in a very bad mood, and I think she might already be drunk.

She screams at us for a solid five minutes, and we're all so stunned that we just let her. She says we're jealous we don't have a boyfriend as cool as hers, that we're jealous she has more friends, that we're jealous she gets better grades than us even though she doesn't go to class.

It goes on for a while until Addy bravely interrupts.

"If you're mad at us, does this mean you're not coming out with us tonight?" she asks.

Nadia rolls her eyes. "Obviously, I'm still coming."

Dear God, I cannot be in the same room with her tonight.

I lean into Reed's shoulder, close enough so that I'm sure no one else hears me, and ask, "Does offer to stay in still stand?"

"Yes ma'am," he whispers quickly.

"Consider it taken."

He laughs, in an obnoxious *'look at me I'm so great, I won and I'm right all the time'* way, so I lightly push him before I walk away, which only makes him laugh harder.

I catch Addy's attention in the kitchen as she pours herself another vodka Diet Coke and I tap her arm.

"Hey, I think Reed and I are gonna stay in tonight instead."

Addy wiggles her eyebrows. "Sexy. Try not to break the bed. The school will make you pay for a new one."

"We're just ordering food and then passing out. This is not a sex thing."

"Keep telling yourself that." She mixes her drink with her finger and takes a gulp. "Oh, Luke is stopping by to pick up his laptop that he left here, I told him we'd leave the door propped open since we'd be gone."

The group leaves not long after, and I tell everyone that isn't Addy that I've developed an onset migraine so I can't go out anymore and I'm just so bummed about it.

I'll never tell Addy, but me and Reed staying in very quickly does turn into a sex thing.

It starts as a way to entertain ourselves in the time

while waiting for our Chinese food to arrive. Reed doesn't even wait for me to change out of my skirt, pushing it up before I can even offer to take it off. Then again, after we eat, we're watching sitcom reruns on my laptop in bed, and he kisses me, and I kiss him, and it progresses from there, naturally.

It's exhausting. We're in bed before midnight.

It's hard to get a full night of sleep with two people in a Twin XL bed. But, it's not the bed keeping me awake right now, it feels like anxiety. Like the anxiety I usually get before going out with my friends, the whole reason I stayed in tonight, won't go away. I toss and turn, and I know Reed's awake too by the way he's breathing.

"I can't sleep," I tell him.

"I didn't wear you out well enough?" Reed smirks, tickling my hip under the comforter.

"No, not like *that*." I laugh. "I am well worn out on that front."

Reed yawns. "Whatcha thinking about then? Something wrong?"

I can hear it in his voice that he's about to fall asleep. I feel bad keeping him awake any longer, trying to explain my bad gut feeling that I can't even put into words.

So I don't bother explaining, all I say is, "It's nothing. I think I'm just worried about my roommates being out without me."

I don't think he even hears me, as I feel his breath and his heart slow from where my head is against his chest. I finally feel sleep washing over me, I'm in that weird state of limbo, when what sounds like the front door opening wakes me up.

I panic for a second before remembering it's just Luke, like Addy said. The bedroom door is closed so I'm not worried about him seeing us and making some stupid comment, so I shut my eyes. Before the door sounds like it's been opened and shut and opened again.

I feel Reed sit up as he moves out from under me, before I see it in the darkness of the room, only a line of streetlights coming through the blinds.

"You heard that, right?" he asks.

"It's just Luke." I try to pull him back down to me and feel his immediate resistance. "Addy left the door unlocked so he could pick something up."

He huffs and puffs, and I'm wondering if I should've told him that it was a burglary instead. He would've reacted better than me telling him Luke is moseying around in my dorm. I'm gonna have to hear about this all week.

On the other side of the door, the sounds of scuffling and drawers opening get louder, but I ignore it. There's an undefinable thud that I blame on our ice maker. The door sounds like it's opening and closing again, and for a second I think it might be Tori. Sometimes, when she sees our door propped open, she'll poke her head in to make sure we're in the room and close it if we've accidentally left it open.

"He's being really loud. How long does it take to grab something, seriously." Reed scoffs, still sitting straight up, on high alert.

"He's probably drunk and doesn't know where Addy put it." I try pulling him down again and am unsuccessful. "Please. Let's sleep."

"The last thing this room needs is drunk Luke walking in and accidentally trashing the place," he says sharply. "You need to tell Addy to stop leaving the door unlocked all the time and if you don't, I will. I don't want you sleeping in an unlocked apartment. It's not safe. I mean, how would you feel if I were-"

"Reed." I sit up and grip his arm in one final plea. "Calm down. I'll talk to Addy in the morning."

Before either of us can say anything else, there's another weird thud and the sound of two voices. Two guys for sure. Definitely not Tori. Reed looks at me, and even with the dim light, I can make out his stern expression. Oh no. Luke has just unleashed a pissed-off version of Reed that I don't see very often. I would find it attractive if I wasn't so tired.

"Luke brought a friend. That's not that big of a deal, right?" I offer.

Reed doesn't respond at first, shaking his head at me as he climbs out of bed, all tense like he's ready to barge out my bedroom door.

More noises from the kitchen sink through the door, the definite sound of something breaking over and over again and laughing.

"I'm going to go tell Luke and his friend to shut the fuck up and get out because we're sleeping. Stay here."

"Stay here? This is *my* dorm he's fucking with. Who do you think I am?"

"My girlfriend who doesn't wanna get out of bed," he says, mocking my tone.

Well, now it's a challenge. I climb out of bed and join him by the door.

"If you're coming with me you have to put on pants," he protests, gesturing to tonight's pajamas, a big t-shirt and underwear.

"You're only wearing boxers!"

"I'm a guy!"

"This whole thing is so ridiculous." I groan. "It's not like we're in a haunted house or something, it's just Luke. Tell him to shut up, and then come back to bed."

Reed smirks. "So now you want me to go out and talk to him?"

"Yes." I resign. "Strong, honorable, brave boyfriend, go tell the idiot man to leave the room so your sweet, innocent, perfect girlfriend can sleep… Better?"

"Much," he says, kissing the top of my head before opening the door.

After he leaves, I linger close to the doorway, hoping to eavesdrop on the confrontation, which starts quicker than I thought it would. Almost immediately after leaving my bedroom, I hear Reed yell, "What the fuck?"

It's frantic and angry, a response that I immediately know is not elicited by seeing Luke look for a laptop. My stomach twists until it feels inside out. Something's wrong.

All I can see is Reed's back, which is blocking my view of whatever he's looking at in the living room. I approach slowly, tapping Reed on the shoulder so my presence doesn't startle him. It has the opposite effect, he jumps and turns around.

"Go back into the bedroom," he says quickly before turning back around.

I'm frozen to my spot, totally baffled. Reed shifts so I can see what he was blocking before, but doesn't let me get in front of him, making it very clear to whoever is in the kitchen that this interaction was going to take place between them and Reed, not me.

Luke is behind the kitchen counter with a nervous expression. Aaron is next to him. In front of him, next to the counter, is a pile of shattered ceramic. They both seem drunk – the wild-eyed, party kind of drunk. I struggle to piece together what I'm looking at. Luke let Aaron in so he could trash our kitchen?

"You," Reed says, pointing to Aaron. "Get the fuck out."

Aaron, totally dazed, runs out of the room like he's being chased. Reed properly shuts the door so that it locks behind him.

Then, he walks towards Luke. "You. Stay the fuck here."

He rushes past me towards the hall closet and comes back out holding our only broom. He throws it at Luke, who barely catches it.

"I'm sorry-" Luke starts before he's cut off.

"Clean it up."

To his credit, Luke cleans it. He walks over to the other side of the kitchen and slowly starts sweeping the broken dishes into a cohesive heap. It's hard to watch.

"We didn't know anyone would be home," he says, once he's almost done. "Aaron had asked me a while ago if he knew where you lived, he never told me why he wanted to know."

"But you know he doesn't like Halle," Reed yells, a stark contrast to Luke's embarrassed whisper. "Yet you still brought him over here. If hadn't been home to stop it, would you have let him break every dish in the kitchen?"

"I'm sorry dude. I didn't know." He stares at the two of us, then at his pile of broken ceramic on the floor. "Do you have like, a dustpan?"

"I didn't see one in the closet." Reed shrugs.

Both boys turn to me, which I guess makes sense because I'm the one who lives here, but I'm just as lost as they are. "Isabel's the only one who's ever swept. I have no clue where it would be."

Luke leaves unceremoniously, leaning the broom against the fridge.

The door shuts behind him with a final thud. Reed and I are alone again.

"I hope I never see that guy again," he says.

Door's Unlocked

It all hits me at once, I feel myself tremble, and my eyes water. I have no idea where it came from. I wish I could explain it. It feels like the entire day's just caught up with me. Reed's suddenly next to me like he noticed I was about to start crying before I even did, pulling me into him.

"It's okay." He tries to calm me down with the exact words I used on him a minute ago, but it's not working. "Shh, calm down. We're okay."

I push off him. It's suddenly all too much. I need to distract myself. I need something to do. I need a task.

"I think I'm gonna make tea," I tell him. "Do you want some?"

"Hal," he says gently, looking at me in total confusion. I get it, I'm confused too.

I take his hand in my own and kiss his palm. "I'll make enough for both of us."

drunk girls

· · ·

I STAND BY THE STOVE AS REED SITS BY THE KITCHEN counter. He glances at the pile of broken ceramic in the corner of the kitchen, which draws my attention to it. We both stare at the heap for what feels like forever, until the kettle screams, knocking us both abruptly out of our daze and back to the present.

"I'll buy you new plates," he says half-heartedly as I turn away from him to take the kettle off the stove.

I shrug him off. "You don't have to." I grab two mugs from the highest shelf on the cabinet for our tea. A mug with my high school's mascot on it for me, a mug with a Jane Austen quote on it for him. Thank God Aaron didn't go for the mugs. I probably would've started crying. Steam rolls off the tea as I pour. "The girls will pitch in and we'll go pick out new ones together."

I slide the mug over to him, and he barely acknowledges it, choosing instead to glare at me. "Really, you should be asking Aaron and Luke for the money. And now, every time you look at the new plates you'll think of-"

Reed's rant is cut short by the loud sound of the front

door opening, making us both jump and turn to our tea, sipping it so that we look cool and collected, like we weren't just on the verge of an argument. The first sip burns my tongue. It's scalding. Plus, it doesn't taste as good as the tea Isabel brews. How is that possible? I used the same goddamn type of tea.

An obviously intoxicated Nadia struts into the room, followed by a stark sober Teddy. He's carrying her heels as she stumbles to the stool next to Reed.

When Nadia pulls her foot up to her lap to examine a blister, her sole is so dirty it's black. She heaves a big drunk girl sigh and rests her head on the cool granite. She almost hits Reed's mug, which he not so subtly moves away from her to the other side of himself. Teddy examines the whole scene with extreme annoyance.

"She had a lot of *fun* tonight, as you can tell," he says to us both, before shifting to address Reed specifically. "I'm sure you've had to do this whole routine with Halle before, right?"

Reed and I stare at each other, both trying to gauge what Teddy's getting at.

Reed turns back to Teddy stiffly. "Not really, no," he says casually. He doesn't elaborate.

Teddy, looking freshly uncomfortable, helps Nadia pick her head up from the counter and leads her to her bedroom slowly, passing the broken plates on their way.

"Why's all this here?" she slurs.

I shrug at her and smile. "Accident."

My answer must be satisfactory, as she leans back into Teddy, and they make it the rest of the way to her bedroom door.

Once it shuts, Reed says, "I'm buying you new plates. End of discussion."

He sips from the mug but keeps his eyes on me until

I nod.

"Yeah, okay," I say. "New dishes would be great."

I settle onto the stool next to him, and we sit in comfortable silence, refilling our mugs from the kettle as needed until it's emptied. I like that my boyfriend will have a cup of tea with me and not force conversation, just listen to the creak and moans of the ice maker together. I like that this is something we would've *never* been able to do freshman year. During freshman year, we were so excited to get to know each other, we never shut up.

Our comfortable silence ends the second we hear clamorous, out-of-pocket sex noises from Nadia's bedroom.

Reed laughs, and I know I should be laughing with him, but I can't. All I can think about is how drunk Nadia was when she came in, *way* too drunk to be having sex, even if it is with her boyfriend. It makes me think less of Teddy. It reminds me of myself last year.

Before I can even form an opinion on the situation, Teddy sprints out of the bedroom, uttering a quick and nearly incomprehensible goodbye to us as he leaves, the front door slamming behind him. Weird. I wonder what happened. They didn't sound like they were fighting.

I hear Nadia's bathroom door shut, the shower turn on, and her crying. If I were her, I would appreciate being checked on, so I knock on the bathroom door. I knock once and get no response.

I knock again, and say, "Nadia, it's Halle. Just checking to see if you need anything."

I hear her take a deep breath in between sobs. "Halle? Can you come in?"

I tug at the doorknob, surprised that the door's unlocked. But if I was upset and drunk and wanted a shower, I wouldn't think to lock the door either. Her crying is much louder now that the door's not blocking the sound.

"What do you need? Do you wanna talk about why you're upset?"

I try to ask the questions delicately. I've been Nadia before. I've been the drunk girl crying in the shower. Being direct with her is the best way to avoid sounding too patronizing or impatient.

Nadia pulls back the shower curtain meekly from where she sits on the floor, looking up at me with big eyes, mascara, and glittery eye shadow running down her cheeks. She breaks out into a new sob.

I feel weird seeing her so naked, even though she invited me in here. I sit down at her eye level on the cold tile, so the ledge of the bathtub acts as a privacy barrier between us. She leans over the ledge and stares at me.

"What's wrong?" I ask.

She gives me a half-shrug. "I think I love Teddy more than he loves me."

I have no idea what to say to her right now.

"What makes you think that?"

Nadia wipes her nose. "I feel like he only cares about the physical stuff anymore."

It's only after she tells me this that I notice the very faint trail of blood in the water, swirling down the drain and disappearing. She keeps talking, but I'm not listening anymore. I feel like I'm gonna be sick.

I think about last year, waking up on a Sunday morning in January to find out I had sex I didn't remember. Being so hungover I could barely see. Going to the bathroom and seeing the toilet paper I used stained red. Crying quietly in the shower so Addy wouldn't hear. I might puke.

I'm able to compartmentalize for Nadia's sake and talk her through her breakdown until her words become incoherent. She's inebriated. I don't know how much of this she'll remember.

I help her take off her makeup. She lets me brush her wet, slightly matted hair and braid it. I pull a pair of pajamas from her dresser and check to see if Teddy's drawer of illegal goods is still in Nadia's room. It is, and it has grown. There are at least seven or eight pill bottles, and I don't feel like sifting through them to see what they are. Teddy is such a dick for dragging Nadia into his nonsense.

Nadia dries herself off on shaky legs, puts the pajamas on, and gets into bed. I ask her if she needs anything and she tells me no, but I put a bottle of water and painkillers on her nightstand anyway.

When I finally make it back into the kitchen, Reed is leaning against the counter, staring at me with his arms crossed.

"Everything okay?" he asks quickly.

"I don't know." I shrug. "I think they were having sex and he did something she didn't want to do or said something to upset her. I didn't press for details."

"What makes you think it was something with sex?"

I swallow and try to keep my composure. "There was blood, um, going down the drain. I don't know what it was from, I didn't ask her about it."

"She okay?"

"I don't know. She's asleep now."

Reed stares at me, expecting more to the story. But I don't have any more to say.

"You okay?" he asks after a while.

"Yeah," I respond, not sure why he's asking. I move to

the sink, bring our mugs from earlier with me, and start washing the dirty cups.

"I think you should talk to Nadia," he says.

My back is to him, but I don't turn around. I talk over the sound of the water running.

"I *did* talk to her."

"No, like in the morning. Maybe you can help her," he says slowly.

"I can't help her."

"I think it's worth a try." I hear Reed sigh behind me. "You said she's been drinking a lot, and that she's been skipping classes, and not acting like herself. And she just had sex that she was way too drunk to have… Sound like anyone we know?"

I do turn around this time, dropping the cup back into the sink. Reed's looking at me nervously, like he's anticipating an argument. I don't have any response, good or bad. He's not wrong. The parallels are obvious. I don't have any advice for her, though. I can't give her a step-by-step way to pull herself out of the hole because I don't even know how I did it for myself. Luck, I guess, combined with hitting rock bottom. I doubt I'd be any help.

"We're not that close," I say.

Reed nods wordlessly as I turn back to the sink. I hand wash the rest of the cups, dry them, and put them all away. Reed sits down on a stool and watches me. When I'm done, I plop onto the counter in front of him. I don't usually sit on the counter. Isabel tells me it's too uncivil for the "vibe" of our room. So it's a good thing Isabel isn't here right now.

Reed's fidgeting with his cuticles.

"Did you ever try to talk about that night? You know… uh, January last year?" he asks casually. It's not a very casual question.

"To you? No."

Reed shakes his head. "To anyone. Addy, Isabel, your mom, a professional, I don't know. Just wondering if you ever talked about it. And if you never did, you might still want to, ya know?"

"It's in the past. It was one night. I got blackout drunk and had sex because I was stupid. That's the whole story."

Reed looks at me sternly. "Halle, you don't drink because of that night. Do not try to tell me it's in the past."

"That's not true! There're other reasons I don't drink. Besides, I'm not like a recovering alcoholic or something. I'm just distancing myself from college drinking culture."

Reed's stone-set face is unconvinced. "Sure."

"It's not like I never want to drink again," I yell, face flushing. Arguing with Reed can feel like this sometimes, like I'm playing soccer with him. He's good at playing offense and defense, in real life and on the field. And I'm bad at both. "I wish I had a better relationship with alcohol. I would love to go out and drink with my friends without having a panic attack."

"Well, why does drinking make you feel like you're gonna have a panic attack?"

I shrug. "It makes me think of…Fine. Point taken."

Reed nods, some of the tension leaving him and his face lightening up a little. I can still see some of the intensity in his eyes though.

"As long as I'm around, I swear nothing like that will ever happen again," he says, "and I plan on being around you for a very long time."

I can't stop myself from giving him a quick kiss. Isn't that the most romantic thing a person can say? To say: I got you, you're safe with me?

"Next time we're out together," I tell him. "Maybe I'll try getting a little drunk. Just a little."

"If you think that'll help."

Before I can respond, the door opens and Addy, Isabel, and Mic walk into the room. I stop them before they can get too far.

"Be careful, there're some broken plates over by the dishwasher. I don't want anyone to cut themselves."

The girls stare, concerned.

"What happened?" Addy asks.

"Your buddy Luke brought Aaron over and he decided to break all of the plates in your dishwasher to get back at Halle for her article. They didn't know anyone was here."

"Oh."

We all stare at each other, no one knowing what to say. Isabel breaks the silence, catching me and Reed up on all the things that happened at the bar tonight while Addy awkwardly shuffles to our bedroom. Even though everyone is laughing at Isabel's stories, there's a cloud hanging over the room. Eventually, we all go to bed.

Reed wakes up and leaves around 7 the next morning so we can both get a few hours of sleep in our own beds. I don't wake up again until 11 when the voices in the kitchen and seeing that Addy's no longer in her bed tell me my roommates are up.

They're all out here, except for Nadia, crafting a large and greasy breakfast.

"Good morning, Hal Pal," Addy says, frying an egg. "How'd you sleep?"

"Dandy," I tell her, reaching for a mug.

Nadia comes out of her bedroom, looking more than hungover. I'm not sure she even remembers last night.

Isabel smirks at her innocently. "How are you, lover girl?" She turns to me as she explains. "This one and Teddy were *all over* each other last night. You know, Teddy's kind of growing on me."

Nadia looks like she wants to fold into herself. She walks across the kitchen, squeezing my hand discretely under the counter when she passes me. I interpret it as both a thank you and a plea not to tell them about what the two of us talked about last night.

the rough draft
. . .

On Thursday morning, Addy leaves for the weekend to attend her cousin's wedding. Missing her is like what I imagine missing a limb would feel like. I don't have to scoot past her doing her hair before class to grab my medicine from the bathroom counter. She's not sitting at her desk, eager to hear me complain about my noon class when I get back. To fill the hole, I work on formatting pages for the magazine until it's time to go to my three o'clock International Affairs lecture.

I settle into my seat like normal, until I notice everyone around me has stapled stacks of paper in front of them.

"Was something due today?" I ask the junior I sit next to. There's no way I would miss a due date. My planner is color coded, *and* I have reminders on my phone for every assignment listed in the syllabus.

She nods. "Rough draft."

Shit. Shit. Fuck. I feel an onset migraine developing. How did I miss this? Turning in our rough drafts are worth fifteen percent of our final grade. I slyly grab my backpack and leave while the girl next to me is distracted asking around for a stapler, and leave the classroom. I don't think I can ever go back. I'm hyperventilating as I walk back to Prez, finally making it back to my room. No one else is home.

I cry for longer than I'd like to admit. Why do I do this to myself? I was doing so well, finally, and I just fucked it all up again. Something is seriously wrong with me. I decide that a nap will make me feel better and fall asleep holding Betty the dog on top of my comforter, my coat still on.

―――

I wake up from my nap to a hand on my cheek. Reed.

"Hey freckles," he says with a lovely smile. "I came by because we were supposed to go to the caf but you were asleep."

Guilt washes over me. I reach over to check the time on my alarm clock. It's almost seven, Reed and I were supposed to get dinner together at five.

"Why didn't you wake me up earlier?"

"I wanted to let you sleep."

I finally sit up and try to rub the nap from my eyes. It didn't help like I thought it would. I still feel like crying.

"I'm really sorry," I tell him.

Reed shakes his head and examines every inch of my face. "What's wrong?"

Damn him for noticing.

"I forgot about a rough draft of an essay I had due in my International Affairs class and felt so horrible about it that I started crying. So I just left class without saying anything to my professor."

He doesn't look as shocked as I thought he would,

which almost makes me feel worse. Typical Halle — watching her screw up a deadline isn't even surprising.

"Shit happens," he says casually.

"Not shit like this! I was finally getting back on track with school, then this happens."

"Hal," he tries to soothe me. "Forgetting about one deadline does not erase all of the hard work you've done this semester. And I promise you if you email your professor, I bet you can still turn the draft in for full credit."

"That doesn't make me feel better."

"Fine. W-W-A-D?" he asks.

"Pardon?"

"*What-Would-Addy-Do*, duh. How would she get you out of your rut?"

I laugh, cackle. "I don't know. Probably make me go to the eight o'clock Pilates class with her."

He stands up from my bed. "Done. Get changed so we can go."

I'm still laughing. "*We?* You're joking."

Reed shrugs. "I've always wanted to try Pilates."

"You so have not."

"Well, maybe not, but if it's what it takes to get your depressed ass out of bed, I'll do it." I scoff and he laughs. "Change and meet me in my room. If you fall asleep again, I swear I'll shake awake you this time."

WE GO TO PILATES CLASS, AND I TRY NOT TO MIND THAT all of the girls are staring at the hot guy in a soccer t-shirt who magically appeared in class today. My only relief is that Reed doesn't bat an eye at any of them. He stumbles during every balance exercise and stares at me in amazement as I breeze through the class. He takes the time to thank our instructor, a grad student who's been teaching this class ever since Addy and I started attending freshman year.

"What now?" he asks.

"Addy and I usually walk a mile on the indoor track and just talk about our days and stuff. But we don't have to do that if you don't want to."

"I'm down."

We walk the track at a leisurely pace, and he doesn't force me to talk about my International Affairs disaster. He talks about the David Lynch film he watched with Ben the other night that he wants to show me. I tell him about the paper I just turned in on *Macbeth* that I'm proud of.

By the time we get back to my room, I'm tired. Drowsy, the way you get when you're a kid and you're so tired you fall asleep at the dinner table in some fancy restaurant on vacation – comfortable and feeling safe enough to rest after a long day.

I collapse on my bed, expecting Reed to join me. But he doesn't, sitting at my desk and opening my laptop instead.

"What's your password?" he asks.

"Seven seven seven seven."

"That's a lame password," he responds, typing.

"Bite me." I sit up with my back to my headboard to watch him furrow his brows at my laptop screen. "What are you even doing?"

"Drafting an email you can send to your International Affairs prof."

Sometimes, Reed's practical kindness almost makes me embarrassed. "You don't have to do that."

He shrugs. "You did it for me."

"What?"

"When I had surgery. You helped me figure out all of my extensions and deadlines."

"That was different. You were hurt."

He looks at me like I'm missing something. "Would you just let me help you?"

I back off and let him type away at my desk uninterrupted. After a couple of minutes, he unplugs my laptop and brings it to me on the bed. "Read that and change anything that doesn't sound like you."

He honestly did a pretty job impersonating me via email – one too many exclamation points, a lot of "sorry" and a casual sign-off. It makes me wonder if I could impersonate him that well. I add some missing information and sent it to my professor.

"I still feel bad I made us miss dinner."

It's almost ten, the caf closes at eight-thirty.

Reed grins mischievously. "Good thing Ross Cafe and Diner is open until midnight on Thursdays."

"What would I do without you?"

We laugh together as we walk to his car, but I mean it.

gas station tequila

. . .

Reed and I's first major fight as boyfriend and girlfriend happens on Friday.

We're in the caf, eating a late lunch, when he tells me he wants to quit soccer.

"Don't be stupid," I tell him in between bites. "You don't wanna quit soccer."

"Yes, I do." He's frustrated with me; I can tell by the way he's playing with his food. "It takes up too much time. I'm burnt out. I'm injured, so I'm out for the rest of the season anyway."

"So?"

He's never complained about soccer to me before, he loves it. He isn't planning on going pro after we graduate or anything, but it'll always be his outlet.

"I don't know, just sucks that's all." He shrugs.

"But you aren't going to quit over it."

"I might. I just feel like you should be a little more supportive," he says.

I'm suddenly not very hungry anymore. "I'm not being *unsupportive*. If I told you I wanted to quit my job, you would say the same things I'm saying to you right now."

"Actually," he says slowly, testing the waters. I look at him skeptically with narrowed eyes, daring him to go on. "I think you *should* quit your job."

"You think I should quit my job?" I'm mad now.

"I do," he says smugly. "They over-schedule you, under-pay you, and you're always stressed out about it. There is no reason for you to stress that much about a hostess job, it's not the ER. And that's because your boss has created this environment where-"

"What is this about, you don't want me to work so I can spend more time with you?"

"I don't care if you work or not, I just think that you could find a job that respects you a little more," Reed says.

I set my fork on the plate, but it comes off a little more hostile than I mean it to.

"I don't know what answer you're looking for out of all this, but you know I would never tell you to quit soccer," I tell him plainly.

"Forget it, I don't know why I thought you'd understand."

"Reed-"

"Forget it."

Neither of us finishes our food.

―――

THE TENSION LASTS ALL DAY. WE BARELY TALK. THE PLANS we had made for Reed to come out with me and my friends turns into a text from him that reads: ***going to a club downtown with the team, me and Ben will still pregame at your place if you want.***

I scoff when I read it. *If you want*? I'm going to kill him.

Luke and Teddy arrive at the pregame with their own packs of beer, setting it on our kitchen table before joining the rest of us in the living room. I didn't know they were invited. Teddy attaches himself to Nadia and they start cuddling and kissing on the couch. I nearly turn to share an annoyed glance with Reed, before remembering he isn't here. And even if he was, who knows if he would be in the mood to silently judge my roommates with me. I guess we're officially in a fight. It's disorienting.

Ben and Reed arrive shortly after, bringing the pizza I forgot I had asked Reed to order earlier in the day, prefight. They greet the room warmly, but when Reed sees Luke, his face immediately drops. His jaw tenses and his back straightens. This might be a problem. Reed and Luke haven't been in the same room since he and Aaron broke in last week.

Reed walks toward the living room and stands over Luke who had been sitting on the edge of our coffee table, and for a moment I think having these two in the same room is going to be a very big problem. But Reed never says anything snarky to Luke. He avoids him entirely.

Isabel and Addy hang their upper bodies out of the kitchen window and smoke a blunt, while Michaela and Nadia take shots of the cheap gas station tequila Addy bought last week. When they offer me one, I surprise myself by taking it. It's just *one* shot to help me shake off this fight with Reed. He's the one who told me I should give drinking a try again. I think he sees me take it, because when I walk back toward the group, he shoots me a confused, but not judging glance. I shrug. He lets it go.

Our worst interaction of the night happens in the kitchen, a little past nine. I think I'm leaning against the counter as I talk to Addy, but it's actually the stove. I accidentally shift in just the right way where my ass turns the knob for the front left burner and before anyone else notices, Reed, who had come into the kitchen for another drink, rushes over and turns the stove off with a quick snap.

"Oh, sorry. I didn't notice," I say shyly, hoping it can help strike up a conversation with him. A conversation that isn't about him quitting soccer, or about Luke.

He just nods, barely making eye contact, and mumbles, "Figured" before opening his beer by knocking it against the counter.

On the other side of the corner, Luke pulls our blender out from a cabinet.

"Margs anyone?" he yells.

"Sure." I shrug. "If you're making them anyway."

Luke laughs mischievously. "Drunk Halle! I like it!"

Luke leaves after two rounds of margaritas, and we all know he's leaving to hang out with Aaron, but no one acknowledges it. Reed and Ben leave shortly after, getting picked up by a senior on the team. Reed barely says bye to me on his way out, settling for a wave. He looks so dumb doing it – he has this weird longing look in his eyes like he isn't allowed to touch me. Like neither of us is ready to forget about our lunchtime argument for thirty seconds to hug goodbye.

When the tequila bottle is empty, plans are made to catch buses to the bar. It's awkward, Teddy being the only guy with us. I wonder if this is how the other girls feel when Reed tags along, I hope it isn't. Teddy and Nadia are in their own little world, and when they do talk to us, it's either about their relationship or to tell some story about this "totally amazing crazy weird" night they had at some party or bar this week. I was already in a bad mood because of Reed, and this is not making me feel any better.

I sulk the whole bus ride, keeping my arms crossed until we finally reach Banks.

The buzz from the shot I took earlier calms me down enough to, shockingly, have a little fun. When Addy says she's ordering a round of shots, I offer to walk to the bar with her and order myself a tequila sunrise.

While we wait at the bar, I see Reed and Ben walk in, half the soccer team with them. I see red. What the hell are they doing here? They collectively seem pretty drunk as they loudly and obnoxiously push together tables and start ordering drinks.

I'm not surprised when Reed pushes through the crowd to stand next to me at the bar, right as the bartender hands me my drink.

"Oh Jesus, here we go," Addy heaves under her breath, taking a large swig of her vodka Diet Coke.

Reed makes himself comfortable, leaning against the bar, before pointing at the drink in my hand with an accusatory finger. "Tonight's the night, huh? Are you planning on getting plastered tonight?"

I scoff. "I don't even wanna know how much you've had to drink tonight."

Reed looks away from me briefly, and when he looks back to meet my eyes again his face is suddenly a little more serious. "I haven't had anything to drink since you started doing shots back at the room and accidentally turned that stupid stove on."

That pisses me off. I can't tell you why, but it does.

"Is this like quitting soccer?" I sneer. "You want my *permission* to drink? You have it."

I leave and Addy follows, looking more confused than I've ever seen her. I chug the drink in my hand and throw it in a trash can before we can even get back to our table.

We don't have a great view of the soccer team from

where we're sitting, but every time I do manage to spot Reed, he has a drink in his hand. I can't tell how drunk he is. Reed gets drunk a fair amount, but if he's ever blacked out, I wasn't around to see it. I sip on a seltzer from the bucket Isabel bought and try to look like I'm having more fun than him.

I would never tell him, but I am glad Reed is here. The drinks I've had tonight are starting to catch up to me, which makes me a little nervous and reminds me of all the reasons I stopped getting drunk. I hate losing control, I hate being sick, I hate doing stupid things, and I hate not remembering my thoughts and actions the next morning. But it is some comfort to know that Reed also knows this about me, and would never let anything happen to me as long as he's in the same bar as me. Even if we're not on very lovey-dovey terms at the moment.

I've forgotten what kind of drunk I am. I'm not a mean drunk, but I am a very stupid one. So, obviously I think the best way to calm my anxiety about being drunk is to order another drink. I just need to be half a level more drunk than I am, and it'll be perfect. Just one more drink will put me exactly where I need to be. I stand at the bar alone, swaying on my feet a little, waiting for a bartender. Someone comes up next to me, and I don't have to look to know it's not Reed. It's Luke.

"What are you doing here? Lacrosse house not trying to roofie girls tonight?"

Luke laughs sarcastically, and very unsuccessfully tries to flag down a bartender before turning back to me. "Let me buy you a drink."

He tries to get the bartender's attention again, but she's too busy with a customer a few feet away. I peer over to see it's *Reed's* order that she's taking. Jesus Christ, I can't get rid of him. He notices me staring and shoots me a cocky smirk that doesn't go away, even when he notices Luke trying to whisper something in my ear about Isabel. I'm not listening to him, I'm watching Reed strut over to us, taking a long, long sip from the bottle in his hand.

He stands next to me, wrapping a casual arm around my waist before kissing my temple and giving Luke a bro-like head nod in greeting. Luke tenses, and the realization slowly dawns that I am about to witness a good old-fashioned pissing match, a classic dick-measuring contest. I have to admit it's fun to watch. I love watching guys get into little tussles, although it feels a little different watching my boyfriend participate in something so primitive and immature. Still, I find it fascinating. Boys say that *we're* bitches, that we're mean and petty when really, they're just as bad.

Reed turns to me warmly, offering the bottle in his hand to me, "You should try this, it's not an IPA, so you'd probably like it."

Nice opening move, Reed, reminding Luke how physically comfortable we are with each other *and* how well you know me in one strike.

I grab the bottle from him and half a sip.

I nod, handing the bottle back to Reed. "I don't hate it."

Reed smiles at me, then looks at Luke, pretending he just now noticed that someone else was around us. Point Reed, for pettiness.

"I was gonna buy the lady a drink, but if you have a problem with that I won't." Luke trails off, waiting for Reed to strike back.

Point Luke, for confidence, I guess.

Reed looks between me and Luke, nodding slowly with a cocky look on his face. If he was anyone else, I would think that he was about to hit him. But I know that's not who Reed is. It makes me nervous, what is he thinking about doing if he's not going to hit him?

Reed leans in closer to Luke, just to be certain he hears whatever he's about to say clearly.

"Buy her all the drinks she wants," he says with little expression. "I'll still be the one leaving with her tonight so… joke's on you."

Whoa. And he has won the dick-measuring contest, in a huge knockout, Reed has defeated Luke. I'm in shock. Reed shrugs and walks away, not waiting around to see his reaction. Luke looks angry, confused, and defeated all at the same time. I give him an apologetic shrug, before catching up to Reed, stopping him before he reaches his table.

"What is wrong with you?" I ask him flatly and loudly, crossing my arms and standing my ground. "You ignore me all night but suddenly when I'm talking to another guy for thirty seconds you decide to act like my boyfriend again?"

"Relax," he says, gently rubbing my arm to try to calm me down, his face still smug. "I was just trying to help you get out of talking to him."

"Help?" I scream, shaking his hand off me. "No, we both know what that was and maybe I'd put up with it any other day, but not tonight when you aren't even talking to me."

Talking takes a lot of air, I feel out of breath and notice that I'm starting to slur my words. I try to walk away but stumble over my ankle. Reed steadies me immediately.

"You're pretty drunk," he says, looking down at me. Any trace of annoyance or smugness is wiped, replaced with the sweetest and utmost concern. It's almost enough to make me forget I'm mad at him. Not enough, though.

"I'm fine." I straighten myself up, but the room spins. "Go hang out with your friends. I'm fine."

"Hal," he protests before I cut him off. I'm a very stubborn drunk. Drunk me thinks accepting help means death by embarrassment.

"I'll see you later."

I leave Reed and he doesn't follow me, though I know if I turned around, I would find him watching me. I try my best to act sober as I walk back to my friends, which takes all of my energy. The walk seems so long.

Why do I feel so drunk? Seriously, did I get drugged or something? It used to take double this amount of alcohol to get me this drunk. The most recent drink I finished isn't gonna truly kick in for another ten minutes, which means I'm about to double how drunk I am. The feeling of impending doom is not making me feel any better.

I have a flashback to earlier in the semester when my roommates took Isabel's Lexapro to lower their tolerance before going out. Oh my god, I realize quickly, I have never been drunk on my meds before. My doctor told me my tolerance would go down, but since I planned on never drinking like this again, I didn't fully process it.

The familiar and unwelcome urge to vomit creeps in. I think I can keep it at bay, at least as long as I get out of here now.

I don't have an exit strategy, I rejoin the table and hope that if I drop enough hints, I can convince someone to come back to campus with me. The only exit strategy I will not consider is asking Reed to leave with me. I know he would, and I know he would be happy to, but I don't like the idea of being the first to cave. I don't want to prove right his suspicion that I need help.

"Are you okay?" Michaela asks once I sit down. "You look really out of it."

"I'm just more drunk than I wanted to be tonight."

"Go pull trig," she says so casually she may as well have said drink a glass of water or something.

"No, I think I need to get out of here, like now," I say.

Hint hint, nudge nudge.

Michaela glances at the rest of the table. Everyone else is having fun. No one else wants to leave.

"Ask Reed to take you home," she says with a shrug. Exit strategy failed. Message received, I am not convincing any of these girls to leave early with me, which is fine. But I am sure as hell not asking Reed to leave with me either.

"It's fine, I'll just call a car."

The entire table objects, telling me I'd be stupid to take a car back to campus alone. Everyone is acting like they're worried about me now, which just annoys me more. It takes some convincing, and a lot of pretending to be less drunk than I am, but I'm finally able to convince them.

"Seriously, I will see you when you get back, and if your plans change just text me."

Isabel stands with me. "I'll come outside with you," she says. "I need a cig anyway."

bruise

. . .

Isabel and I leave out the front doors, and I don't even check to see if Reed notices my exit or where he is.

I open my phone, seeing a text from Reed that I'm too drunk to read. I'm able to successfully call a car, only because it's something so habitual, something I did every Friday and Saturday night of last year, even when I was blacked out. I could do it in my sleep.

Even with the alcohol warming me up, I shiver in the November chill. The distant smell of the sewage makes my stomach turn, reminding me of the primary reason for my escape from the bar. I've put up a good fight, but I realize I'm not gonna make it back to campus vomit-free. I know I'm gonna yack before the car gets here. This is a nice establishment, one that I would feel bad puking directly in front of it, so I duck into the alley next door instead and puke my guts out.

When I pick my head up, Reed is staring at me with his hands in his pockets.

"Too much tequila? You only puke if it's tequila."

He's right, and he knows it, which somehow makes it

worse. All of the drinks I've had are hitting me like a truck right now. I feel like shit.

"Fuck off," I say as I step out of the alley. I see that Isabel is gone and her nearly fresh cigarette is on the sidewalk. I wonder if Reed told her to leave so he could talk to me alone.

Ignoring my rudeness, Reed asks, "You're leaving?"

"Yeah, my ride is about two minutes away. Don't follow, I'm in a bad mood."

"I know. I'm still gonna come with you though," he says. I shoot him a threatening glare, to which he responds, "What? I'm not following you, I just wanna leave too. Call it good timing. You can charge me for half the fare."

He's smirking. This is a trick. He is tricking me into letting him babysit me and take care of me. I am not drunk enough to be tricked.

"No," I tell him flatly.

The car pulls up.

I walk towards it and ignore Reed calling for me. "Halle stop being immature," he says harshly. "You're not going back alone."

The car pulls to a stop, and I fling open the door. Once I'm fully inside the car, I make a show out of dramatically slamming the car door without realizing Reed had put his hand in the way in an attempt to stop me from shutting the door. The door closes on his fingers, crushing them before I have the sense to push the door back open.

He pulls his hand back and tries to shake out his fingers bravely, but he looks like he's really in pain. I can't believe I just did that. I can't believe I just hurt him. I feel like shit, not just from the alcohol now. There's a pit in my stomach growing by the second, and soon it's gonna swallow me whole.

"Reed I'm so sorry," I mumble, almost incoherent as I

try not to cry. "Oh my god. Please get in the car, please I'm so sorry."

Reed stares at me intensely from where he planted. I think he's about to scream at me, but he doesn't. He slowly sits down next to me as I slide over to make room for him in the backseat. He's cradling his fingers delicately as the car finally pulls away from the curb.

"I didn't know you were gonna follow me into the car," I croak after a bout of silence. I'm worried if I speak any louder, I'll cry. I feel an impending breakdown burning behind my nose.

Still feebly nursing his hand, Reed looks at me in disbelief and shakes his head. "If you seriously thought I wasn't right behind you, if you thought I was gonna let you get in this car by yourself… You must not know me as well as I thought you did."

Maybe I don't. Or maybe I do, but I'm drunk. Too drunk to analyze Reed's actions when I've had enough alcohol to barely think about my own. He's right though. I should've known he was behind me. Now, I'm really crying.

I'm not looking at Reed anymore, but I can imagine his annoyed face as I hear him sigh next to me.

"Don't cry," he says without any heart. "I don't want you getting worked up thinking this is your fault."

"It is my fault!" I screech.

Reed doesn't respond. Neither of us says anything until the car drops us off at Prez — when I'm trying to unlock the front door of the building with shaky hands and Reed says, "My fingers will be fine, don't feel bad. They're probably gonna bruise but they'll be fine."

He says it so calmly as if nothing could matter less. I stare at him with my mouth half open. How is he not mad at me? He seems so unattached from all this. So shut down,

I'm worried he's thinking about breaking up with me. Is that why he's not mad at me?

"Jesus Christ, Reed." I snap. "Are you not mad at me?"

He shrugs. "I'm upset but -"

"Act like it then! I don't know if you're trying to guilt-trip me or what, but it worked. I promise you I feel worse about this than I would have if you had just screamed at me."

He has the nerve to roll his eyes at me before casually saying, "I'm mad. *There*. Is that what you wanna hear?"

"No! And don't act like you don't know what I'm talking about. It's like you don't care enough to be mad at me."

Of everything I've said, that's what gives me the reaction I'm looking for.

"What the hell, Halle?" he screams. "Why would yelling at you mean I care about you more? That's fucked up."

"No its not. People get angry because they *care*. Indifferent people don't care, and you seem very indifferent about this."

Reed's pacing now, tugging at the ends of his hair.

"Fine," he spits out. "I'm fucking pissed about this. I'm pissed that I had to chase you around the bar all night. I'm especially pissed that I opened up to you about wanting to quit soccer, something I've been avoiding talking to you about by the way, because I was worried you'd react the exact way you did. Every time *you* make some weird decision, I support you, don't I? Can you not do the same for me? I was just looking for you to say, 'It's okay Reed, it wouldn't matter to me if you quit soccer because I would like you no matter what.' I wasn't *actually* looking for your opinion on that."

He flinches at his own words, but they feel like balm to

me. Constructive criticism feels comforting. We fight and tell each other what we did wrong — that feels normal to me.

But Reed looks like his entire world's been thrown off its axis.

"Halle, I'm so sorry I didn't mean that last part," he says quietly. "Of course, I value your opinion."

He looks at me with an unfamiliar weight, one that doesn't belong in such an innocent argument.

He looks defeated as he rambles on. "I'm sorry, I need some time. Not like breaking up with you time. Just…I'll see you later, okay?"

And then Reed runs, literally sprints, away from the building. I don't have the energy or instinct to chase him. I get the sense that whatever he's freaking out about is something he needs to process on his own. I am also still very intoxicated, and the need to get back to my room and throw up overpowers any thoughts about Reed. But I'm never not thinking about Reed, always. Even when I think I'm not, he pops back up. I'd find it annoying if I didn't like him so much.

Hunched over my toilet, I have no concept of time as I hurl the contents of my stomach. My head throbs, my stomach aches, and I feel the alcohol running through my veins into every part of my body.

I don't realize I'd forgotten to lock our door until I hear it open and close. I involuntarily flinch, remembering the last time someone came into 806 unannounced, but relax when I see it's Reed. He doesn't look any different from the last time I saw him, maybe more solemn. I expect him to say something to me about our fight, or even just to scold me for leaving the door unlocked, but he doesn't. He's silent as he slides onto the bathroom floor next to me. But he ties my hair back into a ponytail and rubs my back until there's nothing left for me to throw up.

Neither of us says a word until I've wiped my mouth and look at him for an explanation. Reed tries to avoid making eye contact, but I follow his gaze as it flits around until he finally gives up.

"If I tell you something, can you promise not to ask me too many questions about it?" he asks slowly, sounding younger than I've ever heard him sound before. "I'll tell you anything you wanna hear about it another time when I'm ready. I'm just tired tonight."

I nod. "Of course."

He avoids my eyes again as he starts talking but this time, I let him.

"I think getting angry makes me nervous," he says quickly. "Because my mom, when I was growing up, always drilled into me that when people get too angry, where they can't control it, they risk hurting someone. She was really, *really* strict about that. So I've always tried to not be that person who was too angry all the time. But that's why I'm so weird about fighting with you, or anyone, and hitting people. Anything like that."

It makes sense but it doesn't. I feel like I'm missing something. But Reed asked me not to press, so I don't.

"I'm sorry," I say.

"For what?"

"Pushing you to fight with me. I would've never if I'd known."

"Not your fault." He smiles sadly. "I never told you."

"But I could have guessed or just figured out that after all this time you've never liked fighting and there must be a reason for that. There're other ways to express feelings besides arguing with each other and-"

Reed shushes me, in a kind way not a condescending

way, and floats his fingers through the ends of my ponytail. "I think you're being too hard on yourself. You're also a little drunk."

"A little?" I laugh. "Try again. I'm starting to think those margaritas Luke was making me were laced or something. But I think it was just my antidepressants."

"Besides that," he says. "How'd it go? Was it better?"

I shake my head. "Something terrible happens every time I drink."

"I'm starting to think that might just be life, babe."

"I can't handle it. I tried, but I can't. Not for a while, at least." My skin feels itchy as I try to look for a way to stop talking about my drinking. "Will you spend the night?"

He nods, and we both wordlessly fall into our usual nighttime routine like nothing's wrong. I change into my pajamas, which are Christmas-printed fleece pants and one of Reed's t-shirts, while he changes into his that he's been keeping in my room for the past week or so. I remove my makeup, and brush my teeth while Reed stands in the bathroom doorway. I go to him and hug him fiercely, a strong grip on his middle, and he kisses the very top of my head.

"Do you wanna go to bed?" he asks me.

"Can we stay up and watch something until everyone gets back? I'm worried my roommates are gonna do something stupid."

"Yeah. I'm gonna grab you water."

I want to argue. I want to tell him that his doing things for me with bruised fingers is getting on my nerves because I should be the one tending to *him*, but it's an argument I know I can't win.

Reed mills about the kitchen, before he joins me on the couch with two glasses of water and an icepack he made for himself out of one of his socks.

I tell him to pick what we watch, and he does, turning on a sitcom rerun, the kind channels only play past eleven o'clock, which is what I would've picked too. I think he knows that. He's sitting up, his thumb is rubbing little figure eights on my forearm as I lean on his chest. I know he's about to fall asleep when his arm starts twitching a little bit, and I know he's asleep when the little figure eights slowly come to a stop.

I plan on staying up until the girls come home, but the last thing I remember is hearing the sitcom's theme song quietly ring through the room. The TV sounds far away.

I wake up when the girls come home around four a.m., without Nadia and Teddy. The bar closes at two.

"Why didn't you text me? Where the hell did you go for two hours?" I whisper.

Reed is still asleep under me, snoring a bit.

"Teddy knows these guys on the club rugby team," Michaela says with a giggle. "So they took us back to the house and invited some of the team over."

"Never again," Addy says.

"Oh please, I already texted that George guy and said we'd be back Friday," Michaela says as she grabs a bottle of water from our fridge. Isabel and Michaela cheer. Addy groans.

Reed wakes up abruptly, sitting up and taking in the scene.

"Everyone make it back alive?" He asks, sleep making his voice sound like a whisper.

"Yep," I answer.

He nods, his eyes barely open as he stands and starts dragging himself toward the bedroom.

"What are you doing?" I ask, following.

"Twin XL sucks, but it beats the couch every time."

international affairs
. . .

THE SOCCER TEAM PLAYING IN THE FIRST ROUND OF THE national playoffs, and Reed is less depressed about it than I thought it would be. At the end of the day, he loves his team more than he loves the thrill or the ego he gets from playing himself.

They host the first game at home, and when Reed asks me to go to the game with him, it's an easy yes. I meet him at the stadium after a study session with some girls in my International Affairs class, trudging up the bleachers with my backpack in tow.

"Hey," I say, smiling as I drop my bag next to his feet. It shakes the whole row.

Reed laughs and picks up my backpack with one hand to measure it and cringes.

"Jesus, what is in there? Did you rob the library?"

"My International Affairs textbooks," I explain. "My prof gave us four different essay prompts and is picking one for the final, but we won't know which until the exam. So I was working on writing essays for each with some girls in my class."

He beams. "Studying for a final before Thanksgiving? Hevko, you're a changed woman."

"Yeah, yeah."

We watch the game together, with occasional comments from Reed on his teammates or explaining why certain plays are considered fouls or not.

"So we get the free kick then?" I ask. "Because the other team had the foul?"

He stares at me, disoriented. "How do you know what a *free kick* is?"

"Believe it or not, I listen to you when you talk about soccer."

He grins and knocks his knee against mine. I've known him long enough to know that translates to *I love you*.

"We need to talk about something," he says during halftime, rubbing his hands together to warm them. "I've been trying to bring it up for a couple of weeks now but keep getting interrupted."

A few months ago, Reed saying that to me would've made me so nervous that I would've broken out into hives. Now it doesn't make me nervous at all.

I have something I wanna talk to him about too — London. I still haven't told him.

"It's actually two things," he adds.

"That's a lot of things," I respond dryly.

He laughs. "Do you have any major plans for winter break?"

I shrug. It's coming up, but I haven't thought about it. "Just going home, I guess. Nothing major."

Reed smiles nervously. "Would you want to come home with me for a few days? You don't have to say yes if you don't want to. Not the whole break obviously, I don't wanna take away from your time with your parents. Plus, I don't think anyone could stand my parents that for long. Just four days or so."

"Yeah!" I don't even think about my answer. This is a better plan than anything I could've come up with on my own.

Reed's nearly blushing as he laughs sweetly at my response. "Okay, then it's a plan now. My parents are gonna be asking for your allergies and grocery list by the end of the day, I swear. They will be so annoying about this."

"I haven't met them yet, so my tolerance will be high don't worry."

He shakes his head. "That will not last very long I promise you."

I grin. "So what was your second thing?"

His face falls a little, not enough to make me worried about what he's going to say, just enough to make him look nervous.

Reed takes a deep breath. "I'm gonna study abroad next fall. I didn't mean to keep it a secret from you, but I didn't sign up until the day of the deadline, and I didn't want to tell you until it was a sure thing."

My jaw literally drops, and I gape at him in complete shock. He opens his mouth to explain himself, obviously flustered or worried I'm mad at him, but I wildly wave my hands at him to get him to stop. I reach into my backpack at my feet and pull out the stack of papers my advisor signed a few hours ago. It's a confirmation of my plans for London to show to the bursar so they can transfer my scholarship for the semester to the study abroad office.

I drop the papers in Reed's hands, and he scans them with a dramatically furrowed brow. I reach up and rub my thumb over the worry lines between his eyes until he relaxes them and smiles at me.

"What are these?" he asks.

"Keep reading." I poke him. "The details are on there somewhere, I swear."

He scans them again, and when he gets to the bottom of the page, he stares at me – a mirrored expression of mine from a moment before.

"You're going to London," he says slowly and softly. "Next fall."

I nod quickly, trying to keep my emotions in check until I can fully gauge his reaction.

Then he finally smiles, a huge grin.

"I'll be at St. Andrews. Scotland. Scotland isn't very far from London. Same time zone. Same nation, technically."

"Scotland, huh?"

"Yeah. Figured I'd spend some time in the homeland. Connect with my ancestors and all that shit."

I laugh at what I interpret to be an obvious joke, but stop when I see he is one hundred percent serious about what he just said. It makes me love him more. My goofball with his totally absurd attachment to his dead distant Jacobite ancestors.

"I'm really happy for you," I tell him.

"I'm happy for the both of us."

Reed explains to me that because of his ACL injury, his coach offered him a fifth year of eligibility that he decided to take. He'll be a red shirt next season, which is how he's able to study abroad. He tells me it's something he's always wanted to do, but never thought was possible because of soccer. He's starting to see the upside of his ACL tear — the opportunities it can give him rather than the season it took away. He tells me it took him a long time to reconcile with missing a soccer season, he hasn't missed one since he was four years old.

His parents are furious he won't be graduating in four

years like every "normal" student, but Reed explained to them that spreading his course load over another three years instead of another two will give him more time to study for the LSAT. They're still mad.

I stare at Reed in total awe as he explains it all to me. I love him so much. I always knew he'd grown as a person in the same ways I have since we met, but I've never seen such a concrete example of it. He speaks so articulately about his choices and his struggles but makes it all seem easy to admit.

I can't get over how crazy it is that Reed and I made the same plan without even consulting each other. We're really on the same page. We were keeping the same secret from each other. It feels like a weird confirmation from the universe that the two of us are gonna turn out just fine.

Still, I try so hard to not put myself in a hole. It's hard not to. I try to think of all the reasons this might not be as perfect as I think it is so I can prepare myself for the possible outcomes.

"You're all tense," he says. "I can practically hear you overthinking, what's up?"

I sigh, trying to keep myself from tearing up. "It's too easy."

Reed looks at me contemplatively before stretching his arm over my shoulder. "So what, did you want it to be hard?"

in the elevator

• • •

EVEN AFTER RETURNING FROM THANKSGIVING BREAK, REED and I have kept up our light workout routine. But today, I'm running late to meet him after class, so I told him to get started without me. I run back to Prez from class to change and grab my headphones in record time.

On my way down, the elevator stops on the sixth floor, just another inconvenience keeping me from seeing Reed as soon as I can.

The doors open to reveal both the last people I expect to see and the absolute last people I want to see – Luke and Aaron. Luke's face immediately pales when he sees me. He takes a step back.

"Hey Halle," he says stiffly. "We can take the next one, it's okay."

I shake my head at him as I notice Aaron holding the door open with his arm. "It's fine, I don't mind. Really."

The last thing I want is a fight with these two. I know if I asked them to take the next elevator, Aaron would say something snarky. I don't feel like having to defend myself to him, I just feel like seeing Reed. And the longer we all stand here, the longer I have to wait.

I nod in confirmation that I'm not lying; it is okay if they both come in the elevator with me and they both step in. Luke hesitantly, Aaron with one long stride. None of us look at each other. I cross my arms and tap my feet as I watch the numbers at the top of the elevator doors slowly go down.

"I still can't believe you said all that stuff about me. It's slander."

The words come unprovoked from Aaron. He sounds proud of himself, like a kindergartner using a big word he learned at school for the first time.

I look at him for the first time, surprised to see he looks more resigned than angry. Like a sad little boy. I don't buy it for a second. I will not be guilt-tripped by Aaron.

"It's not slander if it's true." I shrug, looking away.

Aaron moves toward me quickly, and I barely process the long slur of swears Aaron is saying as he pushes me against the elevator wall. My head hits the metal with a definite thud, and it hurts.

Aaron doesn't look very resigned anymore. I see Luke over his shoulder, staring at the scene with no expression before he backs away to the other side of the elevator.

I think this is the worst of it, until Aaron pushes me again, this time by my hair and straight into the wall, hitting the side of my face against it.

Nothing in my life has ever hurt more. I can't tell if I've blacked out or if I've just closed my eyes. I can still hear Aaron yelling but can't make out what words he's saying. He pushes me back against the wall and I brace for another hit. But it doesn't come.

The elevator doors open with a ding. Aaron is pulled

off of me, and I think maybe Luke finally found a sliver of courage inside him to do the right thing.

"Halle, it's okay. You can open your eyes."

But that's not Luke's voice.

I do open my eyes. It's Tori. She's in the elevator with me. Luke and Aaron are gone. She frantically presses the button for the eighth floor and the elevator starts ascending.

"Do you need to go to the hospital?"

Her words reach me slowly but run together at the same time. All I can manage is to shake my head at her. My head really hurts. Because Aaron just grabbed me and threw me against the elevator wall. That feels like it happened a long time ago now.

"What happened, who were those guys?" she asks.

Of course, Tori wouldn't know who they were. She never knew Luke, let alone Aaron. She wouldn't understand unless I told her the whole story from the beginning, and I do not have the energy for that. I do not want to talk about this. I want to forget this ever happened.

The words in my head finally reach my mouth, but all that comes out is, "I'm fine, Tori."

"Halle," she says in an uncharacteristically gentle tone. "Let me take you back to your room. Or at least let me call Reed for you."

I shake my head. The movement makes me dizzy. I feel like I'm about to black out. Jesus, I need to pull myself together. I can't talk to Reed right now. I don't want Reed to find out about this. The last thing anyone needs to do is drag Reed into this.

"Are you sure you don't need a doctor? You look like you're about to throw up."

"No, I just need to lie down." I try to convince her. "I'm fine. All I did was get hit in the face. I'm not dead."

"Stop," she starts to speak again, but I put up a hand to interrupt her.

"Tori," I say as firmly as I can, though it still comes out shakily. "I just wanna sleep in my bed right now."

The elevator doors open to the eighth floor and Tori has to practically drag me out. When we reach my door, she knocks violently. I hear Addy on the other side yell, "Come in, it's open!"

I imagine she's lying on the couch with Isabel, watching a reality show and reading, Mic is still cooking dinner, and Nadia is on the phone with her mom at the kitchen table — just as they all were when I left the room. I feel a horrible, sinking dread when I realize I'm about to ruin their night. This is an inconvenience to everyone now.

Tori pushes the unlocked door open, and Addy and Isabel both turn their heads to see who just walked in.

Tori leads me to the kitchen table, pulls out a seat from the opposite side Nadia's sitting at, and helps me sit down. I still feel like I can't breathe but sitting helps the dizziness fade. Addy and Isabel are staring at me from the couch. Nadia puts down her phone and stares at me. Michaela stops cutting vegetables and stares at me. No one says anything. Addy turns off the TV.

"Did something happen?" she asks quietly.

Tori tells them what she saw, and she isn't even halfway through her story when all four girls rush to my side. Addy stands beside me, rubbing my back and pulling my hair off my face while Tori talks. Isabel pulls out another chair to face me. Nadia hastily says goodbye to her mom and hangs up her call, and Mic abandons her cooking and sits on the floor next to my chair.

"Two guys did this? *Who?*" Isabel asks, looking to me for an answer, not Tori.

"Luke and Aaron got in the elevator with me. Aaron

said something to me, and I said something stupid back and…"

I can't seem to finish my thoughts. I wish I could pretend I was just telling a story about someone else getting hit in the face to my friends. That this really happened to some other girl that isn't me.

Addy whips out her phone. "I'm calling Luke."

"Don't." Isabel sternly shakes her head, before turning her focus back to me. "Halle I think you need to talk to the police."

Is she crazy? I can barely talk to my best friends about this let alone a police officer. Absolutely not. I just want to forget this ever happened. My mouth feels dry, and I don't have the energy to defend myself. I shake my head. I can tell Isabel is trying her hardest not to show her disagreement as she looks away.

"You should talk to the police," Nadia agrees.

"You could talk to the Title Nine office," Tori adds.

I shake my head again. Does no one get that it would be just as bad? I just want to forget this ever happened and never talk about it again. Addy leaves and comes back to me with a makeshift ice pack, and I feel eternally grateful for our clunky loud ice machine. She tilts my chin up so she can hold the ice pack on my cheekbone for me.

"You're remarkably calm about all of this," Isabel says, looking me up and down.

"She's in shock," Addy responds curtly. "It'll wear off."

We sit in silence for a little while. I finally feel like I can breathe again.

Out of my eye not covered by the ice pack, I register Isabel leaving the room. When she comes back, she's on the phone.

"Hold on Reed, I'm handing the phone to Halle."

Reed? I take the ice off my eye and angrily shake my

head at Isabel. I can't talk to Reed about this. No way. Isabel shoves the phone into my hand anyway.

"Halle?" That is all he has to say to make me burst into tears. He has such a nice voice; he always sounds so kind. I'm really crying, nearly heaving.

Knowing that he now knows what happened is the only thing that can break my bubble. If Reed knows, it's real. This really happened to me. I have to carry the weight of this.

"You're scaring me," he says. "Talk to me, are you hurt?"

No words come out of my mouth. That's enough of an answer for him.

"Fuck, Hal. Okay, I'm on my way over." He pauses. "I need you to tell me you're hearing me, Halle. I need to hear your voice."

I suck in a deep breath as I say, "I'll see you here, yeah."

The silence goes on for so long that I'm about to hang up, until I hear him say, "Hey, I love you. You're gonna be okay. It's gonna be okay."

I'm not sure if he says the last part for me or himself.

The girls don't say anything while we wait for Reed, but they don't leave me. Addy puts the ice pack back on my face once I'm able to dry most of my tears.

Reed runs through the door about ten minutes later.

His hair is matted down with sweat, the same soccer shirt I saw him in earlier today stretched across his shoulders, and his breathing is heavy. He looks a little blurry, and it's not until Reed drops his gym bag to rush to me that I realize he looks blurry because my eyes are filled with tears. I stand and run to him. He meets me and pulls me into him so strongly that he lifts me up. I don't think he's ever held me tighter. I feel him kiss my head once, then twice.

"I'm so sorry." I sob into his chest.

"What?" He pulls himself back so he can clearly see me. "There's nothing to be sorry for, you didn't do anything wrong."

I drop my head, pulling my sobs together, and feel his hands cradle the sides of my head as I shake it. "I just stood there."

He looks so sad. I want to cry again.

Reed speaks to me softly but seriously, "Hey, none of this your fault."

He doesn't know yet that it is. It's my fault for ever letting Aaron and Luke into the elevator. It's my fault for ever writing that stupid article in the first place.

He leads me back to my chair and helps me sit before kneeling in front of me and resting his hands softly on my knees. I'm aware of the presence of my roommates, I can feel their stares, but all I can focus on is Reed.

"Hal, who did this?" he asks darkly, his tone completely switching from the sweet way he just tried to reassure me, into something much heavier. I drop my head, breaking our eye contact. When I don't respond, he presses, "I have a few guesses, but you need to tell me what happened."

His jaw is clenched, shoulders tense. His anger is clear.

I heave deep breaths, in and out, before answering slowly, "I don't wanna talk about it."

Reed exchanges a look with the girls in the room. He looks like he's trying to keep his cool for my sake, but I can tell he's angry. I think he forgets how well I can read him. He softly brushes the spot on my cheekbone where Aaron hit me, and I wince. Reed pulls his hand away quickly like he's just touched a hot stove.

Addy puts the ice pack back onto my cheek, blocking my view of Reed out of one eye.

"Halle," Reed says slowly and heatedly. "At least tell me how you feel. Do you feel like you need to see a doctor? Anything broken? Concussion?"

I shrug. "No. My face hurts. I feel a little nauseous."

"How bad does your face hurt? The bruise is pretty bad, I wouldn't be surprised if your cheekbone is broken. We should go to Urgent Care."

I hear Addy scoff from behind me. "Her cheekbone is not broken."

"It looks-" He tries to argue before Addy cuts him off.

"Which one of us is the nursing major?" she says sharply, and Reed shuts up very quickly. "Yeah, me. Her cheekbone isn't fucking *broken*."

I force a tight-lipped smile. "That's good."

Reed visibly relaxes, squeezing my knee before standing and pulling another chair from the table to sit across from me. Once he's settled, he smiles at me kindly, trying a new interrogation approach. Good cop. "You need to tell me who did this."

I try to wiggle my way out of my chair, but Addy pushes me back into it.

"Uh-uh. You're not allowed to get out of this chair until I'm done icing your face."

"I don't wanna talk about it anymore," I tell Reed. "I just wanna go to bed and forget about it. Can we please do that?"

He's back to being furious now.

"You're *never* gonna forget about this," he says forcefully. "Whether you talk about it again or not. You know that right?"

I roll my eyes, but the action makes the bruise on my face ache. I give up. Maybe if I let Reed have his freakout now, he'll be calm enough in an hour or two to go to bed, and I can actually forget this.

"I was on my way to the gym," I start slowly. "The elevator stopped on Luke's floor and he and Aaron got in and Aaron started talking about how he couldn't believe all of the things I've said about him and how they aren't true."

If I thought Reed looked angry a few minutes ago, it is nothing compared to the look on his face right now. He looks like he's about to explode. He stands up so quickly that he almost knocks the chair over and he paces in very small steps in front of me. I think I see his hands shake, but he starts fidgeting with his fingers before I can confirm.

"Luke was there? Did he fucking do this?" He isn't quite screaming at me, but I've never heard anyone talk louder in my life than he is right talking right now. Especially not Reed.

I stand up too. "No, it was Aaron. Luke didn't touch me, but-"

"But?" Reed cuts me off, raising his eyebrows and waiting for a response.

I feel out of breath again, but I keep going. "But he didn't do anything to stop it either."

"He didn't even try to help you. Ask if you were okay?"

I shake my head, for what feels like the thousandth time tonight.

Reed turns away from me, muttering a quick, angry, and low, "motherfucker," under his breath as he continues his pacing and I stare at the floor. He's shaking.

"You need to go to the police," he yells. He looks at me like I should agree with him. Like his solution is so easy and simple. It's not.

"I won't," I say firmly, trying my hardest to speak as loud as Reed is.

His jaw tenses again as I see his hands clench and unclench at his side. "Dammit, Halle. Who are you trying to protect by not going to the police?"

He's yelling now, and I sit down just to put some space between us.

"Enough!" Addy screams, louder than Reed ever did, pointing an accusatory finger at him. "Everyone in this room was acting perfectly civilized until you walked in. Go out into the hall, and do not come back in until you have calmed the fuck down."

He leaves without arguing, and I cry once he's gone. I'm upset he's so far away. I'm upset he's so mad that he's incapable of comforting me right now. Addy soothingly runs her hand over my forehead as I sob. Isabel sits on the floor in front of me with her hands on my knees, the same spot Reed was in earlier.

"It'll be okay," she tells me. "He's just being a guy. Guys don't like things they can't fix right away. He won't be like this all night. And if he is, we'll kick him the fuck out."

I laugh through a sob as Addy takes the ice from my face.

"You've been iced," she says. "How does it feel? You shouldn't put ice on it again for an hour or so."

"It's better. Thank you."

Addy smiles and Isabel goes to the front door, calling into the hallway sharply. "Time out's over. Ready to act like an adult?"

She doesn't get any response, and she peeks her head down both ends of the hall. "Um, he's not here."

"Fuck," I mumble.

Addy calls Ben, who tells her Reed isn't in their room, but he'll come over to help us figure out where he could have gone.

"Do you not share your locations?" Isabel asks.

"No," I respond.

"Why not? Most couples do."

I shrug. "Never thought to. He lives in the same hallway as us."

"I bet now you're wishing you had."

Ben arrives with Reed's car keys, which he says were on their kitchen counter. So he doesn't have his car, he can't have gone too far without his car. We all take turns calling and texting – no response. A half hour goes by. Then an hour.

"He's pissing me off," Addy says. "He's running away when you need him."

I don't see it that way. He's always supported me when I've needed him before, what would stop him now unless something bad has happened to him? What if he ran into Luke or Aaron and did something stupid?

After two hours of sitting in the kitchen anxiously, a knock at the door makes us all perk up. We all slowly migrate closer, assuming Reed is on the other side, but when Ben finally opens it, it's Luke.

He looks terrible – hair matted, red splotches around his right eye, and a split lip. Ben laughs. I assume the worst.

"What the hell happened?" Addy yells.

Luke points at me. "You sent your guard dog on me."

I roll my eyes. "I did not. Does that mean you know where he is?"

Addy finally catches up. "*Reed* did this to you?"

She swipes some caked blood off his chin, and he winces. Next to me, Ben scoffs.

"Yeah," Luke says. "Like an hour ago."

The rest of us exchange glances – if this happened an hour ago, where has he been since?

Addy starts fussing over Luke, getting band-aids and

more ice and forcing him to sit on the couch, while the rest of us stare from the kitchen.

"Doesn't it bother you that she's helping him?" Ben whispers to me.

"Not as much as it's probably bothering you."

That shuts him up.

Usually, I love to pick apart Addy's weird attachment to Luke, but all I can think about is Reed. I feel sick thinking over the series of events and remembering that I have no idea where he is. Mostly, I'm sick over the thought that my Reed who has a no-violence pact with himself, just broke that, and it's my fault. It's all making me anxious enough to forget about the pain radiating from my cheekbone into my jaw.

The now unlocked door creeps open and Reed steps through it apprehensively. I've never been more relieved. I run to him, realizing how dumb I probably look, and hug him before the door fully closes.

"I'm so sorry," he says quietly. "I did something fucked up and I was too embarrassed to go home."

I pull back and stare at him, confused. "You don't want to go to your parents' over break anymore?"

He stares at me with a new sort of affection that makes me feel lightheaded.

"I meant here. Prez." He looks at the floor and his expression shifts. "I'm not kidding, I did something really fucked up."

I run my eyes over him, looking for injuries or any evidence of a fight, but all I see are a couple of scratches near his temple. Seems like Luke didn't fight back very hard.

"I know," I say.

His eyes dart back to mine. "What?"

Before I can explain, Reed notices Luke on the couch. He walks toward him, and Luke jumps up, a little terrified.

"Dude!" He exclaims. "Stop following me!"

Reed laughs. "Following you? You're at my girlfriend's apartment!"

Luke throws his hands up and shakes his head. "Leave me alone. I'm not the one who hit her."

"You're supposed to be her friend or at *least* friends with her best friend. And you didn't even help her stand up." Reed scoffs. "Get out. You are a pathetic excuse for a man."

The door shuts behind Luke after he storms out. The room is eerily silent.

"Reed and I are going to bed." I creep toward my bedroom, Reed following. "Thank you all for everything."

Once we're finally in the privacy of my room, I sigh in relief.

He sits on my bed, staring at the wall. "I'm a monster."

"No, you're dramatic."

He looks at me like he's about to say something but shakes his head and shifts his focus back to the wall. I sit next to him, and he puts his hand on my knee, his knuckles all red, broken skin.

"You need to tell someone about what Aaron did."

"I can't. I want to forget about it."

"Not telling anyone won't make you forget about it," he says softly. I rest my head in his lap and he runs his fingers through my hair while talking. "This is exactly what you did last year. It was easier for you to pretend having sex you never remembered wasn't a big deal than it was to get help. I can't let you do that to yourself again. I love you too much to let you rot over this."

I know he's right, which might be why it hurts so much to hear.

Still, the idea of walking into the campus police department, telling this story to a bunch of adult men, knowing that I would have to get into the whole backstory of my article, of Aaron's break-in, feels like the last way to solve my problems.

"Please," I beg. "I will deal with it tomorrow I promise. But right now, can you just lie to me and pretend it's not a big deal so I can get a little sleep."

"Sure," he kisses the top of my head as I shut my eyes tight and try not to cry again.

I love him. I really do. I love that he trusts me and my choices. I love that he's not going to try to force me into talking to anyone I'm not ready to talk to, even though he'd rather I did. I love that he hasn't given up on helping me feel better just because I don't want to do it *his* way.

"Can you stay over tonight?" I ask.

"I don't know."

I sit up to see him looking at me nervously. I let him leave me earlier tonight but I'm not letting him out of my sight again. "What?"

He won't look at me. "Because I just decked Luke? I did to him exactly what Aaron did to you, how does that make me any different than him?"

I can't believe this is where this conversation is going. "It's not the same. You would never hurt me."

"But I never thought I would ever hit anyone like that until today, I don't know anymore."

I try to smile at him, even though he is not reciprocating it. "You've never hurt me before, and now you know how bad it would hurt your hand, even if you wanted to."

I catch Reed swallowing a smirk. "Don't even joke about that. I would never hit you."

"There you go, you said it yourself. Let's go to bed."

"Hal, I don't know-"

"Reed Callaway," I stop him quickly. "You're not the same guy that you were when you punched a kid in your preschool class because you saw that's how the big boys on TV solved their problems. You know that right?"

"I didn't hit that kid when I was younger because I saw it on TV," he whispers.

"What do you mean?" I ask cautiously.

"I saw my mom's father hit her when I was in preschool. That's where I saw it. And that's why she was so strict about me getting into fights and stuff. She was worried I'd turn out like him."

My heart aches for preschool Reed. "That's terrible."

"Well, tonight I just proved her right." His breathing gets heavier, and he starts picking at his hair. "I can never go home. I can never tell my mom about this. One time, when I was like nine, I heard her on the phone with my aunt and she was talking about how she wished she didn't have a son because she didn't know how to raise me to not turn out like my grandfather."

I shush him and gently pull his hand out of his hair before he can start plucking chunks out. "Making a mistake doesn't take away all the good parts of you. I don't love you any differently now. I just feel bad for younger you. Hitting Luke is not a drug, you're not gonna get addicted to the feeling of punching someone in the face."

"You're right, I guess," he admits, defeated.

"I'm always right." I tease.

He smiles and runs his finger over my bruise, so light he's barely touching it. I still wince on instinct, not at all on purpose. His smile immediately drops.

He sighs and pulls his hand away. "This fucking sucks."

"Starting to think that's just life," I say, quoting him. He smiles again once he realizes. "We should still go to your parents' over break. And you should talk to your mom about all of this."

"Really?"

"Yeah. I think it would make you feel better. I mean, I know it's scary to talk about it but, you're not nine years old anymore, you know?"

I grab a bottle of painkillers from my nightstand and measure out enough pills for both of us and two cups of water from the tap in my bathroom. We swallow the pills in sync. He sits on the edge of my bed, and I stand in front of him. I grab his head and kiss the top of it. He always kisses me there, and I want him to know how nice it feels.

"I love you. Totally," I whisper.

"Yeah," he says slowly, pulling back a little so he can see my whole face. "I totally love you too."

aftershocks
. . .

ONCE THE DRAMA HAS DIED DOWN, I FINALLY TELL MY roommates about my plan to study abroad.

It's a rare night when we're all in the room together. Addy and Isabel are on the couch – reading, and watching a reality show as background noise. Nadia is starting to bake a batch of brownies, and Michaela is sitting at the kitchen table working on a project. Nadia's been a lot better recently. She's been drinking a little less and hanging out with us a little more ever since that night she cried in the shower. Maybe all she needed was to know one of us was on her side.

When I tell them about London, the words all comes out of my mouth very quickly because I'm so nervous.

They all have nothing but positive things to say, starting with how much they'll miss me and ending with how happy they are for me.

"Not to steal your thunder," Mic says, "but I'm going abroad too! I'm going to Egypt with the archaeology students."

Nadia sighs. "I told my mom other people wanted to go abroad but she didn't believe me."

"Have you told Reed yet?" Isabel asks.

"I did, I meant to tell you guys the day everything happened with Aaron but, obviously got sidetracked. I don't normally tell him things before I tell you."

"Were you scared to tell him?" She follows up. "How'd he react? Was he mad?"

"He's actually also studying abroad. In Scotland. So it kind of worked out."

She rolls her eyes, "Of course it did. Everything works out for you two. It's because you've had sex with him while you're on your period."

"God, Isa!" I yell. Everyone else laughs.

Isabel shrugs. "What? I read it online. It's a love spell. Blood pact type deal."

"Okay." I pick my phone up from the coffee table and grab my coat, on my way to a meeting with my new counselor. "I'm leaving before this conversation gets worse."

"It's true!" She screams as I shut the door behind me, "Look it up sometime!"

I CRASHED MY CAR, TWICE, WHEN I WAS SIXTEEN. THE first time was barely a crash, I hit a parked car while trying to back out of a tight space.

But the second time was bad. A car was in my blind spot at an intersection, and I blew through it and got t-boned. After it happened, I thought I would never be able to drive a car again because I would always be too afraid.

After my confrontation with Aaron, I thought I would never ride in an elevator again. But, just like how I drove my car again the morning after my accident, I rode the elevator again. It was either that or take eight flights of stairs.

I'm riding the elevator back up to my room now, and when the doors open on the eighth floor, I see Reed. Seeing him like this, unplanned, is becoming my favorite way to see him. It always makes my day when we run into each other, I feel thankful whenever we catch each other off guard, and I get to see the happy little look on his face when he sees me.

It's been a couple of weeks since the elevator incident. I think I'm mostly over it, honestly. In the days after it happened, with encouragement from my friends, I told my advisor about it. She referred me to the Title IX office, which referred me to the power-based violence counselor on campus, who convinced me to file a report against Aaron. I told them I didn't want to get him in trouble, that I didn't want to go through all of the drama again, and all I wanted was for him to never talk to me again. But once the case got to the Dean of Students, it was out of my hands.

They said they had to, it was seen as a safety concern for the whole campus, and that they were going to punish him whether I decided to go to the hearing or not. Tori offered to go and tell the story for me, which was far too kind of her, so we ended up going together. I did most of the talking while she sat next to me and nodded.

Aaron apologized at his hearing, which I did not attend and only heard a recording of, saying he was very drunk that night and mad about something unrelated to me. I was just the unlucky person he took his anger out on. I think it's total bullshit. He's on probation with the school and I have a no-contact order against him. But he's graduating in May, so it all doesn't matter much. I'm sure he has some cushy business firm job lined up, and one day he'll have a wife and kids and never tell them about what he was like in college. I've stopped caring.

I only saw the counselor I was referred to twice, and we barely talked about Aaron. We talked about last year a lot. She helped me work through some stuff I've kept inside for way too long, like having sex I don't remember. Turns out, in the grand scheme of my life, Aaron pushing me into a wall is a small trauma. I'll admit I've had bad days. I get nervous doing everyday things since that night. I wish it wasn't true. I don't like going anywhere alone or walking around campus at night.

But, like driving my car again and getting into the elevator again, I think I'll grow out of it. I hope I do.

new years' resolutions
. . .

Cheeks pink from the January cold, Reed and I shuffle into 806 on the Saturday night before the start of the spring semester. We just got back from visiting his family together, and it went better than I thought it would. It's nice to be back on campus, though.

I ended the fall semester year with a 3.3 GPA. High enough to be off scholarship probation, but not high enough to make the Dean's List like I had dreamed of. I had As and A minuses in all of my classes — except for Wells' class. I ended up with a respectable D. I was never able to catch up. It's okay, though. I'm still working on my relationship with school, and I know I have a long way to go. I'll be where I want to be one day.

We've already dropped Reed's bags off in his room and saw that none of his other roommates have returned to campus yet. When we open the front door of 806, we find the opposite is true for my room — I'm the last one of us to arrive.

"You're back, finally," Isabel groans impatiently. "Get ready to go out. We're leaving at nine."

"What are you talking about?"

I scan the room, only now noticing that the girls are wearing all black. Nadia and Mic are wearing black jeans and black t-shirts, but Addy and Isabel are in formal dresses. Addy has a little lace umbrella in her hand that makes her look like she's about to attend high tea.

"We're going to the Laundry Room funeral," she says.

"Did someone *actually* die?" Reed asks.

Isabel rolls her eyes at his sincerity. "No. Laundry Room got busted by the feds for serving alcohol to minors so tonight is the last night they're gonna be open before they're legally mandated to shut down. So everyone's going and wearing all black."

"That's kind of sad," I reply.

"Wow. End of an era," Reed agrees.

"Do any of your roommates wanna come with us?" Addy asks him. "Ben and all of them?"

Reed shrugs. "I'll ask Ben, he'll be back soon. But I think the rest of the guys might not be back until tomorrow."

"Scatter, then," Isabel says. "Start getting ready, I wanna be there early enough to get the coffin-shaped jello shots."

"Alright then," Reed says, walking slowly to the door and kissing my temple on his way out, "Call me when you're ready to go."

Once the door shuts behind him, the girls all jump me, begging for a detailed narrative of my trip to see Reed's family.

"It was fun," is all I give them. "It was good for us."

I'm trying to be more private – call it a New Year's resolution.

My friends don't need to know that Reed's parents were as stoic yet oddly kind as I imagined them to be. They don't need to hear that his mom gave me a kiss on the cheek and a hug when we arrived like I had met her many times. Or that his parents noticed the scabs on his knuckles, and that he talked to them about what had happened with Luke privately while I took his little sisters, Mirren and Mackenzie, out to a bakery. In reality, the girls were taking me out, dragging me by both hands, and showing me around their favorite parts of the old town waterfront. Mackenzie asked to try a sip of my coffee, so of course Mirren had to try a sip too, and they both hated it. My friends don't need to hear about how sweet they were when they asked me about college or how their eyes lit up once I asked them what they were reading in school.

When we came back to the house, Reed was sitting on the porch in the cold without his jacket. Once the girls made it inside, he told me that his mom started crying and said she never knew he had overheard her saying she was worried about raising a boy. She apologized; Reed told me it was the first time she had ever done that. She told him he's grown up to be an incredible person, and him hitting Luke doesn't change that – and she's so sorry that she ever made him think it would.

My friends don't need to know about the dinner he took me to on the Potomac, where we stared at the lights in the distance that he said was Maryland. And they don't need to hear about the day we took the Metro into DC and went to as many museums as we could before our feet started to ache.

Or how at the end of the day, as we took a break to sit on an icy bench, I told him, "I always thought about going to college near DC. But it ended up being too expensive."

"Same. Except my reason for not going was that they're all too close to home."

"Do you think there's an alternate universe where we

both chose schools here and still met and ended up together and are running around the city?"

"Yeah. I do."

My friends don't need to hear any of that. Yeah, that's all for me.

Addy and Isabel convince me to dress up for the "funeral" like them, which means wearing the only black dress I own, the same one I wore to the soccer banquet. Addy helps me straighten the back pieces of my hair that I always miss while I swipe on mascara.

"You're gonna have to keep an eye on Isabel tonight. I think she's planning on fully blacking out."

"Why me?" I ask casually.

She shrugs. "Because you don't really drink anymore so I was assuming you'd be the most sober out of all of us."

I pale. "You noticed?"

Addy laughs. "Of course I did, I'm your best friend."

"I feel stupid for trying so hard to hide it now."

I watch in her the mirror, micro-focused on a thin layer of my hair. "Don't. I get it."

"I never brought it up because I wanted to forget about last year altogether. I know I wasn't easy to be friends with."

She puts the flat iron down on the counter and locks eyes with me in the mirror with her sad doe eyes. "Why would you say that about yourself?"

"Because it's true?"

"None of us have ever, seriously ever, thought of you like that. We worried about you, sure, but you're easy to be friends with. You're a great friend."

She says it casually, but I'm trying not to cry.

We sit in silence as she finishes the last couple of pieces. Eventually, she unplugs the flat iron and squeezes my shoulders. "All done."

Not long after, Reed and Ben come over – not dressed for the theme, which Isabel yells at them for. We all leave for Laundry Room together, which, to no one's surprise, is packed. Busier than I have ever seen it. We fight our way to a table and agree not to stay out too late. But we're out late enough for Addy to get tipsy enough to start touching Ben's arm every time she laughs at one of his jokes (which is often) and for Isabel to come back to the table after a bathroom break and loudly announce that she saw three girls doing coke by the sink.

It's not until we hear Nadia say the doomed phrase that always means a girl is drunk enough to start trouble — "Some bitches here don't know how to say excuse me" – that Reed and I decide it's time to rally the troops and get home.

Once everyone has gotten a glass of water and made it to bed without yacking, Reed and I spend the night in his room. I tell him what Addy said earlier and we debrief the night.

"Was it weird?" he asks. "Knowing they know you're not drinking but still being out with them?"

"I actually kind of had fun. Shocker."

I fall asleep warm and comfortable in Reed's arms, picturing a future where I can have fun with my friends during a night out without drinking. It used to feel so far away, but now, I feel like I'm practically holding it in my hands.

part three
eight months older

"Burn all the files, desert all your past lives. And if you don't recognize yourself, that means you did it right"
Taylor Swift, *Midnights (3am Edition)*

"I have so much of you in my heart"
John Keats, in a letter to Fanny Brawne

london

. . .

St. Pancras station is beautiful. There's no other way to put it. That's how I feel about most parts of London, though.

I've been in London for over a month now, and I feel a little burnt out. The study abroad program has excursion and tourist opportunities for us, and for the past four weekends, I signed up for every single one of them, determined to see every corner of this city like it was part of an assignment. But I haven't seen St. Pancras station until today and discovering another beautiful part of the city feels like an accomplishment.

It hasn't been as easy as I hoped it would be. Being away from home and campus, I have so much more to be homesick for. Whenever I see pictures of my friends getting ready to go out and start missing the smell of fake tan and hairspray on Friday nights — it's hard to remind myself that I'm doing the right thing. But I do, and I stay. The first month flew by, and I'm planning on the rest of the semester feeling a similar way. *Enjoy it while it's here*, I tell myself, *if you waste your time here sulking about living in London, you'll regret it for the rest of your life.*

Reed is the only person I share all this with. It's easy to talk to him. He misses home and campus in the same way I do. It's funny, I was so worried that my studying abroad would drive us away from each other, but it's given us more to talk about. He misses soccer, and though it's still a bit of a touchy subject, his fifth year of eligibility was officially approved last week, which has caused a noticeable boost in his mood. His parents are still mad that he's not finishing his degree in four years like they always pictured, but Reed's working on them.

I ended up changing my major. I never became interested in political communications as I convinced myself I would be someday. It sounds awful, but I simply don't care what other people are thinking enough to work in politics. After many long talks with Julia, explaining to her that I'm not interested in political communications anymore, and I'd rather write an advice column for a magazine or comedic pieces or cultural things, she told me I had nothing to lose by switching my major to plain old communications. My journalism-ish political science classes and the classes for communications have so much overlap, I can still graduate on time. No more grad school applications or LSAT prep to worry about. I thought my grandmother would be upset when I told her I wasn't studying politics anymore. She wasn't upset at all.

The first issue of my on-campus magazine, *Trending*, was published in February. Seeing it in print was the best feeling. I've never felt more accomplished. Reed took me out on a date the next weekend and gave me a framed copy of the issue. I think that's the sweetest thing anyone has ever done for me. I brought it home to my parents' house after moving out of the dorms for the summer, and my mom cried when she saw it. It's currently hanging in my parent's kitchen back in Cleveland. I don't think I'm ever getting it back.

There're only a few days a week Reed and I find time to talk on the phone. We're not on an exact or perfect schedule, so our calls usually happen at the very last minute, and we end up talking for hours. I called him last week, and somehow, two hours later, we ended the call with plans for Reed to leave Scotland for the weekend and visit me.

I haven't seen him since June when he came to visit me over our summer break. We got lunch with my best friend from high school, Emmy, and her boyfriend. It went well. It was weird how adult the whole lunch made me feel. A double date at an upscale bistro, watching Reed and Emmy's boyfriend fight over the check. Terrifyingly adult-ish.

The two of us went to Cedar Point, where I learned that Reed has a strong aversion to any ride that spins and is scarily good at overpriced carnival games. I have the stuffed lion he won that day sitting next to Betty the dog on my bed here in London.

I took him to the Zoo, the Rock Hall, and we ate at my favorite restaurant in The Flats twice. Before he left, we made a pact that we would wait a month before visiting each other while we were abroad.

Today is Friday, the beginning of the fifth weekend of the semester, meaning we kept our pact. I'm honestly surprised, I thought one of us would've caved. It became easier and easier to convince myself in the past month that Reed was going to surprise me and just show up at my door. I'd be getting out of the shower, walking back from class, or getting coffee, and working myself up over this idea that I might just run into him on the street or that he'll show up at my door with flowers. Then I'm disappointed that he's not there. And I have to remind myself that I have nothing to be disappointed about, that I imagined it all.

I haven't told anyone Reed is coming to see me, besides my parents. It feels kind of nice, holding it like a little secret in the palms of my hands, knowing that no one has any expectations of my seeing him or will be waiting for the story I'll report. It's freeing, realizing I don't have to tell my friends every detail of my relationship with Reed like I used to.

On the block outside of the station, it starts to rain. I pull my hood up. I hope he remembered to pack a rain jacket. He must have one. It rains a lot in Scotland too, right? I can't remember. His train was scheduled to arrive twenty minutes ago. I'm scanning the crowds of people exiting the station until I see him.

His eyes, like mine, scan the mass of people crowding the street, not seeing me until I raise both my arms into the air and start waving them. I probably look like a crazy person. But I'm smiling and laughing while I do it, so at least I look like a happy crazy person.

I have the privilege of watching him the moment he recognizes me, the second look he gives me like he has to confirm it's really me before a comically large smile breaks on his face to match mine. Duffle bag in one hand, and a little brown paper bag with tissue paper in the other, he looks both ways quickly before jogging across the street. Crosswalk be damned.

When we reach each other, Reed picks me up fiercely and spins me around while I giggle. He puts me down and we kiss. Something tentative and gentle, exploratory, and I can't help but think of our first kiss at the stupid lacrosse party two years ago. I think of how lucky I felt that I had run into him that night. I think about how different my life was when we stopped talking. I think about how my heart jumped out of my throat when I saw him in Wells' class on our first day last year.

When we separate, I'm already grinning and Reed tucks a fallen strand from my braid behind my ear. "What?"

"Just thinking about how I should've known when I saw you in Wells' class, we'd find our way back to each other."

His eyes pinch shut as he drops his hand from where it had been resting on my jaw. "I have a confession but you're probably gonna hate me after and make me get on a train back to Scotland."

I laugh. "Probably not, but okay."

He half-smirks and looks away from me. "Last year, before registration, I asked Addy to send me a copy of your schedule so I could register for the same section of Wells' class as you."

I scoff, but I'm not mad. I probably would have been a year ago, but not today. "And here I was the whole time thinking it was some sign from the universe. Like fate or something!"

"Nah, Hevko. I like you too much to leave it up to fate."

I don't know if I believe in coincidences anymore, because right now, in Reed's arms, I feel like deep down I've known this moment was coming my whole life.

Our kiss breaks and I smile so intensely, my cheeks feel sore.

This is one of those things that, even in the moment, I know I always will remember.

acknowledgments

Thank you to my mom for being my first editor and the first person to encourage me to keep writing. Thank you to my dad for always asking me "how's the book going?" I am the writer I am because of your love and support.

I wrote the majority of my first draft of this book in my sophomore year dorm, and it would not exist without the five girls I lived with. Ladies of 212 - thanks for all the inspiration and encouragement.

Caroline, thank you for your eagle-eye proof reading skills, ever present enthusiasm, sacrifices you made to read my first draft as a PDF instead of as an iBook, and for always talking about books with me. Madison, thank you for running up to my car window after you read the first chapter to tell me how good you thought it was. That meant so much to me, and your enthusiasm for this book has rekindled my own enthusiasm many times. Alexis, thank you for always liking my posts on my author Instagram before anyone else.

Thank you to my first beta readers: Sophia, Mary Kate, Lexy, Alysse, Cristin, Libby, and Kristin for your feedback in the early stages.

Thank you Dr. O'Leary and Stephen Skiles for keeping me in line throughout my years at Xavier. Thank you Dr. Wyett and Dr. Renzi for everything you taught me about writing and about myself in your classes. Thank you Mrs. Puckett for rekindling my love of reading for fun, and introducing me to the work of Isabel Allende in AP Lit.

Thank you to everyone who has listened to me talk about this book for years and dealt with me not shutting up about it. I'm so excited to share it with you at last.

Thank you Taylor Swift, Jensen McRae, Maisie Peters, Joni Mitchell, Fleetwood Mac, Gracie Abrams, Lorde, Phoebe Bridgers, and Lucy Dacus for making the music I listened to while writing this.

Finally, thank you Reed and Halle for sticking in my head for so long. I know you're not real, but I had a lot of fun writing about you.

about the author

Tessa D'Errico is a senior at Xavier University studying Theatre and English. When she's not reading or writing, she enjoys watching HBO shows, eating various pasta dishes, and talking to her friends about Taylor Swift. *No Coincidences* is her first novel.

instagram.com/tessaderricoauthor

Printed in Great Britain
by Amazon